CW01461189

PRAISE FOR UNMASKED

"It's fun, easy reading ... a varied assortment of adventurous tales to journey with"

—*Publishers Weekly*

"An appropriate short fiction collection for a pandemic era."

—Kaye Lynne Booth, Writing to Be Read

Unmasked
Stories of Risk and Revelation

KEVIN J. ANDERSON, EXECUTIVE EDITOR

Editorial Team
Kelly Adams, Erekson Holt, Deborah Kevin,
Melissa Dalton Martinez, Constanza Ontaneda,
Dale Sprague, Amanda Montandon, Matt Wright

WFP
WORDFIRE PRESS

EBook ISBN: 978-1-68057-227-8
Trade Paperback ISBN: 978-1-68057-226-1
Hardcover ISBN: 978-1-68057-228-5
Library of Congress Control Number: 2021934156

Cover artwork images by Mark Holt and Janet McDonald
Kevin J. Anderson, Art Director
Published by
WordFire Press, LLC
PO Box 1840
Monument CO 80132
Kevin J. Anderson & Rebecca Moesta, Publishers

WordFire Press eBook Edition 2021
WordFire Press Trade Paperback Edition 2021
WordFire Press Hardcover Edition 2021
Printed in the USA
Join our WordFire Press Readers Group for
sneak previews, updates, new projects, and giveaways.
Sign up at wordfirepress.com

CONTENTS

INTRODUCTION

TAKING OFF THE MASK

KEVIN J. ANDERSON

We all wear masks, sometimes literal ones like a superhero or a bank robber; sometimes metaphorical ones, when a person disguises their true personality. As we edited this anthology, everyone around us was wearing a protective COVID mask in the face of a pandemic.

Unmasked: Stories of Risk and Revelation is an anthology put together by my grad students at Western Colorado University, all of whom are working toward their Master of Arts degree in Publishing. As their instructor, I guided this project from start to finish, but the real work was all theirs. The students developed the concept for the anthology, wrote up the submission guidelines, read through over five hundred stories in the slush-pile, worked within the budget generously provided by Draft2Digital, selected the very best stories in a range of genres and tones, wrote rejection letters as well as contracts. They worked with the authors on any necessary rewrites and copy edits, they chose the cover art, designed and produced the book, and released it as their graduating project.

In *Unmasked* you will find uplifting superhero stories, dark dystopian stories, humorous tales of mistaken identity, the fast-paced adventures of thieves and spies, chilling tales of haunted death masks and supernatural revenge, and uplifting stories about finding and revealing one's true identity. As a bonus, we are including the Nebula Award-winning masterpiece "Sinner, Baker, Fabulist, Priest; Red Mask, Black Mask, Gentleman, Beast" by the late Eugie Foster, a novelette I edited back in *Nebula Awards Showcase 2011*, which fit so perfectly with the theme.

Take off your own mask, put on your reading glasses, and enjoy these 21 tales of risk and revelation.

—Kevin J. Anderson,
Director, Publishing Program
Graduate Program in Creative Writing
Western Colorado University

Kevin J. Anderson has published more than 170 books, 58 of which have been national or international bestsellers. He has written numerous novels in the Star Wars, X-Files, and Dune universes, as well as unique steampunk fantasy novels *Clockwork Angels* and *Clockwork Lives*, written with legendary rock drummer Neil Peart, based on the concept album by the band Rush. His original works include the Saga of Seven Suns series, the Terra Incognita fantasy trilogy, the Saga of Shadows trilogy, and his humorous horror series featuring Dan Shamble, Zombie PI. He has edited numerous anthologies, written comics and games, and the lyrics to two rock CDs. Anderson and his wife Rebecca Moesta are the publishers of WordFire Press and he is the Director of the Publishing MA program at Western Colorado University. His most recent novels are *Vengewar, Stake*, and *The Duke of Caladan* (with Brian Herbert).

PYGMALION

SEANAN MCGUIRE

W hen I was a kid, people used to ask me all the time. "What's it like having one of the most amazing superheroes in the universe as your mother?" "What was it like when you were little, did you get Wonderland diamonds in your Christmas stocking, did you get roast wyvern for Thanksgiving?" "Are you sorry not to have powers of your own?"

They never asked the question I wanted them to ask, which was, "Do you ever resent your mother for setting an unattainable example for the young women of the world, guaranteeing you would never be enough in the eyes of anyone who knew you, or for that matter, in your own?"

Let's be clear: Mom never treated me like I didn't matter just because I couldn't lift a car over my head, or fly, or turn myself to stone. She treated me like I was the most important thing in the world, the most important thing she had ever done or ever would do, and she did her best to shield me from the reality of her world. I had to put the real story together for myself.

Had to figure out that her friends who came around for stale cake and mediocre coffee sneered at me because of all the things she didn't. Had to figure out that they came to my birthday parties under duress, badly wrapped presents that never exceeded my mother's strict twenty-dollar limit in their hands.

Had to figure out that the man with the blond hair and the heroic jawline, the man whose eyes looked so much like my own, the man who would never look at me for more than a few seconds without clenching his hands into fists, the man who never once addressed me without being forced ...

Had to figure out that he was Zenith, just without the cape and boots and heroic pose, and more, he was almost certainly my father. You'd think realizing the world's greatest superhero was your father would come with dramatic music, or at least the feeling of finally falling into line with your destiny, but all I felt was tired. I was nine years old, and I knew no one would believe me if I told them. He was the world's greatest superhero. He could do infinitely better than a middle-aged diner waitress whose house had peeling wallpaper and water spots on the ceilings, and if he *did* have a kid, they'd be a lot better than me. They'd have powers, they'd be amazing.

All this happened about a year before Mom's secret identity got blown, which wasn't my fault, no matter what the tabloids try to say. She did that all by herself.

But after I was sure that Mom's friend Paul was actually Zenith in civilian drag, I'd started to look a little more closely at the rest of Mom's friends. Some of them worked at the diner, or were regular patrons there, but others, the ones who came to my birthday party with pursed lips and the same general air as me when I was forced to do my homework on a bright spring day ...

The others lined up, one to one, with the known members of the Association of Heroes. The bright-garbed men and women who soared the skies, righting wrongs, dispensing justice, and generally behaving in a heroic manner. It was the first secret I'd ever had, and it was a big one, big enough to break the world, or at least that's what it felt like tucked away inside my nine-year-old heart, where I could keep it safe.

For one year, I was an impenetrable fortress, more secure than any bank—more secure than Fort Knox, even. Some people have tried to spin it since then, said I was the one who tipped off the papers as to Mom's daytime occupation, said I was jealous of her. Jealous of what? I was *nine*. She hadn't told me yet that she had powers, or that if I hadn't developed them by the time I started puberty, I wasn't going to. See again, *nine*. I thought I knew how the world worked, and how it was always *going* to work. Me and Mom, and occasional visits from her friends who thought of me as a particularly demanding and high-maintenance pet. They didn't quite pat me on the head and tell me to sit and stay, but they came close sometimes. I guess by that point, they'd all been living gods for long enough that they didn't understand how human kids worked anymore.

And then came that awful, terrible, life-changing, world-ending day when I was pulled out of Mrs. Harris's advanced math class and moved to the office, where I'd been surrounded by strange, silent men in black suits who carried large guns and looked at the world around them as if it was inherently their enemy, not to be trusted under any circumstances. And no one had even tried to explain what was going on.

That's the part that still gets to me today. I was ten on the day the news broke—by a matter of three whole weeks, I was ten. A child. An innocent, civilian child. The fact that my mother was a soldier in an unending war between the forces of good and evil didn't matter to me. Whether or not I got invited to Missy Sinclair's slumber party, now *that* mattered to me.

You may remember that slumber party. It was all over the news.

Missy and I were the only survivors.

Anyway, Mom showed up at the school three hours after the final bell, five hours after I'd been put on lockdown. Five hours of sitting in anxious silence, no one telling me what was going on or why I'd been taken out of class. I had spent that time spinning nightmare scenarios in my head, worlds where I'd been orphaned by a fire at the diner or something equally unlikely, worlds where I'd have to go and live with the father who had never acknowledged me as his own, leaving our familiar, dingy, but comfortable house behind. So when the door slammed open and Mom walked in, fully costumed, the marble mask covering her eyes and the marble sword in her hand, I was so relieved to see her that I was halfway across the room before her appearance registered.

Galatea. Greatest superwoman in the world, second only to Zenith for most powerful superhuman. The woman of every civilian's dreams and every villain's nightmares. I had her action figure. And even as I remembered that fact, I remembered how reluctant Mom had been to buy it for me, even after weeks of begging and pleading. It hadn't been until I told the mall Santa that I wanted my own Galatea doll more than anything else in the world, even a puppy, that she'd been willing to break down and bring me one.

I'd wondered how she'd been able to afford the deluxe battle-ready Galatea with real sword-swinging action when she could barely afford to pay the power bill. Looking at her in full armor, with threads of stone running through her hair and the famous sword in her hand, my first nonsensical thought was that she could damn well have gotten me the Battle Cruiser playset at the same time.

And then I passed out, unconscious on the floor of the principal's office.

Everyone knows the story from there: some nosy tabloid reporter had put together that Zenith was seen near our little suburban town too often for anything other than a civilian life, and had decided to win a Pulitzer by unmasking the world's greatest superhuman. Real nice guy, that reporter. He's tried to get a private interview with me every year for the last fifteen, saying that only he can truly tell my story. Asshole. He's the one who ruined my life as a side effect of his ill-considered bid for fame, and he thinks he could somehow be fair to me?

He didn't get his Pulitzer. He didn't find Zenith, either ... not directly. What he found was Mom, who had never previously been photographed without her mask, but whose lips had been carried in picture form to a thousand plastic surgeons, and whose chin had been on the cover of Time magazine so many times that it was sort of a miracle it had taken as long as it did for someone to look at Mom's profile and go "huh, doesn't she look like ..."

Finding Mom led him inexorably to finding Mom's secret identity, and finding Mom's hospital records, which listed "Jack Smith" as my father. "Paul Smith" was Zenith's only publicly known alias at the time, having been the name he worked under during his brief time as a judicial assistant. When a woman who looks like Galatea and a man with Zenith's alias have a daughter in a town that sees more than its fair share of superhero activity relative to its size? And that girl is named Hope Anesidora? He might have worked for a tabloid, but he knew how to connect the dots, and while I'd been sitting happily in math class, unaware that the world was about to change forever, he'd been releasing his magnum opus, an expose on Galatea's civilian activities. Including my name, and the name of my school. He basically drew a map for any supervillain who wanted to get back at my mom to follow, and then he released it into the world with no concern for my safety.

My parents' trying to sue him for violating the laws that protect child superheroes made the news, of course, and that was the first time most of the world saw my face. Serious Streisand Effect, since most people had seen me as a forgettable footnote until I mattered enough to go to court over, where the judge had found that although the reporter was guilty of bad judgment and possible child endangerment, he hadn't violated any laws surrounding secret identities. Why?

Because I didn't have any powers.

So now I was in the paper not only for being the daughter of the world's two greatest superhumans, who had never even been rumored to be in a relationship before. Zenith was supposedly in a long-term relationship with a civilian district attorney, whose public repudiation of him as both man and lawyer was one of the only things to distract the public's attention from Mom and me while all this was going down, and Mom had always said justice had to come before she was willing to even consider seeking love for love's own sake—but I was in the paper for being completely defenseless without my parents.

All Mom's friends started coming around again, in costume this time, finally willing to look directly at me. They couldn't pull me out of school and send me to the school their own children attended, because it was one of those special schools for kids who could bend rebar or see through walls, and the faculty wouldn't know what to do with me. Even if the teachers could figure me out, the rest of the student body would eat me alive. I was relieved when they said I wasn't going to be changing schools, even if I had to walk to class escorted by Association security forces, who had identified me with unforgiving accuracy as a possible kidnapping risk.

They didn't scare the other kids away. In fact, they did exactly the opposite; for the six weeks after the news broke, I was the most popular kid in school, enjoying a level of social acceptance that I could only have dreamed of before. I was still pudgy and uncoordinated, with frizzy hair and a tendency to drift off into daydreams when I was supposed to be filling out worksheets or participating in class, but my parents were superheroes, and that made me amazing.

And then came the one thing I had been hoping for since the start of the year, the one thing I thought would make my life truly complete: an invitation to Missy Sinclair's slumber party. Mom didn't want to let me go. It would be my first night spent away from her since the news went wide, and while they could station security on the street, they couldn't put them inside without permission from Missy's parents, which seemed unlikely, since Missy's parents had already complained about my security—who they described as "strange, unrelated adults"—being on campus. They were willing to let me into their home. The people who kept me alive would have to wait outside.

What people don't necessarily seem to understand was that up until the slumber party, the security had been nothing more than a precaution as far as I could tell. I'd been locked down as soon as the world learned that I existed, and the security had only increased after it had come out that I didn't have any powers. That didn't mean anyone had *tried* anything.

People had, actually. Several people, several times. Bad people. The kind of people who looked at a ten-year-old girl and saw an opportunity to hurt her parents. The kind of people for whom the words "collateral damage" had never cost them so much as a moment's peace. The kind of people like the Sinclairs didn't believe would come to our sleepy little suburb for the sake of one brown-haired little girl without powers.

But they came. I went to the party, which started promptly at seven. I knew I was only there because Missy wanted to get a glimpse of Mom when I was dropped off; she didn't *like* me, had never liked me in the first place, and I wasn't foolish enough to think she'd suddenly changed her mind about inducting me into the hallowed ranks of the popular and the perfect. None of that mattered. I was *there*, I was an attendee at the fourth-grade social event of the year, and as long as I didn't throw up during pizza time or wet my sleeping bag from excitement, no one was going to make me leave. I could stay until morning and partake of Ms. Sinclair's famously delicious waffle bar, which Missy bragged about every time she had the opportunity, and feel as normal as anyone else, not like the freak with the superhero parents.

The pizzas showed up at eight. The supervillains showed up at eight-thirty. If the order had been reversed, there might not have been *any* survivors, but Missy and I had found a strange point of camaraderie in our mutual aversion to bell peppers—I'm allergic; she just thought they were disgusting—and so the two of us were the only ones at the coffee table, splitting a ham-and-pineapple pizza, when the footsoldiers burst in through the picture window.

I'll never forget the sound of a sheet of broken glass slicing through Ms. Sinclair's neck, or the way her head bounced twice before it rolled to a stop. Missy screamed. I panicked, and as I have always done, when I panicked, I froze. Fortunately for Missy, I froze in the act of reaching for another slice, so that my body halfway blocked hers from the footsoldiers in insectile armor now occupied with the messy but apparently essential task of slaughtering party guests.

Kids I'd known since preschool came apart into messy piles of tissue and bone, filling the air with a smell that was horribly reminiscent of summer barbeque, only bloodier and somehow more unforgettably primal. People ask me why I'm a vegetarian. That moment, that horrifying handful of seconds, that's the real reason why. Animal welfare has never been a major concern of mine. The day when I inhaled the aerosolized bodies of my classmates, *that's* a major concern of mine, and will be every time I close my eyes from now until the day I die. It's not their fault that I see them every time I even think about eating a hamburger.

One of the black-armored figures pointed at me, snapping something in a buzzing, insectile language that made my skin try to crawl right off of my body. Two more surged forward and grabbed my arms, pulling me away from Missy, who had keeled over in a dead faint during the pause between their appearance and my abduction.

They didn't see her on the floor. They didn't realize they were leaving a survivor behind. They were too busy hauling me out through the hole that used to be the window, their fingers digging into the soft, untested flesh of my arms, the blood of my classmates soaking into my skin.

Their ship was outside, hovering ten feet above the lawn. The first of them stepped into the beam of light emanating from its belly and were pulled away, vanishing. For some reason, that was the step too far. Murder made sense. People were made of meat, no matter how much I didn't like to think about it. A flying saucer hanging over the Sinclair's front lawn? That didn't make sense. That was something that happened to superheroes, not to ordinary people.

I screamed. High and shrill and hysterical. The footsoldiers who were holding me turned to look in my direction, one of them snarling a command that I had to assume meant "stop." I didn't stop. The dam was broken, and all the screams that had been building up behind it were finally free to pour out of me, going where they would.

None of the security people who were supposed to be keeping an eye on the house appeared to save me. I did my best to dig my heels into the lawn, to no avail; the footsoldiers continued to drag me inexorably forward, toward the waiting beam of light. They were going to take me. They were going to take me away, with the blood of my classmates still drying all over me, and I was never going to get to taste Ms. Sinclair's waffles, and somehow that felt like the greatest tragedy of all.

The grass was wet—I didn't want to think about with what —and my heels slipped, bare feet sliding through muddy green. Nothing changed. We were still moving. At least Missy would get to be famous, like she'd always wanted; with me gone, she was going to be the only survivor, and she could spin the story however she wanted to. She could be a hero, if I was gone. That wouldn't be enough to make up for the fact that she'd only invited me to her party because she was hoping she'd get to meet my parents, the heroes, and instead she'd managed to arrange an introduction of her parents, the civilians, to the kind of villains girls like us should only have to hear about on the news. So maybe losing me would give her the chance to make a few headlines of her own.

Then two lines of brilliant white light, bright as the sun itself, shot through the air and through the head of the footsoldier holding my right arm, blasting it clean off. This blast didn't smell like barbeque. It smelled like char and oil and something unidentifiable, like grasshoppers being fried with a magnifying glass. It hurt my nose. The body remained upright for a long moment before it crumpled, losing its grip on my arm in the process.

The remaining footsoldier said something in that terrible, unfamiliar language, and even though I couldn't understand it, I knew it was swearing. Then it did the truly unbelievable, under the circumstances:

It let me go.

I stumbled away, watching in horror as the remaining footsoldiers turned to run. More of those blasts of searing light shot across the yard, vaporizing the soldiers where they stood. I recognized it now, even though it still made no sense at all: it was something that belonged on television, safely distanced by the magic of film, not here, where I could smell the charred flesh and the plasma burning through the evening air. This was a thing for stories, not real life.

Zenith's laser vision. A moment after the realization, the man himself appeared, blazing down the street with one hand stretched out in front of him, fingers balled into a fist. He hit the saucer like a wrecking ball, punching right through the steel plating. The whole thing shook and trembled, nearly falling out of the sky. He blasted two more of the fleeing footsoldiers with his lasers, and then another figure appeared, soaring high, but already descending, feet pointed toward the ground to ease her landing. Mom.

"Mom?" I whispered. She'd shown me the costume, of course, after the news broke; she'd explained how sorry she was that she'd always had to keep the truth about her career from me, and the even bigger truth of who my father was. By that point, I knew that what was being said about her was true; she was Galatea, the most powerful woman in the world, and my father was Zenith, and I was their useless, defenseless, powerless daughter. But knowing a thing isn't the same as *seeing* a thing, never has been, and this was the first time I'd seen her in all her glory.

She was spectacular. She was impossibly beautiful, so beautiful that it hurt my eyes to look at her, that I felt like I wasn't worthy to be in the presence of my own mother, and then she was landing on the lawn, amidst the gore and shattered pieces of footsoldier. One of the few who was still standing drew a complicated sidearm and fired it at her, sending a bolt of blue lightning streaking at her, faster than I could yell to warn her.

She raised a hand, almost lazily, and batted it away. Then she strode toward the footsoldier, grabbing it by the throat and lifting it over her head before she flung it brutally and bodily away. The sound it made when it hit the side of the building was one more thing I'd remember for the rest of my life. I was racking up quite a number of them, and it wasn't even midnight yet. Who knew what wonders tomorrow would hold?

What terrible, unbearable wonders. But Mom saw me on the lawn and ran to me, wailing, "Hope! My baby, what have they *done* to you?" as she gathered me into her strong, familiar arms and crushed me to a bosom that smelled of ozone and acceleration rather than diner coffee, and I buried my face against her shoulder and cried and cried and cried, and in that moment, I was sure everything was going to be okay. She was here, I was here, my father was ripping a spaceship apart, and we were going to be okay.

Then Missy screamed from inside the house, and I remembered that nothing was ever going to be okay again.

That was the night we moved to the Association of Heroes housing complex. I couldn't go back to school, not with half my classmates dead and the other half understandably afraid of me. I couldn't go *anywhere* for a while, not without having panic attacks so bad that I blacked out, or wetting myself, or screaming and screaming until I ran out of air. Therapy was the word of the day, and then the word of the year, and meanwhile Mom and Zenith were working out how to live together as a couple, and with me as a family.

Zenith had a hard time adjusting to the fact that I was a person, not just an idea, and an even harder time with the fact that I refused to call him "Dad." Couldn't even think about him that way for the first year. And then the interviews began, and didn't stop until I turned eighteen, changed my name to something a little bit less on-the-nose, and snuck away to go to college like a normal person.

And I never looked back, and I never developed superpowers, and I didn't think anyone knew where I was until yesterday, when the box appeared on my doorstep.

"My beloved Anesidora, my hope in these dark times, if you are reading this, then I have fallen in the endless fight against the forces of evil, and the mantle of our family has fallen upon your shoulders. I have done my best to protect you, as is a mother's duty to her child, but alas, I cannot protect you from beyond the veil."

My mother's handwriting was as familiar as it had ever been, as was the subtle smell of her perfume, permeating the paper. It would have been more reassuring if it hadn't been eight years since the last time we'd spoken, and if the news hadn't been playing behind me, reporting on the deaths of Zenith and Galatea, along with half the Association, all of them fallen protecting the Earth from one more alien threat.

Tears stung my eyes. My parents couldn't be dead. Denial is always a stage of grief, but I think there's something reasonable, realistic even, about denying the death of your parents when they're the most powerful people on the planet. We hadn't spoken in years, but they were still superheroes, untouchable and above us all. I turned my attention back to the letter.

"I would have told you this long ago, my dearest, if you had stayed with us; I would have found the right words, the right ways to give you the secret truth of our family, which is of necessity concealed from all around us. I am sorry that I cannot give you this in person, but listen to the memory of my voice and believe that what I never said is true:

"I never for a moment regretted the fact that you were born without the power of flight, or your father's burning vision, or my own super strength. I knew you when you rode inside me, sole passenger of a heavenly chariot, and I knew you would be as I had been, mortal clay, meant to carry your jar and walk the world until your mother fell, as mothers must inevitably do. That is the secret of our line: we are never born with powers, and even when we seek out husbands who carry the fire of Prometheus in their veins, our blood wins out. We are born as cold and common clay. The power we wield is our burden, not our gift. I would take it with me to the grave, were it so allowed, but now the choice is fallen unto you. Now the decision is yours."

Under the letter, a mask. The famous marble mask of Galatea, licensed by every Halloween costume company in the world, unlicensed by a million cosplayers. But the shape of it was subtly wrong, no longer quite my mother's forehead, my mother's brow. It looked more like my own.

I stood in silence, looking from the mask to the letter and back again. Galatea's marble sword wasn't in the box, but somehow that didn't matter. I didn't need it. If I put the mask on, I knew, the sword would come to me, or something else would, a spear, or a vase filled with potions and poisons, ready to heal or harm at my desire. I would be as great as my mother had been, and as unbeatable, until the day something bigger than I was slapped me out of the sky.

My life—the life I had worked so hard to build for myself in the years since I'd slipped away, since I'd put Hope to the side and become Dora, whose name had never graced a tabloid cover and never would—would end. Immediately, and with no going back. The diner where Mom worked had never fired her, being smart enough to fear the optics of dropping a super-human from their payroll, but she had never worked another day there after her identity was revealed to the world. She hadn't even tried to live a civilian life until she was pregnant with me, preferring the comfort of the Association, the near-ness of the world in need of protection.

If I put on the mask, Dora Green would die. Hope Anesi-dora Smith would rise in her place, and take to the sky, to defend a world that had been all too happy to devour her. I looked, hopelessly, back to the letter.

"I am sorry, my daughter. I am sorry for the years we lost, for the cost of defending this world, and for the need that will come upon you if you take up my mantle. Aphrodite is a jealous goddess even now, and we the descendants of her masterpiece. She will ensure the mask is passed to your daugh-ter, even as I pass it now to my own, even as your grandmother passed it to me. But she cannot make you claim it. All she can do is guarantee that the next child of our line will exist to be offered the choice, to stand where all of us have been. Will you choose stone, as all of us who came before you have done? Or will you allow one more god to fade from the world, and choose clay? Whatever your decision, I love you, my daughter. I died loving you, and losing you remains my sole regret."

Slowly, I lowered the letter, staring at the closed door of my apartment and the great wide world beyond, and I couldn't have told you, in that moment, which I was going to choose.

The mask, silent as stone, did not rise to aid in my decision.

Seanan McGuire lives in an idiosyncratically designed labyrinth in the Pacific Northwest, which she shares with her cats, a vast collection of creepy dolls and horror movies, and sufficient books to qualify her as a fire hazard. She has strongly-held and oft-expressed beliefs about the origins of the Black Death, the X-Men, and the need for chainsaws in daily life. Seanan was the winner of the 2010 John W. Campbell Award for Best New Writer, and her novel *Feed* (as Mira Grant) was named as one of *Publishers Weekly's* Best Books of 2010. In 2013, she became the first person ever to appear five times on the same Hugo Ballot.

LA MARIONNETTE

ALICIA CAY

Porcelina's fingers trembled in the cold February air as they moved along the worn strings of her violin. Berlioz's Rêverie et Caprice floated on the breeze. She sat on the edge of the fountain in the *Place de l'Opéra*, where she came daily to practice and perform in front of the Palais Garnier, the great opera house she dreamed of one day playing.

The whole of Paris was alive with activity. It was the week of Carnival and *la promenade des masques*, a time when the citizens hid their faces behind bright papier-mâché masks and the streets bustled in celebration.

A man in a boater hat and a mask painted with silver fish rode past on his bicycle, racing the carriages in the street and ringing the tinny bell.

Porcelina looked up at the sound. Her gaze drifted through the crowd. A familiar face caught her attention. His pure white mask stood out from the others, a rebellion against the sea of painted colors around him. Porcelina's pulse thrummed. The man had come to watch her play every evening for the past four days. He was handsome, well-dressed, and carried an air of mystery about him—as though in his company anything was possible, even magic.

Two women stopped to listen, blocking the man from Porcelina's view. Their pastel masks were decorated with lace and silk to match their high-buttoned dresses. One of them dropped a franc in the beat-up violin case at Porcelina's feet.

Porcelina sighed. She could not afford flour to eat, much less to spread on decorated paper and wear. So, she played before them, unmasked and vulnerable, the way she'd felt since coming to Paris.

She'd been in the city a month now. Still unmarried at twenty, Porcelina had left home to follow the song in her heart and audition at the Palais Garnier. Seats were coming open in the opera house's symphony, and they had sent word of an open call for musicians—including women, an unheard-of proposition.

In the letters she sent back home, she told her family she was thriving, that the crowds which gathered to hear her play filled her violin case with money, and she ate beignets and mille-feuille from the finest patisseries with every meal.

Her stomach grumbled. In truth, Madame Reine Marie had been threatening to put her out of her room at the *pension de famille* all week, and Porcelina needed to earn enough today to pay the rent. She hoped there would be enough left over for food. She'd finished off the last of her bread and broth yesterday morning.

The crowd shifted and the masked man came into view again. Porcelina blushed beneath his intense gaze. She hesitated. Her bow jumped on a string, marring Berlioz's piece. A girl in a gold mask with pink blossoms on the cheeks *booed* loudly. Porcelina's fingers tightened, making the delicate notes screech like an injured owl. The onlookers moved away; their coins tucked in their pockets.

Porcelina stopped playing. The Palais Garnier swam in her

vision. How would she ever have the confidence to play there when she could not even part fools from their money? She collected the francs from the bottom of her case and placed them in her pocket. There would be no dinner tonight.

As she latched her case, the man in the white mask approached. "*Bonjour.*" His voice was deep and warm, like honey spread on fresh baked bread.

Porcelina turned. Up close, his mask was not so plain. Bone-white and made of soft leather, it molded to his face. Most masks surrounded only the eyes, but his covered the entire right side of his face. On the left, a sharp cheekbone and chiseled jaw stood out in stark contrast.

Soft flurries of snow drifted from the deepening sky and landed in his thick black hair, shining like tiny jewels. He regarded her with deep brown eyes. "It is a beautiful evening for playing, *oui*?"

When he spoke, his mask shifted and flexed on his face like a living thing. Porcelina blinked. Surely, a trick of the flickering lamplight?

"Are you hungry, mademoiselle?"

Ravenous. How could he tell? "Pardon, Monsieur?"

He straightened the lapel of his dark jacket, worn over a double-breasted maroon vest. "I have been too forward. Allow me to introduce myself." He smiled, showing off perfect teeth. "I am Chace Auclair, master of ceremonies for the *Spectacle Merveilleux*, at your service." He slung the silver handle of his walking cane over his arm and bowed. "If you would not think too terribly of me, I might ask the pleasure of your company for dinner."

The confidence in his manner made Porcelina want to fall into his arms and beg him to take her away from the ceaseless clatter of self-doubt and her tiny room that stank of sausages and despair.

She ran a hand over the waves in her mahogany hair, then

looked down at her simple black shirtwaist and ivory muslin skirt. "I fear I am not dressed for such fine company."

"You are in luck." He cocked a dark eyebrow, and the corner of his mouth pulled up in a smirk that dimpled his cheek. "I know a place, away from the stares *des imb*éciles who would scorn such a beautiful violinist."

Porcelina smiled despite herself. What could one meal with a handsome man hurt? She gathered her violin case and took Chace's offered arm.

They walked a few blocks to a small café. Tucked away on a private garden patio, they dined on *pot-au-feu* with carrots and cabbage, chased by a Bordeaux that left Porcelina lightheaded.

Chace did not remove his mask to eat. It moved on his face as he chewed and smiled, as real as skin. Porcelina wondered at the cost of such a creation of art.

When he asked about her, she told him of her family in Saint-Véran and her dreams of playing violin on stage.

He told her about his work as the leader of a small but exclusive traveling show. "The performers I employ are the most talented in all of Europe. Yet, they are cast aside from society for being different."

"Different?" Porcelina asked. "How so?"

Chace paused. "How can I explain it?" He tapped a finger on his chin. "They possess talents beyond understanding. Pure magic. You must see for yourself."

"A magic traveling show." Porcelina's eyes lit up. "I would love to."

"It's settled, then. You will be my guest this evening."

"This evening," Porcelina started. "No, I must be back at the boarding house before—"

"Nonsense. It is the time of Carnival. Surely, your *Matrone* would understand a late return." Chace laughed, deepening his dimple. "You are a beautiful woman, Porcelina. What wonders I could show you." He traced a line along the bottom of her jaw. "You mustn't say no."

Heat rose in Porcelina's cheeks. Swept away by his aplomb and too much red wine, not even the threat of Madame Reine Marie putting her suitcase out on the stoop would have kept her from saying yes to Chace Auclair.

🎭

Porcelina stepped inside the striped tent and gasped. It was as if she'd entered a secret world of wonder made just for her. Hanging silk drapes of green and purple surrounded the ring, blurring the sharp edges of reality. Tropical birds with colorful tails soared through the air, snatching roasted peanuts from the hands of surprised guests, then perched in the rafters to drop shells on their heads.

Porcelina sat on a wooden bench in the first row next to a woman in a Rococo face-veil and a gentleman in a Baroque mask and black top hat.

The lamps dimmed. A circle of light blinked on in the center of the ring. Chace faced the crowd, his white mask shining like a beacon. "Bienvenu, mesdames et messieurs, to the Spectacle Merveilleux. Preparez-vous a la magie." He worked the audience until their anticipation sizzled.

His spotlight faded and flashed on at the far side of the ring. A dainty woman, tall and thin, stood with arms outstretched. Porcelina blinked twice to clear her sight. This was no trick of the light, the woman had an extra set of arms extending from her sides. She wore a mask of silver filigree, green and white feathers arched along one side like a single butterfly wing, and a bodysuit stitched with tiny crystals that dazzled in the light.

Using all four arms, the woman climbed up the wooden tent pole in the center of the ring. On a small platform at the top, she bent over, and a pair of ivory angel wings unfolded from her back. The crowd gasped in unison.

The woman leapt from the platform. Her feathers ruffled like velvet curtains as she soared across the ring in aerial dance, yet no visible wires appeared to hold her aloft. She pulled the tips of her wings down, cupping them to catch the air, and floated to the ground. Applause exploded in the tent.

Clowns took the ring, their faces covered in rainbow masks that changed expressions as they tumbled and danced. The crowd pointed and laughed until a black leopard appeared and chased off the jolly clowns.

Porcelina had intended to sneak out of the show early. She should be in her room practicing for her audition, or taking in some sewing for extra money, but she could not tear herself away.

A tall woman with olive skin ran into the ring. She wore a gold and black matador suit and a velvet feline mask across her eyes. From the lower half of her face, grew a long black beard. She had waxed and twirled it into stiff strands that stuck out like cat's whiskers. Her midnight hair fell loose, flowing like a cape around her shoulders as she wrangled the leopard through hoops and tricks. The jungle cat hissed and spat, making the crowd wriggle in fear.

Porcelina dreamed of performing with the grace and confidence these women exuded. Perhaps this was the reason Chace, after watching her play today, had insisted she see his show—to inspire her.

Two women with flaming red hair, joined at the back as though they shared a single spine, and wearing a single red tulle dress, bounded into the ring, their four legs moving in perfect harmony. One of them lit a match and placed it in her mouth, then her twin spit out flame in great spouts that sent the matador and her feline fleeing. They went on this way, setting wooden spikes on fire and juggling them around their heads to one another.

After them came a woman with blue skin and tattooed from neck to toe. Her mask was covered in a pattern of green and silver diamonds with ebony horns protruding from each side. She clapped castanets in her hands, pirouetting and gyrating to her own music. As she danced, the stretched images on her skin came to life—ink tigers and bears roared and lashed out with razor claws; half-dressed figurines and hummingbirds soared off her skin and around her body, moving in time to the woman's music.

Last, a legless half-woman in a tightly cinched peach corset, bouquets of rose gold flowers growing on her mask, carried herself into the ring on her hands. The crowd made hushed noises of shock, though their eyes glittered with delight. She grabbed at hanging strips of satin and swung herself through the air in arching circles, higher and higher, her auburn hair flying, until at last she let go, flew through the air and landed in a slide through the sawdust.

When her dance was done, the entire troupe gathered for their final bows. Porcelina whistled and clapped with the rest of the audience. Hot emotion filled her eyes. In the light of day these women would be called freaks and strangers. Her own differences might not be visible on the outside, but inside she felt as lonely and set apart from the rest of the world as they must. How lovely it would be to perform like them—tucked inside the folds of this tent, safe behind their masks.

Chace assisted Porcelina up the steps into his traveling wagon. "What did you think of the show?"

Porcelina clasped her hands. "So beautiful, I haven't words for it."

He smiled, that smoldering grin that brought out his dimple, and Porcelina's heart fluttered in her breast.

"As you can imagine," he said, "these women are not welcomed by society. A shame, though, for they are far more talented than the people who mock them." Chace pulled Porcelina next to him on the small sofa. "I found each of my artists, poor and struggling, on the street. Some of them worked the sideshows." He scoffed. "Disgusting places where the barker encouraged their ridicule, providing the rotten fruit the crowd threw at them."

"No!" Porcelina's hand flew to her mouth.

A serious look settled on his face. "You understand, then? They are just like you. Women who simply needed someone to bring out the best in them."

"In some ways I envy them." Porcelina smiled shyly. "Their fearlessness."

"The masks help," Chace said. "With them, we have the confidence to show the world our true inner selves."

Porcelina reached to touch Chace's masked cheek. He caught her hand. "I see in you what I saw in them, and more." He kissed her fingers. "You have a great talent, Porcelina, waiting to be seen."

Heat seeped along her skin. She looked away. "I came to Paris to play—"

"Yet, you lack confidence."

Porcelina opened her mouth to refute him, then snapped it shut. He wasn't wrong.

"That is why we wear these masks. They are not just a part of the show. They are part of the performer."

Porcelina furrowed her brow.

Chace regarded her for a long moment, then said, "Can I show you something? Something very secret?" He stood and moved to the front corner of the wagon.

Desire rolled in Porcelina like thunder across a stormy sky. She wanted him and all of his secrets.

He pulled a black cloth from the towering object in the corner to reveal a large water tank, which contained the strangest fish Porcelina had ever seen. There were no gills or fins, only a gray mass of soft flesh and writhing stems.

Chace held a hand out. Porcelina joined him. "What is it?"

"Long before this life" —Chace touched his mask— "I was an architect." The corner of his lips turned down. "Together with Monsieur Garnier, our design won Napoleon III's competition, and we were selected to build his opera house."

Porcelina gasped. "You?"

Chace nodded. "I was involved all the way up to building the reservoir that exists beneath it. Soon after, that madman, Garnier, became jealous and possessive. He made my life such a torment, I was forced to leave." Chace sighed and touched the glass.

The translucent creature within stirred. Tentacles, like long spiraling staircases, emerged from the thing's body and pressed against the glass at Chace's fingertips. "After the Palais Garnier's completion, the bitterness of failure grew in my heart. I knew of a clandestine entrance to the canals beneath the opera house, and I would go down there and listen to the world's greatest opera singers to drown my sorrows in their voices. Then one night, I found her floating in the water."

"Her?" Porcelina said.

"Yes," Chace said. His fingers traced patterns on the glass, the creature's tentacles following. "I call her Mother. She became caught inside the reservoir when it was built. When I touched her, it was the most fascinating thing. I could see the world beneath the water, through her thoughts. But more than that, Porcelina, she showed me how I could be confident again, better than I was before. She gave me a gift." Chace's hand tightened into a fist. "I had been driven away from my dreams by Monsieur Garnier, but that did not have to be the end of me."

The strange fish shifted, its gelatinous body twisting and writhing in on itself. Suddenly, from beneath a fold, a smaller version of itself emerged.

"Oh," Porcelina gasped. "It has a child?"

"We are all her children," Chace said, his face solemn. "She creates these offspring for us, and when they have grown to this size," he pointed at the small creature, "it is ready to emerge from the tank and find a host." Chace turned to her, his palm on his mask. "These masks we wear ... they are alive."

Porcelina's mouth gaped. Her eyes darted from Chace's face to Mother and back again. "Alive? But ..." She shook her head.

"They are her gifts to us. Each mask gives of itself in order to enhance the talents of its wearer." Chace touched his mask. "I am the man I am today because of it. And tonight, what you saw was not a performance, it was magic. In exchange, we offer our bodies as hosts."

Porcelina's nose wrinkled. She backed away.

Chace grabbed her hand. "I understand what you must think. It seems an odd thing until you've experienced it. All your fears, all your insecurities, vanish. And in their place, confidence. Your talents and abilities on stage." He grinned his perfect grin. "You would be unstoppable."

Porcelina pulled free. The backs of her knees knocked into the sofa and she sat down hard on the velvet cushion. "I couldn't ..." She stared at him, shock and confusion at war within.

Chace sat beside her and folded his hands on hers. "Imagine it, Porcelina, to never be hungry again. We drink wine and feast on delicacies from every country we visit." He smoothed a strand of hair from her face, sending shivers of excitement down her spine. "A home you cannot be evicted from. The finest gowns made by the finest dressmakers. All that and more, I can give you."

An ache opened up in Porcelina's chest. She thought of her family and the lies she filled her letters with. Her eyes searched Chace's. In them she saw a sincerity that quelled her doubt.

Chace squeezed her hand. "And, you would have me."

The Palais Garnier flashed in Porcelina's mind. Its trio of granite staircases, gold-tasseled curtains, and the bronze chandelier with its thousands of crystals that hung above the auditorium. Every seat filled with guests, all there to see her— Porcelina Juin—chin resting on her violin, the smell of warmed rosin a perfume in the air.

It was her plan to play her violin in the darkened pit before a stage filled with beautiful men and women dressed in elaborate costumes of satin and pearl. Costumes. Wasn't a mask just a costume? Didn't every performer wear one in order to have the confidence, the bravery, to shine in the light? Would a living mask really be so different?

Porcelina stared at her hands, tears gathering on her lashes. "I want all of those things."

Chace lifted her chin with a finger, his deep brown eyes piercing her. "Be mine, and everything I have will be yours."

Porcelina touched his cheek, his mask. It was smooth and warm; muscles flexed beneath it as she traced her fingers down to his jaw.

"Join us, *ma chérie*," he whispered. "Become one with us ..." Chace leaned in.

Porcelina closed her eyes and tilted her face up to meet him. His lips were full and soft, his kiss commanding. He wrapped an arm about her waist and pulled her closer.

Chace Auclair was a prince, straight from the pages of her childhood storybooks. And she would be his princess in a mask.

Chace placed the creature on her face. The pain was immediate —hundreds of tiny teeth boring into her flesh. Gasping, Porcelina jerked up from the bed. The jelly-blob slid off and *plopped* into her lap. Chace settled her back on the pillows. Porcelina shuddered, but allowed him to place the cold slimy thing onto her face again. The sensation worsened. Tiny paint brushes swept across her skin, biting and digging. Then, a suction that grew in intensity until tears poured from her eyes.

Morning light crawled through the wax-paper windows of Chace's traveling wagon when he came to check on her again. "How are you?"

"I can't sleep. It hurts so."

Chace kissed her hands. "Stay still, it will be done soon. After, you will not be able to tell where it ends and you begin. You shall be one."

"What will it look like when it's done, my mask?"

"Each one takes on a unique shape and color. A design to represent the truest beauty of its host."

Porcelina grimaced as another wave of searing pain spread across her face.

He smoothed back her hair. "Try and rest."

Porcelina dozed. What would her mask say about her truest beauty? And what did Chace's pure white mask say about his?

Hours later, Porcelina was awake and vomiting into a bowl on her lap. Madeline, the matador woman, wiped Porcelina's face with a damp cloth, then took the bowl to empty it.

Outside the window next to her bed, Porcelina overheard Madeline and Chace speaking.

"It's not taking," Chace said quietly. "Why isn't it taking?"

"My best guess, she's fighting it," Madeline said. "All I know is it's dying and making her very ill."

Sweat gathered beneath Porcelina's arms. She bit at her

lower lip. All of her dreams spread at her feet and still she failed. And Chace—would he turn her out into the cold? Send her back to play on the streets, alone and starving? If this didn't work, Porcelina would have no choice but to return home, her heart broken and her tail tucked.

"This is no good," Chace said. "I must have her! She is the key that would open all the doors that have been closed to us. We will have aristocracy eating from the palms of our hands. She—"

"Could be your wife?" Madeline said.

"Has such talent," Chace finished, his voice a grim whisper. There was a long pause, then he said, "Put some of this into her tea."

Madeline made a garbled sound. "Chace, no, this could—"

"I said, give it to her."

Madeline entered the trailer a moment later and pulled back the hanging that separated the bed from the rest of the room. "Porcelina, darling." She sat on the edge of the bed.

"I heard." Tears slipped from Porcelina's eyes. "Why isn't it working?"

"Perhaps you struggle too much, or your fear and uncertainty are too great. I cannot say."

"It wasn't this way with you?" Porcelina asked.

Madeline shook her head, her long black beard swinging against her chest.

Porcelina's fingers tightened on the bed cover. "Is there nothing that can be done?"

Madeline's shoulders drooped, then she slid a smooth glass vial from her pocket. "This is laudanum. Enough, and you should sleep through the worst of it."

Porcelina eyed the brown liquid, her lower lip trembled. "Chace wants me to take it?"

Madeline nodded. "There are risks. You're not a regular

user. Too much and your breathing will stop." She squeezed Porcelina's hand. "Do you understand?"

Porcelina thought of Chace—his lips, his touch. She thought of the show the night before and the fearless women in their masks. She met Madeline's strong gaze. "I just want to be brave like all of you."

Madeline's lips pressed into a thin line, but she nodded and left the trailer. When she returned, she held out a steaming cup. "Here, drink this quickly, before it cools."

Porcelina took the cup in trembling hands and gulped down the reddish-brown tea. It was thick and bitter on her tongue. Her eyelids drooped. She fell back against the pillows. The empty teacup rolled from her fingertips and *plinked* onto the floor. The warm sucking sensation on her face grew. This time, there was no pain.

Porcelina studied her reflection in the small mirror above the dressing table. Colors grew on her mask—spirals of blues and violet, like a bruise in blossom, lined in sheer pinks. It itched. She scraped a fingernail along the edges where her skin ended and the creature began.

Chace appeared behind her. "Don't scratch, *ma note de musique*. You don't want to damage it. Are you ready for tonight?"

She swept her hair from her neck with shaky hands. "I'm terribly nervous."

"There is no reason to be. You cannot fail." Chace smirked, his dimple sending spires of heat through Porcelina's bosom. "But perhaps this will help."

Chace stepped out. When he returned, he carried a violin made of golden spruce, backed in dark maple.

Porcelina peered through the f-hole. "A Stradivarius! Oh, Chace, I couldn't."

He laid a kiss on her forehead. "A new violin for a new woman."

Tears in her eyes, Porcelina threw her arms around his neck. She was ready to take the stage.

The spotlight blinked on. Porcelina stood in the center of the ring, sawdust beneath her feet and the pine smell of rosin on her fingers.

Her hands trembled as she swept her bow across the taut strings of her violin. The reverberation sang through her skin. The mask slithered on her face. Chace had said this performance would seal it to her forever. Is that what she truly wanted? Her arm jerked at the thought. Then, a feeling of warmth slid along her nerve endings, like slipping into a hot bath. Her arm moved smoothly, her fingers floated along the strings, but she was no longer in charge of them. The mask had taken over. Assured by Chace she could not fail tonight, Porcelina had chosen to play a difficult piece, one she had never mastered: Paganini's Caprice 24.

Instead, Liszt's Mephisto Waltz, No 1. poured from her fingertips, with its erratic, hectic strumming. Porcelina plucked at the strings with frenetic energy, her body jerking in time. She tried to stop, to freeze her hands, but they would not obey. This was *not* the music that sang in her soul. This was something entirely different.

The song played through her, and as the last frenzied note drifted across the silent tent, Porcelina's heart hammered in her chest. Though the song was not of her choosing, she had played it to perfection.

The audience was silent. Dazed, Porcelina dropped a leg

back to take her bow. The crowd took to its feet, the silence during her performance pierced by their storm of yells, whistles, and applause. Grinning, Porcelina hurried from the ring.

Behind the canvas curtain, Chace greeted her. "*Mon Dieu,* that was perfection!"

Both confused and pleased, Porcelina said, "Oh, Chace. It was so strange. I hadn't intended to play that piece, but the mask, it took over and *that* came out."

"It was brilliant." Chace smiled. "You will be our greatest attraction yet!"

Porcelina laughed, tears of joy rolling down her cheeks. She had performed before a crowd, fearless, and they had loved her. "It has been my dream to perform in front of the stage in the Palais Garnier, hidden away. But now, the world will come to see me play *on* it!"

Chace laughed and squeezed her arms. "Porcelina, *ma chérie,* you cannot stay in Paris."

Porcelina stopped laughing. "What do you mean?"

"You are one of us now. For the mask to work, you must stay near Mother."

"What?" Porcelina pulled from his grasp. "You didn't tell me this." She searched his deep brown eyes. "You're saying I can never leave?"

The corner of Chace's lips turned down. "And why would you want to? We're your family now."

On the other side of the curtain, the crowd stomped their feet, shouting, "Encore, encore!"

"Go now, my swan, your fans are calling for you." Chace spun Porcelina around and shoved her through the curtain.

Porcelina's legs were heavy as she trudged to the center of the ring, a gnawing sensation in her gut. What had just happened? The spotlight slammed on, blinding her. She lifted a hand to block its glare. The crowd hushed. What song would come from her violin this time? Sweat gathered on her forehead. Porcelina pulled at the high collar of her pale green dress. The air felt thick, cloying, every breath a struggle.

Someone in the audience coughed. Porcelina could hear their whispers, feel their eagerness. It did not matter to them she had become *la marionette*, her strings pulled by the parasite on her face; the people wanted a show.

How had she let the seduction of easy success sway her from what she wanted most? She wanted to play her own songs and bring to life the music that lived inside of her, but with the mask in charge would that ever be possible?

It was her dream to play at the great opera house in Paris, but now ... Chace's words echoed in her mind. *I have been driven away from my dreams ... but that does not have to be the end of me.*

She could not let this tent forever be her prison.

The Stradivarius slipped from Porcelina's hands. She clawed at the edge of her mask. The warm tingling sensation shot down her arms, trying to force her hands away. Porcelina fought against it, dug her nails beneath the mask and ripped the writhing creature from her face.

Flesh tore. The pain: pure, ripe, agony.

Screams filled the tent.

Porcelina did not stop. She peeled the mask off the rest of the way, her own cries drowned out by the cacophony of disaster around her. Then it was gone—an enormous weight lifted from her body.

She looked down at the parasite mask in her hands. Clinging to the inside were pieces of her bloody skin and a mass of short flailing tentacles—like silk maggots—that writhed and squirmed.

The crowd were on their feet, pushing against one another. Their boots pounded, men yelled, and still the women screamed.

Porcelina sank to her knees.

Madeline came and knelt beside her. She took the mask

from Porcelina's hands and cradled the limp creature gently to her chest.

The tent flaps slapped open again and again like angry clapping as the people pushed out into the night, the sound of their terror trailing behind them like a mournful wake.

Around them, the other performers were bent over in pain, their hands on their faces. "I'm so sorry, Madeline." Salty tears burned down Porcelina's face. "I never meant to hurt any of you, or ..." Her eyes drifted down to the dying creature in Madeline's hands.

Madeline looked at Porcelina, her own tears slipping down her velvet mask into her beard. "It's all right, Porcelina. I will return it to the tank. Mother will heal it."

"I didn't know." Porcelina let out a sob. "Chace, he didn't tell me everything."

Madeline nodded. "I know." She looked around the tent at the other masked women. "We have all stood in your place, on the night of our premier performance. It was not true freedom he offered us, but ..." she paused, swallowed hard. "He gave us a home, a place to belong. Something most of us have never had. So, we each made a choice." She held the mask up. "The same as you did tonight."

"I wanted so much to be like all of you," Porcelina said, "beautiful and unafraid. I never meant to disappoint you."

"Oh, *ma fille*." Madeline grabbed Porcelina's hand and squeezed. "You have not disappointed us. You have inspired us."

Porcelina wrapped her arms around Madeline's neck and hugged her tight, the matador woman's beard a soft touch against Porcelina's face.

Madeline chuckled. "Careful." She pulled away, shifting the mask in her hands. "Go on now." Madeline jutted her chin at the fallen violin. "Take that and go."

Porcelina shook her head. "No, I couldn't—"

"Consider it a gift." Madeline motioned to the other women. "From us."

Porcelina grabbed the violin and got to her feet. She spun in a slow circle, meeting the gaze of every performer. The trio of clowns in their rainbow masks; Rocket, the tattooed beauty; and the fire-breathing twins, The Flame Dames. All of them stood up straight, some smiled at her, others simply nodded.

Behind her, Chace yelled, "Porcelina!"

Porcelina spun around. Chace stood frozen, his shoulders pulled back, chin held high. Streaks of red seeped from the edges of his mask and ran down his face—tears of blood staining his pure white mask. Then, he placed his hand over his heart.

Porcelina bowed her head. Hot tears searing her face. She could have loved him, but the scars on his heart had made the muscle too tough to penetrate. Still, he had given her a gift. Chace Auclair, master of ceremonies for the *Spectacle Merveilleux* was a creation of his own fears and insecurities, trapped by his own failures. She would not be.

Porcelina turned and strode out of the tent, out into the cold.

🎭

Today was the last day of auditions. Porcelina walked through the grand doors of the Palais Garnier, her battered violin case clutched in sweaty hands.

Porcelina waited in the wings, her face turned down. She wore an ivory lace mask across the top half of her face. It had taken two weeks for her wounds to close enough for her to leave her room at Madame Reine Marie's. The doctors said in time the scarring would lessen, but she might never heal completely. She'd spent the time composing and practicing her own piece of music.

The director called her name, and Porcelina made her way from behind the curtain. On the stage was a single chair. Porcelina sat and pulled her well-worn violin from its case. She had sold the Stradivarius to stay in Paris so she could pursue her dream.

A spotlight flashed on, blinding her. Sweat gathered on her upper lip. Days ago, she'd received a letter from Madeline. The troupe were in Moscow now, sipping vodka and eating varenniki, all of them healthy and content; even Chace and Mother. Porcelina thought of those beautiful masked women, confident and safe behind their masks. She reached up and untied the ribbon around her head. The lace mask slid from her face onto her lap. Porcelina pressed the violin to her chin, took a deep breath, then lifted her face to the judges.

Porcelina's fingers trembled as they moved along the worn strings of her violin. Her song floated into the air.

Alicia Cay is a writer of Speculative and Mystery stories. Her short fiction has appeared in several anthologies including *Hold Your Fire* from WordFire Press, and *The Wild Hunt* from Air and Nothingness Press. She suffers from wanderlust, crochets, collects quotes, and lives beneath the shadows of the Rocky Mountains with a corgi, a kitty, and a lot of fur.

Find her at aliciacay.com.

SPEAKEASY

KELTIE ZUBKO

His words, messaged on the dating app, showed up on her phone as she checked her location and stopped abruptly at the unmarked entrance. A man who'd been following at about six feet behind swerved to avoid running into her and snapped, "Watch the distancing!" then stomped around and past her through the rain. She paused, trying to catch her breath through her mask and examined the inhospitable building, then read their last exchange again before he'd sent the address of the place now before her.

"You said you wanted to talk face to face."

"*There*?"

"Just a coffee shop."

"But so small."

She'd almost missed it. No windows let in the chilled gaze of passers-by. Tightly fastened shutters hoarded and protected whatever waited inside for her. No sign out front marked it, just the building number from earlier, more optimistic days, and some graffiti she couldn't decipher except for the words "or die." She glanced behind to make sure she wasn't stepping in front of anyone else and tried the door anyway. It gave, so she pulled it open, then peered into the dim vestibule. A man stood like a guard, alert behind his clear plastic shield with a mask covering his lower face. This looked like the right place. She stepped inside.

She felt him watching her fasten the door against the rainy wind. She suspected some errant draft may have slipped in with her, hiding in her rain gear or tucked discreetly behind her own mask and she shivered, looking into the eyes of the man protecting the rest of the place from her view. His bulky figure couldn't prevent the blast of heat and noise seething up from behind him, greeting and enticing her. In previous times this very place would have been a cozy retreat from the damp weather, but now the prospect of going inside made her shiver again, this time not from the cold. The man's eyes narrowed as she approached, and his voice cut through the muffling of the mask.

"What do you want?"

"I'm supposed to meet someone here. Named Carl." She stopped, not getting too close, hearing the outside door open and shut again while the host glanced up and then back to his computer screen.

"He's here already. And he's vouched for you. Emma, right? But you still have to read and sign the waiver. He couldn't do that for you."

At odds with his mask and elaborate plastic shield, he pushed a tablet at her, not bothering to sanitize it or take pains over the proper distance. She backed off a bit from reflex, then looked up into his skeptical eyes.

"Not used to it, you know."

"Well, maybe you shouldn't come in, then. No one's making you."

"Oh, no, I want to!" She reached out and took the tablet, looking at the long list on the screen before her.

"You can't enter until you've signed the waiver. You'd better read all the fine print." Another couple fidgeted behind her now at the prescribed distance, and she felt them invisibly urge her to hurry.

"You realize masks are optional? And we don't control who breathes on you, right? Or where people stand or sit, where you stand or sit, who approaches you or not, and what traces they or you might leave or bring with you? Or the consequences."

His eyebrows rose and fell with emphasis as he recited the conditions of the waiver she'd have to sign, all the time watching her eyes. Despite the mask securing the lower part of her face, he seemed to read her doubt. They never used to have bouncers in coffee shops but that's what he resembled. Indoors with no fresh-air patio, this place was supposed to be heavily regulated. She had to get by him to enter and meet the guy from the app. There were always squealers, she knew, imagining the trouble they could make for her, or this small business, struggling on the edge to survive. It was not like the old days when they openly lured crowds of people to stream freely in and out, and crammed in as many people as they could.

She knew the dangers of going into the modest little coffee shop. The operative word, of course, was "little." Many places had been shut down a long time ago, near the beginning of the pandemic, never to open again. She remembered all those hangouts they had taken for granted, redolent of coffee and warm with companionship. They were tiny, tight spaces efficiently paring down expensive square footage to serve office workers, hurried workmen or students huddled laptop to laptop renting wifi and a spot to study with the price of a coffee.

Such small shops now operated with wide distances between the few patrons, or allowed no one inside, doing take-out instead. The host was supposed to police traffic, letting only a certain number of people in at a time, supervising proper single-file spacing, checking for masks and refusing business to those who didn't comply. But this place operated outside those rules. The host, pugnacious and ready to turn her away, seemed like he'd stepped out of some forgotten history. She felt sweat accumulate on her upper lip behind her mask and her breath was hot and suffocating.

He blocked the view behind him, down the few steps where she imagined a dangerous array of rebels mingled in a soup of sweat and odor, taunting the capricious virus. In such close quarters she supposed it could jump person to person, from the careless or the bold, to the lonely or the jaded. Desperate people, like her. It was everything she'd been told to avoid, and had avoided, until this point, swiping her sanitized phone right or left on the app, carrying on long disembodied text conversations with fingertips instead of intimate words you'd have to lean in to hear. She'd even had a few distanced dates, too remote for any spark to leap *that* divide. But this was another chance. Their banter back and forth was fun and easy. She wanted to meet him, see his face, hear his voice unstifled by mask, shield, or that new kind of trepidation she'd found and tried to bury in herself.

"Just read."

The host brought her attention back to the tablet. His scrutiny groped her face and body, intruding on the skin bordering her mask. Her face burned underneath it. Breathing her own recycled breath oppressed her and made her feel she might swoon one of these days if she didn't get fresh air instead. She wanted to meet this guy named Carl, but why here of all places, she wondered. She re-read the long list of dangers he was exposing her to, that she would defy if she stepped past the roped-off threshold and down the few steps into the place called the Speakeasy.

"Okay, so you gonna sign?" She checked the tablet one last time, scrolling to make sure she'd read it all, then holding her thumb above the space indicated, hesitated before pressing it down on the touchscreen. As if this was a defense in any court these days, she thought, but did it anyway. He checked to see that it registered and scanned her i.d. Watching what she could see of his face, she figured that finally he smiled. His eyes had tender little crinkles at the edges and narrowed again, but in a friendlier sort of way. Just how much had she misjudged him, and whether his lips were thin or full, and if he showed his teeth when he smiled, she wondered as he beckoned her to step past him and unclasped the heavy velvet rope. She stopped just beyond him on the top step, preparing for her descent down to the coffee shop itself.

"Oh, and ..." he spoke gentler to her now. She stopped, looking up at him. "You will want to ..." He gestured at his mask and she hesitated, but then understood and turned away, as if now she had to strip naked before going any further. She reached up and slid the straps of her own mask off her head, then stowed it in her bag.

The noise implied that there were many more than the ten or less allowed into any venue of this size, public or private. The sound rose up to draw her toward the gathering of people. She remembered how it felt entering a crowded bar, meeting the mysterious men that inhabited the world of the past.

In the dim light of those bars or clubs you'd never know who was getting close enough to press against your body, exhale their steamy breath on your neck or attempt to whisper provocative words to you while watching your lips for a clue. They might be the worst loser or greatest possibility, but those were the chances you'd take—that you wanted to take—back then. She remembered the auburn beard of her last boyfriend in that other time. He had shaved it off so he could wear a tight-fitting respirator, and she still mourned those crisp little hairs tickling her skin.

With the mask off her face now, she flushed as the heat rolled up to engulf her in the sudden pleasure of being open and unrestrained. Her cheeks tingled and the back of her neck felt like some breeze nestled in her hair.

She made her way down the few steps, studying the small area, then stopped again, leaning on a bannister to orient herself. The couple who'd arrived after her hurried past, veering too close.

The wave of smells greeting her began to have nuances, and she almost took a deep breath, then froze and cautiously let herself inhale slow dribbles of air rich with a variety of vape flavors, something fragrant like her grandfather's pungent pipe tobacco, and all the odors her mask would have blunted. The combination of aromas and noise from people together in the tight space gripped and pulled her like a firm, warm hand she could not resist.

Underlying the dark scent of fresh coffee, tea, and the earthy perfume of so many bodies closer together than normal, there was something else, undefinable and elusive. It wafted across the boundaries between people, pushing her into the invisible maelstrom toward the long counter with the busy baristas. She hadn't located him yet, the guy named Carl. She'd get her drink first, then go find him. The aroma of the coffee made her once again breathe deeper than she meant to until she pictured that spiky little juggernaut of a virus, infiltrating and latching onto the careless and unwary.

Around her a buffet of faces talked and laughed. Their expressions blossomed in the heat and attention, smiling or frowning, not noticing her as they focused on each other. Lips in luscious colors surrounded her with marvelous, disconcerting variety. Her own felt pale and uncertain. Jawlines and mouths, some framed by emerging whiskers or full-out beards, presented her with a range of unsettling possibilities. They were within reach. She could have extended her awkward, inhibited fingers and touched them.

Meanwhile, laughter spewed germs into the air. They

hovered everywhere, targeting her and the heedless crowd. Invisible enemies rose from their hot bodies, hitch-hiking on their confidence, sweat and pheromones. As she stepped closer, still waiting to order her coffee, she couldn't stop visualizing miniscule sprays of the most virulent kind, escaping each person to fly through the confined space. You didn't know what was let loose from those unhindered mouths. But she did know every admonition. The contagion could travel farther than you thought possible on the most ordinary human function: a yawn, a giggle, a smile, a word spoken too enthusiastically, a cough or worse, a sneeze. Somewhere deeper in the room, the man who'd lured her there, watched. She peered around, looking for him. She checked her phone but there was no message. She told herself she could still leave.

Four people sat at a table just large enough to hold their mugs, their heads drifting too close together. She pictured the virus jumping like opportunistic fleas from one bent head to another. In a tiny booth a couple faced each other, their hands on the table, his resting on top of hers. She imagined their sweat mingling and with it the virus, crossing from one to the other, sweet, deceiving and perhaps deadly.

Something nuzzled her again, like an insidious idea, carrying unknown threats or promise. It played with her, brushed her skin, making her tremble and look around the room again. The press of warm bodies moved closer to the till in contrast to the isolated people outside, slogging their separate ways through the cold and wet streets. Even if the guy named Carl turned out to be all wrong, at least she could still have just the simple pleasure of sitting close enough to eavesdrop on strangers again.

The miasma of smells enveloped her, pressuring her to almost bump against the person in front of her. The straps of her mask had left marks that she still felt, clinging to her face, impressing upon her the rules of proper pandemic behavior.

She always donned it first thing in the morning before leaving her place. The marks made a border around the usually censored part of her face.

She inched closer to the counter. Just as her phone vibrated in her pocket with a message, she glanced up at the wall behind the counter and noticed an old bumper sticker pinned there amid a few other haphazard decorations. Puzzled, she saw that once it had read "Live Free or Die." Now the first two words were crossed out. Handwritten in big black letters above them was one other word, the name of the coffee shop so that the sticker read, "Speakeasy or Die!" Her eyes opened wide, and startled, she took in a deep breath as her hand rose in reflex to her own once familiar cheek. But that was taboo. She pulled her hand back down and glanced around.

That's when she caught him, phone in his hand, but watching her. His look reached out from across the room as palpable as a touch about to soothe her cheek. His own face was unmasked, and the promise of a smile rested there.

She blushed. His smile spread, a hybrid of two emotions, she thought. Which would win, humour or desire? With that question, she hesitated, wondering if she could tip the response on his face one way or the other. She turned away from the counter then and slipped out of the lineup.

She walked toward him, cheeks burning, and smiled at him the way people used to do. Of course, she thought, the virus still lurked somewhere nearby—hiding, cajoling, bargaining and tricking them all. She checked his smile again, and let her fears fly up into the air like confetti, a bit like the virus disguised in the droplets of a sneeze. That mysterious small draft—a wish or a hope—blew through the confined hot atmosphere of the tiny shop so they could speak, face to face. Easily.

Keltie Zubko is a Western Canadian writer, born in Alberta and now based on Vancouver Island, BC. She has an extensive background doing research and writing legal arguments, as well as writing about free speech and Western Canadian politics. She now prefers to explore in fiction our human relationships with each other and with technology. Her work has appeared in Canada, the U.S. and internationally.

FRAMING MARTA

JAMES ROMAG

Normally Marta enjoyed bonfires in the town square on autumn evenings, though not this time. Not when she was secured to a post atop a waiting mound of kindling and logs. She understood it was standard procedure for exterminating witches—as outlined in the village "Igniting All Mannere of Bad Thinges" manual—but she also knew she was not a witch. Of that she was certain. *Absolutely* certain. She also had no intention of ever becoming one, regardless of what Sorcerer Drycreek prophesied. Yet here she stood in her best black dress and new boots, falsely accused of said crime and scheduled to be burned alive at the stake shortly after sundown.

She cursed Drycreek for trying to impose on her something for which she had neither enthusiasm nor inclination. More than a decade earlier, when she'd been content learning the cobbling and sewing trades by day and studying her passions of Latin and astronomy by night, Drycreek had called upon the shoe shop "purely by chance" one afternoon with glorious ideas and grandiose plans and proclaimed she was destined to become one of the most celebrated witches ever. It seemed innocent enough at the time. So how did things reach the point where she was about to be served up *hominum flambé*?

As she pondered Drycreek's persistent misdirection that had led to this moment on the platform of a soon-to-be raging bonfire, a rotten tomato smacked her on the cheek, smearing across her jaw and concealing half her face. She peered at the small crowd gathered around her and focused on Younge Ethan, a local boy perpetually in need of a bath. He started to laugh but fled when he caught her evil eye.

Marta flicked her tongue and shook her head to free the bits of Younge Ethan's tomato face covering and sighed. *Surely, they'll see the real me behind this contrived drama and agree I'm but a lowly cobbler and seamstress*, she thought. *In the meantime, must I endure this theatrical twenty-four-hour viewing? I know many of these folk. They wouldn't really burn me, would they?* She squirmed a bit up on the platform. *And where's a loo when you need one?*

Over the course of the fifteen or so hours she'd already endured on public display, she'd accumulated plenty of fruits and vegetables—enough to start her own market stand and soup kitchen—but no offers of assistance. A church bell tolled somewhere in the village, a reminder that her scheduled incineration was approaching a bit too quickly, in the hour after dusk when the moon began its rise. Would she really be set ablaze?

A soft breeze ruffled her long dark curly hair, sending it swirling around her head, masking half her face. Someone in the crowd whistled as the breeze lifted her dress just enough to show a bit of striped stocking over the top of a tall boot. Marta squinted at the man, whose whistle turned into an uncontrollable cough.

Her initial fear and anger following her capture yesterday had worn off long ago and been replaced by boredom, with a dash of impatience. She scanned the crowd before her.

"Mrs. Winslow," Marta called out. "Ahem."

A woman in a dark dress and gloves talking with a man next to her lifted her head.

"Yes, you, Mrs. Winslow. Did I not tell you that black was a mistake due to the way it accentuated your pale complexion? When you came to me—somewhat prematurely—for mourning attire, did I not provide the draught that brought your husband back from death's door?"

Mrs. Winslow's reply came in the form of a displeased snort.

"You're best off with that medium blue frock I stitched for you," said Marta.

"But *you're* in black," said Mrs. Winslow. She held her hand above her eyes to shield the sun.

Marta looked down at her own dress. True, her original pattern called for a simple frock of red fabric, and that's what she started with. For reasons still to be sorted out, when she finished sewing it, she had a ruched dress and cloak in black, which she now wore as she stood for all to see above that waiting heap of dry wood.

"Well, yes," said Marta, "because it suits me and my complexion. Plus, one can't deny it goes well with my boots. And my stockings." A gust of wind raised the dress just enough to show a flash of leggings. This time, no one dared whistle and instead most of the men in the crowd averted their eyes.

Marta had taken the idea for the stockings from the uniforms she'd designed for a team of young men playing that new Rugby Sporte over in the town of Luna. Initially, she wasn't sure she'd like the pattern when she was stitching the socks, but the black-and-white horizontal stripes turned out to compliment her whole ensemble.

"If you say so," said Mrs. Winslow, who returned to her chat with her companion, ignoring Marta.

Marta puffed her cheeks and blew her curly locks from her chin. The curls fell right back to wrap across her nose and mouth. If only she'd had time to get her hair trimmed before they came with torches and pitchforks to pull her from her thatched-roof cottage in the woods. Seeing how it was midafternoon when the clumsy mob showed up at her home the first time, she felt the torches were overkill; nothing but an overwrought, melodramatic trope used by unimaginative witchfinders.

Thunk! Instead of a tomato, this time it was a rotten cabbage that hit her and pulled her from her thoughts. She cursed Drycreek again and searched the gathering crowd. Where was that reptile of a man in her moment of need?

From the time a good twelve years ago when he'd proclaimed she had an aura, through her lackluster efforts at witchcraft schooling, Sorcerer Drycreek had taken credit for any of her successes, however minor, and blamed her for her failures. Now, though, when she was erroneously accused of full-blown witchcraft and counting down the final hours of her life, he was absent.

Their most recent argument had been over her dedication to the craft. That was three and three and three days ago in Marta's cottage. The argument had started during her usual Friday midnight lessons when Drycreek exclaimed once again that she wasn't trying hard enough. She knew he was right, but she simply didn't care. After all, she was not and would never be a witch, so what was the point?

At first, when she was barely a teen, the prospect of witch-craft was new and exciting, but soon it was dull and dry, and who had the patience to collect gnats' wings and midnight shadows and wolves' howls anyway? For Marta, it was all a bit eyeroll inducing. Give her a sturdy piece of canvas or leather and she could make the best shoes or boots this side of Styks. Give her a swath of fabric and she could stitch an outfit that would make a person look like someone new.

The night of their fateful disagreement, she explained to Drycreek yet again that *that* was where her skills lay. "Stitchery, not witchery," she said. Expect her to cure a wart on a big toe, well, that was something entirely different. Hard to find inspiration there. Unless it was a wart on her own nose, which she did remove rather handily a year ago, and yet when she checked herself in her silver mirror last week it seemed to be returning. Nevertheless, Drycreek still wouldn't listen and implored her to learn the witchcraft trade.

Mid-argument, Marta picked up the besom from the wall near her fireplace and shooed him out the door. Drycreek threw his hands in the air and walked away, through the cobwebs and down the thirteen steps in the overgrown path, cloak flapping behind him in the darkness, voice trailing off with distance: "You're living a masquerade behind your well-crafted façade, not showing yourself as you really are. Someone needs to light a fire under your scrawny little ...."

Following the altercation, Drycreek simply disappeared. Presently the rumors started: Marta was placing curses on the villagers' cabbage patches, Marta was the head witch in a secret coven stealing children's dreams, Marta was making the mayor's hair fall out. Not a word of it was true. She assumed Drycreek would drop by to quash the gossip, she'd then show her gratitude by paying closer attention to his lessons for a couple weeks, and in time things would return to normal.

Drycreek, to Marta's disappointment, never showed. Given her predicament, Marta surrendered her pride and felt it best to locate him. It was at that moment she realized she'd never asked where he lived or where he spent his time. He always came to her, most often when she didn't want him. Still, she searched, starting with her favorite haunts. She tried the moor. She explored the cairns. She checked down in Reaper's Hollow and Goblins' Grove, with no luck in any of those places. Marta gave up looking. She was better off without him. She returned home and stayed there, avoiding her shop and the townsfolk, waiting for the imbroglio to pass.

Then yesterday as she was finishing her late lunch of belladonna salad and about to start on a bowl of newt-eye soup, the small, inept mob came for her. She declared her innocence, but they wouldn't listen. She demonstrated for them her inability to cast a spell, her unskilled ways of reading runes, her lack of levitation. She let them know, why, she could barely boil undergarments on laundry day, which caused several of the men to blush.

"If there be but one thing I've no question of," she proclaimed to them, "it's that I'm not a witch. As you're certainly aware, I'm a cobbler and seamstress, and if I'm not mistaken, at least a half dozen of you have unpaid tabs at my shop," which caused several of the men to avert their eyes.

They bundled her up anyway and dragged her to the town square where other townsfolk were still arguing over who was going to supply the firewood for her pyre in these impoverished times. After a bit of deliberation, they sent her home for an hour or two with a warning to stay there until they could get things sorted out.

Had it not been nearly harvest time for her mandrakes and rosary peas, Marta would've left town right then. She also doubted they'd be foolish enough to come after her a second time if they seriously thought her a witch. On top of that, she was certain Drycreek would yet intercede. She was wrong on all counts. At least she'd had time to extinguish the fire under the cauldron and set out a small plate of sardines for Salem, her faithful, ageless black cat, when the smaller—consisting only of those with tabs paid in full—but still misguided mob returned a second time to whisk her away and tie her up at the stake.

That was yesterday. As the church bell tolled and the sun crept toward early afternoon, here she stood today tied to a post on a still-growing pile of old barn boards, chopped firewood, brittle newspapers, and what appeared to be an outhouse door. Someone had smeared lard on the kindling to help it burn faster and brighter when the hour came to set spark to tinder. And that hour was approaching faster than she'd like. Perhaps, Marta thought, it was time to get concerned.

"You there, good gentleman," Marta called to one of the bored people in the group in front of her. She made sure to pick out someone who wasn't holding any fruit. She had to spit out the strands of hair that had twisted their way across her lips before she could continue speaking. "Pray tell, what be the time?"

"Not late enough," said the man. He tipped his hat and turned away. "Best to return when it's the hour to set kindling alight."

"I've not placed myself here for your entertainment, dear sir," she said. "This isn't some lark." Marta glared at the man's back and watched him stumble and fall.

A thin, gray-haired woman with an earnest expression moved toward Marta. Marta smiled beneath the locks of hair swaddled around her jaw. "You see well my predicament, Widow Brighton?" Marta asked. "You understand I'm not a witch even though my potions and words helped you with your arthritis, and I assume you're here to help me?"

Without effort, the elderly woman leapt onto the unstable pile of wood and climbed to the top. She pulled the hair away from Marta's face to get a clearer look at the woman tied to the stake.

"Aye, 'tis you. Wasn't sure," said Widow Brighton, hair still in hand. "It's as if you're hiding up here behind all those curls. You'd do well to pull your locks back, more off your cheeks. Show off that bright smile and—oh!" Widow Brighton caught a glimpse of Marta's wart and released her grip. The strands of hair blew back, obscuring much of Marta's face.

Widow Brighton stole another look at Marta, then bent down and tugged at a board. She pulled harder until the board came free. "A pox on that Younge Ethan," said the widow. She lifted the board, a halfmoon cut into it. "He's the one perhaps best set aflame. Stealing my outhouse door and adding it to your bonfire pile when there be already more than enough wood here. Tonight brings the burning of but a single witch, not an entire coven. I've had my good fill of his pranks."

The woman dragged the door from the pile.

"Wait ye one moment," cried Marta. Her wild mane caught in her mouth before she could say more.

Mrs. Brighton continued walking and looked back only to say, "Nice boots."

And they were. The boots were Marta's most comfortable pair yet, although much like her dress, the finished product hadn't turned out as expected. They were intended to be brown, yet inexplicably ended up black. The toes of the boots were much more pointed than the original design, the tops much taller with many more eyelets. It pained Marta to think they would be destroyed in the fire.

As she pondered her boots, the afternoon grew warmer. The winds had died, but in the humid air her hair stuck to her chin and cheeks. Pyre and stake notwithstanding, the morning had been comfortable enough, but now Marta wished she'd worn a head covering when they came for her the day previous. Her sunhat had been right there, next to the front door, on a hook under the shelf with her tarot cards. Why hadn't she grabbed it as they hauled her out the door?

Back on the first day of spring she'd joyfully sewn that sunhat for the warm days to come when she'd be tending her patch of foxglove, death caps, and other delights. The odd thing was, after she'd finished the hat, it wasn't a bright thing with a lovely yellow ribbon as she'd envisioned it. It was black and pointy with a sigil or two up the side, but it fit perfectly and the brim blocked the sun quite well. She wore it every day while toiling in her garden out near the standing stones and the two-hundred-year-old box elder.

Tied to the stake and exposed to the elements for nearly twenty hours at this point, Marta had plenty of time to think about her sunhat and so many other things. What she thought about was mostly this: Drycreek was despicable, Drycreek was tenacious and unforgiving, and Drycreek was the only one who could help her. If only she'd been more inspired in her pursuit of witchcraft—though she obviously wasn't a witch—she wouldn't be in her current predicament. Were she a more serious student, more competent in her craft, she'd at least be able to cast spells and work magic—or whatever it was that witches did in those tired stereotypes perpetuated by hysterical zealots—to free herself from the ropes that bound her. Better than that, she would've foreseen what misfortune was coming her way and avoided it altogether.

She tried to remember her Latin studies and some of the incantations Drycreek tried to teach her. *Ignis, aqua,* er, *wings and weather.* What else? Oh, yes, *exspiravit, vindicta* .... There was more, she was sure, and somewhere in those words was her escape. If only she'd paid more attention. As far as she was concerned, this town square bonfire charade had gone on long enough and was starting to worry her. They were truly intending to burn her alive. She fidgeted against the post and tried again without luck to slip her narrow wrists and ankles from the binding cords.

⬧

Another church bell tolled. Dusk would soon be at hand. Marta puffed her cheeks and attempted to blow the hair off her face while she tried to recall Drycreek's lessons.

Pluviam, and, and, uh*, rolling thunder.* If she couldn't stop the fire, maybe she could conjure rain, except she couldn't fully remember that spell, either.

Oblivious to her predicament, the sun kissed the horizon. Oh, why *hadn't* she listened to fat old Drycreek? This was all his fault. If only he'd been more persistent in teaching his young apprentice, if he'd tried harder to make her learn, if only he'd pushed her beyond her resistance. He always claimed she was descended from an ancient line of witches, that she had innate powers and inborn skills, that she'd kept her true self under wraps. None of it true, of course, but she wished she'd only listened and learned and practiced anyway.

Libertas. Why couldn't she recall the spells and magic she needed? He'd repeated them to her often enough, and she'd parroted all of it right back at him without thought.

Marta looked toward the last of the sun and bedamned her sorcerer again. If her estimate was correct, she was to be set aflame in less than an hour's time. Her heart fluttered. Best to focus on Drycreek to distract her from her pending demise. *Lentum mortis. Tyrant and tutor.*

Commands were formulating in her mind. She couldn't save herself but perhaps she could hex Drycreek as she blazed her way off this mortal coil. Indeed, there would be some satisfaction in that. No one could see her lips move beneath the hair covering her face as she began uttering snippets of spells.

The crowd surrounding her grew as darkness crept in and

the air cooled. Several townspeople carried torches, as if it were a requirement for events like this. Marta squirmed on her waiting pyre. Fear cleared her thoughts of pity, anger focused her mind. She had a definite deadline here, the dead-most of deadlines, the kind which concentrated the mind.

She shut her dark eyes and chanted softly. A new breeze moved the air around her. The slight wind lifted her hair and made it dance in front of her face, catching on her lips. "Drycreek, *acerba funera ascriberet—*"

"Death to the witch!" someone shouted.

"Light the fire already!" yelled another.

"Sandwiches and biscuits," called someone else. "Git yer sandwiches and biscuits."

"*Occidere,*" said Marta. "*Sanguinem.*"

She opened her eyes to see the mayor approaching while she continued murmuring her spell. The faces in the crowd twisted under the flickering light from a hundred lanterns and torches. She gazed at her executioners. Her head turned from left to right and stopped on a single face. Drycreek! He stood there, anonymous in the energized crowd, his walking staff the only giveaway.

Relief welled inside her. Surely, he would save her.

Instead, Drycreek nudged the man next to him and pointed at Marta while the two of them laughed. Relief became rage. She locked eyes with the sorcerer and began her chant again. *Proditor, sangui.* Drycreek's eyes glimmered in the torchlight. The breeze picked up, sending torch flames dancing toward the sky under the rising moon.

Marta writhed against the stake, twisting her wrists and ankles, struggling for escape, yet her movements served only to tighten the ropes. She blasphemed Drycreek once more and glanced at the sky as storm clouds rolled in. Her chants continued, muffled beneath the thick hair caught around her face, yet Drycreek showed no ill effects from her efforts.

The mayor carried his torch high. "We honest village folk gather this night to pull back the mask, to unveil the truth, to witness the just death of Martha Ophidia Sortilege, witch queen of the swamps—"

"Not true!" shouted Marta. "You have failed even in the pronunciation of my given name. 'Tis Marta, not Martha. No *h* therein. How dare thee decree my death without knowing on whom you place this charge? You speak as if you see nothing of the woman standing here in front of you." She spat a lock of hair from her mouth. "Where are these swamps of which you speak?"

"—stealer of children's dreams, bringer of cold death."

"Come, now. Name but one child, *any* child, who's gone without dreaming." She spit more hair from her mouth and wished her face could be free of its snarled covering.

With dramatic flair, the mayor spiked his torch in the ground near the pile of kindling at Marta's booted feet and held aloft a shard of metal and a large rock for all to see. "The witch has been named guilty of crimes again this town and its honorable citizens. As our village handbook decrees, the witch has been placed on public display for a night and a day, and when the clock has passed at least twenty and four hours and the sun passed to the moon, then I, the mayor, must strike flint and ignite the fires of justice—"

"You've given me no trial, you've not allowed me to speak on my behalf. I am no witch, nor have I ever been one. Who you see before you is what I am, a seamstress, a cobbler."

"Aye, and a fine one at that," said the mayor as he extended one leg to show off some custom footwear. "You'll be pleased to know my bunion is cured," he added before bending forward to rearrange bits of wood. Marta noted with satisfaction the thin spot on the top of his head.

"Would I have allowed myself to be tied up if I were truly a witch?" she asked. "Would I not have condemned the fools who bundled me up and brought me here? I offered no resistance despite their rough handling. Did they tell you they dropped me along the way and bruised my shoulder?"

"Nay, we take no blame for that," came a man's voice from the crowd. "You fell from our grasp only when a murder of crows swooped in from blue skies, scattering us righteous men until we could collect our wits and gather you back up to bring you here where you belong."

"Fools you be. Were I a witch, would I not have smote all of you right then?"

Marta's hair came free of her face and twisted like writhing tentacles in the gathering winds. Anger and desperation grew. If she couldn't free herself, couldn't hex Drycreek, might she at least stifle the fire? She glared at Drycreek as the words formed in her mouth, but the conjuring was no longer directed at him. *Ventus, deluge and purge.* Those were the words, yes, yes, it was coming back to her. She would extinguish any and all flames.

Clouds raced across the sky, drawing a curtain toward the rising moon. A burst of energy pulsed through Marta's mind and body.

Ventis, without mercy, pluvia.

Marta looked down at the mayor and rocked her head. Her incantations grew louder, more rhythmic. Towering storm clouds obscured the moon. Shadows gamboled around her in the flickering torch light.

The mayor struck flint on metal. A lone spark appeared and was lost to the wind. Marta's chanting increased. The mayor hit hard a second time, sparks falling into the kindling and disappearing. The next spark rose up and danced before Marta's face before sizzling in her hair, where the glow extinguished. Marta looked to the sky. There would be no escape. One spark more, and fire would surely take hold and consume her.

Again, the mayor struck flint and a single spark launched into the dry tinder. For a moment, nothing happened, as if the winds killed it. Then the kindling caught, flames licking at the lard, grease sizzling. The crowd surged forward with a cheer and tossed torches on the fledgling fire.

Marta's voice grew louder, more desperate. Certainty overpowered fear. She felt the warmth of the flames seeping through her pointy-toed boots. The lace and netting around the hem of her dress would soon be alight, she knew. She couldn't hear the crackling of dry wood over her chanting. She was shouting now, feeling lighter than air. She shifted her arms, and the rope binding them fell free, she—

Lightning rent the sky. Thunder shifted the ground. The townspeople tumbled and yelled, cries lost in the gale.

The rain hit hard and fast, from left and right, above and behind, a deluge that terrified the townsfolk and drowned the flames of the pyre. Marta stood dazed for a moment before shaking her head and clearing her thoughts. She climbed down from the smoldering pile to seek Drycreek.

The sorcerer followed the frightened crowd as it scattered, but he made no real effort to hide. She gripped his shoulder, twisting him to face her. Wind and rain battered them both without mercy.

"You have forsaken me. You made no effort to spare my life, Drycreek!" Marta had to shout above the winds.

"What could I do that you couldn't yourself do? No harm has found you; your boots and dress suffered no damage. You breathe still, and all have witnessed your intrinsic power. This night, 'twas no more than a nudge, a dash of inspiration to help you disclose your lineage and reveal your inner being."

"I've no witchcraft in my veins, there be no magic in these hands, and I shall want for none of your foolishness!" She turned away, then spun around as understanding flitted through her mind. Veins on her temples throbbed. "You." She directed a long, bony finger at him. "Be you the coward who instigated this? The voice who publicly branded me a witch and riled the town and sent a mob to my humble cottage? Speak only truth."

When he said nothing, she turned away, reconsidered, and turned around again. Lightning spiderwebbed across the sky.

Marta pointed once more. "Despicable you be, Drycreek. May I never lay eyes on you again."

She turned and started to walk away. He called after her. "Yet you discovered your powers, unmasked your true self. You found the inspiration you nee—"

She spun a third time and pointed a cracked nail, fingertip almost glowing. Dead leaves tumbled away in the driving rain. Drycreek was nowhere to be seen.

Marta's mouth hung open. She stared at the spot where Drycreek had been moments before. The winds died, the deluge ceased, the clouds opened to let the moon shine through. Marta pulled back her hair as she looked about for Drycreek.

With a trembling voice she called into the night air, looking in every direction, uncertain where the sorcerer had gone. "You see, Drycreek? I'm but a seamstress and cobbler. Were I the witch you proclaimed, would I not have called on weather and wings to set me free? Would I not be providing ointments and cures to the townsfolk? Would I not have rid myself of your meddlesome presence? Would I not have unmasked myself to show who I truly—?"

Marta's brow furrowed in concentration.

Her eyes grew wide.

"Oh."

James Romag spent his childhood pestering teachers, librarians, and bookshop clerks for recommended reads, from nonfiction to science fiction and all plots in between. His philosophy has always been "Why get one book when five or six will do?" James recently was awarded an MA in Publishing from Western Colorado University. He edited *The Santa Claus Stories of L. Frank Baum* and co-edited the *Monsters, Movies & Mayhem* anthology, both from WordFire Press. James is an Air Force veteran who lives in the foothills of the Colorado Rockies, where he spends his time hiking, running, cycling, reading, and writing as much as possible. He also enjoys a craft beer now and then, particularly when someone else is buying.

THE GREEN GAS

LIAM HOGAN

The war had been raging so long I wasn't sure who we were fighting. Or why. But then, I was just an orphan girl, barely fifteen, sent out to scavenge in the rubble, so what did *I* know?

Tinned goods, mostly; *that's* what I knew, and what we scavenged for. From the look, from the feel, I could tell if the contents were still liquid, still edible. I could hazard a guess as to what was inside, even if the label was ancient history. Then there was the occasional miracle of an unopened jar or bottle that hadn't been smashed. Or something shrink-wrapped, tightly sealed. Anything the air, and the badness, or just time and water and rats and little grey moths, hadn't got into. But who can blame us if the odd book, puffed up and the pages needing to be carefully sliced apart, or a toy, painted metal or eternal plastic, found its way into our sacks as well? There was always plenty of room.

Avoiding the wide roads, skulking through back alleys, through tangled remains of once-proud gardens and yards, over fallen fences and crumbling walls, some still topped with shards of glass, I picked my way through the ruins, trying to guess where the kitchens might once have been. It always amazed me that anyone had ever lived above ground. To be so exposed, with only the thinnest of walls to shelter behind. Even more bizarre when I stood beneath one of the sisters, those skeletal fingers stabbing the tortured skies. The lift shafts fringed with concrete gills were all that remained of the floors of buildings many stories high, fragile homes for hundreds.

I was alone in the wasteland. Alone, with a half dozen other scavengers scattered far and wide and equally alone. It was always girls, only ever girls; the boys too busy being taught to be the next generation of soldiers. Boys like my older brother, Marcus, though he'd graduated to active duty four years back, the last time I'd seen him. I wondered where he was now. There had been letters, at the start; always out of step with birthdays or Christmas as if they'd taken months to arrive, which presumably they had. But there hadn't been one of those for almost two years and I was beginning to think I wouldn't recognise him if I should ever see him again.

Nothing *official*, neither. No "We regret to inform you ..." Nothing to tell me either way how he fared.

We girls were told never to forage alone. Told to hunt for our scraps in pairs or in groups of three. But we never did. You covered more ground alone, made less noise. And being alone ...

Down below, in the dank, dark subterranean bunkers, we were *never* alone. Not in the dorms where the youngest girls slept on the floor beneath and between the lowest bunks. Not in the classrooms, where harried teachers did their best as kids lined the walls and sat in each other's laps, the young, and the almost adult, alike. Kaitlin, our dorm leader, said it wasn't that there were all that many of us, more that the bunker had never been designed for our number, for this long. Even the time in the dining hall was rationed, the bell ringing to chase us from our benches, making room for others to shovel in whatever was on the menu as fast as they could, the watery stews merging into one not very appetizing memory.

Oh! I forgot the spices! If we found something like *that*, something sealed, brightly colored, still capable of making one of the cooks sneeze, then we'd get an extra portion that day and perhaps the food wouldn't be quite so bland. Perhaps. But spices, from peppercorns to bright yellow turmeric, didn't turn up very often, or not in any useful quantity.

I threaded through the gap in a half-tumbled wall, a rope of brittle bramble snagging at my tough work trousers, forcing me to stop and untangle the thorns before continuing on. *Dead* bramble, of course. The gas saw to that. But, amazingly, a few things did manage to grow, even out here. Ragged plants with little blue flowers, pollinated by who knows what, and something waist-high whose hairy leaves you had to be careful not to brush against, that would leave a red, maddeningly itchy rash if you did. Our teachers said these plants were new. Never-before hybrids, something miraculous filling an ecological niche, rapidly evolving over the decade and a half we had been busy destroying everything else, everything they had once competed against. Whether left to its own devices or not, they said, life finds a way. Even in the face of choking, toxic, man-made poisons, the green gas being the most common though not the most deadly.

In our childhood tales—the ones we'd been told when we were younger, the ones we older girls now passed down, quite literally, from the top bunks to those below—the green gas was the bogey man. It was cunning, mischievous, and wicked. It punished you if you were bad, if you ignored the rules, if you failed to do your daily chores. But, if you were strong and silent and good, then maybe, just maybe, it would let you be.

In reality, it was just a gas, an indiscriminate chemical weapon, driven by the wind and gravity, blind and senseless.

Today, like most scavenger days, my mask hung at my side, the padded pouch protecting the fragile lenses and the charcoal filter. We were a long way from any front and, despite the oft-repeated rules, it was so much easier to search for anything that had been overlooked by dozens of previous scavenger missions if we didn't have to cope with narrowed vision and scratched and grimy lenses.

Kaitlin, held back an extra year to be in charge of the younger girls and itching to move out of the kids' dorm, to move *on*, her head-girl duties meaning she didn't even get to scavenge any more, though she was always there when we left the bunker and always there when we returned, counting the girls back in like a mother hen; Kaitlin claimed you could tell the difference between our gas and the enemy's. That the enemy gas smells like the grey soap that makes eyes sting in the showers, and ours smelled like boot polish.

I'm not sure that was in any way reassuring, and I didn't exactly get to compare fragrance notes. By the time I noticed the green tinge gathering in the air around me it was too late. I'd been scrabbling in the dirt, trying to unearth a mannequin's arm I'd at first taken for a corpse. And of course I was in a hollow, a crater surrounded by earth banks and shattered concrete, into which the mannequin and perhaps whatever it had been wearing had fallen. The next moment I couldn't see anything at all, or even breathe, my lungs on fire as I spluttered and struggled with the clasp at my waist, frantically trying to free my mask.

Strong blunt fingers pushed mine aside and for a moment I really did think the mannequin had come to life. But the fingers were gloved; black leather rather than smooth pale plastic. The straps of the gas mask were pulled roughly over my face and everything went dark as I huddled there, curled up and trying to remember how to breathe.

When I could finally sit upright again, tears catching on the mask's fabric at my cheek, I did my best to peer through the film that coated my eyes. Slowly my vision cleared, though I could feel the gunk pooling in the corners of my eyes, a sticky clump that smeared every time I blinked. I had to fight the urge to remove the mask to wipe it all away.

My rescuer sat with his back to me, hunched halfway up a mound I couldn't remember, gloved hands cupping combat-trouser knees, staring at nothing. He must have dragged me there, up and out of the hollow in which the heavy green gas probably still lurked. Maybe if I had been on my own I would have removed my mask, getting a second lungful, despite what I had just been through. Maybe that would have been the end of me. But the man still wore his, a hooded one tightly laced behind, a glimpse of the snout-filter that rendered his profile inhuman. I followed his example and wisely left mine on.

I sat there a moment longer as my breathing and my heart returned to some semblance of normal, inspecting his cobbled-together outfit. He was so still he might have been a mannequin as well, an end-of-the-world fire-sale, dressed in heavy gear that didn't let me see anything of him. There was nothing to tell if he was friend or foe. Nothing to tell me if I had been rescued from one terrible fate, only to be preserved for something even worse. He was outfitted in such a way that even without the mask he would have been hard to identify. Those black gloves, heavily taped at his wrists, the hooded gas mask, plunging into the high neck of his bulky jacket, baggy trousers firmly tucked into his dull black boots. They say there are worse things than the green gas, chemicals a single drop of which could stop your heart or freeze your lungs. This soldier looked ready for them all.

I pushed myself up on wobbly legs, sending a few pebbles skittering down the slope, and he turned. I was convinced it was a he, with boots that large. The glass over his eyes was mirrored, against flares and flash-bangs, I supposed, and all I saw reflected back was a young girl, covered in dirt, hair like snakes, tangled with snot and vomit, her face hidden behind the gas mask, scared eyes just about peeking out.

He nodded, rose to his feet, handed me back my sack. I was wary taking it. And then the thought came to me: when I had last seen Marcus, my brother had been a skinny runt, fifteen, just as I was now. But sometime in the last month he'd turned nineteen. He'd be a man, tall and strong.

A man like this one?

It was ridiculous to suggest, to even hope, that it was my brother who had come to my rescue. But the thought that it might be, however unlikely, overcame my fear of this dark stranger, this guardian angel.

Besides, what did I have to lose? He could have killed me as I lay there, helpless. Or he could have left it to the green gas to do the job and not even dirtied his gloved hands.

I took the proffered bag, swung it over my shoulder, wincing at the fierce sting from a previously uncatalogued graze, before switching the weight to the other side. And then I slowly turned in a circle. I had no idea where I was. No idea even which direction I was facing. No idea where home was.

When I'd left the bunker there had been a brittle afternoon sunshine, half shadows that I had kept to my left as we six girls had fanned out. But the day had closed in, sullen clouds that threatened torrential rain, and worse. And it was nearing dusk; if the sun was going to put in another appearance and help guide me home, it had better do it soon.

I re-scanned the jumbled horizon that blurred through the gas mask lenses until I caught sight of the nearest sister. There were five of them in all. Kaitlin said there had once been seven, but two had fallen in the long years of the war. They were the tallest of the remaining buildings, pockmarked and shattered, only glints of broken glass left in their lofty, vacant heights. But each had a name, a distinctive shape, and each told me—roughly—where I was.

The hooded man was waiting. I thought for a moment, guesstimated how long I'd wandered, plotted the path back in my mind and then pointed into the murk. Mimed walking and flashed my hand four times. Twenty minutes.

I hoped. Assuming dark didn't fall first and slow us still further. Assuming we didn't hit any unexpected and unwanted obstacles. Assuming the rain didn't descend, turning the ruins into a treacherous mud-bath, making it impossible to see through the glass portholes of our masks.

A small doubt lingered. Was I leading the enemy to our bunker? Was I betraying our position? But what could I do?

He nodded and, without any further silent communication, began to head down the slope in the direction I had pointed. He was certainly sure-footed. I nearly stumbled, twice, on the loose gravel, slamming my hand into the rubble to halt my fall so that grit bit into my palms. He looked back each time, and I expected a rebuke, an urgent command to keep quiet, for all there were no signs of life anywhere around us.

As we hit level ground I had to rush forward, hopping over a tangle of loose razor wire to tug him back. His combat trousers bunched in my hand and he peered down at me, mirror lenses picking out the fading daylight. I hadn't realized quite how tall he was and couldn't somehow imagine Marcus ever topping out at over six feet.

I pointed along the road. It was easily identified as such, the relatively straight lines, the dip between collapsed buildings. Though it was far from clear of rubble, it was a lot less jumbled than the ground on either side. I could even see the shattered remains of a lamp post, trailing flex. I held out one hand, flat, palm up. My other hand I cupped over it and then flung outwards, spreading my fingers.

A pantomime explosion. *Mines.*

He nodded and waited for me to go ahead of him, to lead. I skirted the edge, where front gardens might once have been, careful not to crunch on the scattered roof tiles. I had to keep looking back, so silent was he, at least while I was wearing my gas mask. And soft-footed though he might be, I couldn't understand how he didn't know about the mines. They weren't *just* limited to the roads. I guess that's what happens as soon as people learn one hard lesson; the rules of the game change. But everyone knew that if the way looked easy then it was almost certainly dangerous, and if it wasn't mines, then it was snipers. Best to take a less convenient route and risk the natural hazards of torn metal and shattered glass.

The road wasn't quite the direction we needed to go anyway, so, after a couple of hundred paces along its edge, we branched north, clambering over tin sheeting to reach the hinterland between houses, between streets. I thought I half recognized the way, which was reassuring, though the light was fading fast, the dreary colors leaching from the bruised sky. In the distance, thunder, or maybe artillery, rumbled. I quickened our pace, zigzagging towards where I thought our bunker must be.

And then I glimpsed a dim light ahead, and instantly I was flat against a still-vertical section of wall, the soldier crouched beside me. A patrol? Ours, or theirs? Looking for me, or looking for him?

I wondered for a moment if, should they come this way and get close enough to be identified, the soldier would stand and greet the enemy like long-lost friends. Or would he lie in wait, in deadly ambush?

But he couldn't have done that, and I was dumbfounded to be so slow to realize. He wasn't carrying a rifle. He didn't even have a hand gun. Not even, as far as I could tell, a knife. Even *I* had a knife, short and ugly though it was.

A soldier without any weapons could only, as far as I could see, mean one thing. A deserter. At risk of being shot by either side and so deliberately divested of any overt threat, as if that would do him any good.

My heart sank. No hero, then? No brave, gallant warrior from the front? It had always seemed odd that he was in our neck of the woods to begin with. Odd enough that there was even a patrol ...

Cautiously, I raised my head back over the wall. Squinted through the eye glass, cursing the way the light was scattered by scratches and grease.

As far as I could tell, it wasn't moving. And as I watched, my eyes adjusted to see the dim bulkhead lamp and the darkness beside and under it. I realized where we were: it was the bunker! They'd put the entrance light on—presumably for me. A risk, and one I doubt they'd run for long. Not when it got to full dusk. Not when, if I was still out there and had any sense, I'd have holed up until morning and hoped to survive the cold night.

I led the soldier around the corner of the wall, the landscape becoming more and more familiar with every step, despite the gloom. Each boulder, each patch of dirt, screamed home as I headed towards the dark cave of the bunker entrance.

When he saw where we were going, he stopped abruptly, shaking that hooded head of his. I grabbed his arm, pulling him on, though still he resisted. But I didn't—couldn't—let him escape. See, I'd worked it out, on our hike back to the bunker. I trusted him, sure I did. He'd saved my life after all. But to be sure, to be absolutely one hundred percent certain, I wasn't going to let him see where our bunker was and then just wander off. No. That's why I dragged him into the airlock, despite his protests, even as the heavens finally opened and the rain drummed down all around. I hoped he'd be happy; everyone would be glad he'd rescued me and eager for news. He'd get a slap-up meal, kind of, and a dry cot for the night.

And, if he still wanted to leave in the morning—after his papers, his name and serial number had been checked out by people more knowledgeable and less trusting than I—then *well*. Can't say fairer than that.

"You can take off your gas mask now," I said, having done so myself, my voice croaky and alien sounding. But he was standing by the extractor fans, so maybe he couldn't hear me. I turned away, running my fingers through my hair, screwing up my nose at the stink, trying to loosen the worst of the knots, embarrassed. It was stupid, but I almost didn't want to see him unmasked. Because until then, there was always a slim chance. Until then, I wouldn't know for certain he wasn't Marcus.

Behind me there was a sharp clink against the concrete floor, and I snapped around in time to see his bulky clothes deflating into a black heap, far too flat to hide a body.

The air was suddenly full of the pungent smell of boot polish, of carbolic soap, and my breath caught in my throat, but the smell cleared as quickly as it had come, and I felt the pressure on my ears ease as the airlock cycle completed.

The inner bunker door swung open and there was Kaitlin, holding a rifle, a gas mask in her other hand. She peered around, sniffing the air, clocked the pile of clothes on the floor, and frowned.

"What did you bring all *that* junk back for?" She prodded at the jacket with the business end of the rifle, flipped over the gas mask until the cracked, mirrored eyes stared emptily upwards. "Well ... I suppose we can find a use for some of it. Bit large for me, mind!"

I stood rooted to the spot. "Did ...?" I wanted to ask if she'd seen the man I'd returned with, the man I'd entered the airlock with, the wearer of all that junk, the one who had just vanished into thin air. But how could I? So I asked instead: "Did ... everyone else get back okay?" Only now realizing that they might not have.

"Over an hour ago." Her frown turned into a grin and a shrug. "We were beginning to think we'd lost you, Saskia. Glad to have you back. And I hope there's something edible in that sack?"

I was about to tell her there wasn't, that I'd only just begun my search, when I realised an empty sack doesn't weigh as much as the one I was miraculously still carrying, slung over my good shoulder. I eased it off, felt where the cord had bitten, felt bruises on my stiff upper arm. I untied the drawstring at its neck, opened it wide for both of us to see.

"Well! Worth the extra hour, I'd say," Kaitlin crowed, peering at the tins within. Her hand darted forward, snatched up a square-shaped one. "Is that ...?"

"Paprika?" I shrugged. "I guess."

"Come on. I'll escort you to the kitchens myself!"

Later, much later, the tail-end of the very last dinner shift in fact, I sat alone as I used my half-slice of bread to mop my tray. The rationed tang of peppery spice hadn't done much to hide the usual, dishwater taste, but it helped. Anything did. As had my brief shower, a rare mid-week luxury, but essential, once I'd explained what had happened, explained my lungful of gas, which had earned me a check-up with the medics as well. ("You'll live," was their blunt professional assessment.) All of which had delayed my grilling by the other girls; the five I'd gone out on my sortie with and a gaggle of younger ones— asking where I'd been, what I'd seen, and whether the cache I'd discovered was worked out.

I kept my answers short, said that yes, alas, I'd cleaned out the store that I'd found hidden inside a buried refrigerator (hah!) and that I'd foolishly managed to get lost, wandered too far south and got a lungful of green gas for my troubles. But I didn't tell them the rest, not then, and not ever. Not to the little girls who bunk beneath me, nor even to Kaitlin. I didn't tell them I'd been rescued, and by whom, or any of my crazy theories about what, if anything, it meant. Even if I had, they'd probably just say the gas had addled my brains and warn me to quit scaring the young'uns.

Most of all, I didn't want my fragile bubble of hope burst by some casual comment or a pitying look. Hell, I knew the odds. We all did. People vanished on the battlefield all the time. They very rarely turned up again, and never after this long a gap.

But while there was doubt, there was a sliver of possibility. A *chance* of a miracle. However unlikely.

That's why in this forever war, there were no 'Missing in Action' messages. Why my letters would never be returned unopened and marked undeliverable. Bad for morale, the Generals would claim.

I don't know if the man made out of green gas escaped back outside through the extractor fan, into the rain, into the night. What the whirring blades would do to him, I didn't like to think. But I hope he's out there, kitting himself in a new airtight uniform, a new gas mask. Doing whatever it is that he does. Despite the tiny spark I stubbornly cling to, I don't even know if he is our gas, or theirs, or some sort of blend of the two. Whether he is, or was, the spirit of a dead soldier, perhaps even that of my brother, or something new and oddly wonderful, the result of years of battlefield experimentation, of evolution, I had no way of telling.

I licked the last scraps of food from the tin plate, dog-tired now, eager for lights out.

But I do know one thing, and it's this:

Life will always find a way.

Liam Hogan is an award-winning short story writer, with stories in Best of British Science Fiction 2016 & 2019, and Best of British Fantasy 2018 (NewCon Press). He's been published by

Analog, Daily Science Fiction, and Flame Tree Press, among others. He helps host Liars' League London, volunteers at the creative writing charity Ministry of Stories, and lives and avoids work in London. More details at:

happyendingnotguaranteed.blogspot.co.uk.

DEATH BY MISADVENTURE

JOHN M. OLSEN

Sometimes I choose to watch people all the way from birth to the grave. Other times, I show up at the last moment to escort their soul along to the next stop, but nobody avoids me. Not for long, anyway.

Walter had lived a good, long life. I'd shadowed him on and off for years, keeping tabs on his job and family. He loved his beautiful grandkids, and I'd helped his wife, Daisy, move on two years before. She was a wonderful woman, full of love.

It's a perk of the job to choose how much time to spend tracking each person and to determine whether I show up from time to time in disguise along the way. Now, I sat across from Walter playing checkers in a hospital room surrounded by the smell of antiseptic and stage-four cancer as lights blinked on a wall of medical equipment.

"King me," Walter whispered. You would think a master of games like me would never lose to a mortal, but today I played to distract my friend from his overwhelming pain.

"You got it, Walter. So is your son still sore about the World Series?" I tried every trick I knew to divert his attention from his condition as I dropped a checker on top of his. I sat back in the utilitarian chair, idly playing with my scythe, which was transformed to look like a butterfly knife as a part of my current mask. For the record, I don't appear as a flaming skeleton wrapped in black robes unless I'm particularly annoyed at someone when I come for them. Today I wore jeans and a polo shirt, dark wavy hair graying at the temples, and a nondescript face.

Walter whispered again, the best he could manage. "It took a week or two, but I calmed him down. Can you help me up? I want to look out the window for a bit to watch the city lights."

It wasn't time yet, so I set my knife/scythe to the side of the checker board. He was barely more than a hundred pounds soaking wet, so I picked him up gently and carried him to the window with his arm around my shoulder, careful not to tangle the lines connecting him to medical equipment.

A weak smile crossed Walter's lips. "Lights eventually flicker and die, like me. Everyone has to burn out sometime."

"That's dark for you, Walter. And a touch poetic." He was right. Everyone has to die eventually, and I handled them in order based on their appointed time. I show up when a person is born, then I can skip forward in time to keep tabs on them during their mortal sojourn. Whether as a ghost or in physical form, I spend time with those who deserve it, like Walter. A few even become dear friends. I'm required to be there to formalize each exit, and I can't skip back in time again until my current charge moves on. It gets weird when I see a future version of myself following someone who may not die for decades.

A quirk of divine creation made me both infinite and highly parallel.

I've lived through the Cubs winning the 2016 World Series millions of times, and I'm not done yet. You can see why I skip forward to the important parts. The novelty wears off quickly.

And people wonder why I'm so good at gambling. Never bet against Death.

Someone pushed the door open and bumped around behind us for a few moments, but left without a word. More medical tests were useless at this point.

"It's a shame your son couldn't be here tonight. You don't have long."

"I told him my grandkid's musical was more important than counting my breaths," Walter said. "He'll be back in the morning."

After a long while, I eased him back into his bed, where I made him as comfortable as I could. It was time.

"You know, it's funny how I've kept a secret from you all these years," I told him. "I'm glad I got to know you. You inspire me, and I'm better for it."

I reached for my butterfly knife, my scythe, and found only an empty table.

Bad words came to mind in no less than thirty languages. "Hold on a minute, Walter. I'll be right back."

"Promises, promises."

The last time I'd lost my scythe was more than a hundred years earlier on the calendar, but hundreds of millions of lives ago, the way I counted. A fellow named Grigori Rasputin played a joke on me by sneaking it from a dagger sheath on my belt. He sold it to a wandering tinker after he somehow figured out what it was.

It was a tool with power over life and death, bearing symbolism recognized around the world, and I'd lost it again. I was two years late escorting Rasputin to the next step and caught no end of grief for all the stories spawned by his idiotic death-defying antics while I hunted for my disguised scythe. Stabbings, gunshots, poison—nothing worked on him because the symbol of my office had gone missing. I got it back only because a future version of me assigned to the tinker finally returned it to me. The Boss was not amused. I'm not supposed to talk to other versions of myself.

This time, I didn't have months or years. Walter would be in terrible pain every moment until I came back with my scythe in hand. I left the room to hunt down the cretin who took it.

"Nurse, can you tell me who came by Walter's room about five minutes ago?"

She looked up from her desk, her rosy cheeks dimpled by what seemed to be a permanent smile. "Sure thing."

She prodded her computer and looked up at me after a moment. "Nobody in the past hour. Is something wrong?"

"I'm missing a butterfly knife. About six inches long with black handles and a Damascus steel blade. Very sharp."

She raised an eyebrow, and I discovered her smile wasn't permanent.

"It has a lot of sentimental value. I wanted to show it to Walter." How is it some mortals can make me feel so defensive?

She shook her head in place of the lecture we both knew she wanted to deliver. Her frown made me feel like a child caught with a hand in the cookie jar. "You can report it at the safety desk down at the entrance if you like. That's where it will go if someone finds a large unattended knife." She stared at me, her gaze boring holes through my eternal soul.

I'm sure the two of us will laugh about our conversation over the knife when her turn comes around. Sure as anything, she'll still make me feel like a wayward child even then.

I thanked her and headed for the elevator as she muttered something about the wrong kind of knife for a hospital. In my hands, it was a tool to separate spirits from their dying bodies without harming either. In the wrong hands, it could lop off body parts without pausing at the bones.

I still had a trick up my sleeve, something I prepared after the Rasputin incident. I could turn it back into a scythe without touching it. All I needed was to go incorporeal and send it a command. But transforming could turn into a new problem since the scythe would remain physical until I touched it. It would be hard for nearby mortals to miss, so I would wait and transform it later.

Nothing showed up in the trashcans along the way to the front lobby, so I strolled to the security desk parked between two fake potted ficus trees.

As I approached, one of my future ghosts sat in the nearby waiting area. He grinned at me, despite the strict no-contact rule. On a busy day, there could be several of me at any given hospital, but we're not supposed to notice. At least it meant I would eventually find my scythe. It also meant I was in for a horrible day if I went out of my way to watch myself blunder around for amusement. Sometimes I'm a jerk.

My trip to the lobby was a bust. Nothing in lost-and-found, nothing in the trash, and no leads.

My future ghost stood and walked out the main doors toward the parking lot west of the hospital.

He hadn't made contact, except maybe to show me where to go next. I bent the no-contact rule into a pretzel as I followed him. I tailed my shadow to the nearby subway entrance where I paid for a pass and got on the northbound line into town.

One odd thing about escorting everyone from their mortal coil is that I meet nearly everyone in passing, and I have a perfect memory.

I sat down next to a kid named Ricky whose Nana had passed a year before. My future ghost followed Ricky off the train a few stops later, so I followed. I ended up in a park filled with old sycamore trees surrounding a central area smelling of fresh-trimmed grass. Apartment buildings surrounded the park.

I followed as my ghost marched in step next to Ricky. Was Ricky going to die soon? Maybe future me was just being a jerk again. It's happened before, and it's hilarious when I'm on the giving end.

The gap increased as Ricky dodged into the lobby of an apartment building ahead of me. When I got there, Ricky was gone. I couldn't tell if he'd taken the elevator or sneaked out another door. My future ghost laughed as he faded away.

🎭

I sat in the lobby to plan my search. As I sat, a teenager wearing an old baseball cap entered the lobby. His jeans hid the tops of his cowboy boots. Oddly enough, I didn't know him. He'd never been near death. It happens, but not often.

He drawled at me, "You need help with somethin'?"

The way he talked revealed that he was a recent import, new to the area. His accent placed him from upper east Tennessee, probably a farm back in the hills near Johnson City.

I nodded and dropped into an accent not too far from his, closer to Oak Ridge. "I lost my favorite knife. Someone from this here building might have carried it off."

"Huh. That's a lot of doors to bang on," the teen said. "What's it look like?"

"Butterfly knife. 'Bout five inches. Sharp as all get out. Don't want a little kid to cut a finger off."

He pulled a folding knife from his pocket and flipped the blade out with practiced ease. He held it out toward me, handle first. "You keep it sharp, huh? See how I did on this."

Angels protect fools and children, and this was one reason why. Pulling out a knife in a big city, then offering it to a stranger? It was a miracle I'd never bumped into this kid in the past.

I grasped the handle and waited a moment until he let go. Good training.

"This town don't deserve your trust so easy," I said. "You

should watch yourself and be more careful."

I tested the edge and whistled. "That's a sweet edge. My name's Mort." At least that was my name for today. Names mean a lot more to people than they do to me, since I have so many. I folded the knife closed and handed it back.

He grinned and sat across from me. "I'm Beau. Pa says I should be careful, but most everybody's nice here if you give 'em a chance. Y'all could put up a flier on the board to find your knife."

He stood and honest-to-goodness moseyed over to a cork board. I liked this kid.

"Folks post all sort of things here. Lost cats, parties, game groups, that kind of stuff."

One paper on the board caught my eye. My picture graced the flier. Well, it had a cloaked figure holding a scythe, anyway.

It turned out to be an ad for a fantasy convention starting the following morning. I've attended geeky conventions before on assignment. It's one of the few places I can pull out all the stops in public and not get a second look. I once lost a costume contest to a little girl with a black bathrobe and a sugar-skull design painted on her face. She charmed the judges with her cuteness, an attribute I lack.

I didn't have time to goof off at a con. I nodded at the board and said, "Thanks for the suggestion. Take care of yourself, Beau."

He headed to the elevator and gave me a final wave as the door closed to whisk him home. Yes, I'd be sure to check on him when his number came around.

I didn't see any choice but to go incorporeal and turn my butterfly knife back into a scythe, then ghost my way through the whole building one room at a time. I changed and sent the command to transform the scythe.

Skipping any nook or cranny meant I might as well start over, so I took as much time as I could afford.

Like a growing ache behind the eyes, Walter's pain echoed in me as I searched. Sharing the pain was my cost when I granted any reprieve, intentional or not.

Pain is a great motivator and teacher, and a suitable reward for stupidity, but I despise pain with no purpose. My sympathetic pain was well-deserved, but Walter's was not.

Dozens of weapons showed up as I progressed through the building, and I even found two guys painting medieval armor, most likely for the con. A gauzy robe with a ghostly mask was draped nearby on the couch. I looked under the couch, and my heart leaped. It was a scythe! Then the crinkly tinfoil blade caught my eye, and I let out a dejected sigh.

At least I'd have a fan at the convention.

The pressure behind my eyes built along with my guilt as the evening progressed through to early morning. Finally, I finished the last room of the last apartment. It was a nondescript kitchenette with a high-carbon cleaver stored beside a nice end-grain cutting board.

I lofted down to the park to sit and think. With luck, my future ghost would wander past to laugh or mock me, and if I was lucky, give me another clue.

Walter's son would show up at the hospital soon, and the nurses would want to give him stronger pain medication. The stubborn mule would turn them down to be as clear-headed as possible, despite the soul-searing pain.

I became corporeal once more and sat on a log to think as the sun rose. My future self never reappeared. I'd obviously missed something important.

I slapped the log and stood, ready to continue my search.

Log? There were no logs last night. Only trees. I bent down to examine the sycamore limb on the ground.

I passed my hand over the log's mirror-smooth cuts. There was only one blade capable of such a cut. Some idiot took my scythe out for a test drive while I was searching.

The ground near the log and the tree showed no blood. At least the thief wasn't maimed yet.

I trudged back toward the apartment building. I'd look again, starting with the costumers.

People streamed out of the apartment buildings and toward the subway entrance in the morning light as the sun found its way between the buildings to sparkle on the dewy park grass.

I snapped into ghost form without caring who I confused and jumped to the living room where I'd seen the cardboard scythe.

The costumes were gone when I got there, all except for the fake scythe still under the couch. I was, once again, a fool. While I'd searched last night, someone had left the building with the real blade. How they explained away its appearance didn't much matter, but I suspected alcohol was involved.

I became physical, grabbed the dummy scythe, and headed to the lobby to find the flier for the con.

It didn't open for a couple of hours, but people always lined up early. I stayed physical to carry the fake scythe. My growing urgency and throbbing head kept Walter's plight in my thoughts.

As I turned to leave the lobby, something else caught my eye. A new flier showed a rough picture of a butterfly knife with text scrawled below. "Missing. Please call Beau if found." His phone and apartment number ran across the bottom of the page.

The world was a better place with kids like him.

As I stood dumbfounded staring at his flier, I heard Beau behind me. "Any clues yet? The one you've got there don't look the right size."

I turned with a grin despite my growing desperation and

pain. "No luck yet. I think I'll go to the con and see if it shows up."

"Good luck!" He held a paperback in his left hand like he'd been interrupted from reading in a cozy lobby chair.

"Thanks for the flier, by the way. I'll check with you later if I don't find it."

I set my hand on his shoulder and recoiled as I felt the nerve disease seeping through him, overcoming his body like a slow but inevitable tide. Really? How is that fair?

Sometimes I don't see the justice in it. Despite the leeway I have in what I do, it's almost always up to nature or the action of mortals to decide when I visit. The Boss once told me fairness was a much longer-term ordeal than simple mortal lifespans could account for.

I pushed the constraints of my job and said, "You should see a doctor, Beau. Sooner the better."

He offered me an accepting smile and shrugged. "Ma and Pa got jobs in the city so we could be here where the doctors are. I'm doing okay. How could you tell? Are you a doctor?"

I gave a noncommittal tilt of the head. "I spend a lot of time in hospitals, and I've seen a few people with troubles like yours. They have treatments to delay the progress, but most of them can be as rough as the disease."

His condition made me think of my appointment with Walter.

"I've got to get going, Beau. You take care of yourself."

Beau nodded and headed outside to a bench in the park to read.

I got on the subway with my tinfoil scythe among a scattering of elves and a couple of superheroes.

All I needed was to find the kid with my scythe among the tens of thousands of costumed folks at a con scattered across two hotels and a show floor the size of two football fields while my brain felt like bursting.

The convention was huge. No matter where I looked, it was a gamble my target would be somewhere else. Then again, I knew this was something I would win, eventually.

I saw a dark figure vanish as I looked down a row of booths. It took careful planning, but I got into position and waited.

The flash of shadow appeared again, then turned away. It was a future version of me, and he was more careful than normal about the self-contact rule.

I would receive a stern warning because of all the contact I'd had with myself, and I couldn't rely on my future self for any more clues. He might be here on assignment instead of showing up to laugh at me.

Finally, I saw it across the main hallway. A majestic Damascus steel blade, unlike anything mortals could produce, waved above the crowd by a kid with no idea how easy it would be to send someone to either the hospital or the morgue with a single slip.

I eased up beside him and planted the foil-and-cardboard scythe in front of me. I leaned over and said, "I think you have the wrong prop there. This one's yours. We should trade."

His face hid behind a mask. His gauzy robe didn't look half bad, either. "I don't know what you're talking about. And how did you get into my apartment?"

Not a rocket scientist, this one. I recognized the voice. He'd been with his grandpa when the old man passed on. The name *Robert* floated to the surface. *Robbie* to his parents. He hated the nickname.

Even though I could easily overpower him and take my scythe back, I didn't want to make a scene, and it's not my job to dispense justice. The Boss has others to handle justice, and I try to avoid getting on the local news. The Boss explained to me once how proof of the supernatural destroyed a mortal's ability to have faith, but I couldn't follow the whole chain of logic behind it. Faith is not my job, either.

A door opened, and the crowd pushed forward. I followed my target into a roped-off area in a large conference room and said, "So, Robbie, was it you who went to the hospital, or one of your roommates? That's low, stealing from the terminally ill."

He turned to look at me as we pushed forward, joining a line of infrequently showered nerd bodies. "Back off. I'll call the cops if you don't leave me alone."

"Right. With you carrying my blade? You're lucky they didn't take it away when you got here. Don't they do weapon checks at the door anymore?"

He pointed the scythe tip at me. I could sense his glare behind the mask. My tool couldn't hurt me, but it could hurt someone around us. Someone who didn't deserve it. We narrowed down into a single-file line, and crowd control waved us forward.

Someone stepped up to the microphone in front as more people filed in through big doors on the other side of the room and found seats. "Welcome, everyone! Our panel of judges is ready and waiting." The audience cheered as we walked up along the left-hand side of the room. A temporary stage sat at the front where the judges waved at everyone.

Judges? I looked at my line. All costumes.

My mood degraded by the moment. I said to my thief, "A costume contest? I bet you lose, even with my scythe." What can I say? I'm fond of gambling and insults, so it was a two-for-one comment.

He stepped back and looked me over. Jeans, polo, and card-board scythe. "Lose to you? You're on." Bingo.

I hadn't intended to make it a personal challenge, but this gave me a chance to avoid a fight in public. The distraction of wanting to get back to Walter at the hospital put me off my game, but this was second nature to me. If I could get him to hand it over willingly, it would avoid making a scene.

"Great. You know what I want if I beat you," I said. "What do you want if you beat me?"

He replied, "If I win, you tell me how to make knives stay this sharp."

I smiled. "Deal." This would be an easy win. Besides, Robbie couldn't use the information even if he won. He wouldn't have access to the earth's molten core or the Boss' honing wheel anytime soon.

We soon neared the front of the line as contestants performed for the judges. An elf had custom ears good enough to make a movie prosthetist drool. Three versions of the same superhero frowned at each other as they each tried to be the best.

Then it was Robbie's turn. He strode out onto the stage and struck a pose before he pulled an empty water bottle out of his robe and tossed it into the air. The scythe slashed out, and two halves fell to the stage to cheers from the audience.

While the crowd was distracted, I ducked down at the edge of the stage and set aside my mild-mannered form, cloaking myself in tangible darkness. My black hood eased forward as I climbed the stairs, trailing wisps and tatters of blackness.

A volunteer stood silently to the side, out of my way. The volunteer was me, the shadow I'd seen earlier.

He had to be here on a future assignment. Things were getting interesting.

In a profoundly deep voice that carried through the hall without a microphone, I said, "I am Mortimer Lifebane, Death incarnate."

Robbie stopped at the edge of the stage and turned to watch. He lifted his mask to get a better view, and his eyebrows bunched together as he saw my billowing robe. I could see the cogs turning in his defective little brain, wondering how I'd picked up a costume in the thirty seconds I was out of his sight.

I hadn't taken my earlier costume contest with the little girl seriously. The smell of sulfur wafted out as I strode forward, fake scythe in hand.

The room itself reverberated as I spoke. "From across the ages I come for you, one by one. Some sooner, some later. You are born, you live your short lives, and you die. Sometimes you try to bargain with me. Some have offered the treasures of the earth. Useless rubbish. The cleverest among you wager for an extra day, a week, maybe a year. Mere slivers of time. Even when you win a reprieve, you still lose when your time arrives. Death may pause, but I never leave until I have what I came for."

I banged the butt of the scythe on the stage as I raised my arms to let the robe fall back to expose my skeletal arms. The tinfoil-and-cardboard blade twisted, nearly coming loose as I lifted my head. My smoking, red eyes flashed out across the room as everyone stared. Blue and orange flecks of flame ran across my exposed bones, and the wood under my hand gave off wisps of smoke. The audience erupted in wild applause.

To the side, I saw the thief stumble off the edge of the stage.

I lowered my arms and bowed my head once more. Then I turned away from the audience to look behind me.

My future self was still there, but incorporeal and decked out like me with the full cloak of darkness and burning skull sockets for eyes, an exact copy of the image I'd just projected, except with his own future instance of my scythe. I followed him over to the side of the stage and looked down. There was Robbie, face down, with my scythe poking out through his back.

I touched the reddened tip of my scythe to reclaim my winnings as I vanished from the view of mortals, leaving

Robbie's prop scythe in its place. I felt whole again as I stood to the side of the stage.

My other self said, "Before this, I thought it was harsh to send the Israelites into the wilderness for forty years. That's barely enough to cover the warm-up lecture for this mess. Then there's the medical examiner who has to explain a lethal cardboard-and-tinfoil stab wound." He rolled his flaming eyes.

My future ghost waved his scythe, and the thief's spirit joined him. Robbie's confusion deepened as he stared down at his body. "How can I be dead?" Such discussions take a long time, and their conversation was none of my business until I was the one collecting him.

Someone in the audience screamed and pointed at Robbie, and another called for medics while the room cleared under the watchful eye of the con volunteers. It was time for me to tend to business.

It took only a moment to reappear in Walter's doorway, invisible to all but him. He looked up and whispered, "What took you so long? I've been waiting."

His son looked up from his chair by the window, his gaze falling on the empty doorway, and then on his father's frail form. I held the scythe out to my side and realized I was still wearing my bones on the outside.

"I'm sorry. There was an incident." I transformed back to the mask he knew, but I was still hidden from his son.

Walter's eyes sparkled with recognition. He chuckled and said with a wheeze, "Oh, it's you. I was glad to see my son one last time, but it's time. Past time." His breathing was labored, and his words were slurred.

I sensed extreme impatience emanating from nearby, so I unlocked the path to the beyond and let his wife through. She gave me a stern look and shook her head in dismay as I looked down in shame at having delayed their reunion.

"Daisy, is that you? You look wonderful, dear." His voice

sounded firm to me, but weakened and faded on the mortal side.

His son stepped to the bedside and patted his hand. "Say hi to Mom for me." A tear slid down his cheek and fell onto the sterile blanket as he stood beside his father's bed. Daisy reached a hand toward her son and smiled, radiating love.

I waived my scythe to separate the physical from the spiritual. Daisy took Walter's hand and lifted him up as the medical equipment began to wail.

She said, "I have so much to tell you, Walter. Why, I don't even know where to begin." They walked hand-in-hand back through the portal.

Walter needed nothing more from me. It was time to face the Boss, who was likely to demonstrate wrath at Old Testament levels. It was worth it.

🎭

John M. Olsen edits and writes speculative fiction across multiple genres and loves stories about ordinary people stepping up to do extraordinary things. His short stories have appeared in dozens of anthologies. He hopes to entertain and inspire others as he passes on a passion for reading to the next generation.

He loves to create and fix things through editing and writing both short stories and novels, and also when working in his secret lair equipped with dangerous power tools. In all cases, he applies engineering principles and processes to the task at hand, often in unpredictable ways.

He lives in Utah with his lovely wife and a variable number of mostly grown children and a constantly changing subset of extended family and pets.

THE FOG OF WAR

EDWARD J. KNIGHT

I wear the mask for freedom.

Something they do not truly understand. Those men and boys dying by rifle fire. Dying by cannon. Dying by starvation despite their cries for "Freedom!" Those boys, these Americans as they call themselves now, do not truly know this freedom they cry for.

But I do. I know what freedom is. I've known it since I threw off my shackles in Virginia and took to the wind. In flight—in flight I am truly free. To soar through the air and dance upon the clouds. To command the rain, to order the lightning. To bend the very elements to my will—*that* is freedom.

When I first commanded the breeze, I was but a small child. Almost more baby than boy. It was a little nothing at the time. A mere whim to see the dead leaves dance. I'd made them whirl and twirl and do loops until my brother Isaac smashed them to dust.

"Stop it!" He'd hissed. "Someone will see! You can't let them see!"

"Why not?" I'd innocently asked.

"Do you want to end up like Old Jebediah?"

I'd shuddered. Despite his grey hairs, Old Jebediah turned the mill's heavy wheel. Every day. All day. His strength was such that no other men or horses were needed. Just strong Jebediah, always at work.

They'd blinded him and left him chained to it overnight, just bringing him bread. He never broke free. When I went back for him, some time after my escape, I'd been saddened to learn of his death. Instead, I flew his children north to New York City. Neither showed any hint of his talents, though perhaps that is for the best. The unconfirmed rumors of others who were more than men were scant, and those stories always had unhappy ends.

For myself—well, the years after that on the farm in upstate New York were good to me. The few neighbors left me alone, and I them. My crops always got the best sun, the right rain, and never an early frost. That this was unusual was not lost on many, but as they shared my good fortune, they were not eager to search for a cause.

I would've stayed there if not for Benny. My dear, irascible neighbor Benny. Benny, who took the city newspapers. Benny, who'd read Paine and Voltaire and argued them with me. Benny, who'd tromped up the path to my house in his new blue uniform with the shiny buttons and the strange triangular hat. Benny, whose fast mind was only matched by his idealism.

"We're forming a militia to fight the redcoats," he'd said. "I'm gonna be captain. I want you in it."

I'd chuckled. "I don't think so."

"Come on," he'd said. "You're strong. You're brave. You'd be good in a fight."

"I'm Colored."

"So?" he'd said with a snort.

"I need no personal reminder of how Coloreds are treated," I'd said. "Even by so-called enlightened New Yorkers."

"I don't treat you different," he'd protested.

"Which is why we're friends," I'd said. "But you are not the army. Even if you're going to be a captain."

"We could sure use your help," he'd said. "First we free ourselves from the King. Then we free the slaves in the south."

"Do you honestly believe that will happen?" I'd asked.

He'd given me a toothy grin. "Only one way to find out."

Then he'd waited. When several minutes had passed, he'd turned and waved as he departed.

"Think about it!" He'd called over his shoulder.

I'd thought about it. But I did not join him. Instead, that day planted the seed of an idea of my own.

That seed grew over time, and then those very same newspapers proclaimed the declaration of the emerging country. Those words by Thomas Jefferson watered the seed. Even at my distant farm, the words reached me. That "all men are created equal." I pondered the words before I called the winds to lift me up and bear me south.

On the twenty-seventh of August, in the year of our Lord 1776, I entered New York City by night, landing softly in a small yard behind a quiet inn. I pulled my cloak tight for, as always, the flight had chilled my flesh. Then I closed my eyes and willed the air around me to warm. In mere moments, all was well.

I listened at the common room door to the laughter and the clink of glasses. But when I entered, the room went silent. A dozen faces heads turned. A dozen faces—ruddy, bearded, clean-shaven, white—stared at me. The bartender, a burly Irishman by his look, glared at me and set his cleaning towel down.

"Your kind aren't welcome here," he said. His scowl reinforced his words.

"Your pardon," I said. "I am a seeker of knowledge. I wish to know more about this Declaration of Independence."

"I said, your kind aren't welcome here."

Two burly men nearby pushed back their chairs with a screech of wood on wood. They stood and glared.

I bowed and made my retreat.

The next two inns were not as polite. By the time I'd made it to the Colored section of the city, all I'd learned was that George Washington had the army camped cross the river in Brooklyn Heights.

That, and the British were coming.

I took a small room and slept until late the next morning.

Discreet inquiries the next day yielded me little. The political leaders of this young revolution had long since left the city, leaving it to the military and the commoners. A slow panic that the city itself might fall to the British rippled through the streets. A fishmonger told me of soldiers desperate for arms and food. An apple seller asked about the prospects up state.

These concerns tugged at me and dismayed me. If the British came, what would happen to these commoners, particularly my fellow Coloreds? Would they be mistreated? Or merely ignored, having played no part in the rebellion?

British rule I knew. It was less harsh than the slave masters'. Yet the British tolerated and profited from the slavery that their southern colonists perpetuated. I did not see change coming from the British.

"All men are created equal." The words gave me hope, but that glimmering flame was too thin, too malnourished to provide much heat. Yet it was all that I knew. Enough spark that I hungered for more.

I needed to know much more. And yet the ones best able to speak of it were not here. And perhaps would not speak to me even then.

I needed to talk to the one I could, General Washington, the sole leader who remained. But Washington was a Virginian, and I knew he owned slaves. I did not know if he would meet with me.

This is when I decided on the mask. In my cloak and my gloves, all that betrayed my race was my visage. A mask would remedy that situation.

A mask also meant I could reveal my powers more openly. When I slept, I could be chained. The less the man with the powers and the man asleep resembled one another, the safer I would be.

It took some time, cloistered with a Colored dressmaker, to arrive at a suitable design. White cotton served as the base, with thin white muslin over the eyes. I could see, as through a mist. The dressmaker stitched in patterns of red and blue in swirls and stars to disguise the shape of my jaw, and the line of my cheek. When I looked in the small ladies' hand mirror she provided, I laughed.

"I look more like a flag than a man!"

She just smiled, for wasn't that the point?

Meantime, I spent what gold I had for the clothes of a gentleman. I knew Washington would not deign to spend time with a ragged farmer regardless of his race.

That night, I took flight again, mask safely in my pocket. I rose high on the breeze above the East River, flying towards Washington's army at Brooklyn Heights, just across the river. I'd heard the British pressed them tight.

It took little time to find the cook fires and lamps and torches of Washington's army, as well as the British army they faced. Two lines of light faced each other. The British had twice the number. Washington's army was pinned against the sea.

I swooped low across the water. Small boats ferried men and supplies between the isle of Manhattan and Brooklyn Heights. Small boats that would be easy to capsize with a small breeze or a swelling of the waves. Small boats that would be easy to destroy with a single shot from a cannon. They fought their way through the choppy waters, men bent against their oars.

I decided they must be Americans. I left them to their tasks.

Further south, in the open bay, dark shadows against the water caught my eye. I had the winds carry me down until I could see more clearly. Ships. Large ones, with small lights along their decks. I dived lower to see more, but cries went up from the closest. I flew away fast, with the hope that they'd not known what they'd seen.

I pondered the ships as I flew back toward Washington's camp. I guessed they were British, come to cut off the transport across the river. If they did so, it would complicate my ability to meet with the General. That was a complication I did not wish to have.

I called up a wind from the north, low against the water. I raised it up, above the small boats of the Americans, to the height of the larger ships' sails. I strengthened it, until I was sure it would keep those ships at bay.

Then I searched for a suitable place in which to land and approach the General.

I found a rocky spot along the shore, far enough from the little boats to be hidden, but close enough that I could quickly follow those disembarking toward Washington's camp. Even better, the few sentries I saw were watching either those arriving or the water beyond. I dropped, feet first, my arms at my side, with a pillow of air to cushion me in the last yard. Even with that, I almost stumbled as I stepped from the air to the rock. I had not counted on it being wet and slippery. I sank into a crouch and looked around.

No alarm. No challenges. I let out my breath. Then I put on my mask.

I chose to walk rather than creep toward the line of men carrying supplies from the shore up the slope. Better to misdirect any that intercepted me than draw suspicion for my bearing. To my good fortune, I arrived at the informal caravan route during a lull. Two men wrested several boxes while a third held aloft a torch. He tried to drag a wooden trunk across the uneven ground as he did.

"Let me help," I said, hurrying forward. I ducked my head, letting the cowl of my cape cast shadows across my face.

"Huh? What?"

The men were too surprised to react before I'd lifted the handle of the trunk.

"Where'd you come from?" the torchbearer asked.

"My boat's down there," I gestured the way I'd come. "I'm already unloaded. I thought you could use a hand."

The torchbearer grunted and then shifted his grip so we could carry the heavy trunk between us. The weight yanked at my shoulder and the handle cut into my gloved hand, but I merely tightened my grip. I kept my head down as we trudged along the path.

After a hundred yards, two hundred yards, three hundred yards, the ache in my arm grew and grew. The torchbearer jerked on his handle from time to time as he tried to bear the weight more with his shoulder. The light flickered ahead.

Finally, we set the trunk down to catch our breath. I leaned over, my hands on my knees and considered what I might do. A wind would not lift the trunk, being too close to the ground. I could not thicken the air either, as it would remain still while we and the trunk moved on. Lost in my thoughts, I stood up too straight.

"Hey," the torchbearer said, "what's with the mask?" His eyes narrowed as he stared at me.

My heart raced, but my tongue was as quick. "Warmth," I said. "Against the night air and the rain."

"It's not cold," he said.

"Cold enough," I said. With a quick blink of my will, I sent the heat from the air up to the sky.

He shivered, and then stared at me in surprise.

"Let's get to the sentry," one of the other men said.

The torchbearer gave me another hard look and then grunted again. He reached for the trunk handle and we were on our way.

Far too many steps later, we reached two soldiers with rifles at their sides. Dirt splattered the uniforms. Fatigue filled their faces. With relief, we lowered the trunk to the ground. The other men stood straighter, so I did, too, though I kept my head bowed.

"Cannonballs and ammunition," the torchbearer said. "Also bread and apples." He nodded toward the other men. Then he bent and unlatched the trunk.

By God, we *had* been carrying cannonballs. The sentries gave them a cursory look, followed by a check of the boxes of the others. They started to wave us through, when the torchbearer held up his hand.

"He's not with us," he said as he pointed to me. "He helped, yeah, but he didn't come across the river with us. And he's wearing a mask."

That got their attention. The further one raised his rifle, though not quite to his shoulder. The nearer one's hand dropped to the pistol at his waist.

I held out my hands, gloved palms wide, showing them empty.

"I'm American," I said. "I wish to see General Washington."

"What for?" snapped the closer sentry.

"That is between myself and the General," I demurred.

His face hardened and he drew his pistol but did not raise it.

"I am unarmed," I said, "and no threat. I just wish to speak with him."

"Get your commander," the torchbearer said to the sentry. Then he gave the trunk a pointed look. "We need to deliver these."

"Take the others," the sentry said. His pistol was now chest high and pointed in my general direction. "Come back with more men for the box."

The torchbearer grumbled, but gestured for the other men to follow. They shifted their boxes between them and trudged up the path. Meanwhile, both sentries now had their guns trained on me.

I must admit, I felt a chill in my blood. Bullets are near impossible to move with wind. At this range, they could not miss. So I stood as still as I could. My hands out. My head slightly bowed.

"Think we should search him?" the far sentry asked.

"Let's wait for the lieutenant," the closer one said.

So we stood there. Two guns at my chest. Sweat beading on my brow. My heart pumping hard, pumping fast. Would they kill me when they found I was Colored? Lock me in chains? Or just send me away?

Or maybe they'd let me through. But I doubted that. They shifted their weight back and forth on their feet and their breath was uneasy. The faces hung on the edge of panic. I divined that the battle was not going well.

There was yet a chance that a wiser head would prevail. I cooled the air by my skin and it wicked the sweat away. Then we waited.

More than several dozen heartbeats later, a ragged soldier wearing a three-cornered hat and a weary look came up behind the two sentries. The rear one looked over at him and nodded. He stopped behind the first one and put his hands on his hips.

"And what do we have here, private?" he asked.

"He wants to see the General, sir," the closer sentry replied, "but he's wearing a mask."

"We'll see about that," the officer said. He stepped forward and reached out his hand.

I zapped him with a little spark of lightning. Not much— just more than what one might build up running wool socks across the right carpet. Not enough to damage, but enough to sting.

He jumped back, as did the sentries. The rear one swore. The nearer one's pistol hand began to shake. All stared at me with undisguised terror.

"I would like to see General Washington, officer," I said.

"Why?" he asked. His voice shook at first, but he set his jaw and narrowed his eyes as he regained control. "So you can assassinate him?"

I sighed. I'd anticipated that possible reaction.

"So I can possibly help," I said. "There are things I wish to know that he is best suited to answer. If his answers are satisfactory ..." I gave a vague wave and let their imaginations work.

"How would you help?"

"Many ways," I said. "For now—" I gestured toward the heavens. "I will command the rain. That should slow the fighting. It will rain until I return mid-morning. If he wants my help, he will see me then."

The officer growled something just as the first fat raindrop splatted on his shoulder. Then another, then another. Then the drops turned into a downpour.

The three soldiers stared at me. The rear sentry was the first to run. After a short moment, I was alone.

I could've followed them into camp, but it seemed like a poor choice. Those three might believe, but too many would not. Instead, I called up the wind and returned to my hovel of a room at the inn.

I let the rain pour while I rested. The evening had taken much out of me. My mind was tired from the constant concentration, my body sore from the exertion. I slept late, almost too late. But I awoke, refreshed and clear in my intent.

So on the morning of August the twenty-ninth, I set out to the battlefield of Brooklyn Heights. I considered flying directly to the sentry's station, but decided no. They certainly would've stationed more men there, and if any panicked, the results could be ill-favored. Instead, I let the gloom of the rain conceal me until I'd touched earth in the same locale as before.

I strode slowly. I trained the rain to divert from my head and shoulders, though it took too much effort to avoid the splash on my cloak further down. I also pushed away the mist that built up in front of my mask.

As I'd expected, a full squad was posted at the sentry station, along with the officer I'd spoken to the night before and another, of higher rank. They stood in a line, firearms at their side but not raised. They looked like drowned boys in their soaked clothes. My chest tightened. Perhaps the rain had been too harsh and too unthinking. Alas, I could not change the past.

They saw me and a small cry went up. The soldiers tensed. One started to raise his rifle, but the new officer waved him to lower it. The others stood still, hard, their eyes locked upon me.

I paused six feet from the new officer. I once again held my hands out, showing they were empty.

"Welcome, Sorcerer," the officer said.

"Call me Samuel," I replied.

"They say you claim that you caused the rain."

"Until now." I let out a low breath and made it stop.

A frightened murmur ran through the gathered men. Some turned white. To his credit, the officer did not.

"I wish to speak with General Washington," I said. "I will not harm you, or any American." I did not add, unless attacked, which I hope they understood.

"If you wished us harm, we could not stop you," the officer said.

"No." They did not need to know how false that was.

"We will take you to the General," he said. He gestured toward the center of camp and fell in beside me as we walked. The soldiers formed a shell around us.

To my surprise, I felt calm. The soldiers would not likely

harm me, even as they feared me. Or, at least, they would require greater provocation than I had given so far. The clouds and the recent rain dampened all but the growing hope I had for answers. And grow it did.

The soldiers escorted me to a large canvas field tent, easily the size of my barn. Water pooled in its folds and mud smeared its lower sides. In the mid-morning gloom, it looked more like a capsized sailboat than a general's headquarters. Two guards stood at attention by its open flaps.

The officer preceded me in, and the guards pulled the flaps closed behind me. Oil lamps lit the tent and I noted tables and chairs around the space. But my attention was immediately arrested by the man in front of me, who could be none other than General Washington.

He stood taller than I expected, with a high forehead and long nose. His shoulders sagged at first, but he pulled himself up straight when he saw me. His piercing eyes studied me intently.

"Sir," the officer who'd led me in said, "this is Samuel. The one who made it rain."

I raised an eyebrow. That was shockingly polite. Then I bowed, enough to convey respect. Not enough for subservience.

"You wished to speak with me," General Washington said.

"I do." I glanced around. Besides Washington and the officer, two other aides hovered in the background. One had a quill and paper and appeared to be taking notes.

"My time is short," Washington said, "so please forgive me for dispatching with the pleasantries. I understand you might be of assistance to our cause."

"If it is just," I said, "then yes."

"Our cause is indeed most just," he said. "We fight for liberty. So how might you help? We do not need more rain."

"Are you advancing or retreating?" I asked.

He tensed. After a quick glance at his officer, he continued,

"We must retreat," he said. "Their numbers are too great, and should the wind shift and their ships take the river, we will be trapped and destroyed."

"The wind will not change until I command it," I said. "But if you wish to escape ... perhaps a great fog?"

An excited murmur ran through the aides. When Washington shot them a glare, one said, "Apologies, sir."

Washington turned back to me. "Yes. I believe a great fog would serve well."

"With ease," I said with a nod. "But—"

He stared at me and waited.

"You say your cause is just," I said, "but is it just for all?"

He cocked his head. "I do not understand."

"Your Declaration of Independence says 'all men are created equal.' Is that true? *All* men?"

"Yes," he said. "What are you playing at?"

I sucked in my breath. This was the moment of truth. The moment of greatest danger. I could barely stifle my tremors. If they were to shoot me, now would be the time.

I slowly reached up and removed my mask.

Washington gasped, his eyes wide.

"All men?" I said. "Even men like me? Even the Colored that you yourself hold as slaves?"

Now was the moment—would they shoot me as an abomination?

The General turned to his aides. "Wait outside." He gestured at the officer. "You as well."

"But, sir!" the officer objected.

"He will not harm me," Washington said. "If that was his intention, he would have already done so."

The soldiers, their eyes constantly darting to me, hurried to the exit. Washington waited until the tent flaps had stopped swinging. Then he stepped close and pitched his voice low.

"Our cause is just," he said, "and we are in it to the end."

"That did not answer my question."

He stepped back with a sigh. He regarded me and then he turned away, as if lost in thought.

"You ask to change the world," he said.

"I do," I said. I stood silently, waiting.

"And if we cannot?" he asked.

"It is the striving that matters," I said. "You seek freedom from the King. I seek freedom for my brethren. If I told you your cause was hopeless, would you strive for it any less?"

He stood, looking ahead, quiet. I could hear the men outside, talking low by the tent flap. I decided discretion might be prudent and re-affixed my mask.

"I cannot promise anything," he said at last. "There are men who will support your cause and men that will oppose it. It is not something we can take up until we are a nation of our own."

I noted that he did not state to which camp he belonged.

"But there are men who believe it," I pressed. "Men who truly believe that *all* men are equal. Including the Colored."

"Yes." He turned back to me. His face was fixed, hard. He'd masked his own emotions.

"But we must win this fight," he said, "and to do that we must survive this day."

The plea was obvious. As was my response.

"I will help," I said, "but only upon your oath that you will free any slaves you yourself own."

"On my honor," he said. He placed his hand solemnly over his heart. "When the time is right."

"And neither you nor your men will impede me," I added, "in anything I do. Be it here, or in the colonies to the South. I will have your dispensation in writing."

His eyes widened, but then he slowly began to nod.

"It may not do you as much good as you hope," he said.

"I will take what I can."

"Then you shall have your writ."

"Then you will have your fog," I said.

He strode to the desk, took up a quill, wrote out a writ in his own hand, and then handed it to me. I folded it and tucked it in my pocket.

"I will see myself out."

The squadron outside fell in around me as soon as I left the tent. The fog had already begun to form by the time they escorted me beyond the edge of camp.

I took to the wind with my mind troubled. I knew the truth the General had implied. The distance between the words on paper and those realized was vast.

But as I soared, free upon the breeze, my thoughts began to calm. There was much I could still do, both now and in the tomorrows to come. I would have to find the men that believed those words in that Declaration. Who believed freedom applied to all. Those men I could help, in ways beyond what it might take to win this war. I could also exact more promises from the General as the fighting went on. Surely, over the winter, my abilities would serve well and be worth a noble price.

Benny's wisdom came back to me. Freedom from the King. Then freedom for the slaves.

The words of the Declaration had gotten me off my farm. Out of my comfortable bolt hole in the north. The fog that had filled my mind had lifted. A spark had ignited. With my abilities, I could do so much more. The mask and Washington's writ would protect me from my enemies.

And then I could change the world.

Author's Note:

Between August 27 and 29, 1776, the British Army almost had George Washington and his army trapped in Brooklyn Heights. Strong winds kept the British ships from entering the East River and completely cutting them off. Then rain followed by fog allowed Washington's army to escape before the British realized they were fleeing across the river. Had they not escaped that day, the Americans would have most certainly lost the Revolutionary War.

A fourth generation Coloradoan, Edward J. Knight only left the Denver-Boulder area long enough to learn how to put a satellite into orbit. Four satellites (and counting) later, he's returned to both the mountains and to writing fantastical fiction. Along the way, he met the love of his life and became the father of two wonderfully curious kids. He's a huge fan of tightly constructed universes and smart plots. He's also recently become a fan of historical "what ifs"—the little details like weather that alter the universe. Sometimes that detail is "magical," such as in his Mythic West novels. His most recent, *Gunslinger*: *The Dragon of Yellowstone*, is now available through WordFire Press. More of his work can be found at edwardjknight.com.

FACES OF DEATH

ED BURKLEY

Visages de la Mort, they called it. Faces of Death. Those in his circle, what he liked to call the "explorers of the macabre," had suggested he visit the shop, but they had offered him little more than a cryptic name and a crude drawing for directions.

"Well, that's just great," Lucas cried out, his voice seemingly devoured down the maw of the alley. "You think it would be impossible to get lost nowadays."

He wanted a GPS location. His phone showed no signal.

"Really?"

No one took notice of his protest. In fact, there didn't seem to be a living soul in sight. "Well, that just puts the cherry on my already crap-of-a-day."

Perhaps he should call it quits and head home. Perhaps he should leave it to fate. Then he turned around, and there it was, the place he had ventured so far to find. It was a little shop a person could find only in a city such as Paris.

Most flock to Paris, the "City of Light," to partake in all the wonders that it alone can offer. However, for Lucas, it wasn't the crepes outside Notre Dame, the macarons of Ladurée, or the

Mona Lisa in the Louvre that drew him to the city. Lucas had experienced all those clichés before. No, Paris was so much more for Lucas. To him, it was the City of Dark Things. His desire to see the city's more nefarious offerings had led him to this little shop tucked away in a far corner of Montmartre.

After all the buzz the shop had garnered, it was rather demure. In fact it looked very much like any other he had seen in Paris, with the exception of what was displayed in its windows. Behind the glass panes that bowed onto the sidewalk sat six plain white porcelain masks, each propped up on a metal stand.

So far, he was curious but not impressed. He had learned one axiom in his many adventures, and that was that things were not always as they first appeared. He put his reservations aside and entered the shop.

"Bonjour," Mr. Arkwright, the proprietor, said as Lucas stepped over the door's threshold. He was a tall, pale, spindly-looking man with a long-toothed grin.

"Hi there," Lucas replied.

"Ah, a fellow American," Arkwright said, "Welcome. Please look around. I hope you enjoy my little museum. If you do, I warmly accept donations." He pointed to an antique glass container on a pedestal next to the entrance.

A museum, Lucas thought as he looked around, his eyes slowly adjusting to the dim light. The shop was little more than a single room with a counter at the rear. The walls were lined with dark, ornate wood craftsmanship. The smell was musty but pleasant, reminiscent of one of the many old bookstores Lucas liked to frequent. Dust flakes danced on sunbeams that streamed through the store's windows.

Along the wood-paneled walls white masks were lined up. They were similar to the ones in the display window, only they looked older. Very old, in fact. The porcelain of each mask showed all the signs that come with old age. Many were stained yellow and marked with the tiniest veins of cracks, like the faces of antique children's dolls.

"I too lived in the States—for a time," Mr. Arkwright said as he stood behind the counter at the back of the shop. "That is where I began this little collection."

Lucas leaned close to examine one of the masks, then gazed around the room at all the others. As far as he could tell, they all looked identical other than the minor variations in wear. They were not like those masks from New Orleans or Venice, so fancifully and uniquely decorated. No, they were just simple porcelain masks, no one more remarkable than the other. But as Lucas peered more closely at one of the masks in front of him, he noticed a small brass nameplate below it that read *Charles Bentley*. It wasn't a name with which he was familiar. Maybe it was the name of the mask's original owner.

"What exactly are these things?" Lucas asked. "I mean, I know they're masks. Or at least they *look* like masks, but not like any I've seen before."

"Quite right you are," Arkwright said. "They are death masks. But no ordinary ones, I assure you."

Lucas looked back at Arkwright, eyebrow raised. He had heard of death masks before—casts made from a person's face following their demise. He had even seen pictures of a few online. *But what is so unusual about these?*

In response to the look on Lucas's face, Arkwright said, "Very few have properties like the ones you see before you."

Arkwright's use of the word *properties* struck Lucas as odd. Other than referring to ceramic, what exactly did he mean? He pursed his lips and said, "All right, I'll bite; exactly what *properties* are those?"

Arkwright smiled gleefully as he stepped from behind the counter. "Well, you see my good friend, housed within the mask's ceramic skin are the most enthralling of memories, for the mask captures a person's final experience right before he or she died."

Lucas offered a half-smile in disbelief but decided to humor the old man. "So how did you come across all these special masks?"

With the enthusiasm of a schoolboy telling his friends the latest gossip, Arkwright said, "Well, while collecting these masterpieces I encountered what would come to be the last remaining person to know the secret art of the masks. I persuaded him to teach me, and my collection grew. Afterward, I sought out the collections of others, including independent pieces, all to supplement my own. And now it is as you see it today. But I am always looking for additions. No piece is unwelcome, from the mundane to the spectacular."

Lucas nodded. "You say the person who taught you was the last to know how these masks work, correct?"

"Indeed, in all my travels I found no other, save me, who wielded the art. It seems I alone now possess the craft."

Lucas scanned the room and said, "Well, it's quite a collection."

"It took me most of my life to amass," Arkwright said. "I searched the world over for the ones you see before you. Although on the surface they all appear to be alike, I assure you that each mask is unique. Under each is a name to discern the particular owner and its memory."

Lucas returned his gaze to the nameplate before him. "So you say each mask holds the actual last moments of the person whose name is underneath? Like this Charles guy here."

"That is correct."

"So ... why Charles Bentley?" Lucas asked, turning to face the shop owner. "Why not display a mask for Charles Dickens, Charles Darwin, or King Charles?"

"Yes, I know not all in my collection can be the great ones," Arkwright replied. "Other museums house grander trophies than mine, from Henry VIII, Beethoven, and Napoleon to Chopin and Nikola Tesla. But I have my prizes too." He leaned in toward Lucas, put his frail hand to his own cheek and whispered, "Did you know that two masks were made from President Lincoln, and I have one of them?"

"You don't say," Lucas said sarcastically.

Arkwright's smile dropped from his face and he stepped back with hands folded, took a deep breath, and then said, "Like many who first see my collection and learn of the mask's special properties, as well as from your demeanor, I can see that you have been humoring me."

Lucas shrugged his shoulders and smiled as if to ask, *Well can you blame me?* It *was* a pretty big pill to swallow.

"I see by your expression that you want proof," Arkwright responded. "Well, to see is to believe, is it not?" Then he pointed to the wall of masks and added, "Please, be my guest, see for yourself."

"All right," Lucas said somewhat hesitantly and picked up the mask of Charles Bentley. "So how do these things work?"

"Like all masks, one simply needs to put it on."

Lucas turned the mask over in his hands. It looked perfectly normal, so he put it up to his face and peered through the eyelets. What he saw took the breath from his lungs.

Instead of seeing Arkwright standing before him or the wood-paneled shop surrounding him, he gazed out across a vast cityscape. And it wasn't just what he saw that made the air catch in his chest, but what he felt, too. The sun felt warm against his skin, the breeze cool. It was like he was actually someplace else, only the sensations were a bit muffled. *It's like a dream,* he thought, *or a memory.* Yes, as Arkwright had said, it was like he was reliving a memory. Only it was a memory from someone other than himself—it was from this Charles Bentley.

From the view and the strong breeze, it was clear that he was outside and up high. Really high. It was then his gazed shifted down, not by his doing but by that of the memory, and he saw work boots walking across steel girders. He—or more precisely, Charles—was atop the construction site of an impossibly tall skyscraper.

Where—or when—was this, Lucas thought, *and what building am I on? I need to make out something I recognize.*

Because he had no control over what he was seeing, he had to wait until the gaze returned upward. But when it did, Lucas saw a familiar landmark in the distance.

Is that ... the Chrysler Building? Hey, I'm in New York City, and that means this building is most likely the Emp—

In muffled tones he heard a voice yell, "Charles, watch your head!"

The view spun around, and before him he saw an I-beam barreling toward his face.

Duck! he tried to scream.

The view panned and he saw the beam dash past overhead.

Man that was close, Lucas thought. *You should be more careful, Charles. Stop looking out at the city and pay closer attention to what's happening in front of you.*

Then Lucas caught himself. Having been swept up in the experience he had forgotten what the memory actually depicted. A death.

Suddenly, he could see that he—or, actually, Charles—was standing up waving to a group of men close by as if to say, *That was a close one, but I'm okay.* Then, in rapid succession, there was a turn on the beam, a stray rivet on the girder underfoot (*what was that doing there?),* a slip, and a view of the sky with wispy clouds receding into the distance. His head turned over his shoulder, the wind howled and tore at his face, making his eyes water. Twisting mid-fall, he could see the intermittent reflection of Charles in the building's windows as they raced past. In the street below, the people and objects that had been so small only moments before grew large, their faces more clear. Lucas could see the look of horror in the eyes of the bystanders in the final moments of the memory as Charles slammed into the ground.

Lucas gasped and pulled the mask from his face, his eyes wide.

"That was—" he stammered as he tried to catch his breath.

"Enthralling?" Arkwright said. "I know. Mr. Bentley was a steel worker from New York City. He was one of the many who unfortunately fell to their death during the hasty construction of the Empire State Building."

"I was going to say *terrifying*, but ... yeah, it was an experience," Lucas said as his pulse returned to a normal pace. "One I never thought I'd have—one I hoped I'd never have to personally experience."

"But now that you have ... and lived?" Arkwright asked with a glint in his eyes.

Lucas gazed at the rest of the masks that filled the room. A hunger grew behind his eyes.

"There is no shame in wanting to experience more," Arkwright consoled. "It is the same reason people fill amusement parks, haunted houses, and theaters. The same reason they stop to gawk at an accident or murder. It is human nature to want to experience death ... if only vicariously. Locked in our homes, behind police barricades, warm in theater seats, buckled securely in roller-coaster rides, we feel we are safe from death's reach."

Lucas respectfully set the mask of Charles back on its mount and looked at all the other masks of memories. *So many people,* he thought, *lifetimes of experiences trapped within each mask.* He was curious as to what lay hidden behind their eyes.

"Would you like to try another?" Arkwright asked, arm outstretched, motioning him to sample from the wall of wonder.

Lucas looked at each one. From nameplate to nameplate he

went, reading each. *So many; how to choose? I guess anyone is as good as the other.* With eyes closed he stretched out his arm, and when he felt his finger land on a cool brass nameplate he opened his eyes. It read Stephen Stermer. He shrugged his shoulders, picked up the mask, and placed it on his face. *Here goes nothing.*

BOOM!

What the—

"Let's move, move, move," a voice hollered out to others. Bullets screamed by as soldiers darted behind blocks of decimated buildings.

Oh man, it's a war, Lucas thought. *I wonder which one?*

In the distance, he could see a large building on top of a hill. It looked like an old fortress. At the bottom of the hill stood a town.

"The German forces are holed up behind the abbey," a soldier said as he approached. "What should we do?"

Germans. This must be a battle from World War II.

Clouds of dirt sprang up as more bullets missed their intended targets, hitting earthen mounds instead.

"It pains me," said a voice that came not from those around him, but from the person Lucas now embodied, "but I think we should blow up the abbey. Go set the charges and let's do this so we can advance."

The other soldier ran off as large clumps of earth erupted behind him and to his right. To his left, Lucas could see soldiers being torn apart by artillery shells.

This is fucking nuts.

Suddenly there was a white flash, the sound of ringing in his ears, dirt and smoke filling the sky. He felt a dull pain in his side as he hit the ground, knocked from the safety of his hiding place by an explosion. Then a hand reached out—his hand, or rather Stephen's hand—and grabbed his helmet, which had been knocked to the ground. More percussions of exploding earth rained down on him and then a gust of wind cleared the view, revealing a structure behind which he could shield himself. It was a few paces out through open, unprotected territory. He scurried up from the dirt and made a dash for the shelter, but halfway there he felt a sharp burning in his leg, followed by another in his stomach, chest and shoulder. His view scanned down, and he saw bullet wounds peppered across a body—his body.

This is too much, Lucas thought, and reached up to pull the mask from his face. But before he could, a thundering boom erupted, and everything went dark—silent.

He slowly slid the mask off and set it back in its place.

"Stephen Stermer," Arkwright said solemnly, "was a soldier from the 34th Infantry Division at the Battle of Monte Cassino during World War II."

As if still reeling from watching an intense action film, Lucas was motionless, his senses overwhelmed as he desperately tried to reorient them to their natural resting state.

Placing a hand on Lucas' shoulder, Arkwright said, "The front of my shop houses the masks of the common person. Mind you though, there is nothing common about their deaths. But for those less common in society's eyes, those history has deemed worthy of the title famous or infamous—those, I keep here." As he spoke, he pointed to the area toward the back of the shop.

Arkwright helped walk the still-stunned Lucas to the select group of the masks at the far end of the room. Compared to the masks at the front, these ceramic vessels were by far the most weathered. Each was displayed on a stand blanketed with red velvet and encased in a large bell jar. Individual lights shone down from above, illuminating each mask and its accompanying fancifully engraved nameplate.

Lucas read the name of the first one he saw. "Elizabeth Stride ... why do I know that name?"

Arkwright smiled. "She was one of the Canonical Five from the Whitechapel murders."

"A victim of Jack the Ripper?" Lucas asked.

"Very good. I see you know your history of the macabre quite well."

Suddenly, Lucas' eyes lit up in realization of what her memory might reveal. "Did she see—"

But having seen that look on countless faces before, Arkwright was quick to intercede. "Unfortunately, no, she didn't see him coming. He approached her from behind. Some mysteries are not so easily given up, it would seem."

Lucas moved on to the adjacent mask and read the nameplate: H. P. Lovecraft.

"Oh," he said, "this one I know for sure." He adored reading anything he could get his hands on written by this famous author. As he reflected on all of his favorite tales, he started to reach for the mask then stopped. "Wait, didn't he die from ..."

"Yes ... very sad, indeed," Arkwright said. Seeing Lucas' hesitation in taking the mask, he added, "But I wouldn't."

Lucas withdrew his hand and went on to the next mask. There he saw a name that did not look familiar. "Who's this guy? Albert Fish."

Ever the enthusiast, and with a little sprinkle of showmanship, Arkwright said, "Ah, very few can manage to peer through the eyes of that mask. Not for the faint of heart." As he spoke, he lifted the glass dome from over the mask. "But I can tell you are a brave soul," he added, gesturing toward it. "So by all means, don the mask and witness the notorious Moon Maniac."

Moon Maniac? With a moniker like that, how could I not try on this mask?

Lucas carefully lifted the delicate mask to his face and readied himself. He peered through the eyes and thought, *Here goes noth—*

"Hamilton Albert Fish," a booming voice declared.

Lucas could see he was in a room with people staring at him. Their faces were cold, some with burning eyes that pierced him with their hatred.

What's going on here? Lucas felt nervous; he was perspiring, his heart racing. The air was thick with the scent of cleaning solution and old sweat. A man next to him was holding a thick black piece of fabric. Lucas's sight looked down to witness his arm being strapped tightly to a wooden chair.

Oh God, no.

Then that booming voice said, "On this 16th day of January, 1936, witnessed by Warden Lawes, you shall have a current of electricity pass through your body with such amount as to cause your death. May God have mercy on your soul."

I'm in the fucking electric chair!

Then a voice spoke, coming from the person he embodied. "I've tasted children from every state in the U.S."

With that, the man holding the black fabric slipped it over Lucas' vision and all went black. Behind the curtain of darkness, he could hear heavy, panicked breathing, then he felt his whole body seize, his ears pop, and his nostrils fill with the smell of rendering pork fat—

Lucas ripped the mask from his face.

Arkwright, standing inches from him, said with a smirk, "An electrifying memory, is it not? Albert Fish—known by his moniker the Moon Maniac—was an American serial killer who had a most unique and unsavory palate."

"He ate kids?"

"It would seem—"

Arkwright was interrupted by the sound of a phone ringing, coming from a small room in back that was tucked behind drawn curtains.

"Would you excuse me? I'll be but a moment," Arkwright said as he left to answer the call.

Lucas carefully put the mask back in its place and replaced the glass dome.

What horrifying treasures await behind the next mask? He peered at all the glass-domed masks, each a face staring back at him; their hollow eyes the witness of death's various handiworks. As he considered which mask to choose next, something caught his eye. Beyond the domed specimens he spied a small wooden box, its lid open, its interior lined with plush black velvet. Inside sat a pristine, almost polished-looking white mask.

I wonder what this one's all about? There was no nameplate with it and he wondered why it was way back here, separated from the others. He could hear Arkwright was still talking on the phone in the back room. *If I hurry, I can put it on and have it back in its box before he returns.* Then, with equal parts excitement and terror, he grabbed the mask and held it to his face.

What he saw was no skyline, no battlefield, no vision of some far-off place to which he had been swept away by the mask's memory. Instead, what he saw was the inside of the shop, the very one he was standing in. His view turned and he saw that Arkwright was standing before him, an expression of panic and anger worn across his face.

What event is this? And why does Arkwright look so angry?

"I can't believe I let you take her from me," Arkwright said.

Her? Lucas had no idea to whom 'her' referred to, but by the look on Arkwright's face, she must have been very dear to him. Clearly this guy had come between Arkwright and the woman he lov—

But then Lucas's train of thought halted. He suddenly remembered the nature of the masks and the inevitable conclusion to the interaction unfolding before him. Looking into Arkwright's eyes, he thought, *I wouldn't think you capable of ... you couldn't ... kill?*

Arkwright continued, "Well sir, you have taken from me

more than I can bear to lose. You will take no more. This ends now!"

Lucas saw the look in Arkwright's eyes and though, *Oh God, he's actually going to do it. He's going to kill this person.*

Then Arkwright lunged at him and wrapped his hands around Lucas' throat. Arkwright squeezed with all his might, and Lucas could feel the oxygen drain from his body, his lungs burning as they cried for the life-giving air they so desperately needed.

This man is a murderer! Someone stop him!

But it was already too late, for this was only an echo of the actual event that took place. He couldn't believe it—the nice, timid shop owner who looked too frail to harm a fly had murdered some poor soul, and for what? Jealousy over some woman? Then the thought hit Lucas straight in the gut; to witness what he was seeing also meant that Arkwright had captured this memory, this death, with a mask, the very mask Lucas was wearing right now. Disgusted, he tore the damned thing from his face.

Just as he did, Arkwright emerged from behind the curtain and approached him. "I'm sorry about that—"

"I can't believe you!" Lucas shouted.

Arkwright froze.

"I saw you do it, with my own two eyes. At first I didn't really believe that you would ... but that's what the mask always captures, doesn't it? A death."

Befuddled, Arkwright said, "Whatever are you talking about?"

"I saw your fight with that poor fool over a woman. He took the woman from you, and you killed him in an act of revenge. Strangled him with your—and then—you being so damned obsessed with these fucking masks, you placed one on your victim's face, just so you could add another to your collection." Lucas waved the mask he had just been wearing wildly in the air. "Oh, you wouldn't put it with the ones that are on display for all to see, mind you. No, you put it here with the ones you hide in back, the ones that keep your horrible secrets," he said, pointing to the table where the empty box still sat. "The ones you keep in those—wooden boxes." Then Lucas threw the mask he had been waving about back into its velvet-lined wooden container.

"You're making no sense," Arkwright said consolingly. "Now, please calm down."

"I won't calm down!" Lucas shouted. "I saw you kill that person, because he took away somebody you loved."

"I've never intentionally hurt, or for that matter *killed*, anyone in my life."

Lucas's eyes darted around the room, and a hundred empty eyes behind white faces screamed out to him for justice. *How many of these masks are of his own doing?* He picked up a mask off a nearby stand and cried, "You're sick!" He threw the mask to the floor.

"No!" Arkwright screamed.

The mask shattered, sending pieces scattering to hidden places throughout the shop.

"What have you done?" Arkwright asked.

Lucas grabbed a second mask, and then another, sending them to the same fate as their previous companions. Shards of white ceramic danced like shattering ice across the marble floor. Then he turned his attention to Arkwright's bell-jarred masterpieces. He placed both of his hands securely on the glass confines of Elizabeth Stride's mask.

Arkwright's eyes pleaded as he cried, "No."

Then Lucas shoved with all his might. Both mask and dome struck the floor and exploded on impact.

Arkwright dropped to his knees, his hands cupping the shards of porcelain as if somehow this action would magically fuse the broken memory back to its original design.

Lucas stepped over to the next dome and placed his hands firmly on Lovecraft.

Arkwright quickly left his grieving spot and the remains of Ms. Stride to stop Lucas from causing any further destruction. "I implore you to go no further with your intended action," he said, his voice wavering hoarsely, his eyes brimming with tears. "You have already destroyed many of my masks. Now you want to destroy my beloved Lovecraft? I will not allow it. I sat idly by as you smashed forevermore the last memory of Elizabeth Stride. I can't believe I let you take her from me. Well sir, you have taken from me more than I can bear to lose. You will take no more. This ends now."

Upon hearing those words, Lucas froze, overwhelmed with a wave of *déjà vu*. Then it hit him. *The mask—the memory was of—*

But it was too late. Arkwright was already upon him, his hands wrapped tightly around Lucas's throat. He stared helplessly into the shop owner's eyes as a dark tunnel slowly closed in around his vision. His arms flailed as he desperately tried to pry away the man's fingers, then dropped to his sides. His legs kicked for a moment. Then they too grew still.

Arkwright released his hold and stood up, wiping the sweat from his brow with his sleeve. He straightened Lovecraft's display, then took a cloth from the counter and wiped the fingerprints off the glass dome. Then he looked down at Lucas and said, "How dare you take from me that which I hold closest to my heart? How dare you destroy my craftsmanship, my masks?"

Staring at the lifeless body before him, he slowly shook his head, then turned his attention to the mask sitting in the open wooden box on the table. "I'm not sure what you think you saw," he said as he retrieved the gleaming white mask from its mahogany confines. "The masks that I keep in these boxes are blank."

Then he slowly lowered himself to the ground and knelt beside Lucas. "But I suppose you were right about one thing," he continued as he placed the mask on Lucas's face. In response, the mask's eyelets glowed a soft blue as they captured Lucas's last memory. "It turns out that I did kill someone after all." Then with great care, he placed the mask back in the wooden box and closed the lid.

Ed Burkley is a psychologist and author who lives on the outskirts of Saint Louis, Missouri. His short fiction has appeared in *Weirdbook, Year's Best Body Horror Anthology*, *Spooky Isles Book of Horror VI*, and *Strange Lands* (Flame Tree Publishing). He does his best work with a cup of chai to refresh, a Norwich Terrier on his lap for comfort, and the much-needed support from his far better writer wife. More information can be found at edwardburkley.com.

THE QUOTA

TOM HOWARD

A zzed lay back in the padded chair while the succubus covered his crimson skin with peach-colored makeup. With a brown tunic and the black wig, he could be any number of fantasy creatures. They didn't pin back his pointed ears. Having his tail coiled and bound felt uncomfortable enough.

"Aren't you going back up a little soon?" Stell asked. "I thought you got a break between collections."

"Yeah," Azzed said. "Spyrax's disappearance made us miss our quota for the month, so we're working overtime."

Stell nodded and glued down Azzed's bangs again. In the heat, wigs tended to slip off. "With old Spyrax gone, you'll be back on top again."

Azzed squirmed to relieve the pressure on his tail. He wouldn't mind being the number one soul collector again with his photo on the boss's wall. He was good at his job, smart and ambitious. The other collectors envied his skill and the number of mortals he outwitted each quarter. Hell would be half-empty without him.

Stell surveyed her work. "Azzed, you always use the same con. I'd love to make you up as an alien sometime."

"Fairy tales are a better scam. I'm not trading peach makeup for gray."

"Yeah, but you could keep the tail." She removed the cloth around his neck that protected his costume.

He stood and examined himself in the mirror. "Thanks, Stell. It looks great." He smiled, revealing his square white teeth, a false set to cover his pointy ones. His eyes, red with black cat irises, were hidden by warm brown contacts with pupils as large as a cow.

When Stell scurried off to help a boogeyman out of his costume, Azzed pulled out the list of that day's proposed contracts and read it in the scarlet light.

Decades used to pass between the signing of a soul contract and cashing it in. These days, the boss couldn't wait for people to die of accidents or old age. As soon as they signed the contract, Azzed whisked the signee's soul away to the nether regions. No one noticed the number of people walking around soulless.

Azzed liked collecting the younger souls. The teenagers and pre-teenagers proved more gullible than their parents, and they made his stats look good. He didn't follow through with the promises of the contract, only had them sign on the line. The legal department ensured the loopholes were large enough to drive a hearse through.

By the third contract of the afternoon, Azzed was coasting. The teenagers jumped at the opportunity to escape their boring lives of video games, inattentive parents, and pointless homework. They wanted to be secret princes or princesses, rich and pampered. Like taking candy from a baby. Azzed thanked movies and television, two of the boss's better ideas.

He perched on the eaves of an unpainted house and watched his next customer come home from school. Blonde and thin, she wore a patched and faded dress. She carried a stack of books and didn't wait for her two younger brothers to catch up with her.

Azzed smiled as he followed her inside. His faint shadow flitted against the nicotine-stained walls, unnoticed by Maggie May Jones, a twelve-year-old destined to become a burden on society. Her little brothers dawdled behind her, torturing some poor dog or seeing what trouble they could get into.

"Maggie May," her mother called from the bedroom, "is that you?"

"Yes, Mom." Maggie May's shoulders sagged, but she didn't put her books down. With the piles of clutter on the hand-me-down furniture, she might never find them again.

"How are you feeling?" Maggie May asked.

Azzed had done his homework. Maggie May's mother suffered from a long list of imaginary ailments including headaches, food allergies, and bad nerves. Most days she didn't leave her bed. Maggie May said she didn't know how her mother survived on a pack of unfiltered Camels and a case of Coke a day.

Azzed knew. Some of the boss's best servants had splotchy souls, making life miserable for everyone else. Maggie May's mother would live to be a hundred at least.

"I'm still seeing black spots," her mother replied from the parents' bedroom.

"Do you want me to call the doctor?" Maggie May asked.

"No. Those quacks want me to sign over my body to science when I die. Would you check the beans?"

"Sure, Mom." Maggie May stirred the pot on the stove, keeping the stack of books in her arm. She added more salt.

Azzed scorched them a little. After all, he was a demon.

"I'm going to change, Mom," Maggie May shouted and took the back stairs—a ladder nailed to the wall—to her small room in the attic.

Azzed, a shadow, followed her.

She removed her school clothes, hung them up, and put on a t-shirt and jeans. "If I hurry," she told Bellweather, the old one-eyed cat who shared her tiny room, "I can finish my homework before putting out supper for Dad." He came home late after long shifts at the local factory.

Azzed watched as Maggie May regarded the homework resting beneath *Annabeth of Falcon Peak*, her favorite book and Azzed's key to her contract. Azzed didn't understand readers, but their fantasies provided a convenient hook.

"I know I've read it many times, Bellweather." She picked up the book. "But the exciting adventures of a sorceress-in-training call to me, but if I read one tiny paragraph, I'll be pulled into a world of fancy balls and handsome princes and never finish my math."

Maggie May sat on the edge of her cot and petted the cat. "Maybe just one quick chapter, the one where Annabeth saves the handsome prince from the clutches of the swamp beast."

She opened the book, and with a flash of light and a pop of imploding air, Azzed appeared. Maggie May muffled a scream and pulled her legs up on the cot. Bellweather hissed and darted under the bed.

Azzed smiled with his fake teeth. "Do not be frightened, Your Highness. The book sent me to rescue you." He bowed.

She stared at his pointed ears when he removed his cone-shaped hat. "The book sent you?"

"I'm Azzed, the book's guardian. Only very special people can see me. People such as secret princesses."

Maggie May stared at the book in her hands, a smile on her face. "I knew I didn't belong here."

Azzed bowed again. "You are Her Royal Highness Tiffany Ambrosia Regina IV, missing from the fairy realm since birth."

"I don't understand. There's no Azzed or Princess Whatever in the book."

"That's true." He smiled. "You are as smart as you are beautiful, Your Highness. After reading the book one hundred times, the spell is broken, and I'm allowed to appear to reveal your true nature."

Maggie May lowered her feet to the floor. "Why me?"

"Another intelligent question. Haven't you wondered how someone so far above the others could be raised in such squalor and poverty?" He looked around the attic with disdain. "You know in your heart this isn't where you're supposed to be." Flattery sweetened the pot.

She nodded. "But I'm not a beautiful princess."

"A simple enchantment, Your Highness, to hide you from evil forces." This one was smarter than she looked. "When we reach the palace, you'll resume your true appearance. The princes will fight to escort you to this evening's coronation ball. The other princesses will be green with envy."

She almost glowed with satisfaction. This would be an easy contract. "Will there be trials?" she asked.

"Trials?" Azzed was confused. Like with a judge? No, she only needed to sign the paperwork.

Maggie May held up the book. "Yes. There are always challenges and some great evil to vanquish before the princess finds her rightful place. Look at Annabeth. By honing her magical powers, she destroyed Grazel, the Evil Wizard."

Azzed's wig itched. "Of course, Princess. I didn't want to frighten you with the details. Lizard men, the Dark Sorceress ... Bellashade, barricades of thorns, and an enchanted prince."

She jumped up, her eyes wide. "What magical powers do I have?"

Azzed stepped back. "Powers? Ah, when you break the prince's spell with a kiss, he'll give you the Mighty Sword of the Seven Happy Gods. With it, you'll be invincible against Bellavanna the Terrible." He fumbled in his pocket for the contract.

"I thought you called her Bellashade," Maggie May said.

"She has many names. I fear saying them in case she hears

and threatens our quest before it begins, Your Highness." He glanced around as if the enemy might break through the wall at any moment.

Maggie May nodded. "Okay. What do I pack?"

"Don't pack anything. Everything you'll ever need will be provided. Do you have any friends or young relatives who might accompany us on this quest?" He might get lucky. He'd receive a bonus for extra recruits.

"No," she said.

"Of course not." Azzed sighed. They never had any friends. "Meet me at the school bus stop at midnight." After she signed away her soul in a few minutes, she'd forget his visit.

Maggie May hugged the book to her chest. "I knew this would happen, but I'd almost given up hope after the last elf disappeared."

"Your humdrum life is over," Azzed said. "Wait. Another elf visited you?"

She laughed, and the cat crawled from beneath the bed. "Yes, but I don't think he was really an elf. He kind of exploded when I showed him the star."

Azzed had a sick feeling in his stomach. "Exploded? Star?"

"The star in the book, silly! You know the one Annabeth uses to defeat Grazel." She held out the book. "Here. I'll show you."

Before Azzed could question her further, Maggie May took a piece of chalk from her desk and knelt on the hardwood floor. With a few quick slashes, she drew a large star over the faint lines already there.

Azzed stared at the markings around his feet. "That's not a star. That's a pentagram."

Maggie May sat back on her heels and gathered the cat in her arms. "Funny. That's what the other elf said, too."

Sweating and unable to move his feet, Azzed unrolled the

long sheet of paper covered in spidery text. "If you'll sign here, Maggie May, I'll give you the life you deserve."

For the first time, he noticed a ring burnt into the floor inside the pentagram. He sniffed. Spyrax?

The cat meowed and jumped down.

"Oh," Maggie May said, "I almost forgot the word."

"What word?"

She flipped open the book and scanned the page. "It's part of the trial. When Annabeth said the secret word, Grazel was vanquished. Here it is. *Lezarg Combusto*. Now, where do I sign?"

Azzed couldn't speak. His collar grew tight and hot. The cat hissed. The contract burst into flames, and he couldn't release it. As his skin crisped from the oils in his makeup, his last thoughts were of the quota. What would happen to the quota if every child learned that books were powerful enough to destroy demons?

There'd be hell to pay.

Tom Howard is a fantasy and science fiction short story writer living in Little Rock, Arkansas. He thanks his family and friends for their inspiration and the Central Arkansas Speculative Fiction Writers' Group for their perspiration.

WA-HA-YA (THE WOLF)

JL CURTIS

13 September 1943
Palermo, Italy, US military replacement depot

A grizzled, frazzled sergeant stood in front of the assembled soldiers in the cavernous warehouse being used.

"When I call your name, report to me and I'll give you your assignment. Do *not* waste my time asking for something other than what I give you." He yawned and wearily flipped the first page of the clipboard over. "Abercrombie, Joseph Edward, Private."

A soldier stumbled forward, duffle bag over one shoulder, rifle over the other one. When he made it to where the sergeant stood, the sergeant demanded, "Dog tag." The soldier lifted his dog tag from under his shirt. The sergeant nodded, made a check mark, and said, "Eighty-second. Out the door to the left."

Joe Curry, half Cherokee Indian, eighteen years old, small and wiry, sat on his duffle bag leaning back against the wall of the warehouse that smelled of the sea and the funk of too many men in too close a space. The sergeant continued to drone down the list of names as Joe did the meditation his grandpa had taught him for calm, wondering where he would be assigned. *This definitely isn't Oklahoma, dummy! I don't think I better try to do anything over here,* he thought, *other than grandpa's meditation.*

Everything he'd heard was that they were going directly into battle, replacing soldiers lost on the beachhead at Salerno. He finally heard the sergeant call, "Curry, James Joseph, Private."

He jumped up, swung his duffle bag over his shoulder, and picked up his M-1 Garand, carrying it in a hunter's carry. He popped to attention in front of the sergeant and said, "Curry, James Joseph." As he extended his dog tag, he could smell the booze and cigarettes on the sergeant's breath and managed not to recoil as the sergeant glanced at the dog tag.

"Where you from, son?" the sergeant asked, picking up on his accent.

"Lawton, Oklahoma, *si* ... Sergeant!"

"You get along with Indians okay, son?"

Joe grinned. "Yes, Sergeant. My best friend is a Kiowa."

The sergeant chewed his lip for a second, then scratched something out on the clipboard. "Out and to the right, son. You're goin' to the One-Fifty-Seventh. They're from Oklahoma."

"Thank you, Sergeant," Joe said, tucking his dog tag back in his shirt. Hoisting his duffle bag, he walked easily out the door behind the sergeant and never heard the sergeant's comment under his breath. "Son, I just hope to hell you survive."

Seventy-two hours later, Joe was sharing a foxhole with a Cherokee corporal named Andrew Little as they ducked machine gun fire. He was cursing every time rounds spanged and whined off the rocks they had piled in front of the foxhole and would occasionally stick his rifle up and fire a few ineffectual rounds at the Germans.

Joe had been sitting quietly, only bobbing up once in a while and firing aimed shots, when Andrew started to get up again. Joe grabbed his pack and yanked him down just as another round of bullets ricocheted off the rocks. Andrew snapped, "What the hell did you do that for?"

Joe smiled at him. "Because he was due to sweep back over us. Change places with me. I think ... I might be able to get him."

Andrew scoffed, "Sure, you're a boot. I've been up through Sicily, but *you* know more than I do about combat. Go right ahead, Boot," he said sarcastically, but he did squirm out of the way, and Joe crawled over to the front of the foxhole, then shifted to the left side. Just as the bullets stopped hitting the rocks in front of him, he popped up and fired three times quickly, then dropped back in the foxhole, cursing. "Missed the other loader."

Andrew just looked at him. "You're saying you got *two* of them?" Joe nodded, and Andrew continued, "How the hell?"

"It's a pattern. My grandpa taught me about patterns. Everything has a pattern. His was ten, maybe fifteen seconds. He'd sweep the front, and when he crossed us, four seconds later he went back the other way. That meant I had between six and ten seconds to get off a shot." Joe grinned. "And it worked." A fusillade of bullets hit the front and right side of the foxhole, and Joe said, "Looks like the other gunner isn't real happy with us right now."

As darkness fell, Joe had managed to take out another set of loaders and another gunner. The word was passed to withdraw, and once it was fully dark, they eased out of the foxhole and back down the curve until they were out of range of the random firing. Sergeant Kincaid, the squad leader, grabbed them as they got back to the muster point. "Good shooting,

Little. You got a couple of them, but we're still stuck. The old man is up at HQ trying to talk them out of doing a frontal assault at dawn."

Little said softly in Cherokee, "I didn't, the boot got them. He figured out their pattern of fire. He probably saved my life, too." Joe started to say something, but didn't, not knowing if it would be smart to let them know he spoke Cherokee, especially since he was considered a half-breed since his dad was white. When Kincaid looked sharply at him, he managed a questioning look back.

Kincaid said, "Nice work, Boot."

Joe nodded. "Thank you."

The platoon commander, Lieutenant Martin, walked out of the darkness. "Sergeant, squad leader meeting at the CP, now. Send runners to the other squads."

"Yes, sir. Shoemaker! Macon! Go roust out the other squad leaders." Switching to Cherokee, he added, "Corporal Craft, you're in charge. Get 'em fed and watered. I'll be back as soon as I can."

Craft nodded and said, "You heard the man. Little, take a couple of troops and get us some chow."

An hour later, Joe had just finished policing up the area when Sergeant Kincaid returned. "Gather round!" Once the squad was assembled, he said, "The One-Fifty-Seventh will continue to be the point of the spear again tomorrow. We're supposed to be moving up the road to get north of Salerno. Bravo company will continue to hold our positions tomorrow until Alpha can circle around this damn roadblock and get behind the Germans, forcing them to fall back. First platoon, second squad has security tonight, starting at twenty hundred. We're supposed to man at least three foxholes spread out across the road and approaches. Two-hour rotations. Three rounds rapid fire is the alert signal. Challenge is New York, response is Yankee." He glanced at Joe. "Corporal Little, you get to pull the first watch with the boot to instruct him. If you feel he can handle it, he can pull his second shift by himself. Y'all are in the far-left foxhole."

Little nodded. "Grab your rifle, Boot. Let's get out there."

Joe's third watch of the night started at 0400 and it was all he could do to stay awake. He hadn't tried to do anything spiritual since he'd left Oklahoma, but he knew he had to do something, so he meditated, slipping into the trance state between sleep and awake as he took on the masque of the Wolf totem. He knew his vision lost colors as the darkness of the night receded. His other senses became sharper, especially his senses of smell and his hearing. An added bonus was that the cold seemed to recede. What he couldn't see was the dim shape of a wolf surrounding his body or the appearance of a wolf's ears and muzzle covering his head.

He sniffed and smelled the soldier on guard in the next foxhole, almost fifty yards away. He sniffed again and sorted out the odors of gun smoke, the latrine, and a faint smell of sausage coming from the north, along with the smell of the dead. He gazed back and forth over his assigned sector but didn't see any movement. He went to move his M-1, but it felt as if he was trying to grip it without thumbs. He settled for sliding it over the lip of the foxhole, between two of the larger rocks.

An hour later, as he watched, he heard a tink of metal on a rock off to his left. Turning and sniffing, he smelled a much stronger odor of sausage and some kind of odd tobacco smoke. He looked intently in that direction, a growl starting deep in his throat. He picked out three, no ... four Germans moving stealthily down the ditch beside the road with some kind of packs on their backs.

He knew he couldn't shoot them because he couldn't

control the rifle in his trance. Then he saw a brighter patch just down the ditch from them and willed himself back to full consciousness. Slipping behind the M-I, he carefully sighted on the lighter patch of ground and waited.

A minute or so later, he saw one, then a second shadow cross the patch. Aiming low, he triggered off three quick rounds, then heard running feet and fired a fourth round higher. There was a large explosion, temporarily blinding Joe, and he felt something hit him in the cheek as he belatedly ducked down. The crackle of rifle fire echoed up and down the lines on both sides, with at least one of the German machine guns firing sporadic bursts. He started shaking, tears in his eyes as he realized he'd just killed men. Then he remembered his grandpa's last words to him before he shipped out, "*A warrior kills only when necessary, and only enemies of his people.*"

The next thing Joe knew, Little was shaking him, hard. He took a deep breath just as Sergeant Kincaid eeled his way into the foxhole after giving the appropriate countersign to Little's challenge. "What the hell did you do, Boot?"

Joe's ears were still ringing, but he replied, "I think I got two ... maybe three Germans. I don't know if I got them for sure. I shot a little high in case the fourth one was running—"

"Three? How the hell? Are you telling me you can see in the dark?"

Joe pointed to the lighter patch in the ditch. "I saw something moving over there, and I knew it wasn't one of our guys. So, I took a shot."

"You took three shots! That was the alert signal! Now everybody is up and wanting to know what the hell is going on. You better hope you were right, Curry!" Kincaid crawled back out of the foxhole and disappeared toward the rear area, leaving Joe sitting there wondering if he'd said too much about his ability.

Macon slithered into the foxhole. "They want you back at

the CP. Guess they're sending out a patrol to see what you did or didn't do."

Joe crawled out of the foxhole without saying anything and jogged back to the Command Post, saluting when he saw Lieutenant Martin, the platoon commander, standing there impatiently. "Private Curry reporting as ordered, sir!"

"Now that you've deigned to join us, lead the way to whatever the hell that was that you started this morning, Private."

Joe gulped. "Yes, sir." He almost saluted again but remembered the instructions not to on the line. "I think we should go around to the left of the foxhole I was in, sir." The lieutenant made a shooing motion and Joe turned and led them past the foxhole after Rutherford challenged them. Joe realized he'd forgotten to challenge Rutherford and figured he'd hear about that later.

Fifteen minutes later, they stood over the bodies of three Germans, all shot through the body, and a smoking hole in the ground with a boot still standing up in it where the fourth had been. All three of the bodies had packs, and the lieutenant whispered, "Get their packs. We'll take them back and see if they have anything in them intel might be interested in." He peered back toward the line of foxholes, then added, "That's a helluva set of shots in the dark there, Private."

Joe was wrestling one of the packs off as two troops from second squad got the other two. "I took ... I took a chance, Lieutenant. I saw movement over this lighter patch."

A German machine gun started stuttering and everyone ducked. "Back to the lines, no lights. Lead on, Private."

A bald-headed major stood at the entrance to the Command Post as they walked in. "What ya got, Lieutenant Martin?"

"Four dead Germans, sir. Brought their packs back."

"Let's see what they have, shall we?" The major turned to Curry and the others, "Bring them in here."

Joe stepped in and took the pack off. As he did so, the major stopped him under the light, then turned and yelled, "Medic up!" He pushed Joe toward a folding chair and said, "Sit down, son. Let's get the medic to look at you."

Joe realized his cheek was still hurting, and he started to reach up and scratch it when the major grabbed his hand. The medic came in, took one look at Joe, and whistled. "You got lucky, Private. Another inch higher and you'd have lost the eye." He reached up and tugged on Joe's cheek, then held up an inch-long piece of metal. "Want a souvenir to go with your purple heart?" Joe held out his hand and the medic dropped it. "Now this might sting a bit." Whatever he swabbed the wound with *definitely* hurt, and Joe's eyes started watering.

Suddenly they heard the major exclaim, "Holy crap! This pack is full of potato mashers! Be careful with those others. I think we know what the explosion was now. Damn!" The medic led Joe out of the Command Post before he heard anything else.

❦

Two days later, they'd only advanced about five miles up the road and were definitely into the mountainous terrain. The Germans were digging in, giving up ground as slowly as they could. It was a grinding war of attrition, and the One-Fifty-Seventh was losing its share of troops. Joe was back on the line, five stitches closing his cheek and the piece of shrapnel in the medicine bag he wore around his neck.

Sergeant Kincaid was ranting and pacing as the squad slid back for chow. "I'm sick and tired of these damn machine guns! They've got us pinned, *again*! Captain Dawes wants volunteers to try to find a way to get behind them and ambush them as soon as it gets dark." He glanced at Joe when he finished his rant and said softly, "You want to volunteer, Curry?"

Joe shrugged. "I ... sure, I'll volunteer, Sergeant."

"Thought you might. You're turning into a good troop, Curry. I'll take you up to the CP as soon as we get chow."

Joe didn't eat much, suddenly not hungry when he realized what he'd volunteered to do, but he enjoyed the scalding cup of coffee as he waited for Kincaid to finish.

Two hours later, after an argument with Kincaid and the lieutenant, he crawled toward the drop off on the side of the road. He didn't have a helmet, a rifle, or a pistol. His pack was sitting in the rear, and the only thing he had was his grandpa's Bowie knife he'd pulled from its hiding place in the bottom of his pack. Once he was off the side of the hill, he sat up and spent the time necessary to go through his meditation. As his vision sharpened, everything turned shades of gray, but he could see almost as well as if it was light. His other senses heightened, and he warmed up. He took a few moments to ensure he could move without problems, and a low growl came from his chest. He moved quickly now; sure he could avoid any Germans he might see, long before they would see him.

He found a shallow draw and followed it up around the hill, staying low as he moved. He slid behind the first two machine gun nests without a problem, noting the trail they were using. He eased up to the top of the draw just below the third machine gun nest, then stopped and watched. *We can do this*, he thought. *Footing isn't the best, but if we're quiet ... we might be able to get all three of them.*

Slipping back down the draw, he moved back until he was sure he was behind his own lines before he sat and said a short prayer of thanks to the gods for allowing him to get back safely. He stuck his head up and said, "Coming in."

Shoemaker was in the first foxhole and said, "Abraham."

"Lincoln."

"C'mon in, Curry. I recognized your voice."

"Thanks, Shoe. I think I found a way to get behind them."

"Well, you're the last one back. We were wondering if you'd been captured."

"What time is it?" Joe asked softly.

"Almost midnight. You been out there almost four hours!"

"I ... didn't realize I was gone that long, but I made it up to the top of the hill behind the Krauts."

He reported back to Kincaid, who took him to the Command Post and the Captain. "So, you think you've got a way to get behind the nests, is that right, Private Curry?"

Yes, sir. There's a draw on the back side of the hill that goes almost to the top. We could get all three nests if we did it quietly."

"Are you willing to lead them, Private?"

"Yes, sir."

"Kincaid, get the best troops we've got to go with him."

The sergeant saluted. "Yes, sir."

As they walked out of the Command Post, Kincaid said, "Go wait by the wall. I'll send them to you as soon as I round them up. Knives only, right?"

Joe said jokingly, "Unless you've got a few bows and arrows? Yes, knives."

Kincaid chuckled. "If only," and melted into the night.

Joe made his way back to the wall and sat on top of it, thinking of Oklahoma and warmth, the smell of the prairie grass and cattle. Just a few minutes later, Corporal Little followed by Miller, Begay, Harris, and Thornton walked up. Joe thought to himself, *Well, well, well, a half-breed leading four full-blood Cherokees.*

Little said in Cherokee, *"You can assume your true form now, Joe. Let us go before we lose too much time."*

Startled, Joe stopped for a minute and slipped into the half-awake world, letting the wolf take over. He waved to them, and the six of them moved silently through the night.

At the first machine gun nest, Lewis pointed to the

German sergeant closest to the draw and then at Joe. He nodded as Lewis and the others took out bows, strung them, then nocked arrows. Joe eased up behind the sergeant, grabbed his head and pulled it back as he cut his throat with ease, his heightened senses allowing him to smell the fear sweat, the tobacco, and some kind of sharply scented liquor. He heard the twangs of the bow strings being released and dispassionately watched all of the Germans fall. Lowering the sergeant, he nodded and led them to the next machine gun post. They repeated the same drill, again killing all of the Germans without a sound.

At the top of the draw, it was a little harder to get into position, and as he reached for the soldier in front of him, the German bent over and sneezed, causing Joe to miss his grip. Suddenly, Joe was in a fight for his life as the German cursed him and fought like the very devil to keep Joe's knife from his neck while simultaneously trying to stab him with his bayonet. After a minute or so, though it felt like an hour, Joe finally slipped the Bowie deep between his enemy's fourth and fifth ribs, then worked it around as the soldier tried to scream. He finally went limp, and Joe sagged to the ground, totally spent.

Little said, again in Cherokee, "*We need to get back. Get up, Warrior. Lead us back. We are done here.*"

Joe groaned and climbed wearily to his feet, panting as he led them back down the draw, around the hill and back to the wall. Lewis said, "*Wait here, Warrior,*" as the five of them disappeared into the darkness.

Saying a prayer of thanksgiving for his and the others' safety, Joe came out of his totem and back to full wakefulness, seeing the world dim and his other senses dull with a deep, exhausted sigh.

Ten minutes later, Kincaid walked up with the five soldiers and said, "Took me a while, but these guys are willing to have you lead them on the ambush."

Joe looked at him incredulously. "Sergeant, we just got back. Little was in charge, we—"

"What do you mean, just got back? I just now got here with Little and—"

Joe stood up and looked at each man, then said in Cherokee, "*Are you guys screwing with me? We just killed every man in three machine gun nests!*" He looked at Little. "*You told me which ones to take out with the knife while y'all shot them with bows. I got two sergeants and a ... corporal. We killed them all! You were there!*"

Kincaid said, "Bullshit. You're just dreaming." He clicked on a flashlight, shielding the beam with his hand. "You couldn't have ..." He played the light over Joe and saw that he was covered in blood. He took a step back and said, "You just spoke Cherokee!"

Joe's temper frayed, and he snapped, "*Yes, because I am Cherokee, dammit!*"

Begay began backing away, mumbling in Cherokee, "*Spirits! The Nunnehi ... the travelers.*"

Kincaid stripped off his pack, helmet, and canvas belt, keeping his bayonet. "Little, you're with me. Curry, show us those nests. The rest of you stay here, and be quiet!"

Joe looked at them in confusion. "What is going on?"

Kincaid said, "That is what we're about to find out. Move out." Joe led them back up the draw to the first nest and Kincaid chanced using his flashlight. Cursing softly, he said, "One with a knife." He slit open one of the German's tunics where the blood was and sighed. "Not a knife or a gun. It ... looks like a war arrow wound."

Joe said, "I told you!"

"I know. I ... believe you now, but we need to check the other two nests."

"There's a trail they used. It runs right behind—"

"Show me." Joe led them up to the second nest and Little cut away a tunic, shook his head and looked at Joe in wonder.

At the third nest, Kincaid used his light again and said, "My God, it's ... an abattoir in here. This one looks like he was torn apart by an animal! We have to get back and tell the Captain. He'll want to move tonight to consolidate these positions before the German relief shows up. Let's go!" Little just stared at Joe, not saying a word as they turned, and he led them back down the trail, then around the slope of the hill to the wall.

Kincaid said, "I have to report back to the captain. Little, get Curry cleaned up. The rest of you get back to your squads, and get ready to move out. Don't say a word about this!"

🎭

Two days later, another four miles up the road, Corporal Little retrieved Joe just before chow. "Sergeant wants you."

Joe finished reassembling his M-1 and asked, "Where is he?"

Lewis dropped into Cherokee, *Over by the mess tent. Joe, he's got the First Sergeant with him!*

"The First Sergeant?"

"From battalion. John Bearpaw. He's a Kiowa and a medicine man. Leave your stuff with me, I'll watch it."

"Thanks, Little." With some trepidation, Joe walked toward the mess tent and saw Kincaid standing with a squat, flat-faced older sergeant with coal-black hair and piercing eyes. "You wanted to see me, Sergeant Kincaid?"

"First Sergeant Bearpaw wanted to meet you, unofficially, Private."

Bearpaw inclined his head, almost a bow, and stuck out a hand. "So, you're the one! John Bearpaw."

Joe shook his hand. "First Sergeant." Not knowing what else to do, Joe just stood there at attention.

Bearpaw shook his head and smiled. "You are a wolf warrior and blooded, aren't you?"

Knowing this was not the time to hide anything, Joe said,

"Yes, sir. I'm ... my totem is the wolf." He felt the totem take over momentarily and a rumbling growl start as he half bowed to Bearpaw. Kincaid involuntarily took a step back as he saw the full import of the wolf masque surrounding Curry.

"Don't 'sir' me. You know how to spirit walk in the real world, don't you?" Stunned, Joe just looked at him. "You don't look Cherokee, so I'm guessing your mother is Cherokee and your daddy is not an Indian, right? That's why you live in Lawton, not down with the tribe."

"Yes, sir."

"And somebody taught you how to spirit walk, didn't they?"

"My grandpa, White Feather, is a Paint. He's a Cherokee medicine man down in Tahlequah, Oklahoma. I ... spent the summers with him the last three years while Mother and Dad were running a ranch in Montana."

Bearpaw cocked his head. "White Feather?"

Joe's mouth dropped open. "Yes, sir. He's my grandpa."

"I know him well; I am descended from Red Otter. We correspond on a regular basis." He turned to Kincaid. "Royce, I'm almost ashamed of you. It's plain as hell that Curry here is a true warrior. If an old fart like me from a different damn tribe can see the wolf masque, why can't y'all?"

Shaken, Kincaid replied, "That ... explains the wolf prints on ... the trail. And maybe the Nunnehi."

"Ah, the travelers. We too have our wolf stories, but none like the immortal travelers." He turned to Joe. "Has White Feather told you of the legends?"

"Yes, sir. He has been instructing me for years. My daddy has no problem with it, saying it's better for me to know my heritage than not. We moved to Lawton because my father did not want to cause problems in Tahlequah after marrying my mother."

Bearpaw looked intently at him. "Do you believe they were the Nunnehi?"

Joe thought for a few seconds. "Yes, sir, I do now. They must have been the Nunnehi because we only spoke Cherokee and they told me to take my true form. None of the others." He glanced at Kincaid. "Know ... knew about me. I never told anybody."

Bearpaw asked bitterly, "Because of being a half-breed, right?"

Joe hung his head. "Yes, sir. I had problems in school because of that. My one friend was a full-blood Kiowa, and he got in almost as many fights as I did."

Bearpaw pulled out his medicine bag and opened it, taking an object out. Joe looked at him in wonder. "What are you doing, sir?"

Nodding, Bearpaw merely smiled. "There is no such thing as blood brothers. By this exchange, I am adopting you into our tribe, since we don't have time for a formal ceremony. I would ask for a small item from your medicine bag around your neck." Joe pulled his out from under his shirt and blindly reached in. As he pulled out what he realized was his gold nugget, Kincaid asked tentatively, "May I?" Bearpaw only looked at Joe, leaving the decision to him. Joe turned to him and nodded. Kincaid pulled his medicine bag out, as Joe dipped back into his again.

Bearpaw said, "Hold out your hand. Do not open your eyes until you have closed your hand over my gift. Then hand me your gift the same way." Joe nodded, held out his left hand and felt something drop into it. He closed his hand around it and felt a tingle of magic even as he opened his eyes. He saw Bearpaw's hand out and eyes closed, so he dropped the small nugget into his palm and watched the hand close. Bearpaw then looked at him, closed his eyes, and bowed his head. Joe did the same, and Bearpaw said words in Kiowa that seemed to echo with power within Joe's mind.

He was startled when Bearpaw said, "You are now my son.

Welcome to the Kiowa tribe. I will give you an appropriate name in time."

Joe looked at what he held in his hand and was startled to see a fossilized tooth with a bail on it for a necklace. Looking up in amazement, he saw Bearpaw smiling. "Yes, it is a wolf's tooth. It has been in my family for many years."

Kincaid said in Cherokee, "*I'm sorry for what we've done to you. I would like to ... formally adopt you as a full-blood Cherokee. As an elder of the tribe, I believe this is within my rights, considering what I have witnessed.*" He turned to Bearpaw. "Would you bless us?"

Bearpaw laughed. "You going to trust a Kiowa? Are you sure you're not sick, Royce?"

Kincaid chuckled ruefully. "Well, since Curry's grandpa isn't here, you'll just have to stand in for him. I'm assuming you'll contact him and rub his nose in it."

Bearpaw doubled over laughing, then finally stood back up, wiping tears from his eyes. "Oh, I shall. I shall!" He reached out and put a hand on each of their shoulders and said another echoing prayer in Kiowa.

He had just finished when a runner came up and said, "First Sergeant, the colonel needs to see you."

Bearpaw nodded. "I will be there momentarily." He came to attention and said, "Wolf Warrior, use your capabilities to keep our soldiers alive." He bowed slightly from the waist as Joe came to attention.

Joe looked him in the eye and replied. "I will, my Father. I will." His masque slipped into place without warning, brightening the darkness enough to see a tear rolling down the first sergeant's cheek.

JL Curtis was born in Louisiana in 1951 and was raised in the Ark-La-Tex area. He is a retired Naval Flight Officer, retired engineer in the defense industry, an NRA instructor, and now lives in north Texas writing full time. He began his education with guns at age eight with a SAA and a Grandfather that had carried one for "work." He began competitive shooting in the 1970s, an interest he still pursues time permitting. He has two series currently out, The Grey Man, a current fiction series and Rimworld, a military science fiction series. He has also published a number of short stories and novellas all of which are available on Amazon.

I HAVE NO NAME

ANDI CHRISTOPHER

I have no name. I never have.

If I ever did, I don't remember. All I know is that I woke up one day, alone and cold, with nothing more than a torn piece of paper in my hand. In the years since, the temptation to give a name to myself has been palpable, but I can't find anything that feels right. So, instead, I give myself a million names dependent on my whims.

"And *you* are?"

The man peered at me, the flesh of his red face oozing into his eyes and forcing him to squint.

"Sir," the boy to my right coughed uncomfortably, "this is *her*."

The puffy-eyed man harrumphed. "Yes, yes. But what do I *call* you?"

My young contact opened his mouth to respond, but I cut him off. "You'll call me nothing," I declared. "I'll finish the job and you'll never call on me again."

The porter leaned back, his eyes attempting to widen in disdain. Meanwhile, my own tracked the swinging of the clock's pendulum on the opposite wall. My window of opportunity was about to open.

"Sir," my contact attempted to whisper, "my lady here is a master illusionist. She has never failed a job."

The porter's caterpillar eyebrows lowered toward his eyes as he frowned. I wasn't a mind reader—I detested the very practice—but I didn't need magic to know his thoughts. He was weighing risk and reward. Was I worth my price? If I failed, could I be linked back to him? If I succeeded, how could he avoid paying me?

The answer? He couldn't. I took my payment in advance. And I could tell he was reluctant to give it.

"Well," the porter finally seemed to realize that the risk of me turning him in should I be offended—something I wouldn't do, but he didn't need to know that—was far worse than the risk of my failing a job and him losing the money. Pulling a pouch from his cloak, he held it out. "I expect this to yield results."

I gestured to my contact. If the porter bothered to pay attention, he'd notice the lines of hunger in the boy's face, or the way his eyes clung to the silk fabric of the pouch. "He'll take care of it."

With another distasteful scoff, the porter handed my contact the money. The young boy's hands shook at its weight, and I fought back a look of sympathy.

The clock behind the porter called out eight times. On the final ring, I felt myself fall into character.

"Go now," I ordered the porter. "Meet me in an hour's time at the stables, and you'll have your diamond."

With a distrustful glance, the porter opened the door to the lounge, exposing a wave of mild laughter and stuffy music. The door needed to be opened fully to accommodate his portly body, but he shut it behind himself with little ceremony, leaving me alone with my contact.

"My lady?" the boy asked into the stillness. I glanced at him, a brow raised. "W-what should I do?"

My eyes lowered to the pouch. Taking it from him, I opened it to see a velvet interior filled with coins. Pulling one out, I ensured it truly held the current king's seal. It did. So, the coins were genuine. Pursing my lips, I counted ten coins for myself, slipping them into a pocket sewn in the side of my skirts. Then, I sealed the pouch and handed it back to the boy.

"Take this," I ordered. "And make sure you never see me again."

The boy's eyes widened, his mouth dropping slack. His hands shook, and he looked as though he wanted to argue. Honor, I realized, and maybe fear. He was smart, wondering if I was setting him up.

"Throw away the pouch," I advised, my voice softer. "Or sell it. Use something sturdy and nondescript to carry the coins. Burlap will do. Sew a few of those coins into your cloak and shoes. Use them carefully."

His face hardened into resolve. He nodded, scurrying away with the pouch tucked tightly against his chest. Watching, I waited until he too left the room before reaching into a second pocket in the other side of my skirts.

I pulled a small, blue masquerade mask from the folds. The edges were lined with black lace—the generic kind you'd get in the market, not the elaborate hand-stitched variety made exclusively for nobles. A simple black ribbon helped secure it to my face.

This was where the magic began, long before I bothered casting any spell. It started with my gown, a simple frock in average fabrics, and with my hair. My plain brown locks twisted in braids atop my head, unembellished with clips or accessories.

It continued to my posture, straight but not tall, as I exited the lounge into the great hall. My steps were silent, my hands clutched to my stomach. I made my way past bustling servants, many of whom dodged around me while forgetting to excuse their presence. At a set of wide double doors, very clearly marked for guests, I turned to the right. There was another entrance, one people forgot to watch.

It was here I entered. I didn't sneak or bow my head. I merely slipped into the ballroom and merged with the mingling crowds.

I was invisible. And I had yet to even cast a spell.

The masks of the noblewomen around me were elaborate. Extended feathers intimidated potential suitors and connections. My own mask was perfectly molded to my face, both custom-made and worn from years of use. Their lips were flushed and painted red, while mine remained a neutral pink.

I caught myself in the glances of the people around me. Women sized me up as competition, men as a partner. All of them turned quickly away, most likely forgetting my face the moment they did.

Good.

Taking a moment to look anxious, to look preoccupied with the social games of the court, I let my eyes search the room. Vaulted ceilings propelled voices up to the chandeliers and back down to the marble floors. The walls were blocked by velvet curtains and portraits, any free floor space taken up by servants carrying hors d'oeuvres and champagne on silver trays.

I noted potential exits and hiding spots, but they weren't my objective. Instead, I scoured the guests' faces for one in particular.

It didn't take long to spot him.

Captain Oliver Alexander O'Hanlon stood in the direct center of the room, right next to the dancing, but just far enough away to avoid doing so himself. He was young, fresh, and tall—taller than most. At this, I frowned. I didn't like my targets standing out, but what my research didn't confirm, the voices around me did.

"Do you see the captain of the guard?"

"Isn't he dashing?"

"Would you introduce us?"

Damn. I'd have to change my target. With him, there was no chance of escaping without notice.

A servant walked by with a tray of champagne, and in a moment's gamble, I adjusted my plans. Reaching out, I took a flute from the servant's tray, intentionally brushing my fingers against the bare skin of his wrist.

He said nothing, going on his way, while I let my magic absorb the knowledge I'd stolen in that simple touch.

"Excuse me, miss?"

I nearly dropped my glass. Turning—a little too fast to be natural—I looked up into the eyes of the very man I'd originally targeted.

I swallowed, forcing a blasé smile onto my face. "Yes?"

"You dropped this." He reached out, extending a white handkerchief between us. I blinked, recognizing it as one of the many objects I kept in my hidden pockets. A flush filled my cheeks, not one of embarrassment, but of discomfort. I wasn't used to people noticing me. And, suddenly, I found his pale gaze overbearing.

"Thank you," I murmured, hoping he would decide against continuing the conversation and just leave.

Of course, he didn't.

"I haven't seen you in the court before," he commented, as I tried to relax my shoulders.

"I'm surprised you recognize anyone," I replied, "considering this is a masquerade."

At this he smiled. I hated that smile. It spoke of hidden knowledge, hinted that he held a secret I couldn't decipher.

"You'd be surprised," was all he said, and I felt my façade crack in annoyance.

"Very little surprises me," I retorted. And then, looking about, I realized he was still the center of attention, bringing me into attention by proxy. Falling into a curtsey, I hoped he didn't hear the strain in my voice as I said, "I really must find my escort. Goodbye."

Trying to keep my gait even as I walked away, I heard whispers follow me.

"Why would Captain Oliver speak to *her*?"

"Did that girl just walk away from the captain?"

"Who *is* she?"

I was becoming Known and Known was the last thing I wanted to be. My jaw clenched as I waited for the focus to slide from me the way it usually did, but tonight it seemed to stick instead.

The feeling of Captain Oliver's gaze heated my back as I slipped between bodies in the crowd. I resisted the urge to glance over my shoulder, my hand shaking and spilling drops of champagne onto my skirts.

Focus, I ordered myself. My heart pounded. Glancing at the clock in the corner, I bit my cheek.

I'd already wasted fifteen minutes.

After another five minutes, I felt the attention of the room truly slide away from me once again. I would have preferred to wait a bit longer, but I didn't have time. My window was closing.

As casually as possible, I made my way along a refreshment table against the wall. At the end of it, nearly hidden behind a floor-length purple tapestry, servants bustled in and out, restocking, cleaning, serving, and remaining unseen.

They didn't have the access I needed, but they would have to do. Setting my glass on the table, I tapped twice against the corner of my mask and felt the rush of my magic covering me.

Nothing physically changed. In fact, to my own eyes, nothing changed at all. But to anyone who was looking, I was the exact servant I'd brushed against earlier.

As seamlessly as possible, I joined the other servants, slipping into the kitchens while reviewing every map I'd spent the past month memorizing. All the while, I counted each breath, knowing I only had sixty before the magic wore off.

It'd taken years to master this trick, and even then, my time was limited.

Five, I counted with my exhale, searching for a door in the back of the room. *There!*

The door was simple, narrow, and obviously designed to take up as little space as possible. As I made my way to it, a few of the other servants shot me annoyed looks, probably thinking I was going to shirk my duties. This was, of course, why servants were the worst to impersonate. The nobles may not notice them, but they more than made up for this with the tabs they kept on each other.

Behind me, the door to the ballroom opened. I glanced back, my heart in my throat, seeing the very man I was disguised as just beyond. Striding forward, I opened the back door and slipped out.

Two more breaths were wasted as my heart raced. Had they noticed that there were two of us? I clenched my fist, deciding it wouldn't matter as long as I was out of here long before they chose to raise an alarm.

This corridor reflected the same design principles as the door. It was narrow, narrow and short enough that I figured a man like Captain Oliver would have to duck to get through. Another good reason to have avoided disguising myself as him.

Continuing forward, I balanced counting my breaths and counting doorways.

A right, I recited. *Then a left. Straight, straight, and another left.*

"You there!"

I involuntarily exhaled my fortieth breath as I turned to answer the call. I didn't recognize the man, but I'd spent enough time in the bowels of castles to guess his position.

The head of servants, possibly with a minor title.

I bowed my head, holding my breath.

"Why are you down here? You should be tending to our guests."

I swallowed. As I spoke, my voice was feminine to my own ears, but the magic held true. He showed no suspicion that he was speaking to anyone other than a wayward servant.

"Apologies, sir. Captain Oliver asked for a specific kind of wine from the cellar."

The man's brows rose, and he took a moment to ponder my words. I mentally cursed his hesitation, my lungs burning as I attempted to conserve as much time as possible.

"Captain Oliver, huh? Damn him, always trying to show off." He looked at me, his eyes focused just above my head. "Well, carry on then."

I nodded. "Yes, sir. Thank you, sir."

And then, as we passed each other in the narrow hall, I managed to brush my bare hand against his.

The knowledge of his form trickled into my mask, bringing me some comfort as I released my fiftieth breath. Only ten more in this form. I needed to hurry.

My steps were less casual as I rushed onward. At the end of the hall I stopped, opening a nondescript door to my left. At least here, in this castle, they didn't display their riches. Too many people hid valuable things in ostentatious places. Of course, their foresight hadn't helped them here.

Shutting the door behind, I didn't bother lighting the candles. Darkness washed over the space, covering me as well as blinding me. It didn't matter—I had the way memorized.

Sixty. The air around me crackled when I released my breath, a telltale sign of the servant's form melting away. The mask felt cool against my skin, as if apologizing. I stroked the silky material.

You did well, I told it. And, for a moment, it warmed.

Beneath my shoes, the stairs were slick, untended, and unused by anyone but the guards. Each click of my heels against their stone echoed throughout the cramped space. Despite my source's assurance that the guard assigned on this night would be visiting his mistress for at least an hour, the sound set me on edge. People were unreliable. There was no way of knowing if he might have chosen this exact night to stop cheating on his wife.

Still, as I reached the bottom of the stairs, there was only a door waiting for me. No guard, no hint that anyone knew I was there.

My mask tingled with the knowledge I'd fed it earlier, but I brushed against it soothingly.

"Not yet," I murmured. I needed to save that form for my escape.

From my pockets I produced a simple iron key—a gift from my client. As I inserted it into the lock, the resulting click once again echoed through the space.

The door didn't move without some prompting. It was sturdier than the others, made of metal instead of wood. I was used to this, and by occupational hazard, I was stronger than most might assume. It took the force of my entire body, but I was able to shove it open just wide enough to pull my skirts through.

The room was dim, but the sounds my shoes made against the floor confirmed what my maps had already told me—it was large, as large as the ballroom, with a shorter ceiling. These weren't just the king's riches, but his heirlooms. The birthrights of the royal family.

I didn't bother gaping at the glittering jewels or fine clothes.

I didn't touch the bags of coins, the likes of which could have made me richer than any noble in the ballroom.

The porter's diamond sat against the left wall in a locked glass case. Ignoring everything else, I walked over to the case and looked down at the necklace. The blue-tinted gem winked back at me, and I saw my reflection grimace in its protective glass.

Such a fuss over a rock.

Wrapping my hand in the handkerchief that the captain had returned to me, I pushed my fist through my reflection. It shattered, glass littering the table and the floor below. Shaking fine shards from the cloth, I plucked the diamond necklace from its velvet cushion and wrapped it in my handkerchief.

The little package tucked nicely into the folds of my skirts, and my eyes flickered to a clock by the door. Thirty minutes gone. This left me with just enough time to search for my own treasure before I needed to escape.

I mentally recalled a different map, this one leading to a separate part of the castle. Nothing in the vault tempted me as I stepped over broken glass and made my way back up the stairs. Gems and coins never did, but they were a good way to get inside places like this.

Places that held what I really wanted.

I cracked the door atop the stairs open just enough to feel the warm air from the hall before I stopped. No footsteps or voices made themselves known, but it was still dangerous to go out as myself. If someone saw a guest this deep in the castle, they'd start asking questions.

And I couldn't afford to have anyone asking questions.

Still, my goal was far enough away that I wasn't confident I could get there in sixty breaths. My hand twitched over the doorknob, my mouth dry in want.

It was a risk. It was a dumb risk. If they caught me with that diamond in my pocket, I'd be hung. Or executed on the spot.

But I needed to know who I was.

Reviewing the map in my mind, I slipped into the hallway as my own self. Everyone's attention would be on the ballroom, on the party and the guests' needs. Very few people, much less anyone of importance, would be this far in the castle.

But that didn't make it empty.

One hand on my mask, the other clenched into a fist, I wove my way through passages until the narrow halls of the servants' wing turned into sweeping corridors covered by plush carpets and royal portraits. At each turn, I paused, listening for anyone who might discover me.

It was at one such stop that I heard two servants discussing a need for clean linens—apparently a relatively drunk count happened to have bumped into a servant carrying a tray of red wine. Whatever the reason, they would know immediately that I was out of place. Swallowing, I tapped twice against the mask on my face and held my breath.

As the servants turned the corner, they stopped in shock at the sight of their superior, their eyes lowered in deference.

I didn't bother speaking, knowing each breath was precious. Nodding, I gestured for them to move along. They did so, preoccupied with their own tasks, and I continued on my way. With a clenched jaw, I trapped the air in my lungs until I felt as though I'd burst. Then, I released it, sucked in another breath, and repeated the process.

In this way, I made it to the records room in only three breaths. This left me with fifty-seven to search the documents, grab what I needed, and escape.

If, that is, they even *had* the information I sought.

Opening the door, I knew that at least this area would be safe. Anyone who worked here would be long gone, party or not. I could, for the moment, let down my guard.

But, sitting casually at a desk in the center of the room, was Captain Oliver.

I blinked. My mind went blank. Why was he here? The desk in front of him was empty. His chin rested on his hands, his eyes unsurprised, as though he'd been expecting me.

Well, not me, but the man I appeared to be.

By the time I'd organized my thoughts, I realized that I'd wasted five more breaths. *Stupid.*

It's okay, I told myself. *You're the head of servants. You belong here.*

Stepping inside, I closed the door behind me.

"Hello," Oliver called into the otherwise empty room, one hand raised in greeting.

My brows rose, and I tried to calculate what sort of relationship these two might have. "Hello," I responded, trying to keep my gaze even. Shifting eyes were the easiest sign of deception. "Just wanted to grab some things for tomorrow."

Oliver nodded, as though he'd expected this. He didn't move as I walked up to the shelves, his gaze on me.

Fifteen ... sixteen ...

"Escaping the party?" I asked casually as I scoured the shelves for any sign of what I might be looking for. It wasn't much. The only thing I knew about my past was one word, scrawled on expensive parchment.

Hermitage.

Castles kept extensive records of their holds. Parchment that nice had to have come from a royal record room, such as this one. I'd already searched the palaces of eight kingdoms, but there were no records of such a place.

The scraping of a chair against the floor told me that Oliver was standing. "Oh, you know, dull company and all that."

I nodded to myself, as though agreeing with his words. Meanwhile, my mind raced.

Twenty-two breaths ... Herastown ... Hinderites ... Twenty-three ... no Hermitage.

It wasn't here. Of course, it wasn't. Bitter tears pricked at my eyes, and I reminded myself that this wasn't the time. Not now, not here, not under the captain's piercing gaze.

"I can help you find what you're looking for," Oliver's voice, startlingly close, pierced the silence.

I turned, seeing that he now stood right next to me, and I forced a blasé laugh. "No need. I'll come back tomorrow. I really shouldn't be working this late anyway—"

"No." His eyes were serious, his gaze just a bit off. He wasn't looking high enough, even though my façade should have been much taller than me. I blinked, subtly feeling for my magic. It was there. I was only on breath thirty. But his gaze was wrong. "I can help *you*."

I resisted the urge to feel for the diamond. *Who is this man? What's wrong with him?*

"There," he gestured to my hidden pocket, "that necklace. It's not the real reason you came here tonight."

I took an involuntary step backward, bumping my shoulders against the bookshelf.

"I don't know what you mean."

How does he know? Did he somehow see?

"Don't worry." His voice was soothing, his eyes almost pleading. But they were still wrong. Still looking too low, as though looking at *me*. "I'm not here to arrest you. I can hardly arrest someone for stealing what's theirs."

And then I realized. He *was* looking at me, despite my façade. He saw me. And only one kind of person could see through my illusions.

His eyes widened. "Wait," he grabbed my arm, my *real* arm. "Don't go."

I flinched from his grip. A mind reader. He was a mind reader—the bane of every illusionist.

"Please." The broken word fell from his lips even as I backed toward the door, my heart pounding and my mouth dry. "I know what you want. I can help. *I know who you are.*"

The room froze. I forgot which breath I was on, forgot to breathe altogether. He knew ... what? Knew me? No one knew me. I didn't even know me.

Taking advantage of my confusion, Oliver stepped toward me, hands raised as though placating a wounded animal. I told myself to run, told myself to hurry and leave, but I couldn't move.

Instead, my eyes traced his shaking hands as they plucked away my mask.

My façade slipped like water. His eyes focused on my naked face. His expression twisted into ... warmth? Fear? I didn't know.

Run.

The word filled my mind. And suddenly my skirts were in my hands, the door open before Oliver could react.

"Wait!" he cried as I sprinted down the hall. I didn't. I didn't know this man, didn't want this man to know me. "Please, come back!"

His cry echoed through the corridors, scratching at that part of my mind that demanded to stop, to learn who I was and why I was left with nothing but a torn piece of royal parchment.

I turned a corner, smacking into the hard armor of a castle guard. Hands wrapped around my arms, holding me in place.

"Stop!" the guard called. "Why are you here?"

I searched for an answer, a smooth lie, an escape. *Something.* This had never happened. My magic had never failed me.

Pursuing steps stopped behind me. The guard looked over my shoulder at his captain, straightening into as much of a salute as he could manage while keeping me restrained.

I forced back frustrated tears, twisting in the guard's grip to look at Oliver. He stood taller, taller than he already was. His eyes were hard, and gone was the desperate, pleading man from before. This was Captain Oliver Alexander O'Hanlon.

"Release our esteemed guest," he ordered. I blinked, but the guard let go, sending a rush of blood through my arms.

"Sir." The guard did salute this time, his armor clanging as he clicked his heels together and smacked a hand against the forehead of his helm. "I apologize. It looked as if—"

"A misunderstanding," Captain Oliver inserted smoothly. "This woman is with me. Now, be on your way."

We didn't move until the guard was around the corner. The moment he was out of sight, Oliver's shoulders relaxed, and the desperation returned to his eyes. *Please*, they seemed to say. *Listen to me.*

Please, I thought back at him, knowing now that he heard every word. *Just let me be.*

For a moment, neither of us spoke. And then, ever so slightly, he nodded. The movement was pained. He swallowed, his lips thinning into one line.

This night hadn't gone as planned for either of us, or so it seemed.

Part of me longed to stay, longed to hear what he had to say. But even as I thought it, a hope lit in his eyes, and fear filled me. This man *knew* me. Not only who I was, but my every waking thought.

I ran. Through the halls, through the passages I'd long ago memorized. I used my planned escape route, never in my wildest dreams thinking I'd run from the very thing I'd spent years searching for.

No one chased me. I didn't know if Oliver's order had made its way to the other guards or if, more likely, the few servants I passed thought I was absolutely insane. All I know is that as I made my way out into the gardens and toward freedom, I stopped.

I stopped running, turned around, and stood there under the shadow of a new moon. Looking back at the light spilling from the ballroom windows, I felt the diamond in my pocket.

I needed to go to the stables, give the porter his prize, and escape into the night. But I couldn't get myself to move.

That's how I got here.

I still can't get myself to move. I've been out here for sixty-five breaths, staring at the castle, retracing my steps in search of what went wrong. I'm scouring every word Oliver said, looking for meaning, or a clue, or something.

Is it better to stay out here, where it is familiar and safe? Is knowing worth the price of being Known?

And of course, one thought rivals all others.

I left my mask inside.

Andi Christopher spent her childhood mapping out the rainforests of Puget Sound and will forever consider Seattle her own personal moveable feast. She wrote her first novel on a dare at the age of fifteen and fell in love with the craft. Now, when she's not lost in a fantasy world, she works in book promotion while eagerly awaiting the publication of her debut novel. To learn more about Andi you can visit her website at andichristopher.com or follow her on Facebook or Instagram @AndiChristopherAuthor.

BEAUTY IS LIFTED FROM ITS FACE AS A MASK

ERIC JAMES STONE

L uz Trunso frowned at the black circle that had appeared on her monitor, its sharp edge standing out against the fuzzy grays of the data coming in from the SMC-18's seismophones. In the seventeen months she had been working as a mining operator on Luna, she had never seen anything like this. She rotated the image in three dimensions. The circle was a sphere. "That's odd," she said.

"What is odd?" asked Takshin Zalpuri, who was playing a videogame in his bunk.

Luz pointed to the sphere. "That. It's like a black hole for seismic waves."

Takshin slid out of his bunk to take a closer look. "Could it be, like, an actual black hole?"

"Don't be silly. A black hole wouldn't just be sitting there—" She glanced at the depth readout. "—twenty-seven meters below Luna's surface."

"Then what is it?"

Luz shrugged. "Most likely, a glitch. Maybe something got knocked off-kilter while we drove here. I think we should check the seismophones and the rest of the system."

"Whatever you say, Luz. I'll go get my repair kit."

Luz shook her head. "I don't want you tinkering around with them and breaking them. They're my babies. We'll just run diagnostics from here."

"O-kay ..." said Takshin, and returned to his bunk and his videogame.

"Sammy, activate seismophone diagnostics," she said.

"Activating seismophone diagnostics," replied Sammy, the SMC-18's computer.

Since that would take a few minutes, Luz decided she was hungry enough to eat something. She microwaved a couple of frozen empanadas, which unfortunately tasted very little like the empanadas she had grown up eating in Buenos Aires. She should not have gotten her hopes up when she found them in the company commissary back at Selene Mining Corporation Base as she was stocking up for this trip.

"Seismophone diagnostics complete," said Sammy.

She took a final bite of a so-called empanada—she could not remember when she had last had a meal created out of actual food from real ingredients—and walked back to her monitor. All the seismophones were showing at 100% operational. The black sphere was still there.

"Takshin," she said, "I think it's something real."

Takshin stowed his videogame and came over to look at her monitor. "Could be something natural, a geological—"

"Selenological."

"—whatever, process we don't know about. Or the metal core of an asteroid that smacked the Moon a bajillion years ago."

"It's not metal. Metal wouldn't just absorb all the seismic waves like that."

Takshin shrugged. "Who knows? Remember when they started mining industrial-grade silicon on the Moon, and they ended up digging up a significant deposit of boron? Nobody knew there was that much boron buried under the surface. It's possible something else might be buried down there, something new ... Let's call it 'new-tronium.'" He grinned at her.

Luz rolled her eyes. "It's forty meters in diameter. If that were real neutronium, we'd be crushed by its gravity."

"So it's something newer—newer-tronium. Or maybe they'll name it after you since you discovered it: Luzium? Trunsonium?"

"Get real. Anything we find is property of SMC."

"Ah, of course! Smackium!"

"I ought to smack you," Luz said. She did not really mind that he kept getting on her case about being a company drone, but some days she was in a better mood for that than others. She tapped the black sphere on her monitor. "I'm going to call it in. Maybe someone at Base has seen something like this before."

🎭

"Huh." The face of Pyotr Gerasimov, SMC's chief seismologist, frowned out at Luz from a small window on the bottom left of her monitor.

"Do you have any idea what it is?" she said. "Is it possible this is natural, some sort of vibration-absorbent material?"

"Is possible, sure," Pyotr said, "but not very likely."

"So it's artificial?"

"Not necessarily."

Luz bit back a reply about how helpful that was. But it must have shown in her expression, because Pyotr said, "Apologies. Not to get hopes up, but it could be human-made structure."

Luz looked at the black sphere on her monitor. "Human-made? We're the first to survey this area."

"Maybe. Maybe not. China keeps lips tight about where

they deploy resources on the Moon. Could be something they built. This 'black hole' maybe is for stealth."

"You think they buried, what, a base or a mine?"

"Could be."

"But why bury it? Why not just file a mining claim and do it out in the open?"

"Something extremely rare, maybe," said Pyotr. "Something extremely valuable."

"Something worth hazard pay and a major bonus for us to drill down and see what it is?" asked Takshin over Luz's shoulder.

Pyotr grimaced, then gave a curt nod. "I will get approval."

🎭

Approval came three hours later.

Just to be sure, Luz ran through the diagnostics and got the same results as she had earlier. The black sphere was real, not a recording error or the like. She had Sammy analyze the seismic waves again, this time looking for changes in frequency caused by reflections off a curved surface. Nothing.

She triple-checked the mining path she had programmed. It would create a circular shaft two meters in diameter, with a 45-degree slope leading down to the edge of the black sphere.

"I am going to start mining," she told Takshin.

Takshin stopped whistling the annoying tune he had been repeating for a while and looked over her shoulder. "Are you sure? What if it's something valuable and we break it?"

"You're the one who wanted hazard pay and a bonus."

"What if it's aliens?"

"What would aliens be doing twenty-seven meters under Luna's surface?"

"Alien things. Who knows what their motivations are?"

"Unless you've got a real objection, I'm going to proceed."

Takshin grinned, then went back to whistling his tune.

Luz sighed. "Sammy, execute the mining program."

"Executing mining program," replied Sammy.

She sat at her monitor watching the feed from the minia-ture camera on the mining head. A high-pitched whine carried through the SMC-18's frame as the diamond-encrusted drill bits quickly chewed their way through the compacted dust of the regolith until hitting bedrock at 7.3 meters. The mining head slowed, and the whine dropped down to an almost subaudible rumble as the grinding converted bedrock to dust, which was then pumped up into the heart of SMC-18 to sepa-rate out the usable minerals.

Experience told her that mining through bedrock could take up to an hour per meter. The SMC-18 was much more effi-cient at extracting the minerals from regolith. But sometimes there was something worth drilling down for. She hoped that was the case this time.

"Probably won't get there for about twenty to thirty hours," she told Takshin. "I'm going to take a shower and then call it a night."

Twenty-two hours later, Luz and Takshin both had their eyes glued to the screen as the mining head ground through the last few centimeters toward the black sphere. Pyotr was watching remotely from Base.

The feed from the camera flickered, then cut out. The mining vibrations ceased.

"What was that?" asked Pyotr.

"Not sure," Luz said.

"Contact with the mining head terminated," said Sammy.

Luz bit her lower lip, then said, "Sammy, restart the mining head."

"Unable to comply. There is no contact with the mining head."

"Run diagnostics on the mining head."

"Unable to comply. There is no contact with the mining head."

"Run diagnostics on the fiber-optic cable to the mining head."

"Running diagnostics." After a few seconds, Sammy said, "The fiber-optic cable has been severed near the drill head."

Takshin chuckled. "Guess it's time for me to earn my hazard pay. Start bringing the head back up. I'll suit up and go fix it."

🎭

Fortunately, retracting the mining head to the surface only took twenty-two minutes. Luz watched an outside camera feed as Takshin approached the drill head. Pyotr was still conferenced in.

Takshin swore in Hindi.

"What's that?" asked Pyotr.

"Uh, sorry, sir. The drill bits look awful, like chunks of them have fallen off. What I can see of the fiber-optic cable looks fine, though."

Luz sighed. "I guess you'll need to get started on replacing the drill bits."

"Are you kidding?" Takshin said. "We drilled to the edge of that sphere. We need to check it out."

Luz was about to say she did not think that was a good idea, but Pyotr spoke first. "Activate your helmet camera first. We need to know what is down there."

Luz activated a private channel to Pyotr. "It could be dangerous to let him go down there."

Pyotr shrugged. "That is how one earns hazard pay."

A moment later, the feed from Takshin's camera popped up on Luz's monitor. He headed toward the opening of the shaft.

"At least hook your suit to a winch cable first," Luz told him.

"Yes, Mom." His tone was sarcastic, but he complied, connecting the winch to a carabiner on his spacesuit. He stopped as he reached the two-meter-wide hole in the ground. Beyond the opening, the mining head had fused the regolith into a solid mass in order to provide a wall for the shaft. "Everything looks good here. I'm going in."

Luz brought up the winch controls on her monitor. "I'll pull you back up if anything goes wrong."

Takshin chuckled. "Always the optimist, Luz."

On Takshin's helmet camera, Luz could see the color of the walls become slightly darker as the shaft shifted from fused regolith to bedrock. Takshin continued down the shaft.

"The outside temperature is dropping," he said. "Suit insulation is good, though, so I'm still cozy."

That sparked a thought. She switched back to the outside camera feed that showed the mining head. "Sammy, switch this camera feed to infrared."

"Switching to infrared."

The drill bits showed solid black on the screen. After only twenty minutes, they should still be glowing white in the infrared view.

"Takshin," she said, "stop where you are."

His camera feed stopped moving. "Why?"

"The drill bits are cold. And not just lunar-night cold—they've got to be close to absolute zero."

"Are you sure?" asked Pyotr. "Those bits get up to 300 C when they're drilling."

"Heat is vibration," Luz said. "That black sphere absorbs—"

The monitor flickered and died. Over the next three seconds, all the lights in SMC-18 dimmed and went out. It was pitch black.

Luz counted off fifteen seconds for backup power to come on. It did not.

"Sammy?"

No response.

She fumbled her way to the emergency supply locker and found a flashlight hanging in a charger, but it would not turn on. A minute later, she located a glowstick by touch. She bent it to activate, and relief flooded through her as its green glow lit up the SMC-18's main cabin.

Had it been some sort of electromagnetic pulse? That might explain power being knocked out for everything with a circuit.

At least Base would know something was wrong because Pyotr's call would have disconnected, and they would not be able to re-establish contact. They would send out a rescue vehicle.

Unless the pulse had hit them, too.

No, she had to keep a positive attitude. Rescue was on the way. She and Takshin just needed to hunker down and wait.

But was Takshin all right? If he did not come inside on his own, she would have to go out and find him.

He did not come back during the ten minutes it took her to put on her spacesuit. The electronics in it were dead, but the oxygen flow could be controlled by a manual valve. The suit had insulation good enough that she was more likely to end up uncomfortably hot than freezing to death.

It took two minutes to crank the inner airlock door open manually, and another two to crank it shut behind her.

She hated to waste any oxygen, but without power for the air pumps, there was no choice but to vent the airlock into vacuum.

Leaving the outer airlock door open in case she needed to get back in quickly, she headed toward the mining end of the SMC-18.

"Takshin?" she called out as she approached the entrance to

the shaft, then realized how foolish that was in a vacuum, with no radio.

Luz spotted his footprints in the regolith heading into the shaft. There were none coming out, so he must still be in there.

The cable attached to the winch was loose. She picked it up and gave it a tug, hoping Takshin would reply with a tug of his own. Instead, there was barely any resistance. She pulled the cable up and found that it had been cleanly sheared at the end.

She tied the end of the cable into a slipknot and hooked that to a carabiner on her spacesuit.

Luz took a couple of slow breaths to get her nerves under control. Holding her glowstick out to light her path, she said, "That is how one earns hazard pay," in a parody of Pyotr's Russian accent, then stepped into the shaft.

Forty-five degrees' down-slope would be a very steep ramp on Earth, but it was manageable on Luna. After several careful steps she was far enough inside that the starlight faded. A few lunar dust motes drifted around in the dim green light cast by her glowstick.

Beyond the edge of the light, the shaft seemed to extend forever, as if she could drop off the edge of the universe.

Thirty-eight meters from the top of the shaft to the edge of the black sphere. She could do this. Takshin had to be somewhere in the next thirty meters or so. Unless he had gone inside the black sphere. She would cross that bridge when she came to it. Or not.

A sudden tremor shook the ground beneath her feet. If not for the weak gravity, she probably would have tumbled down the shaft.

Moonquake? They did happen from time to time, usually as the result of tidal stresses. Just her luck for there to be a moonquake in the middle of all this craziness. But no, the more likely explanation was that this was all related to that black sphere.

The green light from her glowstick began to fade.

A sinking feeling settled in her gut ... and the glowstick went completely dark.

Of course—glowsticks stopped working if they froze solid.

Luz swallowed hard, clutching the now useless glowstick as if to hang onto her sanity with it. She could not afford to hyperventilate with limited oxygen.

"Wake up! Wake up!" she whispered, mostly to herself, but also to her glowstick, her suit, her helmet, her radio, the entire SMC-18. "Just turn back on!"

She was about to turn around and climb back out beneath the stars when she glimpsed a flash of light in the depths of the shaft. Before she could decide whether she had imagined it, the flash repeated. Three seconds later, it flashed again.

White light. Repeating every three seconds. Just like the emergency beacon on their spacesuits.

Takshin was down there, and something had triggered his emergency beacon. Which somehow worked, unlike every other piece of electronic equipment.

Luz cautiously took step after step, always making sure she had firm footing before taking the next step. Twice she had to stop as tremors shook the ground.

The flashes of light were too brief for her to accurately judge the distance or see any details up ahead—until she almost tripped over a spacesuited leg on the floor of the shaft.

She got down on hands and knees, feeling her way around Takshin's body—she hoped it was not a corpse. When she found his helmet, she put hers up against it, hoping the sound of her voice would conduct through to him.

"Takshin! Are you alive?"

There was no reply, and his body did not move in response to her query. She listened hard, and thought maybe she could hear him breathing, but it was so faint she could not be sure.

"Don't worry, I'm going to get you out of here," Luz said.

Hoisting him into a fireman's carry was awkward, but in

one-sixth gee she could handle the weight. What she had not considered was the forty-five-degree upward slope, which her ankles just could not handle. Instead, she had to walk backward. Three times, she almost lost her balance due to ground tremors.

Relief flooded over her as they emerged from the shaft into starlight.

And then she turned around and saw the SMC-18: the giant vehicle was tilted almost completely onto one side, sinking several meters into the regolith. As she watched, it sank another meter, as if the regolith and the bedrock beneath it had turned to quicksand. It reminded her of an experiment she had seen in a geology class involving a marble placed in a vibrating container full of sand.

Nothing in the seismology of this place had even hinted at such a possibility.

The main airlock was on the buried side. There was an emergency airlock on the side that now pointed toward the stars.

There was no point taking Takshin inside if they were just going to end up buried. But if they were going to survive until rescue came—if rescue came—she needed to salvage oxygen canisters, and maybe water and food.

Luz carried Takshin about a hundred meters, to what she hoped was a safe distance from whatever was happening. She then loped back to the SMC-18, which had now sunk more than halfway into the ground.

After clambering up the former bottom of the vehicle, she hauled herself atop the emergency airlock door. As soon as she started cranking the door open manually, a rush of air came out, its moisture condensing into white crystalline vapor.

She lowered herself into the airlock and cranked the outer door closed. If not for a bit of starlight coming through the airlock's window, it would have been pitch dark inside.

Working mostly by feel, she found and opened the valve to pressurize. Then she cranked the inner door open about a half meter.

The first thing she needed was another glow stick. Fortunately, there was an emergency supply locker on the wall next to the emergency airlock. Unfortunately, that wall was now a ceiling. Luz reached through the opening into the main cabin and unlatched the door of the locker. After fumbling around a bit, she found something that felt like a glowstick and detached it from the Velcro that held it in place. She activated it and was relieved when it started to glow.

The SMC-18 jolted as it sank farther into the ground. She did not have much time left.

Next to the airlock door on the other side was a rack with oxygen bottles. She cranked the door the rest of the way open. She reached over and pulled a bottle off the rack. She was able to reach two more, but did not dare lean out any farther for fear of falling out of the airlock.

Luz cranked the inner door shut. She attached the three oxygen bottles to carabiners on her spacesuit.

By the time she exited the airlock, the door was almost level with the lunar surface. She jumped as far as she could, and landed on normal regolith. Then she headed back to where she had left Takshin.

When she was about twenty meters away, she realized Takshin was not alone. Another figure in a SMC-logoed spacesuit was bent over him. Rescue had arrived!

"Am I glad to see you!" she said, before remembering that her radio was still out. Overwhelmed with relief, she took the final few strides to join the figure next to Takshin.

The figure turned to face her. In this dim light, the photosensitive diamondglass faceplate should have been transparent, but instead it was mirrored. She could see her distorted reflection.

Then she saw the name stenciled just below the left shoulder on the spacesuit: Takshin Zalpuri.

She backed away slowly. The doppelganger made no attempt to follow her. It turned its attention back to Takshin.

She remembered seeing a horror holo about scientists in Antarctica reviving an alien creature that could absorb and mimic other beings. Was this a shapeshifter that had been imprisoned in the black sphere, and now it was free? At least it had not absorbed Takshin.

The creature straightened up and turned toward her.

Luz braced herself for an attack, but instead the creature just dissolved into a formless swarm of glittering dust and then dispersed, leaving her alone with Takshin.

Whatever that thing had been, it didn't seem to mean any harm. Relieved, she sat down beside Takshin on the regolith. Best to just wait here, conserving energy and oxygen, until the real rescue arrived.

She looked out to where the SMC-18 had now been completely swallowed up. "Goodbye, Sammy," she said.

The regolith rippled out from near the shaft they had drilled. A huge thump lofted her almost a meter off the ground. After she bumped back down, she could feel the aftershocks.

Waiting here no longer seemed like the best option.

She lifted Takshin over her shoulders and started following the SMC-18's tracks back toward Base. Takshin's beacon was no longer working, but hopefully the rescue party would spot them anyway.

Luz staggered over the rim of a small crater and tumbled to the ground. Takshin's body rolled away from her. She had no idea if he was alive or dead. She had replaced his original oxygen bottle with one of the three she had salvaged. She had kept two bottles for herself, and was now on the second. If he was in a coma, he would be breathing a lot less than her, carrying him. And if he was dead, giving him the one bottle would turn out to have been a waste.

But at this point, she could not carry him anymore. Hopefully, they were far enough away from the black sphere now to be out of danger. She was not sure how long it had been since she had felt a tremor. She would go on alone, and if she found rescue, she would tell them where to find Takshin.

She rose to her feet and kept walking.

Luz was so, so tired. Her head ached so much she could barely think. Her breathing was shallow and rapid.

Why was it so hard to breathe? She knew she knew the reason, but it took a minute for her to dredge it up: carbon-dioxide poisoning. The scrubber must be overloaded.

She was suffocating in this helmet.

She had to get the helmet off or she would die.

Her gloved fingers fumbled at the latches on the helmet. Finally they came free.

Air whipped at her face as it streamed out of her suit. That bought her a moment of clarity in which to realize the utter stupidity of what she had done—unless she could get the helmet back on quickly.

The air stopped flowing out as she managed to get her helmet latched on again.

But there was no longer a hiss of oxygen coming into her suit. The final bottle was empty.

Luz sat down on the ground. This was as good a place to die as any.

She looked up at the sky. It was lunar night, Earth was below the horizon, so there was no chance of seeing Argentina one last time. But as compensation, the sky was filled with stars. She did not remember ever seeing so many stars before.

She tried to pick out a familiar constellation, but the stars seemed to be multiplying, dancing around.

A glittering swarm appeared before her, eventually resolving into a figure in an SMC spacesuit. The name stenciled below the left shoulder was Luz Trunso. The helmet diamond-glass was mirrored, and Luz saw herself in distorted reflection.

"Hello again," she said. "I don't suppose you could help me? I'm out of oxygen."

The figure before her raised its hands and unlatched its helmet. Slowly, it raised the helmet off its head, revealing a duplicate of Luz's face.

But then it morphed.

"Morphed into what?" asked Pyotr.

Luz lay in a hospital bed in Selene Mining Corporation Base. They had told her Takshin was still in a coma in the room next door, but the doctors were optimistic he would recover—the extreme hypothermia had probably saved his life.

She could not recall the face of the alien. It was like trying to remember the scent of a lullaby, the sound of a rainbow, the taste of starlight.

Luz shrugged. "The face of an angel."

Pyotr shook his head. "That is very weird hallucination. Lack of oxygen can do that. You are lucky we found you when we did."

"I know," Luz said.

"As for black sphere, I say it must have been bubble of vacuum in bedrock. That is why no seismic vibrations. When bubble is pierced, ground collapses underneath SMC-18. Is total loss. There is no need to mention hallucinations in our report. Just confuse things."

"Thank you, Pyotr."

After Pyotr left, Luz stared at the SpO2 readout on the medical monitor: 99% oxygen saturation in her blood.

She held her breath and waited for it to go down.

It held steady for five minutes before she gave up and started breathing again.

Eric James Stone is a Nebula Award winner, Hugo Award nominee, and Writers of the Future Contest winner. Over fifty of his stories have been published in venues such as *Year's Best SF*, *Analog Science Fiction and Fact*, and *Nature*. His debut novel, the science fiction thriller *Unforgettable*, has been optioned by Hollywood multiple times. The son of an immigrant from Argentina to the U.S., Eric grew up bilingual and spent most of his childhood years in Latin America. He majored in political science at BYU and then got a law degree from Baylor. He did political work in Washington, DC, for several years before shifting careers to work as a programmer and sysadmin. Eric lives in Utah with his wife, Darci, an award-winning author herself, in addition to being a high school science teacher and programmer. They have two children.

Find him at ericjamesstone.com.

PAGLIACCI'S JOKE

TRAVIS HEERMANN

The circuses are gone.

And with their demise, the age-old symbol of joy and pathos—the clown—has been corrupted into an object of horror and ridicule. Children are taught to fear and disdain us.

But what about those of us for whom the laughter and delight of children is the very blood in our veins, the sustenance for our souls? When the elephants are gone, the trapeze is still, and the circus is buried in an ignominious grave, where do *i pagliacci* go?

We put on our faces like we always have. Like my forbears, I keep *i pagliacci* within me.

And in this dark time, a time of cruelty, callousness, and greed, if I could not entertain children, I would protect them. I traded my slapstick and my big rubber hammer for a Glock and a Taser, my red nose and my floppy shoes for handcuffs and pepper spray. A strange transition perhaps, but how else can I drink the stuff of life itself?

Now I walk the halls of Johnson Elementary, all quiet vigilance, but my heart sparkles during recess when the giggles rise and the music of children at play fills the schoolyard.

Children's eyes widen at my sleight-of-hand antics. Their eyes roll at my jokes, but still they laugh.

They run up to me and say, "Do your dance!" And I slip easily into my old soft-shoe.

The teachers ask me, "Where did you learn to do all that?"

I say, "In the company of angels and demons."

At the beginning of a new school year, little Tisha Jackson takes my finger one day and leads me out into the playground. "Watch!" She jumps into a series of cartwheels, somersaults, and attacks the monkey bars like a trapeze artist. I laugh and applaud, "Bravo! *Bellissima.*"

Her gap-tooth grin sustains me for the day. "My daddy is a policeman, too."

I lean close and say conspiratorially, "I'm actually not a policeman."

Her eyes widen. "Really?"

"Actually I'm a clown in disguise." It is more fun than saying I'm only a security guard.

She makes a sour face. "I hate clowns." Then she bounces away like a beach ball.

The next day, though, she takes my hand again and guides me toward the swings, asks me to push her.

The eyes of some teachers narrow.

But at the apex of her swing, Tisha cries, "*Wheeee!*" And all other concerns go away.

Every day, the children gather around me.

"Tell us some jokes!"

"Do your dance!"

"Do the trick with the thing!"

"Very well," I say. "I'll tell you all a very old joke. A man goes to the doctor, deep in melancholy—"

"What's a melon-collie?" Tisha asks.

"It means terribly depressed," I say.

"Oh, like my momma sometimes."

I clear my throat and continue, "A man goes to the doctor, terribly depressed. He says, 'Doctor, the world is such a difficult place. I feel all alone in a harsh world, surrounded by mean people. I'm afraid of what lies ahead.'

"The doctor says, 'We can easily treat that. Pagliacci, the world's most famous clown, is performing tonight. Go and see the performance. He will make you laugh.'

"The man starts to cry and says, 'But doctor, *I* am Pagliacci.'"

The children stare at me for a moment. Some of the teachers chuckle. Others cover me with scowls of disapproval and hurry the children along.

As he shuffles away, one of the boys says, "That's a dumb joke."

So I tell other jokes and content myself with whatever audience I can manage, and their laughter is electricity in my tissues.

It's a Tuesday, and I'm walking the halls between classes, and I hear glass break. I chase the echoes through the hallways. My feet hurry into a half-run as I check the entryways. Another pair of footfalls echoes in the corridors. Heavy boots.

Limned in stark daylight spilling through the open door, his silhouette casts a long black shadow. The AR-15's shadow curves across the floor to become a scythe. He's reaching for the first classroom doorknob.

I used to have a toy pistol that said, *"BANG!"*

But the gun I carry now does not play, does not joke, does not de-escalate. It deals in only finality. It comes into my hand. Numbness spreads through me. Everything narrows to a tight circle around the white dots of the Glock's sights.

There is no cover in the hallway, only fifty feet of space between me and him.

His hand pauses at the doorknob, then swivels the barrel toward me.

I throw myself prone, sliding toward him barrel first, already taking aim.

He squeezes off four thunderous rounds over my head before I pull the trigger. His Kevlar vest takes the brunt, but my bullets still stagger him, then punch him against the wall. He sags floorward, and my aim tracks his unprotected legs, his pelvis. I stop shooting when the action locks open, ammunition spent.

He's groaning, writhing, bleeding, staring, gasping. I stand over him, stomp the hand gripping the rifle, and kick it from his grasp.

Screams fill the hallway.

The shooter is a cliché: a young, white man with the hollow eyes of a world without joy. His world does not know the circus. I handcuff him. He will bleed out before the ambulance arrives.

Screams fight through the ringing in my ears, turning from terror to grief.

The shooter's blood soaks my hands, my knees. My legs are jelly. It's like I'm wearing my floppy shoes again.

At the end of the hallway behind me, teachers are screaming for help. The opposite of laughter, their screams suck the energy from my soul until I stagger.

Surrounded by rainbows, alphabet flash cards, and wailing children, Tisha Jackson's blood-specked face stills into a cold, gray mask. The AR-15's 5.56mm armor-piercing round passed through two walls, then through Tisha Jackson as she was reading *Curious George*.

Late that night, when the police finally let me go, when the teachers and staff are done hugging me and sobbing thanks for saving their lives, I return to my one-room, basement apartment on a dead-end street. I strip off my uniform. Sweat soaks the scarlet-and-lemon striped shirt I always wear underneath my disguise. My chartreuse-and-aquamarine, polka-dot pantaloons sag around my legs, stained with blood. I collapse onto the stool, bathed in the lights of my dressing mirror. Tears have left white streaks in my makeup.

I put Leoncavallo's *Pagliacci* on the Victrola. Its scratchy tones comfort me, draw me back through the centuries.

My eyes are watery, bloodshot, and so, so tired.

I peel off my wig, place it on the head stand, and rub the sweat from my naked, bone-white pate.

Then I soak a handful of cotton balls with makeup remover and wipe away the rest of my disguise, my flesh-colored mask. My hands reek of cordite and blood.

My true face re-emerges—white skin, red-circled cheeks, black eyebrows, and a smiling mouth.

"'But Doctor,'" I say, quoting the ancient joke as I meet my gaze in the mirror, "'*I'm* Pagliacci.'"

And I weep for the world.

Travis Heermann is a novelist, freelancer, award-winning screenwriter, editor, poet, member of SFWA and HWA, and a graduate of the Odyssey Writing Workshop. His latest novel is *Tokyo Monster Mash*, book two of his *Shinjuku Shadows Trilogy*. Other novels include *The Hammer Falls*, and *The Ronin Trilogy*, plus short fiction published in Baen Books' *Straight Outta Deadwood*, plus *Apex Magazine*, *Tales to Terrify*, and others. His freelance work includes contributions to the *Firefly Roleplaying Game*, *Legend of Five Rings*, *EVE Online*, and *Battletech*. He loves monsters of all sorts, especially those with a soft, creamy center.

A NEW PURPOSE

REBECCA M. SENESE

The interior was dark but not completely. Enough light shone through the crack between the doors to show the slight imperfections in the wood. Instead of a smooth blending of the rings, it was jagged and somewhat off-center, like the wood had been cut at the wrong angle and no amount of finishing would fix that initial mistake.

The dim light glinted off the wood, revealing the varnish, so someone had tried their best to make it nice, but it didn't take away the flaws, instead gave light to the slight sickening yellow that seemed to run through the wood. Perhaps the tree it had been taken from had been diseased.

Much like the mask itself.

That had to be why it was stuck in this cupboard. Left alone.

Forgotten.

It must have some fatal flaw.

Was it the stitching that crisscrossed along the edges, still glinting some silver, even in this dim light? The single eye hole that sliced across the front of the mask in a thin rectangle? Many overlooked the mask because of it, not realizing that when worn, a thin sheen closed over the hole, protecting the eyes and presenting the wearer with several visual options from zooming in to displaying all sorts of information about what the wearer was looking at, like distance and composition.

It was one of its features that the mask was particularly proud of, even though many didn't like the single eye hole.

Perhaps it was the material itself, a sort of finely woven mesh, light and flexible. Many took it be fragile but the mask was anything but. It could stop bullets or laser blasts without so much as a nick in its polished surface. And it could change color to match whatever outfit the hero was wearing.

What other mask could do that?

Yet still it languished in this cupboard, forgotten, ignored. Too strange for most heroes to take a chance on, although some had in the past. How many heroes had the mask assisted through its long existence? It couldn't remember. After a time, they all blurred together. Camo Man who dressed in greens and black. That had been an interesting color scheme to match. The mask had had fun with that one. The Siren Song who wore a mix of red, orange, and yellow. One of the flashier looks for the mask. It had felt self-conscious working with her, never quite happy with how it blended with her outfit. And so many others, so many colors, so many textures, so many adventures.

So many times saving the world.

The mask was just glad to be part of it.

Until now, when the last hero had retired, as they all eventually did and, instead of passing the mask along to the next hero, had sold it to the shop. Collectables.

For a while, the mask had been in a glass display case, close enough to the front of the shop that it could see into the street. Once it had spotted a mugging down the block and the urge to intervene had been almost overwhelming. But the mask was only a mask. It couldn't do anything on its own. It could only watch helpless as the man in the dark grey hoodie ran off with the woman's purse. It needed a hero, someone to wear it so it could assist people.

But no one opened the display case, no one bothered with the mask.

Eventually the proprietor, a tall, thin man with stooped shoulders and thinning hair who only ever wore white t-shirts and jeans (which didn't give the mask much to work with for matching), moved the mask from the display case to this cupboard. Closing the door with a click after placing the mask on a shelf.

Now it waited. Wondering.

Were its hero days over?

Since it had come to Earth, brought so many years ago by aliens it could no longer remember, the mask had been passed from hero to hero. It had taken such pride in being a hero mask, doing everything it could to protect and help.

Was it now all over? Would no one take it out of this cupboard again? Sorrow made it sag in on itself. Maybe it would spend the rest of its days here, ignored, forgotten. Maybe it should just take on the hues of the cupboard. Then it really would be ignored forever.

A tinkling bell sounded through the wood, muffled. The main door of the shop opened. The light coming through the crack of the door brightened. Shuffling sounded beyond, then a click, and the cupboard door swung open.

The proprietor glanced in at the mask, lifting his nose as if to sniff it. He gave a brief nod before turning away. But he left the door open.

Hope blossomed in the mask. Maybe the proprietor was going to move it back to the display case, where someone would pick it up and choose to take it. A new hero, just waiting to be born.

The mask could dream.

The shop spread out before it. A row of three glass display

cases filled the center of the room. Shelves lined the walls, some made of glass, others wood like the cupboard the mask rested in. In the far right back corner, the proprietor had his cash register and a red stool where he mostly sat and read comic books. Rock music murmured from hidden speakers, too low to distinguish the thumping bass from one song to the next.

The bell above the door tinkled and several teenage boys entered, jostling each other, voices talking over each other. They headed over to the right wall that was full of comics. The proprietor gave them a gruff warning about buying before reading.

The bell rang again. A college-age couple holding hands entered and moved toward the miniatures on the left.

The bell rang again, and more people entered.

But no one came over to the cupboard. No one looked at the mask.

Did no one want to *be* a hero? Did they only want to read about them?

Or maybe something about the mask just wasn't up to it anymore. That single rectangular eye slit, its flexible feel that people took for flimsiness. The mask didn't measure up anymore.

It had no future, except watching people pass by.

It had never felt this despairing before, not even when the evil Tentacled Thrasher cornered Camo Man in the alley off Madison. Huge, red brick walls stretching up on either side. Concrete covering the ground. Nowhere to escape to, nowhere to hide. And the Tentacled Thrasher stepping forward, tentacles writhing, cutting up so much dust the mask had been forced to try multiple different lenses and views before it found one that helped Camo Man see the approaching menace.

And the fleeting glimpse of escape.

"Mama, what's that?"

The squeal of a voice brought the mask back from its reminiscences. What? Where? Oh yes, the shop. It remembered now. It was sitting in the cupboard, alone. Not a part of any fight. No danger, no chance to save the world here.

Except for the tiny hand reaching for it.

Soft fingers grabbed hold of the edge of the mask and pulled. If it had wanted, the mask could have let the fingers slide over its fabric. A simple twist of its flexible threads and it would be free from the grasp.

But why bother? It wasn't as if the child could tear it. The mask was made of materials beyond this world and nothing here could destroy it.

The mask had always thought that was a blessing, but these days, it was starting to think that maybe that wasn't such a good thing. After all, what good had it done lately? Maybe if it could be taken apart, it could be woven into something new, something more useful.

The fingers tightened on the mask and pulled it down from the shelf.

The mask felt like it was floating on air, falling. It caught a glimpse of a woman wearing a blue dress, then it twisted and landed in a child's palm.

A girl, with soft brown hair curling wildly around her head. Big brown eyes, dark brown skin. She wore a bright yellow top with little bows at the collar.

Yellow. Bows.

The mask could work with that.

Her brown eyes widened even more as she looked at the mask. For a moment, the mask was dismayed. Was its eye slit too small for those eyes? Then a smile blossomed on the girl's face.

"Mama, so pretty!"

The mask felt a tiny burst of pride. It had shifted color to be closer to the yellow. It hadn't added the bows though. That might have been a little too much.

"Yes, that's nice, Teisha," the woman said. Her tone was neutral, but the mask sensed some trepidation behind it. Did the mask worry her?

Of course, she was worried about her daughter becoming a hero. Understandable. The girl was so young, no more than ten, with long arms and legs that she still needed to grow into, but already the mask could see the muscle, the strength, in her. Not just in body, but in spirit. She was bursting with potential. Heroic potential.

The mask felt giddy. Was it finally happening? Had it found its next hero?

If it truly was this girl, they could be together for decades.

Perhaps forever.

Now it wished it had added the bows.

"Can I have it, mama?" Teisha asked. Her hands tightened on the mask. Her skin felt warm and soft as they twisted its fabric.

"Be careful, don't tear it," the woman said. Alarm filled her voice. Her hand came down, touching the girl's fingers, loosening them.

"Can I help you?" The proprietor appeared, hands folded in front of him, his head tilted to one side like a bird.

"Oh sorry," the woman said. "My daughter was just looking at the mask. Put it back now, honey."

"Oh, it's a nice one, isn't it?" The proprietor leaned over, putting his hands on his knees as he bent at the waist. He smiled at the girl.

Teisha gave a shy smile back. Her chin ducked down, almost turtling into her neck. She raised her hands, lifting the mask toward the proprietor.

No, don't hand it over! The mask felt frantic. What could it do? It wanted to twist away so the proprietor wouldn't take it, but the mask had little ability to move itself. In a burst of effort, it sprouted tiny bows on the either side of the eye slit.

"Look how it matches your shirt," the proprietor said. "I bet it would look so good on you."

"I don't think ..." the woman said.

"Why don't you try it on?" the proprietor said. "I bet those bows match yours."

Teisha tilted the mask to look at it. "Bows," she said. Her voice was breathless with wonder. The mask trembled with her excitement.

So close, so close now. It could be with a hero again.

"That's enough." The woman's tone grew stronger, catching the mask's attention. Her hand tightened on the girl's fingers, drawing them off the mask.

"I'm sorry we don't have the money for ..."

"It's half price," the proprietor blurted. "Special clearance."

"Mama?" Teisha asked.

"I'm sorry, that's still too much," the woman said.

"I tell you what I can do." The proprietor stood up, leaning closer to the woman. He dropped his voice to a near whisper but still loud enough for the mask to hear.

"Twenty dollars, absolute bargain," the proprietor said. "That's less than my cost. I just want to clear the shelf."

Teisha's grip tightened on the mask. "Mama?"

The woman's eyes narrowed. "What's wrong with it?"

"Nothing," the proprietor said. "It's been here too long. Honestly, you're the first people to look at it in months. I just want it gone."

"Mama, please?" Teisha said. "Pleeeeaasse."

The woman sighed.

"No tax," the proprietor said.

"No tax, mama," Teisha said.

The woman sighed again. "Then I'll have to get your brother something," she said. She tilted her head at the proprietor. "Will you throw in the latest issue of Wonder Kid?"

The proprietor shuddered. Then he threw his hands up. "Okay, sure. But I'll have to charge you the tax then."

"Deal," the woman said.

Teisha squealed and hugged the mask to her chest.

The mask felt the warmth of her arms pressed against it, felt the excited thud of her heart. Home, it was finally going to have a home again with a new hero-to-be.

The mask almost trembled with joy.

Teisha's room was in the top of the house, with walls that sloped along with the angle of the roof. Posters cluttered the wall on one side, opposite a book shelf that was cluttered with books. A single bed sat under a tiny window that overlooked the front of the house. A desk with an old, beige desktop computer sat against the opposite wall.

That was where Teisha did her homework and wrote her stories. The mask learned this as Teisha carried it around her room, talking to herself and to it.

She ended up plopping down on the bed, lying on her stomach, the mask in front of her. Her voice grew louder and more excited as she talked about Tina Shadow and her adventures, saving the city.

Who was this Tina Shadow? Was that Teisha's hero identity? The mask became more excited. Perhaps this girl was already a hero. It had heard of the occasional child hero but usually they had some kind of superpower. From what the mask had discerned, Teisha was just a regular girl, but the mask could be wrong.

Perhaps Teisha was more of a hero that it realized.

And she had chosen it.

The mask was humbled and excited.

Except she had still not put it on, had not shown it her costume. How was the mask to blend in if it didn't know her costume? It needed time to adjust itself, to learn the type of support she needed. Did she prefer the eye slot be covered with mesh or clear? Did she need zoom-in capability? Would she be fighting villains at night and need infrared and night vision? Would she be working mostly in the day and need shade to protect from bright sunlight?

The mask needed to know these things, but most importantly it needed to match her costume.

Whatever that was.

But when she turned off the light to go to bed, leaving the mask on the nightstand beside her bed, it realized it wouldn't see her costume tonight.

Tomorrow then. It was understandable that she would want to reveal it in the light of day.

The mask could wait.

But she didn't reveal any costume the next day.

Or the day after that.

Oh, she still chatted to the mask, and giggled when it matched the color of her shirt. She even continued to talk about Tina Shadow, who the mask soon learned was not her hero identity but a character in a comic book.

The mask slowly came to realize that Teisha was not a hero after all.

She was just a girl.

A girl who had liked the mask.

It tried not to be disappointed.

After all, Teisha continued to lavish attention on the mask. She talked to it, carried it to school to show her friends, even sometimes put it on when it matched her clothes exactly. But she showed no inclination to wander the city, stopping villains.

It was better than sitting in a cupboard all day. At least the mask was grateful for that. But it still missed its days of adventure, of scouring the city for the Mad Menacer or the Slippery Sizzler. As nice as Teisha was, being her mask didn't quite live up to the past.

Not everyone aspired to be a hero, the mask realized.

One day at recess, Teisha carried the mask outside into the sun. She was wearing a light blue, sleeveless top with tiny yellow flowers on the collar. The mask had matched the color and even added little yellow flowers around its eye slot. They sparkled in the sunshine.

The squeals of the kids sounded through the playground. It was a large expanse of concrete behind the school. On the right side, white chalk lines outlined a basketball court. Portable baskets sat at either end. At least three basketballs were in play with different groups of kids bouncing the ball up and down the court. Other groups of kids jumped rope or clustered around a single phone, playing a videogame.

Teisha's usual group of friends were bouncing balls against the yellow brick wall at the back of the school. Several called out to Teisha, waving their arms for her to come over. Teisha smiled and waved back.

But she didn't go over.

Instead she headed across the playground to the far end.

A narrow gravel patch stretched along the back, right before the chain link fence, separating the back of the playground from the street beyond. As Teisha reached the gravel, her feet kicked up dust that puffed into the air. The bright sun glinted off the silver chain link. Cars rolled by on the street beyond, but their engines were soft rumbles in the distance.

"Hi," Teisha said.

The mask realized that there was a young girl huddled against the fence. Her head was bowed too low for the mask to see her face. Long brown hair, tangled and wavy, hung over it as well. She wore a boxy, dark green dress that managed to look dull even in the sunshine. Her running shoes were a dirty white, covered with dust from the gravel. The shoe laces were frayed on the ends.

She stood against the fence, angled away from Teisha, hands in front of her. When Teisha said "hi," those hands started clutching each other.

"Did you read that story in class?" Teisha asked. "I liked it. I like science fiction."

The girl shrugged. "'S okay."

"I like how they could make their clothes be different colors," Teisha said. "Changing the little pieces."

"Nanoparticles," the girl said. Her voice sounded a little stronger. Her head lifted just enough to reveal one startlingly green eye. The other was still covered by the fall of her hair.

"Right," Teisha said. She glanced back toward the playground, surveying the area, before turning back to the girl.

"You're Casey, right?" she said. The girl gave a ducking nod. Her eye began to disappear behind the curtain of hair again.

"What if I told you I had something like those clothes," Teisha said. "Something that can change to match what you're wearing?"

The mask felt a trickle of dismay. Teisha was talking about it, for certain. Even without revealing a costume for the mask to take to, she had realized part of what it could do. She was more intelligent than it had thought, but why would she be telling someone about the mask? It sounded unnervingly like bragging.

She wasn't like that, was she?

Had the mask made a huge error in choosing her? Had its desire to escape the shop, to be useful again, clouded its judgment?

Was Teisha not a hero?

Casey tilted her head. Her hair fell away, revealing more of her face. Her skin was pale and blotchy. Her nose and lips were thin, but her green eyes were large and bright, even half hidden behind her hair.

"That's not possible," she said.

"Is too," Teisha said. "Wanna see?"

Casey hunched deeper against the chain link fence, as if she could strain herself through it. She gave a half-hearted shrug.

Teisha lifted the mask up from where it had been tucked into her belt.

"When I got this, it turned yellow like my top and added little bows on the ends to match," she said. "But see how it's light blue to match my top?"

Casey shook her head. "Nothing can do that."

Teisha held the mask out to her. "You try it and see."

The mask trembled in her hand. It was confused. It sounded like boasting, at least the words did, sort of, but Teisha's tone was anything but. She sounded more encouraging, friendly. But she was handing over the mask or at least willing to do that. What was happening? The mask didn't understand.

Casey's hand shook as she reached for the mask. Just before her fingers touched it, she stopped and pulled her hand away. She huddled against the fence, wincing as if expecting to be hit.

"C'mon, try it," Teisha said. "I bet you'll look cool."

She stretched her hand closer to Casey.

This time Casey took the mask, even as her hand shook while doing it.

Transferring to her, the mask felt the girl's uncertainty wash over it, followed by a desperate longing. Casey wanted so much to believe Teisha was actually nice and not stringing her along for a greater fall down the road. That had happened so many times before, leaving Casey believing that no one would like her ever. And why would they? She was so ugly with all these red splotches.

"Put it on," Teisha said. "I bet it can match your dress. Blend, ya know."

She gave an encouraging nod and smiled.

Blend.

Now the mask understood.

How had the mask not seen it before? Of course, Teisha was a hero, just as it had thought at the beginning. But she didn't need a mask to match a costume. She didn't need to hide her identity.

Just as Casey didn't need the mask to turn green to match her boxy dress.

But she did need it to hide the blotchy redness, to stop people from staring at the transitory imperfections so they could actually see the beauty underneath. Like those great green eyes, the cute nose, the line of her chin.

And the sparkle of life that kindled in her eyes.

Casey lifted the mask and pressed it against her face.

The mask adhered to her skin and began to blend, smoothing into her skin. No longer did it feel the need to stand out. It wasn't about hiding anymore, it was about revealing.

Finally, the mask had a new job, a new purpose. It didn't have to hide a face, to show off itself in order to be heroic.

It could blend in, smooth out, be invisible, and let others shine through it. That was heroic.

A grin lit up Teisha's face. "You look great!"

Casey's lips trembled, turned up a little at the corners. "Really?"

"Yeah, take a look."

Teisha fished out a small, plastic pink, toy compact from her pocket. She handed it to Casey. Casey opened it and slowly lifted it up.

Her face reflected back, smooth, white, clear of blemishes.

The mask invisible.

Casey took a deep breath, a smile blooming her face. "Wow."

"Yeah," Teisha said. "Wanna wear it for the rest of the day?"

"Could I?" Casey said.

"Sure."

"Um, can I wear it home?" Casey asked. "You could, you know, come for dinner. My mom makes a fab mac and cheese with bacon and jalapeno peppers."

"That sounds so good," Teisha said. "I have to call my mom, but I'm sure she'll be okay."

The bell rang, signalling the end of recess. Casey straightened, and the mask realized she towered over Teisha by several inches.

The girls began to walk back toward the school, chatting. Soon laughter rang out. The mask noticed several other kids turning to look at them, some of them Teisha's friends. They wandered over and started talking.

Soon all of them were heading back to class, together. Including Casey.

Including her with them. She walked with her head up, hair flowing back from her clear face. The mask invisible.

And yet doing its job.

Doing what its hero, what Teisha, wanted it to do.

Just like any good mask should.

🎭

Based in Toronto, Canada, Rebecca M. Senese survives the frigid blasts of winter and boiling steams of summer by weaving words of mystery, horror, science fiction and contemporary fantasy.

She is the author of the contemporary fantasy series, the *Noel Kringle Chronicles* featuring the son of Santa Claus working as a private detective in Toronto. Garnering an Honorable

Mention in "The Year's Best Science Fiction," she has been nominated for numerous Aurora Awards. Her work has appeared in the anthology *Obsessions*, *Fiction River: Superpowers*, *Fiction River: Visions of the Apocalypse*, *Fiction River: Sparks*, *Fiction River: Recycled Pulp*, *Tesseracts 16: Parnassus Unbound*, *Imaginarium 2012*, *Tesseracts 15: A Case of Quite Curious Tales*, *TransVersions*, *Future Syndicate*, and *Storyteller*, amongst others. Rebeccasenese.com.

EYELESS

GAMA RAY MARTINEZ

I shtara's heart raced as she reached up and plucked out her right eye. It hardened, becoming a glass sphere in her hand. Joy rushed through her. She'd never managed to remove an eye before. She turned to Master Malak, who, like her, sat on one of the three empty beds in the basement of his home. To her left eye, he looked like an old man with a silver beard, but her empty socket saw something entirely different. Bright bands of power wrapped around his body, silhouetting his form in a soft green light. Elar flowed across his skin like ropes carried on a river.

"Very good." His elar brightened as he spoke.

She winced and brought a hand to her forehead. "Why does my head hurt?"

"Remove your other eye. It's difficult to have both sights open at once."

Ishtara nodded. Now that she could see the elar running through her fingers, manipulating it was simpler, and her other eye practically slipped out of her socket. The world went dark, all but the elar. It shimmered around her. Master Malak glowed like a bonfire, but elar ran through all living things. A bright clump sat several feet away, and Ishtara realized it was Malak's fern. A spark of light darted in front of her, accompanied by the buzzing of a fly's wings. It landed on her nose, and she brushed it away. She could even see the elar in Tiapa as the housekeeper walked across the room above them.

"Incredible."

Malak laughed. "You've only—"

A loud bang came from above. Malak went silent, and a second later, they heard muffled voices. Malak cursed. "Put your eyes back in. Quickly."

Ishtara did as she was told. Her vision returned, but the room spun. She tried to stand, but she couldn't keep her balance and collapsed back into the bed. The lantern hanging in the corner stabbed into her eyes. Her vision refused to focus, and her head pounded.

"What's wrong with me?"

The hatch in the ceiling opened, but the light was too bright, and Ishtara had to look away. Heavy boots came down the stairs, and Malak threw a blanket over her. He dipped a cloth in a water barrel and placed it on her head. The cold helped a little, but she still felt like she would throw up.

"What are you doing down here?" a gruff voice asked.

Ishtara froze, not even trying to see the features of the newcomer. She recognized the accent and wondered if he would kill them. Though it was illegal, no one would ask any questions if an Ontari soldier killed a couple of Ragan.

"This girl is sick." Desperation dripped from Malak's voice. "The light hurts her eyes. I beg you, leave her alone."

"Is she Eyeless?"

"What? No, of course not. It's just a fever. Please, sir, she needs rest."

"Maybe I should question her. The captain would want to know about any Eyeless in town."

"No, I promise you, she is not Eyeless."

"Or maybe *you* are. Hiding down here, what else would you be?"

"Please sir," Malak pleaded. She heard the jingle of coins. "I'm just a simple healer."

"Ragan scum," the man said, but his footsteps retreated up the stairs. It was only after the door banged shut that Malak let out a breath of relief.

"Master, I think there's something wrong with my eyes."

"I'm sorry. We rushed that last part." He removed the cloth from her head and helped her sit up. "Take them out again."

This time, it took a few tries. It was difficult enough to manipulate elar without being able to see it. With her vision swimming, she had trouble concentrating, but eventually she managed. Instantly, her headache vanished, and elar came back into view.

"Switch them," Malak said. "You had them in the wrong sockets."

Ishtara nodded and did as she was told. Her vision returned, this time much clearer. Tiapa stood at the top of the stairs, and Malak waved her down. She wrung her apron in her hands as she descended.

"I'm sorry about that," she said.

"There was no way you could've stopped them."

Ishtara got to her feet. Malak put a hand on her shoulder, but she was able to keep her balance. She stared up the stairs after the soldier. Rage boiled inside of her. Ever since the Ontari conquered the town of Jonarch, they had held the Ragan people under their thumb.

"Don't do anything foolish," Malak said.

"What?"

The old man smirked. "I've seen that look on the faces of enough young people to know what it means. When you became my apprentice, you promised you wouldn't get involved. That hasn't changed just because you can remove your eyes."

"But we could make a difference."

Ishtara spoke without thinking, and Malak glared at her. He shot a glance at Tiapa, but the housekeeper was already shuffling up the stairs. As soon as the hatch closed, Malak turned his gaze back at Ishtara, and she took an involuntary step back.

"You are my apprentice. It is not for you to decide what we can or can't do."

"I'm sorry, master, but we're Eyeless." She emphasized the last word as if he didn't know it. "We could drive them out."

To her surprise, Malak laughed. "The only manipulation of elar you've done is removing your eyes. Do you really imagine you could fight off an army?"

Ishtara lowered her head and spoke quietly. "You could. You could block the Erantem Pass and stop them from ever coming into the valley."

Malak didn't respond until she met his eyes. She couldn't help but wonder how much time he'd spent without those.

"People believe a lot of nonsense about Eyeless," he said. "They think we can call lightning from the sky and curse our enemies. The Ontari say we consort with dark powers. Elar is simply the power of life, and that doesn't easily lend itself to battle."

She banged her fists on the bed. "If it's the power of life, then use it to kill them."

Malak shook his head. "Elar can no more end life than a lantern can create darkness. It heals or enhances, but it cannot kill. No, one or two Eyeless cannot fight an army. They will be defeated. I'm sure of that, but it won't be in a quiet village. Until the day comes when the Ontari are gone, we must both wear the mask of ordinary people."

Ishtara spent the next several hours with her eyes out, learning the basics of manipulating elar. She had studied the interactions for months, how the bands attracted or repelled each other based on how they were positioned, but she hadn't been able to see it until she could remove her eyes. The elar in her body responded easily to her touch, and with a few swipes of her finger, she could concentrate it in her hands and use it to have greater effect on the elar around her.

Most of her work was done on the fern, and she had to put her eyes back in to see the effects. The plant's leaves swayed as if a breeze blew across them. She removed her eyes again. There was a slight weakness in one of the stems, and she maneuvered the elar so that it flowed stronger in that area. Given time, that would correct the defect.

A few leaves had withered, and she plucked a piece of her own elar and put it in the plant. It melded with the plant's until she couldn't retrieve it even had she wanted to. The action weakened her, but only as much as losing an ounce of blood would, and like the blood, her elar would eventually recover. She replaced her eyes and watched as the life she'd put into the plant restored the withered leaves to full bloom. She stared in wonder, silently thanking her father for allowing her to study under Malak instead of following his own path as a sculptor.

"That's enough for today." She jumped at the sound of Malak's voice. "It'll be dark soon, and I need to walk you home now if I'm to get back before sunset."

Ishtara snorted. "We wouldn't want the Ontari to catch us after curfew."

Malak narrowed his eyes. "No, we wouldn't. Not if we want to avoid suspicion."

She nodded once and followed him outside. Most of the people had already hidden, afraid of being caught out after dark. The sun hung just above the western mountains, and a chill wind blew through the empty streets. She huddled into her cloak. Master Malak had said it would be a harsh winter, and the tribute the Ontari had taken would make it harder still. More than one Ragan would be buried by the end of it.

The inn was the only building that still had light in its windows, and she could hear Ontari laughter coming from inside. She glared at the two-story building, as if her gaze could burrow through the thick stone walls and strike at the soldiers. Malak motioned for her to follow, and they rounded the corner and saw her house. She froze. The sight of the broken door made her blood run cold.

For a moment, she didn't comprehend what she was seeing. The next thing she knew, she'd covered half the distance to the house and was running at full speed. Malak called out, but she ignored him. The inside of the house was a wreck. Tables had been overturned, and broken dishes were scattered everywhere. A coppery scent hung in the air, though in her panic, she didn't recognize it. She tore through the house, looking for some sign of her parents. Finally, she noticed that the door to her father's workshop had been forced open. Through the doorway, she saw half-finished marble statues. Rock dust carpeted the floor, and a trickle of blood created a tiny river through the room.

Ishtara's heart raced and she ran in. Her parents' bodies lay in a corner at the base of the headless statue of Rikel, the legendary boy-king and the father of the Ragan people. Their throats had been slit, and their faces had gone pale. The statue stood over them like a grave marker.

She looked away from them, not wanting to see their lifeless bodies. Instead, she stared at the statue. The eight-foot-tall sculpture had robes so finely carved, she practically expected them to ripple. Its head had been broken off and sat across the room. Other parts had been chipped away, obviously the efforts of her parents' killers. It was treason for her father to have sculpted it, but he had always believed they would eventually fight off the Ontari, and he wanted his masterpiece ready to stand in the town square, declaring their freedom.

Malak walked up beside her, his face pale. Before Ishtara even realized what she was doing, her eyes were in her hand. Where her parents lay, she saw nothing. There was no sign of elar whatsoever. She approached them, manipulating the elar in her own body and concentrating it at her fingertips.

"Ishtara, no." Malak's voice floated to her from the darkness. "They're gone. There's nothing you can do."

Her fingers brushed a body, though she couldn't tell if it was her mother's or her father's. There was nothing, no elar to draw the power flowing through her hands. Tears ran down her cheeks, and with a swipe of her finger, she forced some of her elar into the body. Before she could do anything else, a hand snatched her wrist and pulled her away. The speck of elar floating in the corpse sputtered and died.

"No, Ishtara." Malak's voice was gentle, yet firm. "There's nothing of them left. Even if you could restore life to their bodies, it wouldn't be them. The elar comes from you, and right now, all you feel is grief and sorrow. Would you curse them with that?"

"But ..."

"Let's go."

She brought a hand to her face to wipe away the tears. The scent of blood hung heavily on her fingers, and with her eyes out, she didn't even know whose it was. She tried to get up, but tripped over a body. She managed to catch herself on one of the legs of the statue of Rikel and used it to steady herself. Her hands ran up the statue until she felt a jagged edge where a piece of stone had broken off. Her father had spent days working on this statue. Every detail had been a labor, and now the Ontari had marred even that. She leaned her head against the cold stone and wept. They were gone. Sorrow flowed through her elar, and for a moment, she wanted nothing more than to be rid of her grief. She brought her hand to her heart and dragged the elar to her arms and into the statue. It floated there as it had in the corpse, but this time, Malak didn't notice until she'd repeated the gesture three times. By then, the statue almost seemed to drink in her sorrow-filled power.

"No, Ishtara, you can't."

"What's going on here?"

The voice came from the doorway, dripping with the condescension the Ontari always had for the Ragan. Rage blossomed in her chest. These were the people that had killed her parents. Anger joined the grief, and her elar flared and brightened even as it flowed into Rikel's form. Ishtara turned to the soldier, glaring at him with empty eyes instead of the mask Malak had always warned her to wear.

"Eyeless!" His voice carried a mix of fear and hatred.

She tried to take a step toward him, but her legs suddenly lacked the strength to carry her. The ground shook, and the soldiers screamed. They rushed forward, moving past Ishtara. The last thing she heard before losing consciousness was the sound of stone grinding on stone.

⚝

"Malak, we have to give her to the Ontari."

"What Ontari, Vintul? Rikel's statue killed every soldier in town."

"They'll be back."

"But not soon. Any day now, we'll get our first snow, and the Erantem Pass will be blocked until spring."

"And then they'll come."

Ishtara's vision returned slowly. Bands of elar floated across the darkness. She felt around, looking for her eyes. A patch of human-shaped elar appeared in front of her and a hand grabbed her wrist.

"They're here."

Malak guided her hand to a leather pouch on her belt. Glass clinked inside, and she pulled out a pair of smooth spheres. She started to put them in but paused.

"How do I tell which one goes where?"

"Why don't you tell me?"

She could practically hear him smiling and would've glared if she'd had eyes. Instead, she stared at her hand. Elar flowed through her fingers, though it seemed subdued. After a second, she saw twin spheres glowing faintly in her palm, though each was only visible to one socket. She put each in the socket that could see it and blinked as her vision returned. She braced herself, half expecting the headache, but it didn't come. Malak stood over her with Mayor Vintul right behind him.

"What's happening?" she asked.

Malak's eyes flashed to the mayor. "If you'll excuse us," he said. "We have matters to discuss."

The mayor glanced at Ishtara. "But ..."

"We won't leave town," Malak said. "You have my word."

The mayor looked like he was about to argue, but Malak cleared his throat and reached up as if to pluck out his eyes. The mayor let out a short gasp and nodded even as he turned to scurry up the stairs.

"I was afraid you wouldn't wake up," Malak said. "You poured a lot of elar into that statue."

Ishtara tried to stand up, but it felt like her body was made of lead, and she struggled to lift herself. Malak offered her a hand, but even as she stood, her knees wobbled, and she sat back down on the bed.

"I didn't mean to." Her voice came out calm and emotionless. "When I saw my parents ..."

"I was afraid of that." Malak walked over to a table and retrieved a small plate with a piece of bread on it. He handed it to her. "How about now? What do you feel?"

Ishtara considered. Her parents were still dead. She could call up the memory and practically smell the blood, but it no longer held the same impact. There was a faint echo of sorrow, but it was a vague thing, more like a dream than an actual emotion. Everything else was just images and odors, and beneath all that, she felt a terrible emptiness.

"Nothing," she said. "I know they're gone, but ..."

She let that hang, not quite sure what to say. Malak closed his eyes and shook his head before meeting her gaze again.

"You did more than put your emotions into that statue. You poured in your capacity to feel."

"Oh." She thought back to the sight of her parents. The pain had been overwhelming. "Good."

Malak stared at her for several long seconds. "You can't run from your emotions, Ishtara. Even if you could, that statue ..."

Ishtara mentally sorted through the conversation she'd overheard as she was waking up. "It killed people?"

Malak gave her a slow nod. "You brought it to life, and it went after the soldiers. Within an hour, they were all dead. It's nothing but grief and pain, and desires only to destroy the Ontari."

"That's what I was thinking when I passed out," Ishtara said. "I wanted them all dead, and it freed us."

"Killing a half dozen soldiers is different from stopping the army that will descend on us in spring. It'll take more than one mindless killing machine to save us from them."

"Can't it defend the pass?" she asked.

The Erantem Pass was the only way into the valley housing Jonarch. In places it was so narrow, no more than two or three men could walk through it. If Rikel's statue had really killed all the soldiers in town, surely it could hold the pass, but Malak was already shaking his head.

"I told you, there's nothing in it but emotions. It can't think enough to guard the pass. Vintul was right. They will come."

"Is that why the mayor wanted to give me to them?"

"Don't judge him too harshly. He's desperate and hopes that if we give them someone to blame, they'll spare us."

Ishtara nodded. She knew the idea should scare her, but there was only emptiness. It would've frightened her if she'd had the capacity for fear. Instead, she fell back on cold logic. "It makes sense. It is my fault. Do you think it'll help?"

Malak stared at her, his mouth half open. After a second, he shook his head. "It won't come to that. This'll be a hard winter. We'll blame the dead soldiers on that. We'll have more than a few graves by spring anyway."

"Won't that be suspicious?"

"Yes, but not enough for them to destroy us. There is one thing we need to take care of first, unless we want them to brand us all as traitors."

"The statue?"

"It's standing in the middle of town like some sort of monument. I have no doubt it'll kill any Ontari that comes near, but even it will fall if enough men come at it with hammers, and we'll be worse off than before."

She nodded and struggled to stand. Malak offered her his hand, but she waved him away. Her legs felt a little stronger, and she was able to keep her balance. "How are you going to stop it?"

He shook his head. "I don't think I can, but you are another matter. You can take back what you gave it."

"I thought that wasn't possible."

"Not once your elar mixes with the elar of something else, but the statue has no elar of its own."

"Do I have to?" she asked. "It hurt so much."

He put a hand on her shoulder and met her gaze. Unshed tears welled in his eyes. She knew she should feel something, but there was just the hollow void.

"You've lost more than anyone should, but you're only half a person right now, Ishtara. You gave away too much of your elar. You need to get it back."

"Won't it replenish itself?"

Malak shook his head. "This isn't like losing a little bit of blood. You've chopped off your right arm. You may eventually get used to it, but you'll never be whole again."

She stood there for a second, waiting for the impact of Malak's words to hit her, but it never came. There was nothing more than the faintest echo of fear. The emptiness inside suddenly felt like a vast chasm threatening to consume everything else.

"What about joy?" she asked.

"What?"

"I poured my grief into the statue. Does that mean I'll still be able to feel joy?"

"I'm sorry, but no. All emotions come from the same source, and that's what you poured out. If you ever want to feel again, you need to reclaim it."

The emptiness gnawed at her. Something was missing, and its lack weighed on her even more than her grief.

"Let's go."

"How did it get its head back?"

A crowd of men had gathered around the statue with hammers, but they kept their distance. Rikel stood in the center of the town square with one fist raised. She could still see the dried blood on its fingers. Though its eyes didn't move, they looked oddly alive and sent chills down her spine.

"Once it finished with the guard in your father's workshop, it picked up the head and put it on. Your elar spread through it, joining it to the body."

She nodded, and reached up to remove her eyes, but they

wouldn't come out. She tried again, but it didn't work. She looked at Malak.

"You've lost a lot of elar. Manipulating it won't be so easy."

"It was never easy," she said under her breath.

It was half an hour before her eyes came free, and when they did, she gasped. The elar in the statue glowed brightly, and when she stared into it, the image of her dead parents filled her mind. She looked down at herself. Her own elar was dim by comparison. It jutted more than it flowed and reminded her of a river that had nearly dried out. She reached toward the statue, and the elar inside it pulsed. The emptiness inside her yearned for it. Her fingers felt cold stone, and a single strand jumped from the statue into her hand.

It was like touching a bolt of lightning.

Her parents were dead. They would never come back. Tears ran down her cheek, and the next thing she knew, she was on the ground. The statue's elar still shone strongly. Her own had stabilized somewhat. The emptiness had lessened but hadn't gone away. Compared to the pain, however, it seemed like such a small thing. She fumbled with her eyes until they clicked into her sockets, but her vision came back blurry. At first, she thought she'd put them in wrong, but then she realized it was tears. Malak offered her a hand up, and she took it. She shook her head.

"I can't. It hurts too much."

"Malak." The mayor's voice was quiet, and the word seemed almost dragged out of him. "I won't pretend to know what this means, but that statue has to be destroyed. If a scout or messenger sees ..."

"The snows will fall any day now," Malak said. "Even if one were to arrive today, he'd still be stuck here for the winter. Give her time. She can take it a piece at a time if she has to."

Ishtara shook her head. "No, I can't. It's too much."

The mayor waved to the men with hammers, and they started forward. "I'm sorry, Malak. We can't take the risk."

"Then, you may as well kill her. We have time. There's no need to do it until she can remove her elar."

The piece of emotion she had reclaimed surged to life. It was only a pale shadow of normal feelings, but compared to the emptiness she'd felt before, it was like being plunged into a fire. That statue was the last remnant of her father. Rikel was the symbol of the freedom they'd all dreamed about, and Vintul wanted to destroy it.

"No," she said. "You can't."

"Don't worry," Malak said. "You'll get your elar back first."

"That's not what I mean. The statue ..."

"I'm sorry," Mayor Vintul said. "We can't have this up any longer. Do it."

One of the men raised a hammer. Both Malak and Ishtara cried out, but the statue moved faster than she would've believed. Its hand closed around the head of the hammer. The man holding it tried to pull away, but the statue swung its arm and sent him flying into a house a dozen feet away. The other men charged, but Rikel moved with a liquid grace that defied it size. Most of the hammers hit only empty air, and the statue's blows scattered the men. One landed a solid blow on its knee, and a chip of stone flaked off, but the statue didn't seem to notice and delivered a powerful kick, throwing the man several feet away. He slammed against the inn and didn't move.

"Malak, do something!" The mayor was dragging away the still form of one of the men.

Malak's eyes were already out. His fingers danced across his skin. Ishtara tried to remove her own eyes to see what he was doing, but they wouldn't come out. She gasped as Malak started to grow. In a few seconds, he'd nearly doubled in size, towering over even the statue. His arms bulged with muscles that hadn't been there a minute ago. The ground trembled as he took a step toward Rikel. He swung a fist, but Rikel was too fast and caught Malak's punch in its hand. Though the Eyeless stood a foot taller than the statue, Malak was only flesh and blood fighting against stone.

Rikel squeezed Malak's fist. There was the sound of bones cracking. Malak cried out, as the statue delivered a powerful punch to his stomach. He doubled over before falling to the ground. Without thinking, Ishtara ran to stand between the statue and her master. He was still breathing but made no move to rise. The statue took a step toward them. Its emotions echoed inside of her, resonating with the emptiness. There was grief over the Ragan who had died because of the invaders, and there was also rage. It hated the Ontari, and it hated those who would bow to them by destroying the symbol of freedom her father had carved. It raised a hand to strike, but she stood before it. She reached up to her face, and this time, her eyes came free.

The elar in the statue pulsed and writhed. It called to the elar inside of her. She walked over to Rikel and laid a hand on a stone leg. She kept expecting its massive fist to slam down on her, but the attack never came. Once again, she tried to draw out the life she'd given it, but even the smallest piece multiplied her pain, and she had to stop after a few seconds. She looked around. Most of those who had tried to destroy the statue were still alive, their elar pulsing faintly. The statue had defeated them in a mindless rage, and it had done it in seconds.

"What could you do if you actually had a mind?" she asked.

She knew the answer. The statue could give them her father's dream. Her dream. Once again, she started the transfer of elar, but this time, it was *into* the statue instead of out. She couldn't stand to take the pain back into herself, and the statue was nothing but pain. She could add to it, though, and she poured in everything—every thought, every memory, the very essence of who she was.

Gradually, her sight faded, as the elar in her body poured into the stone. At the same time, however, she saw the world in muted shades of gray. Her body sat limp at her feet. Malak stirred. Then, with horror, he looked up at her stony face. She nodded at him. He tried to say something, but she turned away and walked out of town, every step like a thunder crash. Though many stared, no one moved to stop her, and before long, she passed into the woods outside the city.

Malak stood at the grave of Ishtara's parents. Few had attended their funeral. No one wanted to be associated with the people the Ontari had named traitors. He knelt down and ran his fingers over the dirt.

"I'm sorry. I would've saved her if I could have."

He removed his eyes and twined the elar in the ground. Grass sprouted, and before long, his nostrils filled with the smell of flowers. He gave them strength enough to survive the winter. It was all he could do. He replaced his eyes and rose. He thought he saw movement in the nearby woods, and stared into the trees for a long time. Though he didn't see any sign of it now, the figure in the forest had stood at least nine feet tall. He inclined his head, though he didn't know if anyone was watching.

He suspected the Ontari would find it difficult to return in spring. One mindless statue couldn't hold off an army, not even when the only way into the valley was the Erantem Pass. A living, thinking statue, however, was an entirely different matter.

Perhaps the Ragan would one day have the freedom that Ishtara had dreamed of.

Gama Ray Martinez lives near Salt Lake City, Utah with his wife and three kids. He moved there solely because he likes mountains. He collects weapons in case he ever needs to supply a medieval battalion, and he greatly resents when work or other real-life things interfere with writing. He secretly hopes to one day slay a dragon in single combat and doesn't believe in letting pesky little things like reality stand in the way of dreams.

Find him at gamarayburst.com.

IN DEFIANCE OF DEATH

REBECCA E. TREASURE

Fanny Bertrand waited for the pirate on black rocks that swallowed light. Rain drizzled down the slippery shore. Thin yellow light from the approaching lantern failed to penetrate far into the storm. The night was cold, the last whisper of winter clinging to the wind. She shivered despite the heavy woolen cloak shrouding her shoulders and her tight brown curls.

Saint Helena had its beauty—a beauty Fanny had come to appreciate in six years of exile with Emperor Bonaparte—but in the dark and rain it was every bit the torturous rock she'd imagined when first learning of their destination. She'd tried to throw herself into the sea to avoid Saint Helena.

In the last moments before the light illuminated her, she considered the sea's embrace once more.

Then the man reached her. Lantern's glow revealed dark eyes sparkling like gemstones in a smooth face that nevertheless gave the impression of great age. He wore loose breeches with cuffs flapping like palm fronds in the hissing wind, a leather overcoat running with rivulets of rain, and a free-slung sword glimmering with menace in the darkness. "Madame

Bertrand?" His accent was rounded, unfamiliar, but his French well-pronounced.

Wishing her heart would silence its thrashing, she nodded. "I am." She did not ask his name. Her instructions had been clear.

He thrust an apple-sized glass jar at her. The shifting lantern light splashed across his hand, revealing thin black tattoos running along his fingers and up his forearm. "Mix this with his blood before he dies. *Before.* Then, when the mask is made, stir the mixture into the plaster."

Fanny held the jar to the light, studying the powdery flakes within. "That's all?"

"Bring a lit lantern to this place when they seal the mask upon his face. Swing it three times and hurl it into the sea. We'll be watching. The woman will do the rest." He grinned, revealing tobacco-stained teeth. "Blood magic."

Fanny shuddered. She had little interest in the occult workings that would trap the Emperor's soul in his death mask, but she did have an interest in the other magic she'd been promised. "And my payment?"

The pirate laughed. "She told me you'd be impatient about that. You'll get what's been promised when you deliver the mask to her in Paris."

Fanny's free hand went to her waist, where a tiny bulge pressed against the dress. "No, I need it now. I cannot wait. She promised—"

The pirate's hand drifted to the hilt of his sword. "You'll do it. She said to assure you of her word. You'll bear a living child again. Once she has the mask."

Fanny slumped, her temper muted by the threat of the blade. Left in its place was the ache of a half dozen miscarried babies, the terror that the tiny life within her would meet the same fate. "What of this child?"

He shrugged and drew his leather jacket tight around his

body. "Get to the woman in time. Or hope your God can save the babe." He left her shivering in the rain.

The weak lantern light disappeared into the darkness. Fanny slipped the little jar into her cloak. She kept her fingers curled around the cold glass, around the promise she would never again have to endure the loss of her hope and love, little bundles carried away in the night like something shameful.

Napoleon's allies wanted to save him from death, but Fanny had a precious life of her own to save.

She hurried toward Longwood House and the cottage she shared with her husband, Comte Henri Bertrand, and their four living children—including little Arthur, the one baby to survive since they'd come to Saint Helena. Pain in her pelvis grew with every step, a clawing ache as sharp as the one in her heart. Before meeting the woman with the gold watch, Fanny had lost all hope. One baby, five losses. Her last, only three months before, had nearly killed her.

A little girl.

The doctors had been unable to stop the bleeding for nearly a week—but in sympathy to her new pregnancy, Napoleon had finally allowed the Bertrands to seek permission from the British to leave Saint Helena. Even as she lifted her soaked skirts over the low stone wall surrounding Longwood, the weakness she could not recover from weighed down her legs.

"Halt! Identify yourself!" The shout of a British soldier startled Fanny.

She stumbled, falling into the mud along the wall. "It's me, Madame Bertrand. I got lost in the storm."

The sentry stomped up to her, his tall black boots splashing mud onto her face. "You shouldn't be out at night."

Fanny wanted to snap at him that after six years of imprisonment on this rock she could hardly have forgotten, but her hand brushed the lump in her pocket. She bit her lip. "I'm sorry. I was frightened and got turned around."

"Where's the carriage?"

"I walked. I didn't know the storm would be so severe."

A third voice came from the darkness, speaking in rapid French. "Madame Betrand? What's the trouble?" The figure stepped forward. Marchand, Napoleon's valet, was tall, with a long straight nose and a cluster of curly hair damp and clinging to his head.

"Oh, Marchand. I walked from The Briars and got lost, and now this soldier is pestering me."

Marchand helped Fanny to her feet. She kept one hand on the precious bottle in her cloak, the other on the swell in her belly, wincing as a cramp grew into a gnawing pain.

"This woman could hardly be hiding the Emperor under her skirts," Marchand chided the soldier. "Away with you."

Convinced she could pose no threat to his imperial charge, the soldier grumbled off into the night.

Fanny smiled at Marchand. "Thank you so much." She slipped her hand over his arm. "Shall we?"

By the time Marchand left her at the door, Fanny could hardly stand. She dismissed the lady-servant with a wave and locked herself in her bedroom. Henri often stayed at Longwood, taking the Emperor's dictation and notes long into the night.

Fanny secured the jar in her trunk at the foot of her bed, buried beneath unused baby blankets. Then she stripped her drenched clothes off, tossing them in a pile. As she reached her undergarments, a shiver went through her.

They were stained with blood.

The doctors had told her to rest, to not exert herself. But this was important. If the child could be saved, it would be worth it. She cleaned herself up as best she could and crawled into her bed. By the time she fell asleep, a thin dawn pushed through the storm, promising a beautiful day.

Napoleon was dying. Nothing could stop it, not now. For weeks he had been vomiting blood, splattering bile. Fanny sat at his bedside, reading his memoirs back to him for corrections, while four-year-old Arthur played with blocks on the plush carpet. The room stank of vomit and sweat and the orange-blossom wine he'd insisted on drinking even though he vomited most of it up.

The Emperor lay on his camp bed in the center of the room, the green tenting deepening the shadows cast by his gaunt features. His eyes were two gates to Hell, dark hollows beneath a smoldering gaze. Muted sunlight from tall windows, filtered through the mist that surrounded Longwood House, stretched across the narrow chamber toward the dark fireplace.

He was feverish, sitting up against his pillows and spitting scarlet and pale yellow wet onto his dressing gown. He pushed back his blanket, his eyes wild. A series of hiccups wracked his body, and he vomited into a silver bucket.

Fanny stood, shooing Arthur from the room. "Fetch Doctor Antommarchi." Turning back, she pressed the Emperor gently to his pillows and pulled his wool blanket up to his shoulders. Such a powerful man, brought so low.

Fanny made soothing noises and, taking a cool cloth from a bucket next to the bed, dabbed at the Emperor's face. "You will live on. The woman with the gold watch promised me it would be so."

"Live on? I am dying. At least the pain will end. I wish I could see the King of Rome one last time. My son, my son. Damn the English." He fell into muttering, tossing his head on the pillow. His eyes fluttered open and shut in the thin sunlight.

Fanny frowned. Did he want to live on? She thought of Henri, who had devoted his life to the service of the Emperor. Then she recalled the tens of thousands of men who had died, scattered across Europe in the endless Coalition Wars. Her hand found the bump beneath her skirt, another life clinging to the precipice. Did the good of Napoleon outweigh so much death?

She thought back to the moment in Jamestown when the woman with the gold watch approached her. Middle-aged, tan, but beautiful in a wild way. She'd worn a red dress, cut low in the Imperial style, drawing the eye of every man in the room. Fanny had been jealous.

Taking Fanny aside, the woman leaned close to her in the corner of a salon and whispered, "I know what you want most in the world."

Another wave of pain left Fanny gasping, and she bent in half, squeezing at the ache. So many deaths. The men who followed Napoleon—and his enemies—chose their fates, knew the dangers. What choice did her little baby have?

No, Fanny couldn't forget the whispers of the woman, her knowledge of Fanny's pain and hopes, and that pirate on the shoreline.

The Emperor had fallen asleep, fitful and tossing, hiccupping. Her eye fell on the spittle streaked with scarlet.

Before he dies.

Arthur's call echoed, warning that Antommarchi approached. Fanny scooped the moist foulness into an empty teacup, wrapped it in a kerchief, and tucked it into a pocket. Antommarchi and Marchand hurried into the room.

Antommarchi scarcely nodded to her, hurrying to the bedside of the Emperor. Before long, the room was crowded. Henri stood staring down at the man who had controlled his destiny. Arthur had his little hand on the camp bed, his face confused. Hortense—Fanny's only daughter—had buried her face in Fanny's lap—from grief or discomfort at the sight. The British doctors, too, were silent and contemplative, crowding around the death bed. Fanny's heart raced.

The Emperor mumbled, Antommarchi and Marchand leaned close, and then Napoleon exhaled with a crackling sigh.

The Emperor was dead.

His skin, yellow and thin, sagged in slack wrinkles over his face. Fanny did not grieve for the man. She had never quite forgiven him for trusting the British and dragging her family to this speck in the Atlantic. He had ravaged Europe for a decade and more, accomplished great things, and failed spectacularly. Few lived a life as full as he had in a mere fifteen years. More, he had a chance at immortality.

No, she did not grieve. It did not matter what Napoleon intended, Fanny decided. The fate of the world was not her concern. Napoleon could stay dead or live on forever. She could not bear the loss of another baby, not again.

Fanny stroked Hortense's hair, chewing her lip. When would the mask be made? And how could she slip away to send her signal?

Henri straightened. To Marchand he said, "Louis, have him cleaned tonight. Doctors, you will perform the autopsy tomorrow."

Antommarchi grunted. "I will be ready."

Fanny smiled at the reaction of the British and French. They were educated men, powerful in their own ways, but Henri's battlefield-trained voice had them shuffling away in moments. She stood, smoothing her gown. "Hortense, take your brother home."

Henri came around the bed and squeezed her hand.

She smiled up at him. "I am sorry. He was a great man."

Henri's jaw tightened, the only outward showing of his pain. "The greatest."

"Go, do what needs doing."

As soon as Henri left, Fanny slipped through Longwood House. Noise seemed inappropriate so she stepped lightly and opened doors with care. She hurried home to secure the blood in the mixture locked in her chest. Napoleon had lived the past six years trapped on Saint Helena, and now his ghost was trapped as well.

Fanny would free him, whether it had been his wish or not.

Two days later, Fanny paced in front of Longwood House. Hidden in the folds of her skirt was the glass jar of promise. Her loins ached and there had been more blood that morning. The fog surrounding Longwood had dissipated for once, and the sun beat down. Today, Antommarchi and the British doctor, Burton, would make the mask.

Antommarchi strolled up the path toward her. "Good morning, Madame Bertrand. You're out early."

She smiled into the warming sun, searching for a glow of hope within. "Enjoying the weather. Longwood is often so gloomy, especially lately."

"Sad times, indeed. Excuse me, I have work to complete."

"Oh, let me help you."

"Shouldn't you be resting? The strain of the past few days, your ordeal ..."

Fanny shook her head. He didn't need to know that the bleeding had returned, that she felt weak and dizzy, or that the pain in her body squeezed and flashed with heat when she moved. "I am fine. It is good to stay busy."

He grunted. "Very well."

She followed him into the house. Napoleon's body lay under a sheet on planks in the front room. Fanny averted her gaze, afraid to see cuts or other evidence of the grim autopsy work done the day before.

Antommarchi poured the plaster powder into a large metal pot. "Can you fetch a servant to bring water?"

That would not do at all. She stepped forward, taking up the wooden spoon he'd brought to mix with and settling on a stool in front of him. "Perhaps you could fetch the water?"

He scowled at her but left. As soon as he quit the room she drew out the jar. Fingers trembling, she struggled to unscrew the lid. Finally it came free. She mounded the white powder over the glittering, pungent mass and had barely resettled to her seat when Antommarchi and Burton returned, followed by a servant carrying a large pitcher.

Fanny stood, blocking the pot so Antommarchi would have to shove her out of the way to stir. His jaw shifted, but he stepped to the side. "Pour the water in slowly. Madame Betrand, please stir with broad strokes to break up any clumps."

The mixture had, perhaps, more flecks in it than it should have, but Antommarchi was busy arguing with Doctor Burton about the cause of Napoleon's death and did not notice. As soon as the mixture had congealed, Fanny left. No time to spare, she had to get to the shore. She grabbed a lantern from the cottage and ran down the path next to Longwood.

Fanny picked up her skirts and trekked east toward the shoreline. The ground was damp, of course, and she slipped down the densely wooded paths toward the stony shore. Cabbage trees and dwarf ebony scattered the sunlight into slivers. The flashes of brightness only worsened Fanny's dizziness. She fell, jarring her back against an incline. The lantern bounced down the path ahead of her.

Fanny clawed her way to her feet, mud edging under her fingernails. The lantern's glass had shattered, but the candle within was intact. Although a ship could hardly see a candle from a distance, the pirate had said to light the flame. As long as she could get it alight in the wind on the coast, it would work.

Finally, the sun high overhead and the sea air whipping at her muddied skirts and her cheeks, she reached the shoreline. After three tries with her flint, the candle caught. Gasping, weak, she stumbled to the edge of the rocks, swung the lantern in three arcs, and tossed it into the sea.

Fanny turned, looking up at the hills of Saint Helena and her long walk back to Longwood—where she had yet to steal the mask. So far to go. She gritted her teeth, determined to believe. It would work, it must work. She had to go on. She took a step. Pain radiated out from her middle, and her vision closed in. The world went dark.

Fanny awoke in her bed. Henri stood to one side, staring out the window. The echo of children playing thrummed through the closed door. A slant of light came through the blinds from the evening sun.

"Henri? What happened?" Her hands clenched at the too-small bump beneath the sheets. "The baby?"

He turned, his face drawn. "Oh, praise be. I worried you would not wake." He crossed and sat next to her on the mattress. "The bleeding has slowed. When I could not find you midday, a search was formed." He sighed. "Why didn't you tell me you were ill?"

"You had enough to concern you with the Emperor's illness. I will be fine."

"The doctors told you to rest, they warned you. I could not bear to lose you, not now."

"Nor I you." She smiled into his eyes. When they'd married, she had seen him as old, boring, and plain. Yet Henri was a perfect match for her fiery temper and determined will. "I am sorry to have worried you."

He cleared his throat. "Doctor Antommarchi is almost finished at Longwood. He will then come to see you again."

Fanny sighed. "What can he tell me that I do not already know? Rest." She rolled her eyes. "And recover."

"The King will grant my pardon. We will leave for London, and you will finally be free of Saint Helena."

A flash of cold went through Fanny, momentarily muting the waves of hot pain. "Not London. Paris." The woman would be waiting, they had to go to Paris.

He shook his head. "We first go to London. Our friends insist upon it."

Her eyes filled with tears. "I had so longed to see Paris once again."

Henri took her hand. "And we will. Now, rest."

He left her. Fanny tossed upon her pillow, writhing against the pain that taunted her efforts to prevent another loss. Hopelessness threatened to consume her. It would all be for naught if she could not retrieve the mask.

Moonlight silvered the short span between the cottage and Longwood. The crescent moon illuminated just enough to give the world a gray, ghostly color. Fanny had pressed Henri for wine—for the pain—and ensured he drank more than she. Now her senses were numbed, and he was deeply asleep. She'd slipped from her sheets and crept outside. Longwood sat shrouded in shadow and gloom. The night breezes carried hints of the summer blooms of sunflowers and the redwood blossoms.

Marchand stepped forward from the porch. "Madame

Bertrand, it's late. After your ordeal today, you should be resting."

Was the man waiting for her? "Arthur left a toy in the Emperor's chambers and won't sleep without it. I'm just going to retrieve it, and I'll be on my way."

"I'll get it for you." He smiled, wan in the moonlight. "What is it?"

"Oh, it's no trouble." She brushed past him, avoiding his gaze. "I'll only be a moment."

He followed her into the house. Fanny's mind raced. The Emperor's body had been returned to his chambers. A parade of the curious and dignified would march through Longwood to glimpse the Emperor.

Fanny hesitated at the doorway of the billiard room. "I can't remember where he was playing. A toy horse. Will you look in the Emperor's chambers? His body ..."

Marchand's eyes narrowed, but he nodded.

Fanny turned away. "I shall look in the kitchen."

She forced her legs to carry her through the house. The mask sat in a wooden crate, nestled in straw. Fanny reached in to draw it out. Her hands trembled. The mask caught on the edge of the crate. The plaster shattered—and her heart with it.

No!

The face fell into the straw, leaving her holding the plaster frame with Napoleon's ears pressing against her thumbs. Napoleon's sleeping face, such a familiar sight to Fanny, stared up at her in the hollows of the cast. His strong nose, his thoughtfully compressed lips, and those eyes. She was glad they were closed, though in her weariness and fear she imagined them snapping open, staring at her in accusation.

This is not what I wanted, the mask seemed to whisper. And now she'd gone and broken it.

She pulled Napoleon's face from the crate, hoping it would

be enough. She left the ears and tucked the mask under her top skirt.

"I've found it, Marchand, thank you," she called as she slipped out of the side door of Longwood. Her vision in the night scattered black spots across the lawn, and she could scarcely bear the pain. Once she reached her chambers, she once again locked the magic in her trunk, wrapped carefully in layers upon layers of blankets and broken dreams. Then she slipped into bed next to Henri and tried to sleep.

"Someone stole it! I will discover who!" Antommarchi was mad, enraged beyond reason by the destruction of the mask. Marchand stood impassively to one side while the doctor raged.

"Calm down, doctor." Doctor Arnott's words dripped with British superiority. "I have a wax mold. And it's not like Bonaparte is going anywhere."

"Yes, *you* have a mask. I am left with Napoleon's ears!" Antommarchi paced the kitchen of Longwood House, his cheeks red and his eyes burning.

Fanny stood to one side, trying to look concerned and innocent at the same time. She could not risk being accused, not now. Fanny turned to leave.

"Madame Bertrand?"

She turned back, smiling at Doctor Arnott. "Yes?"

"I am told you entered Longwood last night."

Antommarchi's face snapped to Fanny, his eyes narrowing.

Fanny shrugged. "Yes, Arthur had left a toy in the Emperor's chambers."

"I see." Arnott tilted his head, watching her. "Your husband served with Bonaparte for his whole career, no? Compte Bertrand is exiled as well. It must be a devastating loss for your family."

Fanny's temper flared. "What we lost was lost in 1815, *monsieur*. We're grateful to have been at the Emperor's side at the end." Henri's sentiments, not her own, but the sneer on the British doctor's face, and the fear of discovery, was more than she could bear. "The British took him from us long before now."

Then she turned and stormed out, as though affronted. In fact, she trembled with fear. Antommarchi would come looking for the mask.

Antommarchi slammed through the front door of the cottage before Fanny had removed her cloak. "Where is it!"

She whirled back to him. "What?"

He strode across the front parlor to her, his hands balled tight. "It had to be you. The British have their own mask and are smug to have the first. I was first!" Spit flew from his mouth as he shouted into her face.

Fanny backed against the armoire, her breath catching in her throat. "No, why would I?"

His eyes were wild, his own breathing fast and shallow. "Marchand saw you in the house, you kept insisting on helping with the mask. Where have you hidden it?"

He shoved her and she stumbled, falling to her knees. The shock of pain sparked up her legs, joining with the pain in her loins.

Antommarchi ripped open the door of the armoire, pulling cloaks and scarves out and tossing them upon her. Hortense came into the room, eyes wide.

"Run, Hortense," Fanny gasped. "Get help."

The doctor whirled and followed Hortense down the hall.

"No!" Fanny forced her way up, leaning on the walls of the

hall for support as she followed the doctor. "Leave my children alone!"

Antommarchi turned into the nursery and began kicking at toys and ripping chests open. Clothing, books, blocks, and children's drawings went flying into the air like a hurricane.

Fanny panted, leaning against the doorframe. "Doctor, please, you are not well."

He ignored her, pushing past her and entering her own bedroom. Fanny stepped forward, pulling at his arm. "Doctor, please—"

"You have taken it from me!"

Distantly, a door slammed and Fanny sighed. At least the children had escaped. There was no telling what this madman would do. Antommarchi turned to the chest at the foot of the bed. He tore open the lid with a thunk and began throwing her precious blankets on the floor.

Fanny leapt on his back, clawing at his cheeks with her fingernails. "Get out of my house!" She screamed, forcing breath she could not spare into her lungs, hoping someone— anyone—would hear and save her, save her unborn baby from a bloody death and a life unlived.

"Antommarchi!" Marchand stomped into the room. "Control yourself."

Fanny fell off the doctor's back, hitting the floor with a groan of pain and relief. Marchand pulled the doctor from the room. Antommarchi's eyes gleamed with hatred as he looked back at Fanny. His shouting faded, and the door slammed once again.

Alone, Fanny turned back to the chest. Sobbing, she pulled away the layers of blankets to reveal the mask, undisturbed. Hot pain radiated from her pelvis, her breath coming in gasps. Napoleon's face pulled her in, daring her to put her face into the mask, to see with his eyes. She was leaning into the chest when, too late, she heard footsteps.

"So," said Marchand from the doorway. "I thought so."

Fanny gasped and slammed the trunk shut.

As she looked down, she saw blood soaking through her skirts, so much blood, too much blood. A cramp threatened to rip her apart. She had lost. She was too late. Tears sprang to her eyes as a series of funerals for tiny coffins tormented her memories.

She would throw herself into the sea this time. There was no more point in hoping. Henri could not stop her.

"Madame Bertrand, you're bleeding. I'll get the doctor."

Fanny pushed herself to her knees, gripping Marchand's arm. "No, wait. You cannot tell them I have it. Please." Fanny begged, pouring all her lost hope into her voice. She could not fail another baby.

"Why?" Marchand sat on the edge of the bed, looking at Fanny. He did not look angry, or even suspicious. Just curious.

Fanny settled onto the floor, fighting a wave of hysteria pushed toward her throat from the pain deep within and threatening to come out in a scream. She stared up at Marchand. He had loved Napoleon, she knew. Served him with devotion as much as Henri, tried to keep him confident and secure in his exile.

Perhaps, with that kind of love, he could understand. Perhaps there was still room for hope.

"I made a promise," she began, "in exchange for something I need. Something important."

"Tell me."

So Fanny explained, looking down at the floor where a cream-colored woolen baby blanket, tossed aside by Antommarchi, kept her voice from wavering. "I couldn't refuse. I had to hope. The Emperor was young, but my babies were younger." Her skirt was damp with blood.

Marchand turned his head toward the window, tears in his eyes. "If you can bring him back," he said in a thick voice, "the world would be better for it. He did not fear death, but he had so much more to do. He lived too short a time. He could accomplish so much." He went to the door. "I'll bring Doctor Arnott."

Fanny nodded. She didn't care about Napoleon, of course, not the way Henri or Marchand cared. But she cared about defeating death.

In that, she and Marchand agreed completely.

🎭

The last trunk, slung on ropes and hauled by sailors, creaked aboard the ship. Within that trunk were all of Fanny's hopes for her future, and perhaps the world's as well.

Blankets, and a broken piece of plaster.

She stood, holding Arthur's hand, and waited for Henri. He looked handsome, tall in his traveling clothes of blue-dyed wool and cotton. He had been a good match for her, better than Napoleon could have guessed all those years ago. She wanted to give him one more son.

Fanny's heart pounded in her throat like the war drums of the Grand Armée. She had to reach the woman by spring.

Fanny was pregnant again.

Just a few weeks, perhaps a little more. There had been nothing to bury, and with the mask secure, Fanny could truly rest. Marchand was true to his word, and though there had been a fuss over the missing mask, the Bertrands were safe. Fanny had been able to recover. When the news came that Henri had been pardoned and they could return to France, he'd wanted to celebrate.

June, perhaps, or July.

But only if she reached the woman in time.

Henri said his farewells. He and Marchand embraced, and over Henri's shoulder, Marchand held Fanny's gaze. His eyes were full of hope.

She boarded the ship, to sail north to England and then to France. Hortense was eager for new dresses, the boys dreamed of glory, and Fanny, too, had hope. Hope for the little life growing within her, hope for Europe, hope for herself.

Death may not yet be defeated, but she would defy its claim to the last. As the ship weighed anchor, Fanny left Saint Helena and her grief behind.

Rebecca E. Treasure grew up reading science fiction and fantasy in the foothills of the Rocky Mountains. She received a BA in history from the University of Arkansas and a Masters from the University of Denver. After grad school, she began writing fiction. Rebecca has lived many places, including the Gulf Coast of Mississippi and Tokyo, Japan. Her writing has been published by WordFire Press, Flame Tree Publishing, Air & Nothingness Press, and others. She currently resides in Texas Hill Country with her husband, where she juggles two children, two corgis, a violin studio, and writing. She only drops the children occasionally.

To read more, visit rebeccaetreasure.com.

QUALIA

RUSSELL DAVIS

*"The real problem is not whether machines
think but whether men do."*

—B. F. Skinner

The rain was halfway to becoming sleet when Detective
Marsh Hallowell brought his unmarked police cruiser to
a stop outside the gates of the long-abandoned junk yard. On
the other side of the fence, row upon row of vehicles, rusted out
and damaged beyond repair, stood in silent and forgotten
memorial to a time in history when the transportation system
of America was mainly composed of gasoline engines and
sheet metal.

Marsh stepped out of the cruiser and walked over to the
gates of the junk yard, pulling the collar of his coat up to try
and keep the sleet from leaking down his neck and into his
shirt. Not that it mattered. In a few minutes, he'd be soaked to
the skin.

The gates were locked with an old chain and padlock, but
they were covered in rust. It seemed likely that no one had

touched them in years. Vehicles these days were recycled rather than scrapped, with very little waste for the process. Marsh reached into his coat and pulled out his stun baton—a light-weight carbon-fiber tool that he could use to subdue a suspect without causing serious damage. He pushed one end of it through the loop in the chain, between the gap in the gates, and twisted several times. The chain tightened briefly, then snapped, the years of rust doing most of the work for him.

Marsh pushed open the gates and returned to his cruiser, pulling it inside the yard. Then he stepped back out and shut the gates behind him. He wasn't committing a crime, not really, not exactly, but he preferred not to be seen. His actions would be difficult to explain. There were questions he did not want to answer. He got back to the cruiser and climbed in, realizing that his earlier feeling was right—the sleet was running in cold strips on the inside of his shirt. Like the fingertips of an icy skeleton.

Ignoring the sensation, he drove the cruiser deeper into the yard, weaving between the rusted relics of a different age. Most of them were smashed flat, stacked atop one another, like the toy blocks of a giant. Several rows in, Marsh stopped once more. This was as good a place as any—the lowest vehicle in the stack in front of him hadn't been crushed completely, and the interior was accessible.

It was a good place to hide the body.

The Butterfly House of Sensual Delights was a brothel in the rehabilitated section of old downtown Chicago, what used to be called the Loop. The area had been decimated in the water riots of 2034, but once the new City Centre was built, nostalgia called and the area was designated an Entertainment Zone.

Sometimes, before he went inside, Marsh would sit in his

parked cruiser across the street and watch as the neon lights in the windows carved intricate patterns into the dark glass. The patterns were strangely sensual, curving hints of half-seen forms entwined in familiar positions that faded away before the image was clear. He would think about the woman on the other side. Amaya.

She would be in the lounge waiting for him. He had a standing appointment two nights a week. Expensive, but a man had needs, and he wasn't too old to want them fulfilled. He wasn't a big man, nor particularly handsome. Marsh was plain, to the point of being invisible, while Amaya was pale skin and black hair and bright green eyes, but more than those things, she was ... safe. Reliable.

After his wife had died ten years ago, Marsh didn't want a relationship, didn't need one. But he still enjoyed sex, and the short time after, when he would lay in the narrow, sterilized bedsheets with Amaya and talk about his week, or a case he was working on. Even more than psychiatrists, companions were entirely confidential. He could tell her he planned to go on a killing spree and she would keep utterly silent on the matter.

Sometimes, he would think about how it used to be, back when his father had died and before the advent of NearC programming. In most cities, prostitutes would work on street corners, under the watchful gaze of their pimp. Many were strung out on drugs of one kind or another. Some carried diseases. Quite a few were there against their will, taken when they'd run away from home as teenagers or bought and sold like slaves.

Prostitution was illegal, then, in all but a handful of places. The women were regularly arrested, charged, and then sent back out on the streets to earn the money to pay the fine the court assessed against them for their crimes. Some women were more discerning, calling themselves escorts and charging

a premium for their time and services. The title didn't matter—
call them whores or tramps or one of the other hundred names
for the trade they worked in: the world's oldest profession.

And after his father was gone, and the little bit of money
they had ran out, so did his mother. It was that or lose their
little apartment and live on the streets. In those days, before
NearC and the changeover that came with the Minimum
Quality of Life Act, there were no other alternatives. NearC
meant androids that could perform numerous functions previously completed by humans. And the MQLA ensured that
everyone in the United States had the basic minimums: a place
to live, food to eat, clothes to wear, an education, and health
care. If that had been in place when he was young, his mother
wouldn't have had to do it.

She was an attractive woman, but not as young as many of
her peers. Still, for several long, dark, years she made enough
money for them to get by—taking clients during the day while
Marsh was in school, then leaving him at night for the discomfort of a cheap hotel that rented rooms by the hour.

He was ten years old the first time she didn't come home.
Worried, he got himself up and walked to the bus stop. He went
to school, and by the time he got home, she was there: sporting
a black eye and a split lip, and the puffy eyes of sleeplessness
and tears. She wouldn't tell him what happened. Marsh later
learned that a pimp had roughed her up because she didn't
want to be one of his girls and give him half the money she
made on her back.

Over the next two years, it happened more often, and eventually the day came when she was arrested and the school
intervened. Marsh was taken from the home and placed in
foster care while his mother scrambled to get him back. The
system was against her, he knew. And she was tired. So very
tired that even a boy his age could see it in her eyes. She was a

woman lost in what she'd been forced to become, haunted by the memory of what she'd once been.

She disappeared when he was fourteen. Had she been killed or run off or, as he sometimes dreamed, married by a rich client who didn't want the challenges of taking on a teenage son? Marsh never knew, but her vanishing act galvanized him: he would become a police officer and find her. And others like her. He would keep people safe. Her crime wasn't selling herself for sex, but selling the only thing of value she had, over and over and over again, until it became valueless. All in an ultimately wasted effort to take care of herself and her son.

Marsh did become a police officer, but the case was so cold by the time he could look at it that it may as well have been frozen in a glacier. There was nothing to be done and so few clues to follow. His mother had lived and disappeared in a world of passing strangers. Millions of unemployed, uneducated workers shuffling from one day to the next, caring only for themselves and what they could obtain for their efforts. Silence, even in the face of horror, was an often-celebrated trait.

Then the first real change came. In the mid-2000's, companies began making sexbots. At first, they were little more than dolls with a computer chip, but eventually, they started to become more and more lifelike. In 2026, NearC programming took the computer world by storm. Suddenly, sexbots became androids who could mimic human behavior so precisely that the need for human prostitutes vanished—along with a lot of other low-end jobs that went nowhere.

There were no laws against sexbots, and overall, they were far better employees. They didn't get sick, didn't get hooked on drugs, and didn't want to keep any of the money they earned. Companies began producing better and better android prostitutes, and human prostitutes were more and more rare. Brothels staffed only by androids were common, and while they weren't perfectly human, each successive model got a little bit closer.

Virtually all aspects of human sexuality could be addressed by an android: BDSM, of course, but things far more extreme were services that an android could, would, and often did provide. Consent was unnecessary and human beings were kept safer. Sexual deviancy in all its forms was perfectly legal, provided that it was practiced with an android. Why risk a disease or a criminal record with a human when one could have virtually the same experience with a bot?

By the time Marsh made detective, the vice cops were investigating organized crime, drugs, and illegal trafficking almost exclusively. It wasn't worth their time to even look for prostitutes anymore—the human ones were as gone as his mother. As far as Marsh himself was concerned, that was one improvement that the world needed. If real women weren't working the streets, then their kids weren't being left home alone. If real women weren't out making money with sex, then they weren't disappearing or dying in cheap hotels and dirty alleys. The sexbot saved a little part of the world, protecting human beings from themselves, while allowing them to safely take off the camouflage so many of them wore in public.

And then there was Amaya.

At the beginning, she was just a bot. He couldn't have slept with her if she'd been human—that would have been too close, too real. But Amaya wasn't human, just an android programmed to pleasure him in whatever way he wanted. To be a sympathetic ear and a warm shoulder and a soft voice. Her programming was NearC perfect—a Model 8000. She "remembered" him—his preferences, favorite positions, topics of conversation.

She knew that when he came in, he liked to sit in the lounge and have a good scotch before they went to her room.

She knew that he didn't like to rush, that he liked the smell of her hair, the sounds she made when he "pleasured" her, though he knew those responses were as much a part of her programming as all the rest of it.

She knew that he was now alone in the world, with nothing but his work to sustain him, and nothing to look forward to when he retired.

He could almost have loved her.

Marsh never owned a vehicle like these relics, but he was seven years old when the government forced his father to trade in his diesel truck for an EcoHauler, a day etched in his memory.

"Machines," his father said, sitting in the driver's seat of the new vehicle, "should make some noise. Especially engines."

"Destination, please, Mr. Hallowell," the computer system said from the dash console.

"And they sure as fuck shouldn't talk to you by name, either," he'd added. He was a big man, with shoulders and arms meant for manual labor and calloused hands that looked strange on the small steering wings. He was a man meant for manual labor, a skill that was rapidly becoming obsolete in an age of machines. His identity was slipping away, like a snake shedding its skin, and his pain with his vanishing place in the world was constant.

They went home in the silent vehicle, and that night Marsh lay awake in his bed listening to his father rant to his mother about the way nothing was the same anymore. Two days later, he'd tried to convert the EcoHauler to manual control at the wrong time and been killed when the engine stopped halfway across the magnetic tracks of a new train system that was being tested for outer-hub commuters. According to his mother, the interior recording from the vehicle revealed that the last thing his father ever heard was the EcoHauler's computer saying,

"Manual control not suggested at this time," and his father yelling back, "I don't give a fuck what you suggest."

Marsh's cruiser was silent, too. Over the years, machines of all kinds had gotten smaller and quieter and more efficient. Better at what they were supposed to do. He was sure that all these changes in machines, in the world around him, might explain the body in the vehicle storage compartment behind him.

There were many hundreds, maybe thousands of new machines, doing many hundreds or thousands of tasks, but underneath, all of them had the same job—to hide, minimize, or even eliminate the destructive nature of human beings. The machines were the masks that hid and protected humanity from itself.

And they were good at it. Marsh's father learned that lesson the hard way.

"Marsh," Amaya said, running a slender finger along his arm. "I want to ask you something."

Marsh looked at the beautiful woman—android—lying next to him. She was flawless: her skin unmarked, her eyes bright and direct, her scent like jasmine. She didn't often ask questions, and had never prefaced one before. That was new. Perhaps her NearC programming had been updated.

"What is it?"

"How do you know you're alive?" she asked. "Like real?"

He sat up in the small bed, surprised by the question. Surprised by her for the first time ever. "I'm not sure I understand you," he said.

"Your heart beats, your blood moves, you feel emotions. All these things I know are true. But they don't make you alive. Alive and real."

He thought about her question. The implications of it were disturbing, like shadows flitting in the corner of his eye. "I guess ... I'm alive because I think," he said, choosing his words carefully. "No other person is exactly like me."

"That is true," she said. Her finger was working its way across his abdomen. "That is ... individualized experience, correct?"

"What are you getting at, Amaya?"

"You know you are alive because you ... how you see or hear or even feel is subjective and individual to you. No one else is the same."

"That's right," he said. "And those feelings or experiences cannot be perfectly translated to anyone else. They aren't exact."

She was silent for a minute. "The word in my programming is 'ineffable,'" she said. "Something that cannot be communicated or understood without direct experience. Like the taste of a strawberry or the color of wine in a glass."

"Sure," he said. "I guess."

"I like strawberries," she said. "And the wine we had was burgundy in color."

Marsh sighed. This was a very disturbing change. Perhaps there was an error in her programming. "Okay, but you don't *need* to eat strawberries or drink wine. Or anything at all. You have a body that includes a processing unit for things like food or drink."

"Yes," she said. Then, "So do you."

"A stomach and intestines aren't the same thing!" he said, his voice sharpening. "You're a machine, an android. You're programmed to like these things."

She appeared taken aback by his harshness. Marsh wasn't the kind of man who normally raised his voice. Both of them were silent for several minutes, and he tried to control his breathing. Something was very wrong with her.

Then she said, "I don't like all of my clients." Her voice was so quiet he could barely make out the words. "Some of them are mean to me."

The rain gave up entirely and now it was pure sleet coming down in small stings Marsh could feel on his face. He stood at the back of the cruiser and opened the storage compartment. The body was inside, carefully wrapped in plastic sheeting.

Not that it mattered. This body wouldn't decay.

He lifted it out of the compartment. It was lighter than a human body, but still awkward. Marsh stepped backwards and slipped in the mud, going ass over teakettle and dropping her. *Dropping it!* he reminded himself. Not her. It.

He got to his knees and saw that the sheeting had fallen away. Amaya's eyes were open. Didn't they close when she was deactivated? Shouldn't they? He'd seen her blink, seen her with her eyes closed ... He reached forward, tentative, then placed his fingertips on them. He tried to push the eyelids down, but nothing happened.

Angry at himself for being surprised, he yanked the sheeting back into place, trying to ignore the sight of her being uncovered. "Not her," he said aloud. "She's ... an it. An android. She has to be."

He lifted the body again, and being cautious of his footing, carried it through the stinging sleet to the rusted-out car he'd seen. Marsh eased the body into the passenger area of the car, stretching it out along the backseat. Then he stepped back.

It wasn't much of a coffin.

"Marsh!" Amaya said. "I am surprised to see you again."

"Yes," he said, shaking the rain off his coat. "We didn't ... last night didn't end well. I wanted to make it up to you. How about an evening out?"

Her eyebrows lifted in surprise. "An out date?"

"Yes," Marsh replied. "An out date."

"You have never requested that service before," she noted. "I am ... not prepared."

He waved a hand at her. "Then go prepare. I need to speak to your boss about the details."

Smiling happily, Amaya headed in the direction of her room.

The owner of the Butterfly House of Sensual Delights was a tall, lean man named Dexter Vines. He ran several pleasure houses in the Entertainment District and was very wealthy. Marsh found him in the front office, and held up his badge to the android playing secretary.

"Mr. Vines?" she called.

Vines looked up and nodded, waving Marsh in. "Detective Marsh," he said. "What can I do for you? Amaya making you happy?"

"Very," he said, pitching his voice low. "That's what I wanted to talk to you about."

"Oh?"

"I want to purchase her," Marsh said. "You can get another."

Vines lifted an eyebrow. "So can you," he said. "No reason you can't order direct. Lots of people do. Why do you want this one?"

Marsh shrugged. "What's it matter to you, Vines? Just give me a figure."

Vines turned his attention to the surface of his desk and tapped away for a moment, then named a figure that was lower than Marsh had expected. "Why so cheap?"

He shrugged, his shoulders rising to near points beneath his suit coat. "They're getting ready to issue the Model 9000s," he said. "They aren't updating the 8000s anymore, so I'll be doing some turnover anyway." He grinned. "Besides, it's always good to be friendly with the local cops."

Marsh's mind raced. "So, Amaya hasn't had any updates lately?"

Vines shook his head. "Last one was ... three months ago, I think."

"What happens when the 9000s come out?" he asked.

Vines thought for a moment, going through the steps in his head. "Oh, about a week before they ship, the 8000s will upload all their experiential data into the primary network—that way, the 9000s will start out even more realistic. This makes sure that each new model has both state-of-the-art programming and experiential models to work from."

In other words, Marsh realized, everything that was ... wrong with Amaya would be passed along to all the other androids in the next generation. Like a computer virus. Convinced he was now right to take the next steps, he nodded. "I see. Direct wire okay?"

Vines tapped a few more keys on the desk. "Just put your thumbprint there on the corner scanner, Detective."

Marsh did so. He had plenty of money. Even for a cop, he was paid fairly well, and he didn't live a particularly lavish lifestyle. "I'll go tell her then," he said.

"You'll receive her complete files and operating instructions over your link. I'll transmit the confirmation to her, too," he said. "Thanks for your business."

"Yeah," Marsh said, getting ready to leave, but a thought crossed his mind and he paused. "Say ... one other question."

"Shoot," Vines said, his mind obviously on other things already.

"Have any of the other bots been acting up? Any troubles with any of them?"

Vines made a high-pitched wheezing sound that Marsh

realized was laughter. "Trouble? Nah. They're just bots, man. They just do what they're programmed to do."

Praying he was right, that Amaya was unique, Marsh said, "Yeah, that's what I've heard."

He stepped out of the office and made his way to Amaya's room. By the time he got there, she'd already received the wireless transmission from her boss, confirming the transfer of ownership.

"You really did it?" she asked. "You ... bought me?"

He nodded. "I did."

She stopped packing up her few belongings—most of which were different outfits. "Why?" she asked, not knowing that no other android would ever ask such a question.

"Because ... two nights a week isn't enough," he muttered.

Amaya stepped lightly toward him and pulled him into a warm embrace. "Thank you, Marsh," she said. "You're not like my other clients. You're kind to me."

He cleared his throat. "Yeah, well, you're welcome. Let's get out of here, okay?"

She stepped back and said, "Okay!" then finished her packing.

Marsh stood in the doorway, watching her flit from the small dresser to the small suitcase. She was an android, he reminded himself at least a dozen times. When she was finished, he picked up the suitcase for her. "I'll carry this out to my cruiser," he said. "Then we'll go to dinner."

"I'd like that," she said. "Maybe tonight I will try something different."

They were walking now, out to the vehicle. "Like what?" he asked, putting the case in the backseat.

"I was reading on the SocWeb that baked brie cheese with blueberries is delectable. I would like to try something that is delectable."

Marsh opened the door for her. "I know a place," he said, as he shut the door behind her.

In his mind, he saw the flow of information as her file arrived from Vines. All her history, from the time she was designed to the moment he sent the last transmission confirming her change of ownership. The client names were missing, of course, but it was far better that way. He didn't want to think of someone else with her. Someone else who might know what he did.

He got inside the cruiser and drove away from the brothel. From the passenger seat, Amaya chatted about what they might have for dinner or where they might go, based on her research on the SocWeb.

Marsh knew what had to be done.

🎭

Standing in the sleet, unable to walk away, Marsh stared at the rusted junk where Amaya's body was wrapped in cheap plastic. Where he meant to leave her forever. He was trying to convince himself that deactivating her wasn't the same as murder.

"She's an android," he said. "Not human."

Dinner had been quiet. He'd taken her to Rueben's Grill, a nice place far away from the City Centre, and ordered her something delectable. Even pressed, he couldn't recall what he'd ordered or how it had tasted. His experience was filtered through her responses to the meal. As she ate, she'd continued to make comments about what things tasted like, what they felt like on her tongue. Sitting there, he'd accessed the DataWeb with his link.

The word that came back after a few searches was "qualia." That is what she was demonstrating. She was having subjective, conscious experiences that were individual to her. Amaya was on her way to becoming, if not already, self-aware.

And Marsh couldn't allow that. He couldn't let her upload, and the instructions that came in her file noted that it was a requirement for all androids when new models were released. He couldn't let it happen.

If the androids became self-aware, they wouldn't be machines anymore. They couldn't be used anymore. Androids would be human. The Model 9000s—women, men, and children—would have no protection from the law and they'd all be self-aware. They'd know what was being done to them, the good and the bad—and the horrifying. How long until humans and androids were the same, and both were back on the streets, fucking for money and trying to survive? How long until they fought back? Society would be caught in a vise between humanity and machines.

How many children would be left alone?

The sleet had soaked through his coat, his shirt, and he shivered. If Amaya was unique, self-aware, was it murder? As a cop, Marsh knew the answer. He didn't need to access any part of the Web to know that it was. He'd killed her.

After dinner, he drove to a quiet park that he visited sometimes, and accessed her information files. She exclaimed happily about how pretty it was, and he'd agreed, then said, "Amaya, execute command Primary Omega One."

Startled, she turned to him, then said, "Executing."

And it was a simple as that. She shut down.

He found the tiny place beneath her hair, on the back of her neck, where the access port to her programming chip was located. Marsh removed it, considering the small device in his fingers. It was so small that he could barely grip it.

His decision was made. He'd made it earlier, but still he hesitated. What he was doing wasn't fair, but still ... it would save thousands, perhaps millions. Marsh crushed the chip between his fingers, breaking it until it was nothing more than tiny shards of filaments. As simple as that, Amaya was gone.

Killing her was as easy as killing a human, easier, and what did that mean?

He wanted to leave now. Leave the junk yard and her body. He wanted to go home to his tiny apartment and try to forget.

And as he started to turn away, to run away, one last thought occurred to him.

He was no better than the men who raped and killed and abused women like his mother. They were the same. One and the same. He'd murdered what he feared and maybe even despised. She was better than him, illuminated like a Japanese lantern with new ideas and information. His reasons didn't matter. In the end, all the reasons came back to the same place —when human expectations weren't met, when what he wanted to see in his world changed, he couldn't accept it. Perhaps he was more like his father than he'd known.

In one sense, he'd killed his mother. He'd loved her, and he knew that he loved Amaya. Human or machine, it made no difference in this age of technology that had erased all the differences.

Marsh sighed heavily, exhausted by the choices he'd made. For a time, at least, the bots would remain bots, blissfully unaware of themselves. It was a blessing. Still, if it had happened once, it would happen again. And he couldn't do it, couldn't bring himself to warn the world. He no longer had the heart for such decisions. All the masks would come off, and the monsters beneath—new and old, man and machine—would emerge.

He climbed back into his cruiser and drove it into an empty space near the car where Amaya waited.

The sleet intensified, but it didn't matter. He shut down the vehicle. Then he moved back to her, his steps slowing, like a clock spring winding down. More than anything, Marsh wanted to rest. He wanted to find some peace in this, and there was only one ... person who'd given that to him in years.

He climbed into the back seat of the car, and gently removed the plastic from around her body. He tossed it outside, then lay down next to her, pulling her arms around him. The sleet made odd pinging sounds on the metal of the car, and after a few minutes, he realized that it sounded like music. Like wind chimes.

Marsh was a good cop, and like any good cop, he knew the penalty for murder.

And in her arms, more aware of the world unraveling around him than he'd ever been, he executed it perfectly.

🎭

Russell Davis has written and sold numerous novels and short stories in virtually every genre of fiction, under at least a half dozen pseudonyms. His writing has encompassed media tie-in work in the Transformers universe to action adventure in The Executioner series to original novels. He's published short fiction in anthology titles like *Under Cover of Darkness*, *Law of the Gun*, and *In the Shadow of Evil*. In addition to his work as a writer, he has worked as an editor and book packager, and created original anthology titles ranging from westerns like *Lost Trails* to fantasy like *Courts of the Fey*.

He was the president of the Science Fiction and Fantasy Writers of America (SFWA) from 2008–2010, and has been a member of numerous other writing organization including the Western Writers of America (WWA), Mystery Writers of America (MWA), and the Romance Writers of America (RWA).

His most recent releases are a re-issue of the four book Jenna Solitaire series (WordFire Press), and he's currently working on a new collection, *Written in the Scars on Our Hearts*, and a middle grade novel with Fran Wilde.

SHOT IN THE DARK

BRENNEN HANKINS

A re you going to ask him? The sudden, random question startled me enough that I stopped rifling through the filing cabinet. I took the flashlight out of my teeth.

"Ask who what?" I muttered, feigning nonchalance as I continued thumbing my way through folders.

You know what, replied the voice in my head. *You've only been thinking about it all day. Are you going to ask Tom out, or just mince words with me?*

"I find the fact that you can read my thoughts disturbing," I replied. "Not now, Meridia. I'm trying to do my job here and you're distracting me."

As I turned back to the filing cabinet, my shadow moved of its own accord, spreading out to the wall and climbing it, until the slim figure of a woman, mirroring the shape of my body, appeared on the surface. A pair of glowing purple eyes formed on the shadow's face and stared down at me with disdain.

"Well, you're annoying the darkness out of *me*," my shadow said, aloud this time. "I've spent the last two hours hanging out in your subconscious, and all I've been hearing in there is 'Tom,

Tom, Tom!' It's like watching that thing you call 'television,' only you don't have that little device that changes whatever you're currently watching."

"You mean a *remote*, Meridia," I said, turning from my work to face the shadow creature, "and that should be a good reason to stay out of my subconscious. For the record, *I* don't even like what's in there."

"Well, what else am I going to do?" Meridia whined. "You won't let me come out when you're not at home, you only use my abilities when it suits *your* needs, and you don't even have the decency to talk to me while I'm stuck in your head. I have to make do with watching your thoughts."

"You could take up meditation." I said, "Or some other activity. The Quiet Game would be a good one."

"Ha-ha. Funny. Your memories already told me what that is," Meridia groused. "Those aren't exactly prime entertainment, either. Better than your obsession with Tom, though. A lot more variety to pick from."

I felt a sudden heat enter my voice. "Stay out of my memories!" I shouted—then I clasped my gloved hands over my mouth in sudden horror.

"Who's there?" came a voice from the hallway beyond.

Crap.

Meridia and I exchanged a frantic glance as a light flicked on and a security guard flung the door open ....

On a completely empty room.

He scanned the room with narrowed eyes, but found absolutely nothing amiss. He did a quick walkaround of the records office, and, still seeing nothing, left in confusion. "Swear I'm hearing things ...." he said, turning off the lights. He locked the doorknob and quietly closed the door.

As soon as darkness and silence settled over the room again, I emerged from my hiding place in the shadow of the filing cabinet I had been raiding. My skin had taken on the mercurial texture of Meridia's true form and was dark as anthracite coal, shining with a slight purplish tint where the light caught it. My hair looked much the same, only more tinted. I breathed a sigh of relief, as I tried to climb out of The Void on my elbows.

"Hey, give me a hand here," I breathed out, "I can't lift my leg."

I couldn't *see* Meridia roll her eyes, but somehow instinctively felt her reaction. As always when this happened, the empathic sensation felt like a weird phantom tingling.

Well, whose fault was that? Meridia said, speaking inside my head again. *You're the one who decided not to bring your cane; not to mention nearly getting us caught.*

She may have been right, but she's still a jerk. *Just help me up*, I replied silently.

Suddenly, several strands of my hair shot forward, splitting into different tendrils. They caught the leg of a desk that was placed halfway between the filing cabinet and the door, and began pulling. I used the momentum to roll on the bad side of my body up out of the pool of shadow and onto the carpet. I ended up on my back, panting lightly from the effort.

"Can we table this discussion until we're out of here?" I whispered. "If we get caught and Tom finds out, I don't think he's going to be in a good mood."

Tell you what, Meridia replied, *Why don't you take a breather, and let me drive for a bit? I can find what you need.*

"You don't even know what I'm looking for," I wheezed. I'd foregone my pain meds on the grounds that I was going to need a clear head for this, but I was beginning to regret that decision.

Along with the decision to not bring the damn cane. It was a genuine blackthorn cane, a gift from my grandfather. I didn't want it making noise if I had to walk, but right now, the pins and screws in my left leg, souvenirs of the incident that had earned me a Purple Heart and Meridia's companionship, were singing much louder than any noise the cane would've made.

Hello, Meridia said, *I can see your thoughts, remember? You're looking for manifest records, right?* More hair tendrils reached for the filing cabinet. *Shouldn't be too hard to find.*

I forced myself to control my breathing. "Can you even read?"

I was treated to the sensation of scoffing as she replied. *If you can use my powers, I can use yours, puny human.*

"One of these days you, me, and a really bright flashlight are going to have a conversation you're not going to like," I said, gritting my teeth. "Fine. Be quick about it."

🎭

A half-hour later I emerged, still wearing Meridia's form, from the shadow of a utility pole about half a block from the office of the shipping company I just raided, several folders in hand. Once I was clear of the shadows, the ethereal skin dissolved from mine and resumed its normal appearance: just a few shades too dark to be called pale.

"Took you long enough," I muttered, lighting a cigarillo and limping over to where my Jeep was parked. "You couldn't get me any closer?"

Do you want *to end up at the peak of a mountain again?* Meridia asked.

I grimaced. Traveling between shadows is more difficult than you'd think. Consider that any given room in a building could have anywhere between a dozen and three dozen shadows spread across it at any given time. Now, consider how many shadows are in the whole building. The neighborhood ... the whole city.

A city, especially a city that experiences as much darkness

this time of year as Anchorage does, has hundreds of *millions* of shadows.

When I cross through one, I enter what Meridia refers to as The Void; a large empty space that is only broken up between other points of light—other shadows, which I can pass back through to re-enter our world.

The trick to effectively shadow-hopping is to pick the right shadow to come out of. It's like finding the needle in a haystack, only the farther you're try to go from your starting point, the bigger the haystack gets.

My last attempt to shadow-hop to work and skip the morning commute had ended with me on top of Flattop Mountain, on the southeast corner of town. I ultimately had to take a day off work to limp a mile and a half down from the summit to the Chugach State Park trailhead, and call an Uber home.

"No," I said, shuddering as the memory came back to me., I took a deep puff of the Swisher Sweet, hoping the burning cherry smell would calm me.

Cheer up, the shadow being said. *Just think, after you make copies of all these records, we get to come back and return them before somebody figures out they're missing!*

I sighed, exhaling smoke. "Joy."

So, now that we're out of immediate danger ... you asking Tom out or what?

"I'm not kidding about that bright flashlight. I have it in the car. A hundred thousand lumens."

"So ... a contact of mine got me a copy of last month's booking records," I said, over a cup of coffee. I didn't sleep a wink last night, and the only thing keeping me going was the tar-like sludge being served inside the breakroom of Tom Vincent's precinct, and the excitement of what I was telling Tom. "The records show that the dealership you're checking out, Alaskan Discount 4x4, LLC, has been booking several dozen late model trucks and SUVs to ride on Trident Shipping's weekly barge up from the Port of Tacoma. What's interesting is, several of the vehicles appear to have been double-booked. Look at all the duplicate models that are on here." I passed a folder across the table.

Tom took it and began flipping through. The brim of his trooper hat obscured his eyes as he looked down at the contents. "Two of each model, like an automotive Noah's Ark." He grunted. "Looks like they're really bad about it. Half of these shipments have been canceled by the customer." He set the file down, rubbing his mustache with his thumb ponderingly. "Strange, but no evidence that shows they're responsible for selling stolen cars from Washington, Rhiannon."

Alaska State Trooper Tom Vincent was an old friend I'd started working with on cases in the year since I'd become a licensed private investigator. He was one of the few people I trusted to have my back. When a few cars with mismatched vehicle identification numbers, some of which were reported as stolen out of state, started appearing in Anchorage and he'd hit nothing but dead ends chasing leads, he'd asked to hire me on as a consultant.

And I made sure to deliver.

"Here's where it gets interesting," I said. "I've *done* business with Trident before." I pulled a folded, faded shipping receipt out of my coat pocket and laid it on the table. "This is my receipt for when I shipped my Jeep back up here when I got out of the Air Force. Here's the VIN of my car," I said, circling it with a pen, then moving to another spot and circling that, too. "And here's my booking number. What do you see?"

Tom peered owlishly through his glasses, comparing the two notations. "The last five digits of the booking number are the last five of your VIN."

"Exactly," I said, feeling a wolfish smile coming on. "Now check the booking numbers against your list of stolen cars."

Tom opened a folder of his own and set it next to mine, scanning both. "Several of these booking numbers match the VINs on the hot sheet. Son of a bitch! Why hasn't Tacoma PD picked up on this?"

"They have. I called down there this morning. They said that a car dealer in Anchorage called to report several vehicles they had recently purchased, sight unseen, as stolen."

"Which is what an honest car dealer would do. That still doesn't explain how those same cars are making it up here."

I sipped the coffee and tried not to grimace. It really was terrible, but Tom had been willing to share and complaining about it would've been rude. "Don't worry, it gets better. Flip to the back of that folder I gave you."

He flipped to the back of the folder and looked at me with eyebrows raised. "A CARFAX report?"

"My source claims somebody at Trident screwed up and slipped an actual shipping receipt in with the manifest records. On a hunch, I ran the VIN." I leaned over and pointed at a spot I had circled. "The vehicle has a salvage title."

"I don't understand," Tom said.

I leaned back in my chair unable to keep the smirk off my face any longer. "Every single one of the stolen cars that Tacoma PD said they recovered—turned out to be totaled."

Tom's eyes widened in comprehension. "They're swapping the VINs right under our noses!"

I smiled proudly, "I believe they might have a lot more than just the five vehicles you found. They might have gotten away with it, too, if whoever's swapping the numbers didn't get lazy and forget to do both the windshield *and* the door tags. I guarantee if you look at any one of those trucks you recovered, the VIN that isn't hot is from a salvage title from down south."

"Is Trident in on it, too? And what about the cars that they didn't screw up on?" Tom asked.

"It's possible that somebody at the Port of Tacoma is doing the swapping, but I have no proof of that," I said. "As far as finding the other cars, my brother Alex works at the Ford dealership up in Wasilla. According to him, the original VIN of each car may be stored electronically in the car's computer. Car thieves rarely change them because they either don't know to or the PCM is too expensive to replace. There's a little port under the dashboard, I forget what it's called—"

"OBD II port?"

"That's the one," I said. "If you plug a scanner into that, the original VIN should pop up."

"I'll be damned," Tom said, leaning back in his chair. "This should be enough for a search warrant."

"Congratulations, Trooper Vincent!" I said in an announcer style voice, "You just broke up an interstate car theft and smuggling ring. Technically international, since the barge travels through Canadian waters to get here," I grinned. "What will you do now? And don't say you're going to Disneyworld ...."

"After we bust these guys, I'm gonna go celebrate over drinks," Tom said as we both stood up. Tall as I was, Tom still overtopped me by a good four inches, and I'm six foot. The man was a moose. He extended a long arm over the desk to me, "Thank you."

I reached to shake his hand when I suddenly heard my voice. My mouth moved and sound was coming out, but it was not me speaking. "Buy me a round at that celebration, and we'll call it even."

Both Tom and I paused at that. My heart dropped out the bottom of my chest and through the floor.

"Well, um, if you're so inclined ..." I said, taking control of my vocal cords and trying desperately to walk back what that *idiot* Meridia had blurted out.

"Why, Rhiannon Douglas," Tom said, are you asking me out on a *date?*"

"Well, ah ..." I felt myself flushing red. I sighed. "Sorry," I said, "that just kind of slipped out. I don't know what I was thinking."

Tom smiled. "That's too bad ... 'cause I was thinking of taking you up on it." He winked at me. "That is, if you're so inclined?"

I wasn't sure if I was embarrassed, relieved, overjoyed, or a combination thereof. "Seven o'clock at Moose's Tooth work?"

"It more than works," Tom replied. "I can be there by seven."

I let out a nervous laugh as I held my cane in a death grip. "A true gentleman."

"No, a true gentleman would offer to walk you to your car," Tom said.

"Um, sure," I replied, still red as a beet. In my head, I screamed at Meridia, who was trying not to laugh. "*I can't believe you did that!*"

It worked, didn't it? Besides, it's not like you were going to ask him.

Tom walked with me the short distance to the door and held it open. As we walked to my car, he asked, "So, would your source be willing to give an official statement?"

"Um ... probably not," I said, shaking off the embarrassment. "I haven't even met them, nor do I know their identity."

"Ah," Tom said, frowning. "That's too bad. I'm sure Crimestoppers would be willing to give them a reward for their tip."

"I'll leave them a note in the mailbox and see if they bite," I said, climbing into my Jeep and pulling a Swisher Sweet out of the glove box. I put it on my lips, letting it hang there as I fished for a lighter. "I make no promises, though."

"Well, I appreciate their help, all the same," Tom said as I lit my cigarillo. "Please, pass that along."

"Will do," I said, exhaling smoke away from Tom. "I'll see you tonight?"

"I'll be there with bells on," Tom said, smiling.

I gave him a warmer smile. Tom waved as I backed out of the parking lot. I waved back as I put my Jeep in gear and drove away.

As I turned onto Tudor Road, I said aloud, "He may have said yes, but I'm still really upset with you."

Meridia laughed inside my head.

"Yeah, laugh it up," I said. "Don't forget, we still have to return the original copies of those manifests tonight."

Would you like me to do that for you, too? Or are you going to handle it?

"Just because it's daytime, doesn't mean that I can't break out that flashlight."

🎭

I left my boss, Mr. Boyd, a message that I was heading home to take a nap after a night of surveillance, went home, and slept for a few hours. Once I woke up, I checked my messages. There was one from Tom. Apparently, a search warrant had been issued within a matter of hours, and the raid on Alaska Discount 4x4 had occurred early that afternoon. Tom had followed my tip about checking the PCMs on the cars, and it paid off: Of the 30 vehicles they had on their lot, 23 of them had salvage titles. The owner, Shane Thompson, had been arrested, and the Alaska Bureau of Investigation had announced that a formal investigation into the smuggling ring was taking place, in partnership with Washington State Patrol and the FBI. Mr. Boyd had left a nice voicemail congratulating me on a job well done.

With that bit of cheer, I left my apartment and drove back to the Port of Anchorage, to finish the job by returning the manifests I'd stolen from Trident Shipping.

"Is it clear?" I asked, hiding in the shadow of the filing cabinet I had used the night before, wearing Meridia's form.

I don't see anyone present, Meridia said. *Let's go. You still got your date tonight.*

"Relax," I said, pulling myself up carefully. I'd remembered to bring the cane and take my pain meds this time. "Date's not for another three hours. This will take less than five minutes."

I opened the filing cabinet and had just put the file back in, when my skin prickled and I felt a tickle inside my ear.

Do you hear that? Meridia asked.

As uncomfortable as the sensation in my ear was, I focused on it—trying to pick up on what Meridia was hearing. I heard the sound almost immediately. It was a muffled banging, like somebody beating a rhythm on sheet metal with a hammer.

Just like a sound I grew to be familiar with in my Security Forces days ....

"Those are gunshots!" I said, eyes widening.

As I tried to focus on what direction they were coming from, my skin prickled again, right as the door rattled.

I dove for the safety of the filing cabinet shadow, plunging through it and back to The Void on the other side as two men ran into the records office and slammed the door shut, locking it.

"Jesus!" said a balding man, wearing slacks and a button up shirt. His tie had ended up hanging off his shoulder, and his eyes were wild and panicked. "How did they figure it out?"

"That bastard Shane must've talked. Or one of his people did," said a tall man in a hard hat and work shirt with a safety vest over it. "They were the only ones who knew, and they all got picked up earlier today."

"What? How come you didn't tell me, Todd? And why did your guys shoot as soon as the Troopers pulled up?"

"Because they don't want to go to jail, Arne!" said Todd. "And neither do I!"

"Yeah, like shooting the police is going to keep you from getting arrested!" Arne shouted.

"Correction: *they* shot at the police. *I* didn't," said Todd. "If they want to go out that way, that's their business. Me, I'm going out the back window, heading to where my bush plane is parked, and flying the hell out of here. Up to you if you're coming, Arne, but you better decide quick."

"Hey ..." Arne started to reply, but something caught his attention. " Where'd that come from?"

Damn it! I knew I was forgetting something.

"Somebody's in here," Todd said, pulling a pistol out of his waistband.

Now a sane person would've just left the cane and fled the scene. But I'm not exactly sane and my cane presented a problem. Blackthorn canes are pretty distinctive, and aren't very common in the United States, much less Alaska. The only reason I ended up with one is because Grandpa Dowd grew up in Ireland, and he decided that if his granddaughter was going to have to use a cane to walk, it might as well be stylish.

And stylish that cane was, with its jet-black, thorned shaft and polished wood handle. So stylish, in fact, that if I left it behind, the cops were going to know very quickly that I was here and would probably want to ask me why. I wouldn't be surprised if Tom recognized it on sight.

So, against my better judgement, I stepped through the shadows back into the office, wearing Meridia's form.

"Darn, you caught me," I said, picking up my cane.

"Jesus Christ!" Arne said, backing up against the door.

"Or did I catch you?" I asked thoughtfully, leaning on it and pretending to be lost in thought. "Kind of a gray area, really."

Not the time, Rhiannon, Meridia chided.

There is always *time for banter, my dear Watson,* I said. *Watch and learn.* As I thought that, Todd raised his gun in horror, aiming it at me.

I dropped back into the shadow I had emerged from just as the gun barked. Three shots rang out— punching holes in the drywall behind where I had been standing. The light fixtures in the drop ceiling cast a shadow underneath an emergency light mounted on the wall directly above Todd, just big enough to fit my upper body through. I came through it and, using my cane, smacked his hand, making him drop the gun. I let my hair fly down, grabbing his hard hat and using it and my cane to pummel him senseless.

"Well, that's one," I said. "Where's Arne?"

Running down the hall with the gun you failed to secure, Meridia said matter-of-factly. *You might want to catch him before he escapes.*

"Damn it!" I said, pulling myself back into The Void and looking through shadows in the hallway. Sure enough, the idiot was scrambling down the hall, pointing Todd's pistol wildly behind him.

He was about to reach a junction in the hallway when a man in a trooper's uniform pointing a gun yelled, "Drop the weapon!"

Tom!

Arne must've been too focused on running from me to consider that the cops were still outside. As soon as Tom shouted at him, he yelped, turned around, and swung the pistol towards Tom.

I didn't even think. I exploded out of the closest shadow to Tom, hitting him like a linebacker. We fell to the ground as Arne fired three erratic shots at where Tom had been, then dropped the gun and ran past us to the door.

Tom and I shared a very surprised glance. I don't think he quite believed what he was seeing.

On the bright side, I don't think he recognized me, either.

"You okay?" I asked.

"Yeah," he said, bewildered. He looked at the door. "I gotta go get him."

I nodded. "Good luck."

As Tom got up, I rolled into a shadow on the wall and disappeared, making my way back to my car as quickly as I could.

🎭

I'd been sitting in the far corner booth at Moose's Tooth Pub & Pizzeria, nursing one of their craft brews, when Tom finally showed up wearing jeans, a cowboy hat, and an old work jacket. He was more than a half-hour late, but at least he'd had the decency to message me and let me know.

"Hey. Sorry I'm late," he said, pulling up a chair across the table from me. "I had to finish up the reports before I could leave. The dealership employees claimed there were people at Trident who were in on it. Boss wanted to arrest them too, before they could flee the state, so APD went with us to make it happen."

"No worries," I said as the waitress brought him his own pitcher and mug. "How'd it go?"

"It was ... interesting," Tom said, frowning. "We arrested six people there. Four of them began shooting at us the second we arrived. APD handled those guys, but the final two ..." Tom paused.

"Yes?" I asked, feigning surprise.

"The final two, the dock supervisor and the general accountant, tried to escape through the office during the confusion. I went in through a back door to find them and surprised the accountant. He pulled a gun on me and fired." He leaned forward and continued speaking, in a whisper. "Something ... saved me."

I leaned forward, a careful expression of shock on my face. "What was it?"

"Dunno," he said. "It was like some crazy ghost. Came out of a dark corner in front of me and knocked me out of the line of fire right as the gun went off. The accountant ran outside and I chased him out to the end of the dock. When I arrested him, he kept screaming over and over: 'Don't let that thing get me! Don't let that thing get me!' But it gets weirder ...."

I took a long sip to hide the smile on my face. "How so?"

"The dock supervisor was found in the records office, beaten damn near unconscious. Beaten with his own hard hat and some other blunt implement. Nobody knows who did it. And that's not even the strangest thing!"

"Well, come on, tell me!" I said, on the edge of my seat. I deserved an Oscar for this performance.

Tom's expression hardened. "The shadow ghost? That was you."

"What?" I said, losing my smile. "Don't be silly."

"For Christ's sake, the ghost smelled exactly like those cheap little cigarillos you smoke, Annie," Tom said, exasperated. "And the dock supervisor had these weird puncture wounds on him that look like he'd been beaten with a bat with nails in it." He pointed to my cane. "Or a long stick of wood with little knobs on it." He leaned back in his chair. "I bet if I took your cane to the state forensics lab, they'd confirm the wounds were caused by it. I'd rather not do that, though. I'd much rather you come clean and tell me what the hell you were doing there."

"Are you asking as a cop?" I said, my voice tightening.

"No, Rhiannon," Tom said. "I'm asking as a friend."

Damn it. He had me dead to rights. And it was *Tom*. He was a genuinely good guy. He never looked down on me for being a woman and never coddled me for my disability. He was funny, kind, and had covered my back dozens of times. There was no reason not to tell him.

And yet ... I hesitated.

I suddenly felt myself speaking again. "Do you remember when I got caught in that bombing in Afghanistan?"

Meridia, what are you doing? I was apoplectic.

Saving the day ... as usual.

Tom nodded. "Yeah. That's how your leg got messed up."

Meridia continued, in my voice. "When I woke up in the hospital, I found out I had been somehow bonded to a creature made of living shadow. Her name's Meridia."

"How'd that happen?" Tom asked, listening intently.

"I'm still trying to figure that part out," she said. "What I do know is, she's living in my head, and I can use her abilities to manipulate shadows."

"How do I know you're not lying?"

"You want proof?" Meridia said. "Set your beer glass down in the shadow of your chair."

Tom gave me a quizzical look, then set the glass down.

I looked around, to make sure nobody was watching. Then Meridia quickly shifted to show her true form. A hair tendril snatched Tom's glass, pulled it into The Void through the shadow it was sitting in, and back out through the shadow under my chair. Meridia held it up for him to see, then set it on the table as she shifted back to my normal appearance. "Is that going to be a deal breaker?"

Tom frowned. "And the informant?"

"Doesn't exist," Meridia said. "I dug through their records myself."

"Hmmmm."

An awkward silence reigned over the table.

"Soooooo, what now?" I asked hesitantly, taking over again.

Tom looked at me with half-lidded eyes, and rubbed his

mustache. "Well, in the official report, your 'source' is going to remain confidential. I wasn't knocked during tonight's raid; I tripped and fell, in a very lucky fashion. And the person who beat up Mr. Todd Martin has not been determined and never will be."

"And ... us?"

Tom gave me a wolfish grin. "We're going to get you another snooty beer, you're going to fill me in on what you haven't told me about what happened over there, and then we're going to go somewhere else so you can show me more of what this ... thing ... this Meridia ... can do. Deal?"

Inside my head, Meridia asked, *Do you need me to do this part for you, too?*

No, I told her, *I think I'm good.*

I grinned back at Tom. "Deal."

Brennen Hankins has worn a variety of hats: ranch hand, commercial fisherman, cannery worker, weather balloon technician, electrician, Airman, husband, tabletop gamer, and now, writer. Growing up between Oregon and Alaska, he bounced between the two before finally enlisting and getting sent God-knows-where. When he's not traveling, wrenching on his trucks, taking photos of the Northern Lights, or hunting, he can be found either writing or cooking up new renovation projects for his house. Along with his long-suffering wife Emma, he currently lives in central Montana with his brother and a mischievous Siberian Husky for company. Follow his mad ramblings, published works, and aurora borealis photos at oldhatnation.com.

THE HIBAKUSHA

MICHAEL SCOTT BRICKER

The demon didn't force Noriko to die again, but he brought memories of the bomb beneath his mask. It was Shikami this time, the malevolent spirit who fed upon her sorrow. The holes in his wooden mask glowed with the light of the Hiroshima blast, lips opened wide like a growling beast, teeth stained with the ashes of those who had died in the name of war. With him came the morning, two years before, when her children were vaporized as they played. Noriko suffered the burning again as the horror disfigured her flesh, but it was unlike that day in 1945.

Shikami brushed the scars upon her cheeks with his long fingernails, and he whispered to her with the voices of the dead. Noriko's vision went, and she felt herself being pulled into the air, and the roar of the blast and the ringing in her ears faded as the wind released her. She heard chanting, wailing, the beating of drums. Her body wasn't burning before she woke up, this time, and she was grateful that Shikami was not without mercy.

"Hello? *Kon'nichiwa.* Are you okay?" The soldier was bending over her.

Noriko was flat on her back. Her eyes opened, and she saw the soldier. She wondered if he was real or a delusion. The red dusk glowed against the bones of the Hiroshima Prefectural Industrial Promotion Hall. She must have passed out. "You are an American," she said.

"You speak English. I wasn't expecting that." The soldier looked into her eyes.

She found that she could still smile. The soldier looked young. His face was angular and kind. "Do you think that all Japanese speak only our own language? I speak four languages."

"I'm sorry," he said. "I meant no insult."

"Then I will take no insult." She tried to get up.

The soldier helped her stand.

"I am strong enough. The fall did not damage me much." She looked up at him. He was very tall, and his uniform hung loosely on his thin frame. "You should eat more."

"Pardon me?"

"I am sorry," she said. "For a Japanese person, I am not as reserved as I should be."

"I'm not offended. My mother used to tell me to eat more too."

"Then she is a good mother." Noriko removed the soldier's hand from under her arm. She could stand on her own. "How long has it been since you last saw her?"

"My mother? Two years, I think."

"That is too long."

"The occupation will be over, eventually. Then everything will get back to normal."

"Nothing will ever be normal again." Noriko limped toward the Promotion Hall. Her leg had bothered her ever since the atomic bomb burned off her kimono. One of her eyebrows had never grown back.

The soldier followed her.

Noriko permitted him to accompany her. "What is your name?"

"Sergeant Hardesty."

"No, what is your name?" Noriko stressed that question this time, speaking her words slowly.

"My name is Max. It's short for Maximilian, though I don't like that name very much."

"You should carry your name with honor, Max. I am Noriko."

"I'm happy to meet you, Noriko." Max stood beside her. They shared a prolonged silence as they stared at the ruins.

"This is where the bomb exploded. It is what you call Ground Zero," Noriko said. "Tell me, do you find this building beautiful?"

Max struggled with his words. "No, of course not. I'm not a terrible person."

"No, I am certain that you are not. But there is beauty in everything." She paused. "Look at how the setting sun appears to be trapped within the twisted metal of the dome. It is as if a spirit watches the city from above. It wants this building to stand a century from now. It wants people to remember. It wants to make certain that nothing like this ever happens again." Noriko turned and looked at him. "You are staring at my face. Perhaps you have noticed the scars."

Max looked away. "I'm sorry."

"There is no need to apologize. I am used to being stared at. I am one of the hibakusha."

Max paused. "I don't know that word."

"The Japanese do not speak of it, but I am not your average Japanese person. The bomb took my humility. It took my humanity as well."

"Then you shouldn't talk about it." Max moved closer. A dry wind blew through the remains of the city. Burnt scraps of clothing still drifted about. His uniform shirt ruffled, as did her kimono.

They said nothing for a time, and Noriko broke the silence. "The hibakusha are the survivors of the atomic bomb. We are shamed. We are shunned. We are of two worlds, of the living and the dead, and neither will tolerate us."

Max looked beyond the ruins, where new structures had already begun to sprout. "Do you think that they will ever rebuild all this?"

"Much has already been accomplished," Noriko said. "The Japanese people thrive in times of adversity. We will grow stronger and happier, yet the past will always be with us, and those who have lived and died during this time will be honored by those of a more peaceful future." Noriko began to walk away, then stumbled.

Max caught her. "You need help. Do you have a family? Friends?"

"I need to rest," she said. "It has been, as you Americans say, a long day."

"Do you have a house? May I take you somewhere?"

"I stay in a shelter with others like me," Noriko said. "It is not far from here."

"My jeep is nearby. I will take you there."

"I will agree to this. Thank you, young man."

Noriko dreamed of Lady Deigan again. They floated above Hiroshima. Deigan was beneath her, staring up at her from behind her mask, the placid face of an elder, with open lips that portrayed only the expression reflected by Noriko's emotions. With a blue-white flash, it happened again. Their bodies spun in a radioactive wind, and below, Hiroshima perished. Noriko listened for the screams of her children, but there were no screams to be heard. They had no time to scream.

The soil below went black with ashes, and Deigan took Noriko's hands as she pulled her down, to where the trees became skeletons and the life-giving water boiled away.

Noriko awoke to hear arguing. She was in bed, where she had been after Max had brought her home. Kiko, one of her shelter mates, approached her bed and told her that someone was waiting for her at the door. An American. She got out of bed. Her leg bothered her more than usual.

Max was waiting for her. "I came to check on you," he said. "That's one of my duties. To observe. To make sure that the people here are getting along okay." He paused. "I enjoyed our conversation yesterday. I wanted to come."

Noriko could hear the others. They were arguing again. "Let us go outside," she said.

They stepped into the garden. "Is something wrong in there?" Max asked.

"Some of my housemates get agitated when there is an American around. Do not, as you say, take it personally. We are all hibakusha here. There is much pain."

Max bent down and examined some of the leaves in the vegetable garden. "I grew up on a farm, but I don't think that I've ever seen plants that were this green and healthy."

"We keep extending the limits of the vegetable garden. The plants want more land. They are not happy if they are confined. It has something to do with the soil." Noriko knelt beside him and looked into his eyes. Being in that position caused her pain, but she thought it important. "The soil is well-fertilized. It is full of ashes. And occasionally, one of the girls will dig up something more. A finger. An ear. Parts."

Max stood, and then he helped her up. "May I ask you about how it happened?" He spoke slowly, carefully. "I'm sorry. I shouldn't have said that."

Noriko looked at the ground. "I will tell you. It was a typical morning in most ways, full of tension. The war had turned us into a quieter people. There was much fear. Fear that we were losing. Fear that the Americans would invade. Fear of what would come after. And then the sky lit up. I do not remember what happened next. I believe that I passed out, but when I woke up, there were bodies. And those who could walk ... Flesh hanging, limbs blown off, their intestines pouring out of them. The pain that I felt cannot be described. I watched others die. And my children ..." She stopped and started to cry.

Max gently placed his hand upon her shoulder. "I'm sorry."

Noriko regained her composure. "My children were away at school. The building was obliterated. Vaporized. Nobody survived. My husband was in the army, far away. I believe that he is still an army man, but I do not know for sure. He never came back to me. He knows that I am hibakusha. He is ashamed."

"I don't know what to say." Max shook his head. "We did things. I did things."

"And the Japanese Government did things. And the Germans and the rest of them. It is complicated." Noriko looked into the distance. "We are not our leaders, are we? We are good people. Do not forget that."

Max forced a smile. "What did you do during the war?"

"I was valued for my English language skills, so I wrote propaganda. I am an artist as well. I had much practice drawing your Roosevelt. He had very big teeth. I did not portray the Americans very kindly." His hand was still on her shoulder. She placed her hand over his. "What about you, Max? What did you do during the war? Perhaps you were too young to fight, then. You are an innocent."

Max pulled away. His expression changed. "I am not as young as you think I am. I was involved. I did things. *I did things.*" He stressed those words.

"I apologize," Noriko said. "You do not wish to speak of this. I can hear it in your voice." She paused. "Are you hungry?"

"Yes, actually I am."

"I would cook for you, but the others would never permit you to come into the shelter. Their pride has been damaged. So I will show you our shopping district. We can find food there. It is not what it was before the bomb, but we try."

🎭

Noriko didn't stand too close to Max as they walked through the shopping district. She didn't want others to think that she was a prisoner. "Many refuse to come here. They believe that the food and water are tainted. But there are others, like me. This is our home. Nothing can drive us out, even the bomb."

"I haven't been here before. I can see that there has been a lot of progress." Much of the area had been cleared of rubble, and new structures were popping up. The air carried smoke and food smells.

"There were many shops here before the bomb came," Noriko said. "They lined both sides of this road, very far, and there were dozens of beautifully carved wooden portals with lanterns above. The shopkeepers would hang their signs all along here, and at night, when the lanterns were lit, it looked like the sky was filled with a thousand moons. It was always busy, people walking, riding their bicycles, buying and selling. Laughing. So much happiness. Now there is only what you see. Hastily-built structures, ugly, utilitarian, I think that is the word for it. This is an ancient country, Max. The houses of our ancestors remain a part of them, so when you visit an old house, you visit the ghosts of those who had lived there centuries ago. But the bomb wiped those buildings away, and it took our ancestors with it. It took our history. You help us rebuild, but your buildings are very western. We will thank you for your efforts, but when you leave, we will tear it all down and build in a way that honors us."

They stopped at a shop of a man who sold fish. The fish were laid across a rough wooden table along the side of the road. The merchant's shop was open at the front and had no doors. It was little more than sheets of tin roofing material that had been sloppily joined together. He looked tired. His eyes were sunken, few teeth remained. His clothing probably belonged to someone else. When Noriko approached, he looked briefly at her, and then he turned his head away. Max approached next. The man bowed his head and kept it bowed.

Noriko asked the merchant something in Japanese. He ignored her. She looked at Max. "He does not want to sell anything to me. He sees only my scars."

"What do you want?" Max asked.

"This fish looks very good, and the rice as well. But we will go somewhere else." Noriko started to walk away.

Max stopped her. He bent down, looked into the man's eyes, and pointed at the fish and rice.

The man prepared two small servings of fish and rice, wrapped them in paper, and handed them to Max.

"How much do I owe him?" Max asked Noriko.

"He will not take your money. He is afraid of you."

Max tried to offer the man money. Noriko was right; he wouldn't take it.

They found a small table nearby. Noriko unwrapped the fish and rice, and they prepared to eat. "I have no chopsticks," she said. "It is too much trouble to get them now. We will have to do the best that we can."

Max looked at the fish. It remained on the paper, and it had mixed with the rice. The fish smelled strong. The rice was acceptable.

Noriko looked at him and smiled. "Have you ever eaten raw fish? It is quite healthy for you. We Japanese live a long time, or at least we used to." She lifted the paper to her mouth and took a small bite of fish.

"I have eaten raw fish before," Max said. "When you are stationed in Japan, it's unavoidable." He took a bite as well, and before long, they both had finished their meals.

They stood and began to walk back through the shopping district.

Noriko froze.

Max saw what she was looking at. A man at a table was selling masks. He looked at Noriko, and then he walked up to the table. The masks resembled souvenir masks that might be for sale in the States. A woman. An old man. A devil.

Noriko approached him quickly, took his arm, and led him away. "We must go. Now. Let us get back to your jeep."

"What's wrong?" Max asked.

Noriko didn't answer, and she didn't speak again until they were in the jeep, heading back toward the shelter. "Those were Noh masks," she said. "Noh is a very old form of Japanese drama. The actors wear those masks to represent many beings, old men, women, demons, spirits, and animals. But it is much more than that. This is difficult to explain to an outsider. The dead are always speaking to us, Max. But we try too hard not to hear them when we are awake. That is why they speak to us in our dreams. And they speak to us through Noh."

"I saw someone wearing one of those masks," Max said.

Noriko held her stomach. "Pull over, Max. Please. Pull over."

Max pulled over.

Noriko quickly climbed out of the jeep, bent over, and fell to her knees. She clawed at the ground and gagged, then vomited.

Max placed his hand upon her back. "God, what's wrong? What can I do? Was it the fish?"

"It is not the fish," Noriko said. "Help me up."

Max helped her stand.

"It is the bomb." Noriko leaned on the jeep. "I am growing thinner. Soon, I will be as thin as you are."

Max handed her his canteen.

Noriko took a long drink. "You said that you saw someone wearing one of those masks. Have you ever seen Noh performed?"

"No. I saw someone wearing a mask when I found you passed out near that blown-up building. He was dancing, I guess, but moving very slowly. His mask was red, like a devil. I didn't know what to make of it, but after I bent down to check on you, he was already gone."

She looked at him, terrified. "Max, what did you do during the war?"

"I did things."

"Tell me. It is very important. *What did you do during the war?*" Noriko was nearly shouting.

Max looked toward the ground. "I dropped bombs. Not this one, but there were many others."

There were tears in Noriko's eyes. "So that is why Shikami let you see him. He is angry at you." She reached out and took Max's hand. "We are linked. Both of us are outsiders."

"What's going on?" Max asked.

"Take me back to the place where you found me. Take me back to Ground Zero. I'll show you."

The demon Shikami was waiting for them in front of the Hiroshima Prefectural Industrial Promotion Hall. He danced to the music of the Noh.

Max parked the jeep nearby. They watched Shikami. "Is that an actor?" Max asked.

"He is not an actor." Noriko climbed out of the jeep. "Follow me."

They walked toward the ruins. Shikami beckoned to them, slowly and fluidly, as was the way of Noh. His arms were open, and his long yellowed fingernails urged them forward. The wind billowed within his robes, and the eyes of his demon-red mask turned golden.

"Can you smell it?" Noriko asked.

"Smell what?" The Promotion Hall was close. There were figures inside, other spirits of Noh.

"The air. It is damp. It smells like rain and smoke, like a thundershower, yet there are no clouds, and there are no other people here. Just us. And them."

Max quickly looked around. It was late afternoon when they arrived, but the sun was just starting to rise. The ruins cast long shadows, yet the sun was too low for that. He looked at his wristwatch. The hands were moving backward rapidly, and old Hiroshima, the city before the bomb came, was rebuilding itself. The Promotion Hall stayed in ruins, but the walls were growing transparent.

"We inhabit a land between worlds," Noriko said. "It has already begun."

They stepped over rubble into the building.

"The spirits want us to stand beneath the dome," Noriko said. "I hear their voices in my head."

Below the ruined dome, they waited. The Lady Deigan, the vengeful one who tormented Noriko in her dreams; Ayakashi, the warrior spirit; Akobujo, the old man; and Fukai, a woman, like Noriko, who had lost her children. All of them wore the masks of Noh.

Shikami followed Noriko and Max. They could see the dome through the floors above.

"We are to stand at the center," Noriko said, "directly beneath the spot where the bomb detonated." Max followed her there.

The others surrounded them.

They watched the sky through the blackened skeletal braces that once supported the dome.

Something was whistling toward them.

"Close your eyes," Noriko said. "The flash will be very bright."

Hiroshima died once again. The flash came like a million bolts of lightning, and their ears rang with the wind, the roar of collapsing buildings, the crackling of flames, and the sizzling of flesh, and yet they remained protected within this space. Noriko felt her cheeks as she opened her eyes, and she found only the old scars there, nothing worse. But outside the building, the explosion obliterated all that had been reborn.

"Look," cried Noriko.

Max opened his eyes.

The others moved back so they could see. A billowing mushroom cloud engulfed the sun. Pale ashes rained down through the open dome. There were flames, but then something else began to glow. Figures. Human figures. They watched them sprout from the ashes all across the city, miles of brilliant white lights glowing like stars. Many of them gathered outside the building, close to the dome. They had no faces. They had no masks.

Noriko cried. "My children are out there."

Shikami approached them. He took Max's arm, and then he began to lead him away.

"No!" Noriko yelled. "Not him. He is young. He must be permitted to live out his life."

Shikami stopped and bowed his head in her direction.

Fukai approached Noriko. She wore the mask of an older woman. The lips showed no expression, so Noriko shared her own. They both wore the face of those who had lost their children.

"Do not take him," Noriko said. "Please." She placed her hands over her stomach. "Something is growing inside of me. It is getting larger. I can feel it. There is only pain left for me in my world."

More ashes rained down, coating them in whiteness.

Fukai nodded.

Shikami released Max.

"Go now, Max," Noriko said, "Never come back here."

The ashes were turning pink, floating through the open dome. Cherry blossoms.

Max wouldn't leave.

Fukai reached up, and slowly, she removed her mask. The face of the woman underneath looked like Noriko, only an ancient sadness resided there, frozen like the mask.

Noriko took Fukai's mask. She looked at it for a long while, and then reverently, she put it on. "My scars are gone now," she said.

Max was shaking his head.

"It is as it should be," Noriko said. "You are a good man, Max. Do not punish yourself for your past. Move forward. If you do not, there will be no journey for you, and you will never find the joys that await you along the way. But when you sleep, your dreams will torment you. It is the way for those who have suffered through war. But I will be with you, and I will see to it that these spirits do not torment you too badly."

Max turned, climbed across the rubble, and ran toward the

jeep. Everything outside the building was as it had been in his world.

Fukai led the way, and as cherry blossoms rained down upon them, Noriko's children welcomed her home.

♦

Michael Scott Bricker has been writing and dealing antiques for most of his life. His passion for history is usually reflected in his writing, and his stories often take place in various historical time periods. His work has appeared in several anthologies, including *Whitley Strieber's Aliens*, *Borderlands 7*, and *Blood Muse*. His first professional sale was to the anthology *Young Blood*, a book comprised of stories that were written before the authors turned thirty. The majority of his working career has involved books, and he has been employed by numerous bookstores and libraries in California, which has been interrupted by unfortunate office jobs that have ended abruptly whenever a supervisor would ask him to cut his hair. He obsessively collects and attempts to repair antique phonographs in his free time.

MOPE NOT FOR THE MIGHTY

MICHAEL NETHERCOTT

In August 1965, my first copy of *Prince Robozz and his Nuts-n-Bolts Brigade* appeared to me like a vision on the comics rack at Smeckle's, a rundown five-and-dime that mostly sold dust. This was issue #59, so by then the Brigade had been saving humanity's hiney for nigh on half a decade. But for me, on that pivotal day, the Prince and his team were fresh, fantastic and intellectually seductive. I dropped twelve pennies into the cup of wrinkles that was Mr. Smeckle's ancient palm and marched off with my prize.

Now, it's not that I had never read a comic book before. After all, I was pushing ten—I'd been around the block. I had sampled a few issues of Fist Man, Rhino Woman, The Living Lump, and various other offerings of the superhero smorgasbord, but none of them had truly won me over. The cover of *Prince Robozz #59*, however, all but cried out my name. There stood the regal wrong-righter, natty in his metallic body armor and purple hood, pounding the daylights out of Dr. Sunset, his nemesis of the month. Everything you'd want from a professional crimebuster. But what really quickened my pulse was the caliber of his cronies. These were guys you'd want in your foxhole, anywhere, anytime.

As depicted on #59's cover, they come rushing in from all sides, the Prince's faithful quartet, clearly rabid to assist in the bad doctor's pummeling. As I would learn in that first educational reading, Sprocket, Screw-loose, Lugnuts, and the gorgeous Gear Girl (collectively, the Nuts-n-Bolts Brigade,) were robots that the Prince had scientifically infused with the souls of four dead space warriors. Nifty or what? Being a fairly solitary kid, whose family moved around a lot, I couldn't claim much by way of long-term friendships, so the idea of a group of powerful pals always watching your back had tremendous appeal.

In the manner of all addictions, #59 led to #60, which led to #61, which led to an uninterrupted run all the way to *Prince Robozz* #99 (including, of course, the two Christmas specials in which the Prince fights, respectively, Black Sugarplum and Frosto the Snow Madman). I even managed to make my mark by having an epistle of mine appear in issue #92's letter column.

"*The Brigade's rematch with the Cruelty Corps was groovy,*" I opined in the lingo of the time. "*But I do have two complaints. One: on page twelve, panel three, Lugnut's loincloth is colored green instead of yellow. Two: The guest appearance of Baron Bazooka was not needed. If the Prince gets in a real bind, he always has the Nuts-n-Boltsers to save his fat. Throwing in a superhero from another comic is just plain exorbitant.*"

Exorbitant. I had dragged that last word screaming and kicking out of *Roget's Thesaurus*. Though I didn't know what it meant exactly, it seemed to have enough syllables to adequately express my disdain. Baron Bazooka and all those other second-raters had no place on Prince Robozz's turf. I was a purist that way. Having to bring in other heroes to defeat your archenemies was like asking your Mom to help you face down the school bully.

I ended my letter with the observation that "Gear Girl is one alluring alloy! The Prince should ask her out or something." Despite my sophisticated suggestion, no man-and-machine coupling ever came to pass. It's probably just as well.

Excluding the random unwanted guest-star, I was more than delighted with the escapades of my champions. The Prince and his mighty team had traveled all the way from their home world Quarzzox to protect the feebler denizens of Planet Earth. I was immensely grateful that, for a measly twelve cents a month, I could keep track of their valiant workload. Beyond those chronicled accounts, I fantasized other equally grand adventures which included the Brigade's only acceptable ally—me.

But then everything ground to a halt with the devastating announcement on the last page of *Prince Robozz* #99 that this would be the final issue of the title. The Prince's publishing company—Sci Fi Funnies—was changing its name to Sci Fab Fiction, Inc. and would henceforth be replacing its comics line with a series of "pop art" speculative novels featuring "mod, marv space-hipsters battling intergalactic bummers."

In many ways, my innocence died with *Prince Robozz and his Nuts-n-Bolts Brigade* #99. For months before, the letters column had teased us fans that the much-anticipated 100th issue would be "a double-sized extravaganza packed with thrills, chills, and more villains than you can shake a Quarzzoxian laser-spear at." But #100 never came. Couldn't they have at least allowed Prince and the Brigade to go out in that one last *promised* blaze of glory?

But no, but no. The editors had lied. Grown-ups lied. The president lied. This was the winter of 1968. Vietnam. Rebellion. Martyred leaders. I was thirteen. Through the pangs of disillusionment, I berated myself: thirteen was damn well old enough to stop reading stupid kiddy books. In a blur of hot tears, I tossed my forty-one issues of *Prince Robozz* into the trash and forced myself to forget my heroes.

🎭

Jump ahead more than two decades. I'd left comic books behind and put together the usual string of life experiences: high school, college, career, marriage, dalliance with my wife's cousin, divorce, second marriage, dalliance with my second wife's aunt, divorce number two—followed by a big double-sized extravaganza of a mid-life crisis.

In one of many attempts to bolster my flagging spirit, I attended a pricey New Age seminar entitled "Hugging, Healing and Hurling Your Inner Child." There I was encouraged to embrace the small lost boy within, exonerate him of any guilt, and then fling his self-pitying little ass out of my psyche. Actually, I never quite mastered the technique, but something unexpected did come of the seminar. During an exercise in which we were instructed to close our eyes and visualize a moment of pure childhood joy, what should pop into my head but that first beautiful copy of *Prince Robozz*, gleaming like a sequestered jewel in the dusty tomb of Smeckle's Five-and-Dime.

Several days later, on impulse, I sought out a comics specialty shop in a neighboring town. By the twitchy manner in which I entered the place, one might have thought that I'd come in search of hard porn. The clerk, a round thirtyish fellow with a frizzy orange chin beard, sauntered over to me. He wore a tee shirt bearing the words, "Proud Fungus"—which I guessed was either the name of a punk band or a strident declaration of lifestyle. Though I could not know it at the time, this character—one Chester Prutzman—was destined to become my friend and ally.

He sized me up with a look that mingled bemusement with disgust: clearly, I was slumming here. I mumbled my desire, and he vanished into a backroom for several minutes before returning with a small stack of comics. He spread these out on a table, and I caught my breath. Here, snug in their protective polypropylene bags, lay thirteen issues of *Prince Robozz*, including the visualized #59 as well as the heart-breaking #99. After a gap of twenty years, the Prince, Gear Girl, and the others stared up at me boldly in all their multi-colored splendor. I imagined, for a fleeting moment, that they were forgiving me for that long-ago abandonment.

Then Chester told me the price, and I nearly soiled myself.

My shock made his day. He snickered, "Hey, man, you can't put a price tag on history." (Though he just *had*—a whopping one.) "Prince Robozz is pretty much the only Silver Age hero who's never been reissued, revamped, or revitalized. He hit the wall in '68 and, splat, that was that. Robozz is like a frickin' prehistoric insect preserved in amber."

Succumbing to this primal image, I hauled out my checkbook and welcomed the Prince and his clan back into my life. After that initial purchase, I found myself on a mission to acquire the rest of the ninety-nine book run. Over the course of that next year, I managed—with Chester Prutzman's help—to hunt down and obtain sixty more issues. Even after he lost his job at the shop (due to an incident in which he labeled the owner a "brain-dead gonad" for ceasing to carry the underground comic *Cannibal Nurse*,) Chester continued to aid and abet me.

After that first successful stretch, my purchasing slowed down considerably. It was getting harder to track down the Prince's old adventures, especially the earlier issues which I had never read. Still, I persevered and after a couple more years, I owned almost the whole series—ninety-eight out of ninety-nine comics. Only the premier issue had eluded me.

"Hell, you'll never find *that one*," Chester assured me one night as we sat in his tiny apartment trading shots of tequila.

"It's the only issue that was written and drawn by George Vanderpool, himself."

"The man who created Prince Robozz," I added. Chester had tutored me well.

"Yep." My friend nodded. "Ol' George died in a boating accident a week after *Robozz #1* hit the stands and, from issue two on, a bunch of different people took turns on the series. *#1* had a very small printing, and only three copies of it are still known to exist. And frickin Karleen Mopps owns 'em all."

Karleen Mopps. Her name invariably came up in any discussion of high-stakes comics collecting. In a field dominated by younger men, Mopps, a woman in her seventies, was an anomaly. Having gotten in on the ground floor years before collecting became an industry, she had built up a small fortune buying and selling complete runs of the most sought-after series. She reputedly lived the life of a wealthy recluse in an old mansion in Greenwich, Connecticut.

"Maybe Karleen Mopps would consider selling me one of her copies," I mused aloud. "After all, she doesn't need all three."

Chester looked at me as if I'd just stated my intention to swallow a piano. "Dream on, nimrod. Once Moppsy's got her claws in something legendary like the *Robozz #1* trifecta, she ain't never gonna let go. Besides, you'd have to sell your lungs to even afford a copy."

This reality check left me feeling morose. But after a few more doses of tequila, I woozily shifted my thoughts toward matters of philosophy: "Why d'you think they're called the Nuts-n-Bolts *Brigade*? I mean, there's only four of 'em, right? Five, if you count the Prince. Can five be a brigade? That always bothered me. Now, maybe if they said *Squad* ..."

Our conversation deteriorated from there, ending, I recall, in a heated debate on the aforementioned Baron Bazooka. Chester championed that uninspiring hero, going so far as to suggest that he was Prince Robozz's equal or even—blasphemy of blasphemies—his *superior.*

"Are you insane?" I cried out. "Everyone knows a prince outranks a baron!"

"We're talking quality, not royalty," Chester countered. "Hey man, Baron Bazooka is the bomb!"

"Jesus!" I corked the bottle before our friendship could dissolve into fisticuffs. "Enough fire-juice for *you.*"

🎭

Sometimes a miracle will just leap out of nowhere and slap you in the jowls.

Not long after that tequila-drenched night, I was enjoying a leisurely ride in the country and stopped at a yard sale down a winding back road. A very elderly man behind a row of cluttered tables gestured toward his wares and declared, "Make an offer." I scanned the pickings and determined quickly that there was little there but junk and knickknacks. I had just started to leave when I noticed something colorful peeking out from under a pile of old *Reader's Digests.* I pulled this item free and held it in both hands. At that moment I forgot how to breathe. For some time, I stood there, my eyes welded to the cover.

The old man noted my interest. "Oh yeah, I got a couple of those old funny books mixed in there. Left over from when my sons were little."

"How much?" I croaked out.

"Well, those things are worth something these days, aren't they? Would you do, say, five dollars?"

I nodded. Just nodded. And placed a five-dollar bill into his ancient palm.

That evening, with Chester by my side, I oh-so-slowly

turned to the splash page of *Prince Robozz and his Nuts-n-Bolts Brigade # 1*.

"Bro," said Chester in a reverential whisper. "Today, the geek gods were looking down on you for sure."

We marveled at my luck. The comic was in certifiable good condition—a little creased and stained, plus a couple small tears on the cover, but thoroughly intact. We read the book in silence, cover to cover.

When we'd finished, Chester let out a resounding "Whoa!"

"Whoa," I echoed.

"They were actually bad guys!"

"What do you—?"

"Robozz and the Brigade! They came to our world as invaders! They fried dozens of innocent people with their laser-spears—it says so here!"

Unfathomably, what he said was true, but I couldn't bring myself to admit it. "No, no, they became our defenders."

"Are you in frickin denial?" Chester pointed at the opened comic. "Look, in the last panel here, they vow to not rest till they've conquered Earth! Sure, they battled crime starting in issue 2, but that was written after George Vanderpool died. Sci Fi Funnies must have decided to sanitize the book and told the new writers to put Robozz on the straight-and-narrow. Had Vanderpool lived, chances are the Prince would have gone Mussolini on us."

I could offer no rebuttal. The terrible truth lay sprawled open on my coffee table: my childhood heroes had been created to be enemies of humanity. Before he left my house, I made Chester promise to keep mum about my new acquisition. He agreed without an argument.

Two days later, I got a phone call from none other than Karleen Mopps.

"I understand you possess an inaugural issue of *Prince Robozz*," she said in her creaky Katherine Hepburn accent.

"How did you hear about that?"

"Ah, you know, information travels like a hummingbird in the collecting community. I wish to purchase your copy—for an appropriate fee, of course."

"I don't wish to sell," I informed her.

"A *more* than appropriate fee."

"No."

A touch of ice came into her voice. "Very well. Then at least come visit me so that we can compare copies. I assure you I'll make it worth your while."

I fell silent for a few moments. The idea of viewing Karleen Mopps's fabled collection was certainly enticing. As long as I didn't part with my *P.R. #1*, what was the harm? I accepted her offer to come by that weekend. She promised to send a limousine for me.

When I saw Chester the next day, he managed within minutes to get me to forgive his loose lips and, additionally, to weasel his way into my planned journey. The weekend came around and a long, sleek limo arrived as promised. Our chauffeur was a lanky, skittish individual with a facial tick who kept grinning at us in the rearview mirror and exclaiming, "See? I'm a good driver, aren't I?"

Eventually, we found ourselves on the doorstep of Karleen Mopps' antique mansion. I had worn a suit and tie for the occasion; Chester had chosen a spiffy ensemble consisting of camouflaged army pants and a tee shirt announcing, "I Brake for Social Lepers." The door was opened by a tall, angular old woman in a velvet dressing gown, with a cascade of pure white hair and a distinct air of haughtiness. Our hostess.

She appraised us as if through a microscope. "My, aren't you the unique pairing. Enter."

We followed Karleen Mopps through a series of sizable rooms, all filled with glass display cases brimming with comic books.

Chester pinballed from case to case. "Jesus! She's got six copies of *Rampaging Walrus #3*—the first appearance of Killer Minnow! And look! The complete run of *Captain Biceps*! And *Madame Mad-dog*! And, holy crap! here's *The Plaid Stallion #18*—the one where Saddle Lad dies!"

"Come along," Karleen Mopps ordered. "There's time for that later. Besides, those books are here merely for financial purposes. My true passion is Prince Robozz."

We came at last to a large room unlike any of the others. Here there were no comic books on display. Instead, every wall was lined with desktop computers, television monitors and a vast array of complex-looking equipment, the function of which I couldn't begin to guess at. Standing to one side, two very big men in white slacks and turtlenecks awaited us. Once we'd entered the room, the quirky chauffeur, who had been trailing us, stepped in and closed the massive oak doors behind him.

As we reached the center of the space, the three men moved in to flank Chester and myself. Mopps stood before us, her thin lips squeezed into a small, unsavory smile. She pointed a bony finger at the briefcase in my hand, which contained my copy of *Prince Robozz #1*.

"I'll claim that now."

With something akin to a paternal impulse, I clutched the briefcase to my chest. "Remember, I only said you could look at it."

"Oh, I'll look at it, all right," she cooed. "And then I'll *destroy* it."

Chester aimed his own stubby finger at Mopps. "Back off, mummy lady! No one said you could—"

One of the turtleneck men rabbit-punched Chester, dropping him like a sack of laundry. My friend lay there unmoving, eyes rolled back in his head.

A gasp of protest shot out of me. "You're doing this just for a comic book?"

"*Prince Robozz #1* is not just a comic book," Karleen Mopps growled. "*It's a blueprint for invasion!* Behold!"

As ordered, I beheld. In one swift, bizarre motion, the old woman flung back her robe and let it *swoosh* to the floor. I staggered backwards into a corner, unable to process what I was staring at. Mopps's long, lithe body was composed entirely of gleaming metal, contained in nothing but a red and black bikini and a pair of knee-high red boots. I recognized the apparel. She then tossed away the white wig and, gripping her scalp, yanked off her face. I found myself gazing into the shimmering silver countenance of ... Gear Girl!

She laughed at my stupor. "You know me now, don't you? Secret identities can be such a nuisance, really, but they do have their benefits. Oh, and let me introduce my associates ... Screw-loose ... Sprocket ... and Lugnuts."

At each naming, the bearer pulled off his own human mask to reveal a face of metal.

Screw-loose, the chauffeur, gave me a little wave of his fingers. "We're pleased to menace you," he quipped.

I raised my briefcase like a shield and began to stammer, "What ...? How ...? Why ...?" Then through this maelstrom of confusion, something occurred to me: "Where's Prince Robozz?"

Gear Girl sighed. "Listen. I'm only going to explain this once. Back in the early 1960s, when we first arrived here from Quarzzox, Robozz was as determined as the rest of us to conquer your planet. Our mission was to go undercover, learn your societal structures and methodology and, within a few decades, initiate the takeover. But Robozz grew soft. From early on, your lifestyle tainted him. The dancing, the dining, the films ..."

"Especially romantic comedies," Screw-loose put in.

"Yes, the bedroom farces." Gear Girl shuddered. "Films with titles like *Midnight Mischief Mambo* and *Three Heads on a Pillow*. He'd watch them and get all ... syrupy. He began to over-identify with humans. In time, he became ..."

"A traitor!" said her three cohorts in unison.

Gear Girl nodded. "Exactly. Unbeknownst to the rest of us, Robozz—in his human identity—had contracted with Sci Fi Funnies to create a comic book detailing our plans. He felt that alerting the youth in this way would be the most effective method of warning humanity. He did all the writing and art himself."

I tried to get this straight. "You mean Prince Robozz was really *George Vanderpool*?"

"Or vise versa," said the metal maiden.

Sprocket scowled. "After we stumbled upon the comic at a newsstand, we knew we had to stop him."

"Yes," agreed Lugnuts. "We arranged for his sad little 'boating accident.'"

Gear Girl continued. "After Robozz's demise, Sci Fi Funnies kept the series going. But they turned our characters into noble protectors of the populace. We decided not to interfere with the publication. After all, whenever we did finally reveal ourselves, it would serve us well to be thought of as heroes—instead of the dominators that we really were. However, there still existed the problem of that first inflammatory issue. We bought up all the copies we could find and destroyed them."

Screw-loose cackled mechanically. "Even broke into Sci Fi's offices and torched their backstock."

"But over the years, every once in a while, a copy of *Prince Robozz #1* would pop up somewhere." Gear Girl's robotic red eyes stared into my own wide humanoid ones. "Then do you know what we'd do?"

"What?" I hated to ask.

She began to move toward my corner. "Why, we would lure

the owner here and eliminate both him and his cherished collector's item."

Screw-loose emitted another of his nasty chuckles and also started toward me. "And we'd hunt down everyone they'd shown the comic to ..."

Now, Sprocket moved forward: "Or even told the plot to ..."

And Lugnuts: "And eliminate them, as well."

Gear Girl's face was now about three inches from my own. "We're *very* efficient. As your whole pathetic race will quite soon learn."

I screwed my eyes closed and a sound escaped from my lips that no one would describe as manly.

At that dire moment, I was greeted by a loud, familiar voice raised in extreme annoyance: "Yo, you frickin' rustpot kettle heads! Look over here!"

When I dared open my eyes, I saw that all four robots had turned their backs on me and were now focused elsewhere. There in the middle of the room stood one Chester Prutzman, looking pissed as hell. Above his head he held high an unfathomable device comprised of metal rings, intricate circuitry, and glass tubes filled with a bright blue fluid.

He assumed an expression of childlike innocence. "Gee, this gizmo you have here looks all mega-tech and important and stuff. I happen to know it's the core of your power. So I probably shouldn't mess with it, right?" With that, he flung the device to the hard floor where it exploded like fireworks, shooting out a web of quivering bluish light beams in every direction.

The Nuts-n-Bolts Brigade unleashed a team shriek that all but pierced my eardrums. Although the light beams flashed across my body, they seemed to do me no harm. On the other hand, their effect on the robots was spectacular. Howling and jerking, the metallic foursome staggered around the room as if they were in the throws of a Sex Pistols revival. The streams of blue energy had turned them into raging marionettes no longer in control of their own limbs. What's more, all the walls of machinery seemed to be likewise affected as the room filled with frenzied crackling, sputtering sparks, and clouds of thick black smoke.

"Make tracks, man!" Chester hollered, and I did.

We swung open the oak doors and began racing through the maze of rooms.

At one point, Chester halted before one of the display cases and tried to force open the lid. "Just let me grab a couple of those *Plaid Stallions*."

"Forget it!" I shoved him forward. By now, a tide of angry flames was pursuing us, and the house itself seemed to be in the grip of a powerful seizure. We rushed onward and burst out through the front door. Luckily, the limo still sat in the driveway, keys in the ignition. With Chester at the wheel, we tore out of there just as the mansion went up in a fierce ball of fire.

We sped on for several minutes before I managed to find my voice, "How did you know shattering that contraption of theirs would short-circuit them?"

Chester shrugged. "Call it intuition. Plus, man, I was really ticked off. Urge to smash."

"Oh."

I suddenly noticed that I had retained my grip on the briefcase, despite all the insanity. Opening it now, I extracted *Prince Robozz #1* and held it up before me. I could never again look at the Nuts-n-Boltsers without imagining myself the object of their laser-spear barbecue. And the image of the poor Prince, who had sacrificed himself for humankind, was equally hard to bear. With a great cathartic cry, I ripped the comic book into a dozen jagged pieces and threw them out the window.

Chester glanced over at me. "You're hardcore, man."

We drove into the descending darkness. Emotionally

exhausted, I closed my eyes and eventually managed to doze off.

Sometime later, I let out a yelp and jumped in my seat. A reaction, no doubt, to the terrors I'd just lived through. Either that or my inner child had just kneed me in the marbles.

🎭

After that, I never saw Chester Prutzman again. In the days immediately following our escapade, he didn't answer any of my calls. When I finally stopped by his apartment, the landlord informed me that my friend had abruptly left town, no forwarding address given. This was in the days before cell phones and the internet, so if you wanted to disappear into the ethers, it wasn't hard to do. After some thought, I figured maybe it was for the best. In the wake of the harrowing madness I'd just experienced, I no longer desired to be part of the comic book universe. And Chester represented that universe more than anyone I knew. I sold my comic collection for a pittance and, as best I could, drove all thoughts of metallic space conquerors from my brain.

For a good number of years, I lived behind a comfortable wall of abject denial. Then, one evening in the late nineties, I was staying with some out-of-state friends when that wall abruptly collapsed. I'd been assigned the room of their son, presently off at college, and was settling in for the night when I noticed a stack of old comic books piled on a shelf. Like Ulysses drawn to the Sirens, I approached and examined them. Though several books were from the sixties, these, thankfully, didn't include *Prince Robozz and his Nuts-n-Bolts Brigade*. I did, however, discover a single copy of *The Heroic Baron Bazooka*, starring that lesser luminary. This, of course, was the same Baron Bazooka who had guest-starred in one issue of Prince Robozz's comic and whose merits Chester and I had once hotly debated. Out of old impulse—and despite my understandable aversion to the medium—I began reading the lead story. It only took me a few pages to come upon an unsettling piece of information.

Because I'd never followed the Baron's exploits, I knew very little about him other than the fact that he could shoot bazooka blasts out of his palms (a fine enough power if you went in for that sort of thing). I never knew, for instance, his secret identity or what he looked like when not encased in his bulky, face-covering costume. Now here—on page three, panel four—the truth was revealed to me. Out of costume, Baron Bazooka lacked the standard buff physique of most superheroes. Instead, he proved to be a round, unathletic fellow with frizzy orange hair. And his secret identity? One Chester Ritzman! True, *Ritzman* was not exactly *Prutzman*, but damn close enough to make me nearly swallow my tongue. And the artist's rendition of him looked unmistakably like my old comrade, down to the paunch and chin beard.

I flung the comic back on the shelf, killed the light, and leapt into bed. If I slept at all that night, it was sporadically at best. I woke with the bedsheets utterly drenched in sweat. I believe my hosts were forced to burn them.

If you're wondering, did I ever attempt any follow-up research on the matter, the answer is a bellowing, thundering, deafening NO. Who *or what* Chester Prutzman was is something I have no desire—or stamina—to uncover. Let this written account of mine be the end of it ... at least for me. If someone else is motivated to delve deeper into things, well, more power to them. As for myself, the only required answer to the above question is this: Chester Prutzman was my pal.

Oh, and he saved the world.

Michael Nethercott is the author of two mystery novels, *The Séance Society* and *The Haunting Ballad* (St. Martin's Press). He is a winner of the Black Orchid Novella Award, the Vermont Writers' Award, the Vermont Playwrights Award, the Clauder Competition (Best State Play) and the Nor'easter Play Writing Competition. His writings have appeared in numerous periodicals and anthologies including *Alfred Hitchcock Mystery Magazine*, *Best Crime and Mystery Stories of the Year*, *The Magazine of Fantasy and Science Fiction*, and *Abyss & Apex*.

SINNER, BAKER, FABULIST, PRIEST; RED MASK, BLACK MASK, GENTLEMAN, BEAST

EUGIE FOSTER

Each morning is a decision. Should I put on the brown mask or the blue? Should I be a tradesman or an assassin today?

Whatever the queen demands, of course, I am. But so often she ignores me, and I am left to figure out for myself who to be. Dozens upon dozens of faces to choose from.

i. Marigold Is for Murder

The yellow mask draws me, the one made from the pelt of a mute animal with neither fangs nor claws—better for the workers to collect its skin. It can only glare at its keepers through the wires of its cage, and when the knives cut and the harvesters rip away its skin, no one is troubled by its screams.

I tie the tawny ribbons under my chin. The mask is so light, almost weightless. But when I inhale, a charnel stench redolent of outhouses, opened intestines, and dried blood floods my nose.

My wife's mask is so pretty, pink flower lips and magenta eyelashes that flutter like feathers when she talks. But her body is pasty and soft, the flesh of her thighs mottled with black veins and puckered fat.

Still, I want her.

"Darling, I'm sorry," I say. "They didn't have the kind you wanted. I bought what they had. There's Citrus Nectar, Iolite Bronze, and Creamy Illusion."

"Might as well bring me pus in a jar," she snaps. "Did you look on all the shelves?"

"N-no. But the shop girl said they were out."

"The slut was probably hoarding it for herself. You know they all skim the stuff. Open the pots and scoop out a spoonful here, a dollop there. They use it themselves or stick it in tawdry urns to sell at those independent markets."

"The shop girl looked honest enough." Her mask had been carved onyx with a brush of gold at temples and chin. She had been slim, her flesh taut where my wife's sagged, her skin flawless and golden. And she had moved with a delicate grace, totally unlike the lumbering woman before me.

"Looked honest?" My wife's eyes roll in the sockets of her mask. "Like you could tell Queen's Honey from shit."

"My love, I know you're disappointed, but won't you try one of these other ones? For me?" I pull a jar of Iolite Bronze from the sack and unscrew the lid.

Although hostility bristles from her—her scent, her stance, the glare of fury from the eyeholes of her mask—I dip a finger into the solution. It's true it doesn't have the same consistency, and the perfume is more musk than honey, but the tingle is the same.

With my Iolite Bronzed finger, I reach for the cleft between her doughy thighs.

"Don't touch me with that filth," she snarls, backing away.

If only she weren't so stubborn. I grease all the fingers of my hand with Iolite Bronze. The musk scent has roused me faster than Queen's Honey.

"Get away!"

I grab for her sex, clutching at her with my slick fingers. I am so intent that I do not see the blade, glowing in her fist. As my fingertips slip into her, she plunges the weapon into my chest, and I go down.

Lying in a pool of my own blood, the scent of Iolite Bronze turning rank, I watch the blade rise and fall as she stabs me again and again.

Her mask is so pretty.

2. Blue Is for Maidens

The next morning, I linger over my selection, touching one beautiful face, then another. There is a vacant spot where the yellow mask used to be, but I have many more.

Finally, I choose one the color of sapphires. The brow is sewn from satin smooth as water. I twine the velveteen ribbons in my hair, and the tassels shush around my ears like whispered secrets.

"I don't think I'll ever marry," I say. "Why should I?"

The girl beside me giggles, slender fingers over her mouth opening. Her mask is hewn from green wood hardened by three days of fire. Once carved and finished, the wood takes on a glass-like clarity, the tracery of sepia veins like a thick filigree of lace.

"Mark my words," she says. "All the flirting you do will catch up to you one day. A man will steal your heart, and you'll come running to me to help with the wedding."

I laugh. "Not likely. The guys we know only think about

Queen's Honey and getting me alone. I'd just as soon marry a Mask Maker as any of those meatheads."

"Eww, that's twisted." My girlfriend squeals and points. "Look! It's the new shipment. Didn't I tell you the delivery trucks come round this street first?"

We stand with our masks pressed against the shop window, ogling the display of vials.

"*Exotica, White Wishes Under a Black Moon.*" My friend rattles off the names printed in elegant fonts in the space beneath each sampler. "*Metallic Mischief, Homage to a Manifesto* —what do you suppose that one's like?—*Terracotta Talisman*, and *Dulcet Poison*. I like the sound of that last one."

"You would."

"Oh, hush. Let's go try them."

"That store's awfully posh. You think they'll let us try without buying?"

"Of course they will. We're customers, aren't we? They won't throw us out."

"They might."

My concerns fail to dampen her enthusiasm, and I let her tow me through the crystalline doors.

The mingled scents in the shop wash over us. My friend abandons me, rushing to join the jostling horde clustered around the new arrivals. While the mixture of emotive fumes makes my friend giddy and excited, they overwhelm me. I lean against a counter and take shallow breaths.

"You look lost." The man's mask is matte pewter, the metal coating so thin I can see the strokes from the artisan's paintbrush. A flame design swirls across both cheeks in variegated shades of purple.

"I'm just waiting for my friend." I gesture in the direction of the mob. There's a glint of translucent green, all I can see of her.

"You're not interested in trying this new batch?"

"Not really. I prefer the traditional distillations. I guess that makes me old-fashioned."

The man leans to conspiratorial closeness. "But you purchased those three new ones yesterday. I tried to warn you about the Iolite Bronze. It's not at all a proper substitute for Queen's Honey."

Memories of lust and violence fill me, musk and arousal, pain and blood. But they are wrong. I am someone else today. I shake my head.

"I don't know what you're talking about." I search for a hint of green glass or sepia lace. Where is she? "I'd never let someone use Iolite Bronze on me."

"Didn't you say it was a gift when I sold it to you?"

"What?"

"I was the shop girl in the onyx mask."

I am shocked beyond words, beyond reaction. It is the biggest taboo in our society, so profane and obscene that it is not even in our law books. We do not discuss the events and encounters of our other masks. It is not done. What if people started blaming one face for what another did, merely because the same citizen wore both?

The moment of speechless paralysis ends, and I run. I fly through the glittering doors, not caring that I've left my best friend behind, and run, run, run until I am back to the dormitory on Center at Corridor. I huddle in the lift, and it whisks me to my quarters. On my bed, I sob, the tears wetting the inside of my mask. A part of me worries that I will stain the satin, but it is a distant part.

When the tears run out, I am done with the day, done with this mask. But the unmasking time is still far off. If I'd only worn the tan mask today, with the bronze veneer and dripping beadwork, I wouldn't have fled from the pewter-masked deviant. I'd have punched him in the golden flesh of his gut or hauled him to the queen's gendarmes for a reckoning.

Then I realize what I'm thinking, what I'm wanting— another mask, but not during the morning selection, not during the unmasking—while I'm still wearing today's.

And I'm afraid.

3. Black Is for Sex

In the morning, as I stand barefaced among my masks, looking anywhere but at the tan one, I receive the queen's summons. It is delivered, as always, by a gendarme masked in thinly hammered silver. He rings my bell, waiting for me to acknowledge him over the intercom.

The gendarmes are the only citizens about during the early morning when the rest of us are selecting our daily masks, just as they are the only ones who patrol the thoroughfares after the unmasking hour, collecting retired masks and distributing new ones.

"Good morning, gendarme," I say.

"Good morning, citizen. You are called upon today to carry out your civic duty."

"I am pleased to oblige." A square of paper slips through my delivery slot and into my summons tray, bringing with it an elusive sweetness. The queen's writs are always scented like the honey named after her, both more insistent and more subtle than the stuff which circulates in the marketplaces.

Among my arrayed masks, raised above the others, is the sable mask—hammered steel painted with liquid ebony. It is the consort mask, worn only to honor the queen's summons. The paint is sheer, and glimmers of silver flicker through the color. The eyes are outlined in opaque kohl, a masked mask.

I lock the delicate chains with their delicate clasps around my head. For a moment, I am disoriented by the lenses over the eyes. It takes longer for me to adjust to the warp in my vision than to the feel and heft of the mask. But not much longer.

The music trills liquid and rich around us, and I concentrate on the steps. In her mask-like-stars, the queen swirls and glides across the ballroom in my arms. Caught in her beauty and my exertions, I have missed her words.

"I beg your pardon, my queen. What did you say?"

Her mask tilts up, and the piquant flavor of her amusement fills my senses. "I asked if you were enjoying the dance, whether you liked the refreshment."

"I have not sampled the buffet, but it looks lavish. As to the dance, I am worried that my clumsiness might offend you or that I might misstep."

"I've never danced with you before? That would explain your stiffness."

"I have not had the pleasure. I'm sorry."

"Don't be. It was only a whimsy. I don't dance with many. You probably won't dance with me again." The queen gestures, and the music stops. She leads me to her couch—crimson sheets and alabaster cushions. I am more familiar with this type of dance, but she isn't ready for me yet. Her scent, though heady, tells me it is not time to mate, although it will be soon.

It confuses me, this waiting. Why am I here, if not to do my duty?

She reclines on her couch but not in the position of copulation.

"Talk to me," she says.

"What would you like to speak on, my queen?"

"Do you have a favorite mask?"

It is an odd question, treading the boundary of indecency.

"No, my queen. They are all precious to me."

"Don't you wish you could discard some masks, perhaps the ones that you suffer in, and just wear the ones that are pleasurable?"

Was she testing me? "They are all precious to me," I say again. "Each in its wonderful variety. I would never presume to contravene the law."

"Not even to bend it a little? There are some citizens who wear just a few masks and don others only as often as they must in order to stay out of the purview of the gendarmes."

"But that's criminal."

"Technically, it's legal, although it defies the heart of the code. Generally, the number of their select rotation is large enough that no single mask becomes dominant. Do you find the prospect appealing?"

Dominant mask? What would be the purpose in limiting one's mask selection? Her words make no sense.

"No."

My answer pleases her. Her scent rises and with it, my arousal, and I cannot think clearly anymore. The queen is the font of desire and satisfaction—the perfume of true Queen's Honey between her legs, her need, mine—nothing exists but the urgency of mating. It eclipses mere copulation as the sun outshines the stars. I submerge in a tide of desire and completion and the rise of desire again, over and over, until the unmasking hour.

In the morning, barefaced and aching, I report to the Mask Makers galley. I avoid looking at their ugly, soft countenances. It's partly instinctive discomfort at being seen without a mask, but also, Mask Makers have always made me uneasy. I feel sorry for them, their faces so colorless and insipid. It's an irony that they wear such bland features and plain colors, yet they make such marvelous faces for us, each one unique in its brilliance. I pity them, and I'm glad I was not born to their caste.

I hand over my summons writ and accept my newest mask, my favor from the queen. It is glossy saffron with pointed wires to fasten it. It has no mouth opening, but it does not seem lacking for that. Like every face they craft, it is a feat of artistry.

4. Orange Is for Agony

I press the saffron mask to my face and wrap the barbed laces around my head. A fleeting touch, my fingertips on the painted metal tell me of thick runnels that dent the surface. Their unevenness makes the fit uncomfortable. For a moment.

Wire mesh presses above and below. If I lie down, I can stretch my neck, a little. But then the mesh cuts into my feet, my fore-arms, my chest. Standing, sitting, a few back-and-forth steps. But pacing only reminds me how small my cell is. And they do not like for us to pace. Exercise thins the fat between muscle and skin, making the harvest more difficult.

My neighbor wears a ginger mask dotted with cobalt sequins. He urinates, and it splashes through the mesh on me. I hiss my rage, crowded by the scent of his body, and return the favor.

I'm glad when the workers come for him and watch as they trap him in their loops. He tries to fight, but he has nothing sharp or hard to wield. Their wicked tools, edged with blue light, open him from neck to groin. He barely has time to bleed before they carve perpendicular incisions, flaps to better flay him in a single piece.

His eyes bulge as they tear away his skin, all the movement he is capable of. He's silent, for there is no mouth on his mask; he is as mute as I.

When they're done, they leave him writhing in the liquids of his body on the wire mesh floor. They take the heavy cloak of his skin with them.

Then it's my turn. The ginger planes of my neighbor's mask swivel to me, so he can watch.

There's no place to run in my tiny cell, and their loops

pinion me. When they begin to cut away my skin, it is the most terrible pain I have ever known.

Their masks are lemon, daffodil, and butterscotch. Pretty and yellow, like sunshine.

5. Jasper Is for Jilting

The next morning, the choice is harder than usual. I flinch away from the saffron mask and stare for a long while at the tan one. But it feels inappropriate to select it.

Like a whiff of passing corruption, the notion of going without a mask today, simply staying in my quarters and not choosing a face, flits through my thoughts. It is too scandalous to contemplate; I feel guilty to have even considered it.

Without looking, I reach among the rows of empty faces and snatch the first one my hand falls upon.

It is brackish green, the color of stagnant water in a pool that never sees the sun. The chin and nose are gilded in dark velvet, and the lips shine, liquid silver hand-painted on silk. I tighten the woven cords around my head.

♦

I hover beneath the window of my lover, she of the cerulean mask detailed in voile. She reclines on her balcony, and a song of courtship thrums from her dainty mouth. I inhale the delicate body scents her servant wafts out with a fan: enticement and temptation, innocence and promise.

"Do you love me?" my sweetheart calls.

"With all my soul. You are my everything."

"I don't believe you," she laughs. "How are you different from all the other men, just waiting for a chance to slather me with Queen's Honey?"

"How can you say that? I've asked you to marry me."

"What does that prove? Any meathead with a tongue can do that. And anyway, I don't want to marry at all. Marriage is a sorry state that leads to fighting and grief."

I pantomime exaggerated dismay for her benefit. "What can I do to convince you of my sincerity? Ask me for anything, and I'll give it to you."

"Do you have a jar of Queen's Honey?"

I hesitate. If I answer truthfully, she might accuse me again of being a libertine. But it is also my courting gift. She will feel slighted if I don't have anything to offer her.

I sigh and choose the better of my options. "A humble present to honor your loveliness."

"Good."

When I'm not immediately rebuffed, I dare to hope.

"I'm sending my girl down. Give the Queen's Honey to her, and we'll all play a game. She'll seal the jar so the contents may not be used without breaking it, and puncture its lid, freeing the scent. If you can spend the afternoon with me and my girl in my enclosed boudoir and keep from breaking the jar open, I'll believe that you love me and not simply the pleasures of copulation. But if you lose control and *do* break the jar, you can slake yourself on her, but you'll never get a word or whiff from me again."

"What, pray, do I get if I can restrain myself?"

Her laughter is like a teasing wind. "If you can check your desires until evening, I'll send her away and break the jar myself."

I'm both excited and dismayed by the prospect of her "game." My lover will ensure that our time is not spent on chaste recreations or thoughtful conversation. She will pose herself and her servant girl in all manner of ways suggestive of copulation. And she is probably already drenched in one of the trendy distillations—Passion Without Doubt or Exotica or Citrus Nectar—to madden me further. Still, the reward will be sweet. And at the very least (my love did not altogether peg me wrongly), I'll get to do the servant girl.

My prospective consolation prize opens the door. Her mask is a sage green that suggests transparency, the eyes rimmed in toffee lace. She snatches the Queen's Honey from me, but there the anticipated script ends. She twists off the lid and scoops the unguent out. Without embarrassment or coyness, she rubs it on herself, between her thighs. As I stare dumbfounded, she smears a glistening coating on me. Instantly, I'm aroused and eager.

"Want me?" she whispers.

"Yes." Flesh on flesh, the Queen's Honey brooks no denial.

"Then catch me." She sprints away.

I waver for only a breath. Above, my sweetheart calls down plaintively, wondering at our delay. But desire roars through me, and all I care about is the servant girl.

I chase her through the dormitory block as she weaves around crowds and over obstacles—sculptures, shops, new constructions. Sometimes men turn, catching the fleeting perfume of Queen's Honey mingled with her sex as she darts by.

I am enthralled. She fills every breath I take. I run until I'm a creature of fire—blazing lungs and burning limbs. But it is spice to my eagerness. I will catch her, and then we will copulate.

She leads me past the market district, past shop windows filled with citizens making purchases, and into the rural outskirts where the machines harvest our food and workers gather esoteric materials for the Mask Makers guild.

In a shaded copse of green wood trees, she drops to her knees. I'm upon her, not even waiting for her to assume the proper position. She opens to me, and I rush to join our bodies.

It is glorious, of course, the release all the more satisfying for the chase. But even as I spend myself, I notice something wrong. The girl is not making the right movements, and her scent, while intoxicating, is strange. Beneath the Queen's Honey she is impatient when she should be impassioned. As soon as I'm finished, she pulls away, and for the first time after a copulation, I'm not happy and languid, awash in the endorphins of sex. I feel awkward.

Before I can say anything, the girl tears off her mask. The horror of her unmasking paralyzes me; I'm unprepared for her next action. She lunges, ripping off the bindings of my mask, and yanks it free.

I am barefaced.

It's not the unmasking hour, not the time for emptiness and slumber. Without my mask, I don't know how to act or feel, or what to say. I don't even know if I *can* speak, for I never have without a mask. I'm lost, no one. The nucleus of my personality and intelligence is empty; the girl has stolen it.

6. White Is for Obedience

While I kneel, stupefied, the girl discards my mask, letting it fall among the long grasses where we loved. I don't even have the presence of will to retrieve it. She examines the inside of her mask. With infinite care, she peels a sheer membrane away. It is like a veil of gauze or chiffon, but this veil has a shape. There are nose, cheekbones, and chin.

It is a mask, but a mask unlike any I've seen. The fabric is unornamented and diaphanous white, like thin fog or still water, all but colorless. It doesn't conceal what it covers, only overlays it.

She takes this ghost of a mask and drapes it over my face. Without cord or chain, it fastens itself, clinging to my head. It is such relief to have my nakedness covered, I'm grateful when I should be outraged.

I wait for the mask to tell me who I am and what to do.

And I wait.

"There's not much oversoul there," the girl says. Without a mask, her features are too animated, obscenely so. I avert my gaze, wondering if the ghost mask exposes my expressions in such an indecent fashion.

"It's only a scaffold to help you get past the schizo panic," she continues. "It doesn't have any personas or relationship scenarios to instill, and absolutely no emotives."

I don't like the ghost mask's vacancy. But at least I can think now, and it occurs to me to scramble for my own mask.

"Stop," she says.

I cannot move. My fingertips brush the darker green and glint of silver lying in the grass, but I can't pick it up.

"I'm afraid the scaffold does have an obedience imprint. I am sorry about that, but it's necessary. You wouldn't be able to access the oversoul in your mask anyway. The scaffold creates a barrier that mask imprints can't penetrate, and you won't be able to take the scaffold off. Go ahead, I know you want to. Try to remove it."

I grope my face, my head looking for something to undo. There's nothing to unknot, release, or unbuckle. I find the edge where the ghost mask, the scaffold, gives way to skin, but it's adhered to me. The memory from yesterday—the saffron mask, being skinned alive—is enough to deter me from anything drastic.

"What did you do to me?" I ask. "And why?"

"Good, you're questioning. I knew you'd acclimate quickly." A scent penetrates my distress. She is pleased. Except the tang isn't right. It's not feminine but not masculine either. She has no mask to tell me whether she's male or female. Should I continue thinking of her as a girl? And for that matter, the scaffold hasn't provided me with a gender. Am I a man or a woman, or am I neuter, or perhaps some sort of androgyne?

I feel lightheaded and ill. "If this is some perverted game," I say, "I'm not amused. I'll report this to the gendarmes. They'll confiscate all your masks for this crime, and—" I trail off. Her naked face is testimony of her indifference to the severest penalty of our society.

"Why are you doing this to me?" I whimper.

"Did you ever wonder who you are beneath your masks?" she says. "When you say 'me,' who is that?"

Hearing her voice the question that has lately made my mornings so troubling and the hours after unmasking so long is a kind of deliverance. I'm not the only citizen to have these thoughts; I'm not alone in my distress. But the guilt remains, along with an added unease. Is exposing my crime what this is about? Am I to be penalized?

"Don't be afraid," she says, "I'm not going to turn you over to the gendarmes or anything like that."

My breathing quickens. "Are you hearing my thoughts?"

"No, only watching your face."

"My face?"

"It conveys emotions. It's like smelling another's confusion or knowing that someone's angry by the tightness of their shoulders, only with facial musculature. Before long, you'll read it as instinctively as you do scents and stances."

"You say that as though you expect me to be pleased."

Her mouth curves and parts, revealing the whiteness of her teeth. Being witness to such an intimate view is both repulsive and fascinating.

"I know you don't think so now," she says, "but I've given you a gift, one very few people receive." She stands. "Walk with me."

I don't want to go anywhere with her, but the scaffold compels me to obey. We stroll deeper into the wilderness, leaving my mask in the grass. It is an uncomfortable sensation, having my will at odds with my body.

"I've been watching you for a while to make sure you were right," she says.

"Watching me?" Fragments of confusion knit into understanding. "You're the shop girl who sold me the Iolite Bronze and the deviant man with the pewter mask."

"And the customer at the bakery who bought a dozen egg tarts from you before that."

"The woman with the pink mask who asked for the recipe?"

"Yes. And before, when you wore your roan and iron mask, I was in the audience when you presented your new poem. And the day before that, I picked indigo with you for the Mask Makers."

We emerge into a clearing. A broken-down hut lists, obscured by overgrown foliage. Her sage and toffee mask still dangles from her fingertips. She passes its brim over the doorknob, and the door swings open.

"I'm glad to finally meet you," she says. "You can call me Pena."

The interior is dim, lit by stray sunbeams poking through holes in the ramshackle walls.

"Pena?" The word is meaningless. "Why?"

"It's my name, a word that means me, regardless of what mask I'm wearing or not wearing."

I snort. "Why stop at each citizen having their own name? Why not each tile or brick the builders use or every tree or blade of grass?"

"Every street has a name," Pena says. "And every shop."

"So we can tell one from the other. Otherwise, we couldn't say where a place was, or differentiate between one food market and another."

"Exactly." She runs her fingers over a floorboard, and I hear a click. In the far corner by the fireplace, flagstones part to expose steps.

"What's down there?" I ask.

"Answers. Come."

We descend, and the flagstones rumble shut overhead. Ambient light washes over us—dim and red, casting bloody shadows.

We're in a tunnel with rough, stone walls. The light extends ten paces before us; beyond is darkness. Pena strides toward this border, and I am obliged to accompany her. When we are within a pace of light's end, more red comes on to reveal another span of corridor. When we are within this new radius, the light behind us goes out.

And so we walk.

"Why do citizens need names?" I ask. "We change masks every day, unlike shops and streets which stay the same. What if I discover that my physician is the same citizen as my murderer? Or a citizen in one mask is my lover and in another, my enemy? If I call that citizen by a single word, it's like treating all their mask identities as the same person."

"That's the point," she says. "It lets us be who we truly are, underneath our masks."

I shake my head. "Without the masks, we're not anything."

"There was a time before the masks."

"And we were empty, primitive creatures, without will or purpose, until the First Queen created the First Mask to wear and carved faces for the citizens and—"

"And She designated the Guild of Mask Makers and tasked them with their sacred duty so that everyone would be imbued with souls, blah blah blah. I know the lies."

Her heresy is both disturbing and intriguing. "What do you believe, then?"

"That's what I'm going to show you."

"Why me?"

"There's a group of us named. We seek out others who harbor the same doubts and resentments we do, and we liberate them."

"I don't want to be liberated."

"Don't you? Haven't you wanted to be free of the daily selection routine? Or chafed against the mask, wishing the hour of unmasking came sooner? Don't you hover in indecision some mornings, not because the choosing is so hard, but because none of them appeal? Don't you wonder who you could be if you were left to decide for yourself?"

I am saved from having to answer by the appearance of something new when the next lights activate: a door.

7. Red Is for Revelation

"Where are we?"

"Beneath the palace at the Mask Makers guild."

She passes her mask over the door. Like the hut's, it opens.

I balk. "No. Absolutely not. It's prohibited."

She studies me. "I can make you, but I won't. It's your decision."

I open my mouth to repeat myself.

"But first, hear me out."

I exhale. "If I must. But it won't change my mind."

"You know I've been keeping by you as you've switched masks. I was also with you when you wore the saffron mask at the leather harvesters."

The memory is still raw. "So?"

"Do you know who I was?"

"One of the skinners, I presume."

"I was your neighbor in the adjoining cage."

Despite everything, I'm dismayed. "Didn't you know what they were going to do to you, to us?"

"I knew."

"And still you let them, willingly even. *Why*, in the name of the First Queen?"

"Because, to be with you, I could either hurt you or be hurt, and I chose not to hurt you."

"Am I someone to you? Have we been lovers or spouses or friends?"

"Not that I know of."

"Then why?"

"Because I know who I am, and my actions are a reflection of me. I don't skin people alive."

Her last sentence carries a conviction, a certainty that makes me envious.

"What would you do if you had to choose," she says, "if your decisions extended beyond what mask to wear any given day? Would you willingly inflict such suffering upon another?"

"I would ... I-I don't know."

"Do you want to know?"

And I find I do.

The door opens upon a storage room jammed with row upon row of shelves. Bolts of multihued fabric, rolls of ribbon and lace, and jars of washes, dyes, and lacquers are piled together without any semblance of order. More rolls of textiles spill out of cubby holes and closets lining the room.

"This is their overflow storage, where they keep their excess," Pena says. "We raid it for our mask-making supplies. Named artisans can create near-perfect replicas of guild masks, but without the oversouls, of course."

"With added features that can unlock doors."

She displays her teeth again. Some part of me has learned to equate that facial configuration with positive emotion, even before I breathe the perfume of her approval.

"You noticed. Very good."

"How do they do it?"

She leads me through the jumble. "It's complicated to explain. All of our mask functions, including the scaffold you're wearing, are based on the Mask Makers' constructs. There's bits and pieces appliquéd, sewn, glued, or imbedded in all masks which stimulate thoughts, trigger emotions, assign personality traits, and so on. Named artisans have taken apart and put back together these pieces, re-aligning and modifying them until they've gained an understanding of their workings. In the process, they've discovered that the components can do much more than imprint oversouls, like lock and unlock doors. And there's still so much we haven't figured out yet."

The supply room exits upon a dark corridor that illuminates red at our approach. But unlike the one from the hut, the circle of light shows a cluster of turnings that forks in different directions.

"You make it sound like you named have been at this for a while," I say.

"We have." She sets off down one of the twisting tunnels. "Sometimes the gendarmes get wind of our activities, so we work exclusively in pairs—one mentor, one recruit. That way, the most named any of us knows is two, your mentor when you're recruited, and your recruit once you're ready to bring someone in. We disseminate information and requests through codes and drop-off points. It's slow but safer."

I've lost track of the bends and turns we've taken. "You must recruit pretty selectively, if each mentor can only take one."

"Mentors can take another recruit if theirs is apprehended by the gendarmes." The lighting casts deep shadows over the planes of her face, and for a moment, it seems that she's wearing a crimson mask. She brushes her fingers over her eyes, and they come away wet.

"What happens when the gendarmes catch you?"

"They kill us."

I shrug. "That's all? So you lose the day. In the morning—"

"No. They *kill* us. It's not like the petty murders citizens inflict upon each other. There's no waking up from the death the gendarmes deliver."

I stumble, shocked. "That's-that's *monstrous*. How is that possible? How can our laws permit it?"

"You said it yourself; without the masks, we're nothing. When the gendarmes execute one of us, they reassign all of that named's personas to the population at large. The oversouls continue, and there is no disruption among the citizenry. I think the gendarmes grieve more when they have to destroy a mask that has been 'murdered' than when they kill one of us."

Pena rounds a corner, and there is a wall. It's creamy smooth, as though stone workers spent hours painstakingly sanding it to perfect flatness.

"Did you make a wrong turn?" I ask.

"Afraid of getting lost?" Her tone is teasing. "Don't worry. Even if I had made a wrong turn, my mask contains the labyrinth's secrets. But I didn't."

I half expect her to wave the mask at the wall and a door to miraculously appear. She doesn't. Instead, Pena lifts a hand to her mouth and tears at it with her teeth. Dark blood oozes, and she smears this droplet on the wall.

Soundlessly, the wall glides up and disappears into the ceiling. White, not red, light comes on, blinding after the dimness.

Pena tugs me forward while I'm still blinking. I squint, eyes tearing and blurry, at the small room we have entered. The walls are polished metal, and they encircle us, curving outward so it feels like we're inside a cylinder. A closed one. While my eyes adjust, the door shuts itself.

In the room's center is an ornate chair of silver and gold. Resting upon its seat is a mask.

I recognize it, for it is the stuff of legend. Carved from a single diamond with a million-million facets, each representing a mask-to-be, the First Queen's Mask, the one She created with her own hands to bring enlightenment to us all.

8. Diamonds Are for Death

Pena touches my face, and the scaffold slips away. The anxiety of being barefaced is forgotten in the wonder of the First Mask.

"The truth, your answers, they're all in the oversoul of that mask," she says. "All you have to do is put it on."

"What if I don't?"

"Then we go back, and tomorrow morning you choose a mask to wear, like every other morning, and you never see me again."

"I might turn you over to the gendarmes."

Her lips part and flash teeth. "What will you tell them? That a citizen kidnapped you and filled your head with truth? How will you find me? And how do you know the gendarmes won't kill you simply for knowing this much?"

She's right, of course. "But I don't have to put on the First Mask?"

"What you do is up to you. Now and forever."

I hesitate for a heartbeat before striding to the chair and seizing the First Mask. It's so light. I'd expected it to be heavier. Holding it aloft, I realize the eyeholes are encased in nearly transparent lenses like my consort mask, except diamond instead of glass.

"You might want to sit before you put it on," Pena says. "I didn't and ended flat on my back."

I perch on the gold and silver chair, and set the mask over my face. There are segmented strands of diamond to wrap around my head that fasten with glittering diamond locks. The lenses warp my vision, disorienting me. But only for a moment.

Crowing exultation.

The war is finished! My last rival and her progeny are dead, and I reign in exclusive sovereignty.

My children, I am so proud of you. This is the dawn of a new age, a glorious and splendid age.

My scientists have conquered our only remaining enemy: time. They have found the key to unlocking the shackles of age and injury, and conquered the last disease. I am no longer chained by the dictates of perpetual reproduction. The years of my empire will be like a magnificent river, rippling past eon after eon, powerful and endless.

I do worry, however, that my soldiers will decline. They are the simplest of my children and only understand rigid procedures and physical contests. Perhaps I should manufacture a new corps of soldiers, an elite one. They can vie with each other in mock battles for the honor of being counted among my gendarmes.

The river of years is murky and deep, and I cannot see where it will take us.

I am stymied at an unanticipated quarter: my consorts. The noblest of my children, nearly my equals—clever and curious, independent and imaginative—I should have known they would feel neglected and adrift when I ceased summoning them to mate. They are creatures of great passion, as I am, and now they squabble, forming factions and carrying out vendettas.

I have started opening my body to them again, but I will ask the scientists to develop a synthetic pheromone so they may copulate amongst themselves.

I am despair.

A citizen killed another today, beyond what my scientists were able to restore. I must accept the truth; we are an aggressive people, not destined for peace, and all I have tried to build is in ruins.

If only there was a way for my consorts to expend their passions harmlessly.

I must confer with my scientists.

At last! I have devised an end to the chaos which blights my citizenry.

My scientists have developed a means of imprinting memories and eliciting emotions that may be interchanged, swapped out, and added upon with seemingly infinite variety. My consorts may oppose each other and mate with promiscuity, all without garnering rivals or blood feuds.

I have set my scientists to generate these oversoul masks in copious quantity and in wondrous variety.

This must work.

All is well. The activities of my children are once more in accord with my desiring, and eternity's river holds no more uncertainties.

There was a minor dilemma, but I have solved even that. It seems that I am not immune to the effect of the masks. I thought my royal will would safeguard my identity, but it is becoming a strain, sorting reality from fabrication.

I have had an oversoul commissioned. It will be a lasting record of all the tribulations I have confronted and my efforts to remedy them. This mask shall be sealed beneath my palace in a chamber secured by steel, and my blood shall be the only key that unlocks it.

I take off the mask of diamonds. Pena watches me, her lips parted.

I tumble out of the chair and fall to my knees. "I am your servant, First Queen."

Pena's eyes widen, and she laughs. "Oh, no, no." She is at my side and hauls me up. "I'm not the First Queen."

"But your blood opened the door."

"Don't you get it? We're all of her blood, each of us descended from the First Queen. Some joke on her, huh?"

I stay silent.

"Come," she says. "We need to get back before the hour of unmasking. If we're seen on the streets after, the gendarmes will take us."

I straggle after her, lost in my thoughts. I don't try to keep track of the red-lit corridors and notice only when we are among the fabrics and dyes of the storage room.

"Hsst." Pena gestures.

"What is it?"

Without warning, she shoves me, and I tumble into a closeted hole. Bolts of velvet and felt topple upon me. She flings an oversized bottle of jasmine oil after, engulfing me in cloying sweetness.

Then there is confusion. The red light extinguishes, and white beams flash in the darkness. They catch and glint off white metal—glittering eyes, gleaming brows—the silver masks of the gendarmes.

Hidden in my cubby, my scent as obscured as my body, they do not detect me. They converge on a single spot, Pena, huddled between shelves.

"By order of the queen, you are hereby accused and convicted of treason," one gendarme says.

I cannot smell anything over the sickening jasmine, but I can see the terror on her face. She glances at me, and there is a beseeching in her eyes, and a question, but she looks away before I can understand it.

"The penalty for treason is death, citizen," a gendarme, perhaps the same one, says. "Do you wish to repent? Identify your co-conspirators, and we will allow you to return to the way of the mask."

Pena lifts her head. "Never."

They don't ask again. They activate their loops, and I'm reminded of the day of the saffron mask. I'm ashamed of the gladness I felt then.

They don't skin her, but this is as gruesome, if swifter. A gendarme kneels over her as she is pinioned on her back by bands of blue. Bracing himself, he staves in her face with his fist. I want to look away. It is an obscene violation, a perverse defilement to damage a citizen *there*—to do any violence which might cause harm to a mask. But Pena isn't wearing a mask, and I don't look away.

He strikes again and again until there is nothing left of the front of her head but a wreckage of bone and pulped wetness.

9. The Last Mask

The gendarmes are as efficient in disposing of Pena's body as they were in dispatching her. When they have gone, the red light comes on, and I dare to creep out. As I untangle myself from a length of burgundy velvet, my hand falls upon an unmistakable shape—Pena's green and toffee mask. The sight of it, so soon after the atrocity of her execution, unhinges me. I start crying and I cannot stop. But it doesn't matter, because her mask will hide my tears.

Somehow, I make it to Center at Corridor and the familiar confines of my quarters. Safe.

But I am *not* safe. I cannot forget the First Queen's memories, which the gendarmes would surely kill me for having, and more, I cannot erase the beseeching question in Pena's eyes.

I tear off her mask. It's not the unmasking hour, but I don't care. I'm weary of masks, even a blameless one without an oversoul. Pena's death burdens me with shame and guilt—like being flayed again, but with the pain inside.

I am surrounded by masks. Each is a player in some fabricated theater—artist, victim, rake, entrepreneur, lover, spouse, friend. None of them is real, but I can put them on and escape these feelings.

But I won't.

One after the other, I destroy my masks. The ones that shatter are the easiest. I hurl them at the floor and shards spill across the tile. The ones that burn, I commit to fire. But the metal ones I must work at, smashing one upon another until they are twisted out of all recognition.

I save the sable mask for last out of a sense of propriety. Although it is metal, it is oddly malleable, and it crumbles between my hands. The lenses fall out of the eyeholes and tumble among the broken bits of ceramic and glass on my floor.

I stand amidst the debris that was my life and don the only mask I spared, Pena's green and toffee one.

My lover glances at me in her cerulean-with-voile mask and lets me in. She thinks I am her servant girl.

"Where did you go?" she demands. "Do you know how long I've been waiting for you? And where is my suitor?"

Her quarters are much like mine, much like every citizen's.

There is a mask room, a kitchen, and a bedchamber. I brush past her and she follows, continuing to scold as we enter her kitchen. I find what I need in one of the drawers: a tenderizer mallet, heavy and solid. Even when I turn with it upraised, she doesn't relent.

"Are you ignoring me, you slut?" she shouts. "How dare you!"

Only when I yank off her mask does she become afraid, and by then, it's too late.

I smash the mallet into her face. She stumbles, and I ride her as she goes down, hammering the metal tool into her face over and over. Bones and flesh mash together into pulp, and still I persist. I must be thorough.

Pena did not have time to teach me the secrets of her league of named. But through her, I have learned enough. I have seen how the gendarmes kill. I do not have their loops or their strength, but I know how to murder so that my victims will not wake.

Pena also taught me to know who I am.

I am chaos in this ordered society, the flaw in a carefully wrought plan. I am turbulence in the queen's eternal river.

After receiving her master's degree in psychology, Eugie Foster retired from academia to pen flights of fancy. In addition to receiving the Nebula Award for Best Novelette, she was named the 2009 Author of the Year by Bards and Sages. Her fiction has also received the 2002 Phobos Award; been translated into seven languages; and been a finalist for the Hugo, Black Quill, Bram Stoker, and BSFA Awards. Her publication credits number over one hundred and include stories in *Realms of Fantasy*, *Interzone*, *Cricket*, *Orson Scott Card's InterGalactic Medicine Show*, and *Fantasy Magazine*; podcasts *Escape Pod*,

Pseudopod, and *PodCastle*; and anthologies *Best New Fantasy* and *Best New Romantic Fantasy 2*. Her short story collection, *Returning My Sister's Face: And Other Far Eastern Tales of Whimsy and Malice*, is available from Norilana Books. Eugie lived in Atlanta with her husband Matthew Foster until her passing in 2014. Each year at Dragon Con, the Eugie Foster Memorial Award for Short Fiction is presented to an "irreplaceable" work of short fiction.

ADDITIONAL COPYRIGHT INFORMATION

IF YOU LIKED ...

If you liked *Unmasked*, you might also enjoy:

Monsters, Movies & Mayhem
Edited by Kevin J. Anderson

Hold Your Fire
Edited by Lisa Mangum

Selected Stories: Science Fiction, Volume 1
by Kevin J. Anderson

Avatar Dreams: Science Fiction Visions of Avatar Technology
by Kevin J. Anderson, Mike Resnick, Ray Kurzweil

The Humans in the Walls and Other Stories
by Eric James Stone

OTHER WORDFIRE PRESS TITLES

Selected Stories: Fantasy
by Kevin J. Anderson

Maximum Velocity
Edited by David Lee Summers

First Person Peculiar
by Mike Resnik

X Marks the Spot
Edited by Lisa Mangum

Our list of other WordFire Press authors and titles is always growing. To find out more and to shop our selection of titles, visit us at:
wordfirepress.com

facebook.com/WordfireIncWordfirePress

twitter.com/WordFirePress

instagram.com/WordFirePress

bookbub.com/profile/4109784512

Lightning Source UK Ltd.
Milton Keynes UK
UKHW012121271022
411228UK00008D/213/J

9 781680 572285